DEFENDER OF HISTORIES

THE WITNESS TREE CHRONICLES, BOOK 1

HALEY WALDEN

MORAVON PRESS

Defender of Histories is an epic fantasy set in a medieval-reminiscent world. Learn more about its themes and tropes at authorhaleywalden.com.

ISBN: 978-1-7353431-2-9
(Paperback Edition)

Published by Moravon Press

Developmental Editor: Allison Martin
Copy Editor: Jolene Perry

Cover Illustration: Saint Jupiter
instagram.com/saintjupit3rgr4phic

Additional Illustrations: Danaye Shiplett
danaye.com

Map Artist: Cartographybird Maps
cartographybird.com

Author Headshot by Jessica McIntosh Photography
jessicamcintosh.net

BOOKS BY HALEY WALDEN

The Witness Tree Chronicles
    1- *Defender of Histories*
    1.5- *Ballad of Stallions*
    2- *Keeper of Keys*
    3- *Vow of Magic*
    4- *Sovereign of Clans* (Coming Soon)

Tales of Rodhlan
    1- *Ruse of Heirs*

~

Stay up-to-date on bookish news and happenings:
www.authorhaleywalden.com

Follow the author on Instagram, TikTok, and Facebook:
@authorhaleywalden

THE FROZEN ISLANDS
THE IMMORTAL WATERS
LA'HAYN
RIV'ANA
SVA'CERA
ITELORIA
PORT OF RASU
CAPITAL CITIES
CITIES AND TOWNS
MINOR SETTLEMENTS
THE SALTSWEPT LANDS OF THE
OLYRAN SEA

TAI'KARA
RIKU'S BORDERLANDS
KINGDOM OF SOV'IS
LA'FREYAN'S WILDS
LORJYN
PORT OF NAJYN
THE STRAIT OF ULAN
WHERE THE MUDFLATS EMERGE
RODHLAN
IATHIUM
FORTRESS HALGEIR
CATACOMBS
MORAVON RIVER
VA'HESK
THE MEADOWLANDS
ÉNNA CARAVAN
ACTON'S COVE
RODHLAN RIDGE

For my children.
Never let the world extinguish your flame.

CHAPTER I

Silira Mór lay her quill down reverently and flexed her aching fingers. She felt stiff and hunched after hours of painstakingly copying the decrepit historical manuscript that lay open on her ink-stained desk—a relic of the Archive of the Dome, whose high stone stacks surrounded her on every side. Beside the old tome sat the transcription she'd just completed, daubs of wet ink still glistening on its final words.

Lira held her dark brown curls back, leaned over the book, and blew carefully on the ink, watching as the last droplets dried on the parchment. She gave the page a final once-over before gingerly closing the cover.

The scent of the fresh parchment and newly bound leather ignited memories of her first clumsy attempts at transcription. As an adolescent apprentice, she'd had a habit of smearing the ink with her quill hand as she clumsily copied each line. Her master, Lord Irem Énna—the elderly Defender of Histories— had been patient with her, providing endless sheets of clean parchment for her to practice her calligraphy. Even now, as a full-fledged historian, ink stains perpetually marred the entire side of her right hand.

She looked to her left, where Aidryn Tarlach was hunched over his own transcription. For a moment, she watched him work; his dark hair fell into his eyes as he scratched his quill deftly across the page. His usually close-trimmed beard looked more unkempt than usual, and he chewed the inside of his cheek as he wrote.

Lira waited until he paused to dip his quill into the ink pot on the corner of his desk, then rose. She stretched, rolling her stiff neck before hefting the heavy volume with an unladylike grunt and another glance in Aidryn's direction. As she sidled past his desk, she whispered, "Finished," with a satisfied smirk.

Aidryn cursed under his breath, momentarily flustered. "I suppose I can't win every round."

"You don't." She laughed, heading toward the stacks.

"Three out of the last four," he said, not bothering to hide his smile before returning to his work.

She moved between the rows of desks where the other archivists worked, crafting scrolls and tomes with cautious hands, steady gazes, and shoulders as stiff and rounded as hers. Six apprentices filled the desks, all focused solely on the tasks set before them. Lira often wondered if, like her, they preferred to perform such isolating work in the quiet company of others.

Lira padded across the ornate floor, a mosaic of bloodstone and onyx tiles, as she made her way to one of the many towering shelves that lined the circular perimeter of the archive. She placed the new book on the stone shelf, running her fingers down its spine one last time before she returned to fetch the original from her desk. It was an economic history of her city, Iathium: the capital of Rodhlan.

Springtime's relentless rain showers had saturated the earth above them, bringing a dampness to the archive that was so thick, Lira could taste it. The wide, open stairwell that led to the

Dome's main floor usually kept the air in the archive fresh, but today the space smelled musty and stale. She paused by a burner in the center of the archive to light fresh incense, carefully placing it inside the burner—a bronze miniature of the great Dome in the heart of Iathium.

Lira relished fitting pieces of Iathium's history together like a puzzle, working each new bit of information into the whole, connecting catalysts and events across families and centuries. She understood why and how each law, each war, each ruler, and each structure had come to be. Her understanding came easily, but her position as a historian had been hard-won.

Though she'd always been fascinated by stories of the past, Lira's father had turned her history lessons into a game of strategy when she was a child—a game she'd never tired of, and never stopped longing to revisit. Even now, scouring books and scrolls for missing pieces of truth felt less like work, and more like reliving a happy memory.

After five years of working as an apprentice, then being promoted to historian, Lira still marveled at the intricate stonework surrounding her. She had never seen anything else like it: a massive cavern that had been fashioned into the stacks, chambers, and nooks where she spent most of her hours reading, researching, and transcribing. The craftsmanship was so skillful that she had to look twice the first time she learned that the handiwork was solid, unbroken stone.

As she rounded the side of her desk to reach for the book, Aidryn leaned toward her and swiped his quill across her forearm, leaving a spit of thick ink on her pale skin.

"What was that for?" she hissed, putting the book down to rub furiously at the ink, but succeeding only in smearing it all over her palm and arm.

"What did you do to cross Lord Irem?" he whispered, raising a dark eyebrow. A smile tugged at the corner of his mouth.

"Why did you—" She huffed, using her linen apron to scrub at her palm, cringing as the ink began to stain the clean cloth. "What do you mean, what did I do? I never cross him."

Aidryn tilted his head, leaning sideways to glimpse the book that rested on her desk. Lira moved to hide the book's title, but it was too late.

"*Economics of Ancient Iathium*," he mused, brushing strands of brown hair away from his eyes—a striking blue in contrast. He ran his fingertips over his beard in mock deliberation.

"If I were the one assigning manuscripts—" he pointed with his quill— "I'd say you were being punished."

Lira raised her chin. "Well, I'm not. Besides, it was stimulating."

Aidryn leaned forward conspiratorially. "Since when did you like economics?"

"I'm no economist," she replied. "But clearly, the Defender trusts me with the most challenging titles."

"I don't know about that," he whispered with a wicked grin, closing his manuscript to reveal its title: *Rowan's Mathematical Anthology, Vol. 2.*

She muttered an insult under her breath as she snatched her book from her desk. Aidryn chuckled, turning back to his work.

Lira wouldn't openly complain to him about the bore of a book; Aidryn enjoyed baiting her too much to give him the satisfaction. But she did wonder, just for a moment, why the Lord wouldn't have given a book like this to one of the apprentices. After all, their sole task was copying the texts, not reading them.

Most apprentices were brought into the archive as artisans through a competitive selection process. They were valued for their artistry with ink and quill, their storytelling prowess, and their musical skill. Oral historians, bards, and artists with archival training were known to amass great wealth in Iathium, whose elite would pay handsomely to see and hear the stories that had built their city and given their families power.

For many apprentices, the archive was merely a place to pass through and hone their craft while learning some of the city's histories. Then, they moved on, teaching through their art. Others learned to bind and re-bind tomes, remaining in the archive as curators to preserve artifacts and manuscripts that had fallen into disrepair. Still others, like Lira and Aidryn, chose to master the histories and teach the apprentices.

Iathium's people placed great importance on oral histories, in part, because they were woven tightly into their culture. Only a few historians and select members of the elite classes could read and write in Athi, the common tongue. Illiteracy was fashionable, and though Lira had quietly challenged this cultural norm over the years, the consensus seemed to be that art and performance were the most enlightened ways for the public to receive knowledge.

Some nobles kept illuminated manuscripts in their homes as symbols of affluence and tokens of the city's storied past. Aidryn's family had two in their home, which they displayed proudly in the entrance hall. Only specific, sanctioned manuscripts were allowed outside the archive, and they were considered to be more decorative than useful.

Lira made her way across the archive toward the inner chamber. The smaller, circular room within the archive was reserved for Lord Irem, Lira, and Aidryn—the only historians in residence.

Rare, first-edition manuscripts were stored in the chamber, as well as tomes and scrolls that had been removed from public access long before the rest of the archive was sealed. Lira longed to get her hands on the records that had been locked away for centuries. Aidryn had once suggested that Irem had access to scrolls and tomes written in the four clans' indigenous languages, but she wouldn't believe it until she saw them for herself. The clans' languages had long since been deemed illegal to write or speak, for fear of treason—and she had never laid eyes on one.

Certainly, if Irem indeed knew something of the ancient languages, he would pass that knowledge down... but not to her. At twenty-one years old—two years her senior—Aidryn had already been chosen as Irem's successor. There were records Lord Irem and his heir had access to that no one else would ever see. It pained Lira to know she would always be left wanting for knowledge. Though Aidryn was more than worthy, and though she tried not to dwell on it often, she couldn't help feeling envious of him.

When she reached the chamber, its massive wooden door was closed, so she rang the tiny bell that hung beside it. Its tinkling echoed through the wide, open archive; several of the apprentices glanced behind them before turning back to their books.

A friendly, wizened voice called from inside: "Enter."

She pushed the door open and stepped inside, shutting it behind her. Irem was hunched over his desk, quill scratching feverishly. The mingling smoke and incense—more pungent than the sweet-smelling kind she'd lit in the archive—were more overwhelming than usual, so she took a moment to collect herself before speaking.

The chamber also contained stone stacks from floor to ceiling. Its floor was covered in the same tiles of bloodstone and onyx that swirled and twirled into a tight central spiral, dulled from years of neglect, in contrast to the mirror-bright floor in the open archive. Glass lanterns adorned the walls, their flames flickering, and an iron chandelier was suspended in the center of the chamber, filled with burning candles of varying sizes. Wax accumulated on each candle holder and overflowed from some, as evidenced by the blots that had dripped onto the floor below and hardened there.

"Good afternoon, Lord Irem," Lira said, bowing her head.

The brown-skinned man looked up from his work, squinting at her through his spectacles. Lira knew the expression well, for she wore it often; hours of staring at manuscripts made it difficult for her eyes to adjust when she was ready to focus on a person, an object, or another task besides reading and writing.

"Ah, Silira," he said. "Impeccable timing." His dark eyes twinkled, the laugh lines that framed them deepening.

"Impeccable?" she asked teasingly, hefting the book onto a stack of originals at the end of Irem's desk. "The illustrations took longer than I expected, but I still have time to work on the scrolls you mentioned."

"No need," he said, waving her off. "We have more pressing matters." He glanced at the timepiece on his desk: a small, delicate gold pendulum that looked as if it had been quietly ticking since the days of Riku, the benevolent Rí who founded ancient Iathium.

"Yes, sir," she said, tapping her fingers on the stack of manuscripts. "What—"

"We are expecting a visitor," he said. "Come, help me stand."

Lira braced Irem's elbow as he struggled to rise from his stool. She reached for his cane, passing it to him. The elderly lord steadied himself, raising his chin to glance back toward the door. "Lock us in."

She crossed the room hastily to engage the lock. "But I thought—"

Tapping from beneath the floor at the chamber's center silenced her. She whirled, eyes widening. "What's that?"

"Our visitor." Irem chuckled, hobbling toward the source of the noise. He used his cane to tap a pattern into the tiles, the sound billowing into what seemed like a booming echo. Lira couldn't say whether the sound was truly that loud, or she was merely nervous.

Irem stepped back as the center of the spiral opened with a groan, revealing a stone staircase. The flickering of a lantern made its way upward, cresting the edge of the floor and flaring as its bearer entered the chamber.

The Rí.

Lira gaped at Iathium's supreme ruler as he lowered his lantern. Rí Eremon's long, black hair was tied at the nape of his neck. The eye-popping azure, gold, and violet of his silken robe caught her eye, its rich fabric shimmering in the candlelight. He flashed her a wide smile, as if he'd known her for years.

"Good afternoon, Silira," he said, in a voice as rich as the blueberry-filled chocolate candies Lira hoarded on holy days.

She opened her mouth to speak, but her lips and tongue had turned to sandpaper. Instead, she blinked once. Twice.

At nineteen, Eremon was the youngest ruler Iathium had seen in two centuries—the same age as Lira.

"Well, aren't you going to say something, Silira?" Irem chuckled.

Lira didn't realize she'd been moving backward until she bumped into Irem's desk and crashed down onto his stool. Her backside throbbed as she averted her eyes and dropped haphazardly to one knee, the hard tiles sending a painful shock up through her leg. She tried to hide her cringe, her face burning.

"I beg your pardon, my lord," she stammered, trembling.

"Eremon," he said, offering his hand to her. She took it awkwardly, letting him pull her to her feet.

Eremon was far more handsome than she remembered from her few brief, distant glimpses of him at the few feasts and ceremonies her father, Arlen, had allowed her to attend as a child; she tried to be subtle as she noted his high cheekbones, full lips, and the soft angles of his eyes. Today, he was disarmingly casual. The wide sleeves of his thigh-length robe were rolled up to his forearms, and he had replaced his usual black trousers and boots with loose-fitting pants and sandals.

"I'm honored, Eremon," Lira echoed.

His name rolled off her tongue with ease; like ordinary citizens of Iathium, she had never spoken it aloud without his title attached. Still, it felt oddly familiar.

It was becoming quite a challenge for Lira to hide her surprise at the entire situation—his nearness, the fact that he was speaking to her, and that he'd just asked her to call him by his given name. She knew she was gaping at him, and though she was horrified at herself for doing it, she couldn't seem to stop.

Eremon smiled briefly, but shifted his gaze toward Irem, as if deferring to the older man. Lira took a step back, putting a more appropriate distance between herself and the young ruler.

"I apologize for shocking you, Silira," Irem said as he moved to clasp Eremon's hand in greeting. "Eremon asked to see you on quite short notice."

In that moment, Eremon seemed more like one of the elderly man's charges than his highest authority.

"Lord Irem couldn't refuse," Eremon quipped with a wry grin. "Besides, he's been telling me for years that I should meet you face-to-face. I'm glad I finally listened."

"Years? I—I beg your pardon?" Lira sputtered.

"You're an incredibly talented historian," Eremon began as he crossed the chamber, setting his lantern beside Lira.

She held her breath as he leaned casually against the desk, inches away from her.

"I've observed your work for some time," he continued, "and I wanted a proper introduction. Besides, the three of us have something important to discuss."

"Thank you," she said, lowering her gaze again, "but why?"

Eremon brushed his fingertips across book bindings on the stacks next to him. "Your passion for our histories is unparalleled. Inborn instinct like that is rare."

He turned to face her again, his expression alight with excitement. "Why *wouldn't* I want to meet someone like you— someone who would preserve the histories of my city with such care?"

His ash-gray eyes bored into hers with an intensity that made Lira's stomach twist. She laced her fingers together tightly, suddenly unsure of what to do with her hands—or the rest of herself, for that matter. She shifted her gaze from her mentor to Eremon, then back again. Clearly, Irem expected her to speak for herself; she worked her jaw uncertainly.

"I can't truly say, my lord."

"Eremon." He gave her a gentle, long-suffering smile. "Lord Irem says no one else in the archives understands or retains these histories like you. You commit every detail to memory like your life depends on it."

"Th-thank you," she stammered. "I have loved our histories since I was a child; my Da and Lord Irem taught me well."

Eremon nodded. "I used to beg my father to let me abdicate when I was a boy. I wanted to be apprenticed here instead."

Lira's eyes widened; for a moment, she imagined a younger Eremon occupying a work space next to her in the archive— two apprentices studying together under Irem's tutelage. She wondered what it might have been like if Rí Corlan had allowed his son to give up the throne, and how Eremon would have gotten on with her friends.

The thought of Eremon's father brought memories of her own Da rushing back. Images of the grim-faced sentries who brought the news of Arlen's death to her threshold seven years prior flashed through her mind. Corlan had been aboard the same ship as Arlen, sailing for Iteloria on a mission whose purpose had never been disclosed. The late

Rí's body had been returned for burial, but Arlen's was never recovered.

"I'm sorry you weren't able to join us here," Lira said, shoving down thoughts of her father. "I would have enjoyed studying alongside you."

"As would I," Eremon replied.

Irem cut in. "But private lessons in the chamber are the next best thing, are they not?"

Eremon smiled warmly. "Yes, sir. After hours, as we do."

"I've never seen you here after hours," Lira blurted.

"Because you haven't been permitted in the chamber after hours," Irem scolded gently.

Lira's cheeks heated, but she tried to laugh off her embarrassment. "That's true, unfortunately."

Eremon clasped his hands behind his back. "Let's get right to business, Silira. You're familiar with the spoken histories of our clans, are you not?"

"Yes," she hedged, heart pounding. She resisted the urge to drag her sweaty palms down her apron, suddenly too aware of the mess of ink on her hands. "My grandmother, Skelly, told me the old legends when I was a child, but I've focused my studies here on recorded histories alone—not folklore."

Eremon crossed the room again to stand before her. Lira shrank at his proximity, and heat rose to her cheeks. She wasn't accustomed to feeling this enamored of anyone; it was normal for her to interact with members of court and the nobility from day to day at the Dome. Beyond the city's upper crust, Lira had plenty of experience dealing with clan leaders, dignitaries, and important people from outside Iathium.

But standing this close to Eremon, she could barely utter a coherent sentence.

"Do you remember Skelly's stories?" he asked, breaking through her thoughts.

She swallowed hard, forcing herself to reluctantly say, "I do."

Memories from her last trip into the southern mountain range flooded her mind; it had been seven years since she'd visited Skelly there. Her grandmother was a lively storyteller who preferred to live in her own imaginary world of fantastical lore. From time to time, Lira's uncle Gerallt—master of Clan Mór and a tradesman who often visited Iathium—tried to persuade Lira to visit them in the mountains, but she had little interest in doing so.

Here in Iathium, Lord Irem was like a grandfather to Lira. Otherwise, Lira's inner circle was small. She and her younger brother, Talfryn, had lived alone together in Iathium since their mother had remarried three years prior.

Iva Mór had abandoned Iathium for Clan Beran's overlord, Artur Beran, and had disappeared into his isolated fortress in Rodhlan's northeastern territory. Lira resented her mother for leaving, especially to embrace Beran's backward culture. Artur and his people were preoccupied by intimidating outsiders, and seemed to have no real interest in anything apart from their own traditions.

Eremon crossed his arms, his voice breaking through Lira's thoughts. "You really think of Skelly's stories as lore?"

A little laugh escaped her lips. "Of course. What else would they be?"

"Histories—silenced and long-forgotten. There are few people in Rodhlan who remember them." Eremon sat on one of the stools by the desk. "Lira, Irem tells me you're a most trustworthy historian—that you have a willing mind and open heart to receive what I'm about to tell you."

Lira's pulse quickened; what could he possibly know that she hadn't already studied, beyond the restricted knowledge she'd craved for so long?

"I'm willing," she said quietly.

Eremon's attention snagged on Irem's timepiece, and he

watched its pendulum tick down the seconds before he spoke again.

"Few ancient records exist in the common tongue. And as you know, we've kept no tomes in the clans' languages here in the archive for centuries—or on the continent, for that matter."

Lira couldn't help feeling a bit frustrated. She wanted to tell Eremon that she knew all these things, but she held her tongue and let him continue.

"Have you ever wondered why we have so little information about the years before Rí Nami's reign—about Iathium's early days? Or about why my forefathers restricted reading and encouraged illiteracy in the name of culture?"

Coming from Eremon, these statements sounded horribly oppressive. Although Lira had always taken issue with the Dome's stance on literacy, she'd still understood Iathium to be a place of prosperity and diversity, where clanspeople and city-dwellers alike could share space. She'd believed—perhaps foolishly—that the inclusion of histories in art and culture made them more accessible to everyone.

Lira felt ashamed to answer, "I really haven't questioned any of it deeply."

Dread stirred deep in her belly; trying to understand what Eremon was saying to her felt like deciphering a faded manuscript page. He didn't respond, but instead appeared to be waiting expectantly for her next words.

"Everything I've studied—the written and oral histories—" Lira continued weakly, her thoughts growing foggy—"nothing seems to have been left out..."

"A lie, sprinkled with a little bit of truth, is more believable." Irem regarded them both. "All of the city's histories contain just enough truth to go unquestioned."

"You're telling me that our histories are lies," she said flatly.

She'd meant for it to come out more like a polite question,

but she couldn't produce the right inflection. The thought that her beloved father's stories and games could have meant nothing —she felt herself breathing rapidly. Her father's lessons and the histories she'd refined here meant *everything*. Da had taught her the foundational truths that helped her excel in the archive.

"I'm sorry, my girl," Irem said, as if reading her racing thoughts.

"We know this isn't easy to hear," Eremon added gently.

Lira stilled, her shoulders tensing. Frustration replaced her confusion as she met Eremon's gaze.

"Why are you telling me this?" she demanded.

"Because the time to reveal the true histories is near," Eremon answered, unbothered by her sudden boldness. "And we need your help to do it."

"What true histories?" Lira huffed a disbelieving laugh and shook her head. "Iathium is truth, and truth is freedom," she recited—but saying the familiar phrase felt more like a deflective tactic than fact. She tried to ignore the pang in her stomach.

"A pledge we repeat to cover the lies," Eremon said earnestly—almost pleadingly. He leaned toward her slightly, as if he wanted to give her a glimpse of his emotion; as if, somehow, sharing it would erase the dread coiling in her belly.

Lira straightened, raising her chin. "That's not possible. It can't be."

"It is," Irem said. "But we didn't have the proof until recently."

The Defender gestured behind him. Two new bookcases sat in a dark alcove, each shelf covered by iron bars and padlocked for safekeeping. Rows of unfamiliar manuscripts—at least one hundred—filled the cases. Some were crumbling like the book she'd transcribed today; others were beautifully bound in emerald, blue, and crimson leather, stamped with bronze and silver filigree.

"Where did these come from?" Lira breathed.

"Iteloria," Eremon answered carefully, studying her expression. "Our fathers were trying to retrieve them when they were killed."

The words seemed to flow from his mouth at an excruciatingly slow pace—yet they slammed into her, knocking her breath out in a ragged rush. She wrapped an arm around her middle, the other hand rising to her mouth as tears clouded her vision.

"It has taken seven years and many failed attempts to get them to Rodhlan," she heard him continue, "but they're finally here, and now we have evidence."

Lira bit the insides of her lips, willing herself into some semblance of composure. Eremon tried to say something else, but she held up a hand and whispered, "I need a moment, please. I'm sorry."

She ducked her head and hugged herself tightly, rushing past the two men to stand nearer to the unfamiliar books. Curling her fingers around the bars that separated the tomes from the outside world, she squeezed her eyes shut and took several shuddering breaths.

Lira's father had been her most ardent supporter when she began her apprenticeship at the archive. He had been the one to kindle her love for Iathium's history, and was the most vocal detractor of Skelly's stories.

"It doesn't make sense," she whispered thickly, afraid to raise her voice any louder for fear of sobbing in front of the Rí.

"But it does."

She jumped, startled; Eremon had moved quietly to her side.

"It makes sense because your father was loyal to Iathium. So, when the crown had need of his help, Arlen was willing to serve—even if he didn't fully understand." Eremon lay a tentative hand on Lira's shoulder. "Just like his daughter, I hope."

Lira didn't want to meet his eyes, but she forced herself to. "I can't imagine Da dying to dismantle Iathium's histories."

"Not to dismantle, but to rebuild," Eremon said softly.

Now, she looked to Irem, her eyes pleading. She felt helpless; if anyone else had challenged the histories as Eremon was right now, she would have set them straight. But standing before the highest authorities in the city, she could barely formulate an appropriate reply.

"I love the stories of this place and what our city stands for—what I thought it stood for." Lira's voice trembled. "Please, help me understand."

"Your father was made privy to information that changed his mind about a great many things," Irem said, his expression full of pity. "I'm sorry he was never able to tell you himself."

"Why would your father have wanted an armorer's help retrieving these books?" she asked Eremon. "Da was no archivist, and he was no seafarer, either."

The disparate pieces of the story still didn't fit together. She had always imagined that her father had been killed in some effort to gather secrets of the Itelorians' armor, weaponry, and battle tactics. As Rí Corlan's head armorer, Arlen had designed and crafted the sentries' chain mail, plate, and weaponry. Logic had led her to the conclusion that his death had been associated with his work.

"Our fathers found they shared more interests than the city's welfare alone," Eremon answered.

Lira shook her head. "What could they have possibly—"

"They were equally invested in your futures," Irem interrupted, giving Eremon a stern look. "If that meant clarifying the existing histories, they were willing to risk their lives to do so."

Eremon pressed his lips together and nodded in agreement. He looked conflicted for a brief moment before he spoke again.

"If it isn't too odd for me to say..." Eremon traced the delicate wrought iron on the shelf. "I recall seeing you the day we buried my father. I thought of you as a strange sort of friend who knew how I was feeling, though we'd never met."

Lira remembered being acknowledged by the head sentry at Rí Corlan's burial. Eremon and his mother, Raní Macha, had remained still and silent—except for a brief moment when the boy had locked eyes with Lira. At the time, she'd imagined some unspoken bond of shared grief between herself and Eremon, though it had been years since she'd spent time thinking about it.

Apparently, Eremon felt the same.

She swallowed the lump in her throat, turning her attention back to the litany of questions crowding her mind. "Who recorded these? How did they escape discovery?"

"A small band of scholars left Rodhlan to preserve these old volumes a thousand years ago, far from the city's reach. They also managed to secure a number of Itelorian records and religious texts documenting Rodhlan's history from their point of view."

"Who here can translate records from Iteloria?" she asked, her eyes widening in awe.

"I can," Eremon answered.

Lira sized him up with renewed curiosity, but looked back to Irem. "What about the others? The clans' languages are banned; who could possibly speak or write in them?"

"All in good time, Silira," Irem soothed.

"Forgive me, my lord, but is there time?" she asked, hastening across the room to stand before her mentor. "You're saying that our histories are lies. Yet we're going to leave the apprentices in the dark? And what about Aidryn? Shouldn't he be here? He is my superior, and—"

"Aidryn is older than you, Silira," Irem replied, "but he is not your superior. And, he has given his notice. He will not be pursuing a position as my heir; therefore, he need not be here for these meetings."

Lira felt like she'd been slapped. "Why would he do that?"

Aidryn had always been with her here; how could he give up inheriting Irem's title? How could he abandon her?

"He has asked to gather oral histories from the clans," Irem answered, "which will require extensive travel. I have agreed to his request."

"How much does Aidryn know?" Lira pressed. "How much am I allowed to discuss with him?"

"Please keep this discussion within these walls for the time being. You may ask him about any plans he has for travel, but everything else..." Irem shrugged. "It's vital for you to understand that Aidryn knows all he needs to, at present."

Lira almost choked on her own words as she managed to say, "I see."

Once again, Eremon had followed her across the room; Lira knew he was carefully reading her responses, her body language. She had long since lost the ability to mask her expression.

Irem grasped her shoulder firmly. "Don't look so downtrodden. He isn't leaving for good."

Lira shook her head. "I can't help it; it's too much all at once."

Eremon's body shifted ever so slightly in her direction, as if he wanted to offer her some kind of comfort. After a moment, he stilled, his face the picture of impassive restraint.

His voice was calm and even as he said, "None of this is easy to hear. I imagine someone who loves Iathium as much as you do would be just as heartbroken. And equally heartbroken to know a friend won't be shouldering the burden alongside you —at least not as you'd hoped."

She tried to let his words comfort her, but it was no use. Her throat was still too tight, her shoulders too tense. A painful knot had long since formed deep in her belly—the place where she always held her anxiety and grief.

Irem rested heavily on his cane. "Eremon, perhaps you could tell Silira what role she will play in all of this," he said gently.

Eremon nodded once at Irem, then turned his focus back to Lira. "I would like you to record your grandmother's stories in Athi," he said. "As the next Defender of Histories, it will give you a start on writing your own historical records."

"The next Defender?" Lira whispered.

Of course; if Aidryn was giving up the post, she'd be next in line. The realization numbed her senses. She fumbled through her next words. "If what you've told me is true, then I don't really know our histories as I ought. I have much to learn before I could truly be your Defender."

"I think you'll find the true histories much easier to grasp than you realize," Eremon replied. "Besides, no one else in Lord Irem's charge will know the old tales from Clan Mór. Those stories are a critical part of this endeavor."

Lira stared at her hands. It was hard to believe that Irem and Eremon regarded those ancient clan stories as viable parts of history—the stories she'd long since discarded, though each had impressed itself upon her memory anyway. She fumbled behind her for the stool she'd stumbled into moments earlier, when her most pressing concern had been how to conduct herself in Eremon's presence.

"I don't know what to make of this," she said. "It's too much. And—pardon my candor, Eremon—but if the rulers have been lying for this long, how do I know you won't lie to me?"

Irem looked shocked, but Eremon took her jab gracefully.

"I understand why you feel that way," Eremon said. "Imagine how Irem felt, after so many years of teaching false histories to countless apprentices."

The Rí moved closer to her and reached for her hands. His soft touch jolted her skin, and heat crept up her neck. He continued quietly, imploringly. "Imagine how I felt, as your ruler."

"*Nineteen years*, Ere—forgive me." Lira fought the urge to avert her eyes, glaring steadily into his instead. "For most of my life, I have worked to preserve these stories—to ensure they're passed down. I gave up my family and my childhood, all for these histories, and you're saying it was for nothing. You're saying I failed."

"No, Lira, I failed you," Eremon said. "I have failed my people, but no more. Now is the time for us to act, to expose the truth. Irem has earned the clans' trust; I believe they will also come to trust you in time."

He didn't release his grip on her hands. Both men regarded Lira expectantly. She glanced from one to the other, the wild cyclone of panic fading into a steady thrum. Irem had never given Lira a reason not to trust him. And here was the supreme ruler, standing alongside the elderly lord in solidarity.

For a moment, Lira felt ashamed of lashing out. She sighed, feeling some of the tightness melt from her shoulders with the release.

"After everything you've told me, I don't think I can refuse," she said.

"Of course, you can refuse," Eremon said, squeezing her hands lightly. "But I know your love for Iathium. I've never known of anyone as dedicated to this place as you are, with no ulterior motive. And I believe you have an important role to play in the future of Rodhlan.

"Silira," he urged, "allow me the honor of anointing you as the next Defender. Take up your quill and help us give the truth back to our people."

Eremon was one breath short of begging. Lira tried to hold his gaze without wavering.

Tentatively, she asked, "Why me? Why do you need my help to right wrongs that I had no part in?"

"Because you play a unique role here," Eremon said. "You
—"

"There is no time to explain it all tonight," Irem interrupted
kindly. "Eremon is expected at council. But for my part, Silira, I
know you to be empathic and diplomatic. You perform well
under pressure. And when the time comes, you'll be able to
lead our apprentices and our people to the true histories in the
gentlest way possible."

The elderly Defender's eyes shone as he added, "You have a
heart, Silira. That is, perhaps, the most important reason of all."

Part of her wanted to flee; but another, more insistent part
demanded that she negotiate her terms. If she was going to
learn the truth, she wanted to have a say in how it happened.

"If I agree to this," she hedged, "I want to learn as much as I
can, as quickly as possible. I don't want to be left in the dark
about any of it—not any longer."

"Agreed," Eremon said hastily, before Irem could counter.
"As quickly as possible."

"Within reason," Irem added.

Eremon stood before Lira; he had never let go of her hands.
For a moment, she wondered why she hadn't bothered to withdraw. He brushed his thumb over her fingers, then gently
squeezed them as he leaned in imploringly.

"Please, Lira," he breathed. "Help us."

He felt like an anchor, she realized—the one thing teth-
ering her to the room. Eremon truly seemed to be the ruler
she'd always believed him to be. But she'd spent her life
defending a lie, so he would need to prove himself true.

Lira looked into his eyes again, searching for any shred of
deceit, but she could find none. She was silent for a long
moment before she answered, her breath ragged, her thoughts
unmoored.

He's telling the truth.

I don't want it to be true.

How is it possible?

Da died for this.

"I can find no lie in you," she forced out. "I don't believe you will share what you know unless I agree to help, so I will. Teach me the truth my father was willing to die for."

The last words came in a rush; if she let herself pause again, they might not have come at all. She released Eremon then, pressing a trembling hand to her mouth.

Eremon nodded, looking relieved.

"I'll perform the rite," Irem said. "There's no time to waste."

"Let me, Lord Irem," Eremon said, releasing Lira to withdraw an amber vial from his robe pocket before meeting her eyes again. "I would like the honor of anointing you, Lira."

Irem deferred, his gaze sliding to Lira. "If Silira wishes it, then the task is yours."

"Of course," Lira agreed.

Lira stood before Eremon as he uncorked the familiar vial.

"This is the oil I was anointed with when I ascended the throne seven years ago," Eremon said. "I want you to know that I don't take your commitment lightly."

The whole scene felt both surreal and too ordinary, all at once.

"What do I do?" Lira whispered.

"First, kneel," he answered.

Lira obeyed. Eremon locked eyes with her; her breath hitched when he lowered himself to the floor before her.

"Allow me to treat you as an equal," he whispered, turning her trembling palms upward as he placed a drop of oil in the center of each one. "One historian to another."

He anointed the crown of her head with a smile. The oil was fragrant and earthy—like incense wafting through the clean, verdant air of her childhood mountains. A tear slipped down her cheek.

"Close your eyes," Eremon said softly, tipping the vial

against his fingertips. He carefully anointed her forehead and eyelids, his touch barely a flutter on her skin.

"That's it," he whispered.

Lira opened her eyes; Eremon was so close that she could feel his breath on her face. She gasped lightly at his nearness, praying he couldn't hear her racing heartbeat.

"Repeat after me," he said, pocketing the vial and cupping her cheek. He brushed the tear away with his thumb. "I, Silira Mór—"

She blinked hard, struggling to steady her voice, but she did not shrink. "I, Silira Mór—"

"Upon my master's death or departure—"

"Upon my master's death or departure—" She could hardly make herself repeat it.

"Do hereby assume the anointed title Defender of Histories, and solemnly swear to uphold the truths of Rodhlan."

Lira took a deep breath, suppressing her tears again. She repeated the rest of the vow slowly, careful not to stammer.

Eremon fixed a steely gaze on her. "This must remain secret for now, Lira. I know you understand."

Lira nodded numbly. She bit her lip, sinking back on her heels. "What happens now?"

"You will continue your usual duties, with additional training morning and night," he answered. "First, we'll teach you what we've learned. Then, the three of us will work together to record and translate what we can."

Irem clasped her shoulder, squeezing it lightly. "I'm proud of you, my girl. I know we've left you with more questions than answers, but let's take one day at a time."

Eremon stood, then reached for Lira. She let him clasp her hands and pull her to her feet, wobbling as she got her bearings.

"Th—thank you," she said.

Eremon's warm smile nearly sent her crashing to the floor again. "It was an honor, Lira," he said. "I'll see you soon."

With that, he picked up his lantern and descended the staircase. Lira stared after him until the flickering light faded and the tiles closed around the entrance.

CHAPTER 2

Lira collapsed against the chamber door, closing it more loudly than intended. The bang echoed through the archive, disturbing the apprentices who lingered over their work. Startled, they broke from their binding and calligraphy, turning to gawk at Lira as she crossed the large room.

Offering them an apologetic wince, she moved mechanically toward the massive spiral staircase that led to the main floor of the Dome. She ached to get home, where she could wrap herself in a warm blanket and sort out her racing thoughts away from prying eyes.

Lira bounded up the first few steps before Aidryn caught her by the arm. She whirled, grabbing the wide railing to steady herself. Even on a such a damp day, he smelled faintly of warm spices and the fresh, open air of the meadowlands—where he'd no doubt been out riding before he arrived at the archive.

"You forgot this," he said, holding out her leather satchel. "I packed your quills for you. I know you have your own method, but it's getting late."

She took the satchel from him, slinging the strap over her

shoulder and resisting the urge to dump out the bag's contents and repack everything the way she liked it. "Thank you."

"What, no tongue-lashing today?" He raised his brows, moving closer to study her face. "Lira, what's the matter?"

"Nothing. Irem was burning incense again," she answered. "It makes my eyes water."

It wasn't really a lie; the perfume was particularly torturous in the archival chamber, which trapped the fragrant smoke in a stifling haze.

Lira skipped several steps, eager to avoid his searching gaze. Aidryn caught up with her easily, matching pace with her. She was tempted to speed up, but she was already practically running.

"His incense is a special kind of putrid," Aidryn said from her side. "No idea where he finds the stuff, but it should be a punishable offense."

Lira tried to outpace him again, lengthening her strides as she moved up the stairs. She only exceeded in becoming winded, while Aidryn matched her pace effortlessly.

"I'm in a hurry," she huffed breathlessly. "I was supposed to meet Caitir ten minutes ago."

Lately, Aidryn's sister—Lira's closest friend—had been preoccupied with private tutors and her handmaiden duties to Eremon's mother. Lira's meetings with Caitir had become a rare treat, and she was worried her friend might be gone by the time she arrived in the courtyard. She needed the distraction and laughter today; it would help her stay composed until she arrived home.

"I'll come with you," he offered. "We're all going the same direction."

"If you like," she answered, voice flat. She fixed her gaze on the stone steps, willing away the tears that pricked her eyes.

"Lira," Aidryn pressed, "please, let me help."

Lira's shoulders sagged, and she stopped climbing for a

moment. Aidryn stopped, too, leaning expectantly against the wide stone banister.

It had always been easy to hide her feelings from Caitir, who was too aloof to notice the occasional dark moods that overtook Lira. But Aidryn had always been able to see even the subtlest shifts in her demeanor and was quick to ask questions —which Lira usually rebuffed. Today, though, she sagged resignedly, too exhausted to put him off.

"I just need to get home in one piece. Can you help me do that?" she whispered, her chin trembling.

Aidryn's brow furrowed, but he nodded and began to move. "Come on, then."

It will be difficult not to speak with him about the histories, she thought as she followed, *but at least he already knows I'm taking his place. Perhaps there's no harm in talking about that later.*

Lira wished she felt ecstatic about the anointing. It should feel like a victory, but instead, she felt shocked and hollowed-out. Perhaps she could justify prodding Aidryn about it under any other circumstance, for the sake of stoking their competitive rapport—except he'd given up the title. Essentially, he had handed the post to her. That meant she owed him something.

A pang of annoyance struck her; she didn't like feeling indebted to anyone.

Aidryn and Lira continued up the winding staircase in silence. As they climbed higher, the stifling quiet of the archive gave way to the bustle of the Dome's ground floor. Afternoon sunlight bathed them in warm gold as they shouldered their way through the crowd that pushed toward the courtyard. Lira squinted as her eyes adjusted, her long hours underground a stark contrast to the vibrant daylight.

Gently curving panels of intricately etched glass stretched upward around them, a deceptively delicate-looking intrados that opened into a wide, stained-glass oculus above them. The entire Dome was made of glass panels so thick that only the natural light filtered through them, distorting the images on both sides.

Along the inside of the wide corridor were windows that displayed artifacts from ancient Iathium. Statues, clothing, lanterns, jewelry, tools, and other relics were carefully arranged on stone shelves behind panes of thick, clear glass. Members of the archival staff—usually the curators—periodically cleaned and restored these items.

Lira had once been allowed to assist Iona, the head curator, during her apprenticeship. She vividly remembered the older woman's sharp reprimands when she handled a diadem without gloves. The problem had not been that she touched the jewels bare-handed, but the fact that she'd imagined a history for the item—and made the mistake of voicing it while she worked.

"Do you suppose Riku's wife wore this once?" she'd mused, carefully polishing each stone. "Dark hair—auburn, perhaps, with flecks of gold that caught the sun. Mother of Iathium, friend of the clans, giver of light—"

Iona had cut her off and marched her straight to Irem, claiming that Lira's wild imagination was distracting her from the work at hand. Irem had just smiled at Lira, winked discreetly, and promised Iona he would discipline the girl.

But rather than disciplining Lira, Irem lifted her apprentice restrictions and gave her full access to the books in the archive—though she hadn't been tasked with artifact preservation again. Lira still didn't know what to make of the incident.

She remembered Aidryn's flustered sputtering when she had joined him at the research desk the next day with a stack of scrolls, a newly minted historian. He had spent the first half of that year ribbing Lira about their age difference, and how she would have to wait an extra year to catch up.

Funny, how their roles had reversed. She wished her

promotion to Defender hadn't relied solely upon Aidryn's decision to give up the role.

Lira busied herself studying the shapes and patterns of the people and objects until Aidryn asked, "Are you cross with me?" He stood between her and the door, as if daring her to pass without answering.

She narrowed her eyes. "I will be if you keep interrogating me. Besides, it isn't something we can talk about here. Now, *move.*"

The words came out harsher than she'd intended. Lira winced, then added a clipped, "Please."

Aidryn raised an eyebrow. He leaned against the door and pushed it open, holding it for her as she passed in a huff.

"You're welcome," Aidryn said.

Lira saw a glint of shimmering fabric near the courtyard gates and trotted toward it, Aidryn at her heels. Caitir was perched on their usual bench, impatiently twisting the ends of her thick, golden hair between her fingertips. Her gown, a few shades darker than her hair, was luminous in the sun.

"Lira!" Caitir beamed. She rose to kiss Lira's cheek.

"I'm sorry I'm late," Lira replied, returning the kiss.

"Let's hurry," Caitir said breathlessly. "I can't miss another appointment; Mother will never let me hear the end of it."

"Your hair is beautiful," said Lira. "Tell your mother the stylist can rot."

Aidryn kicked a pebble down the walkway. "That's what I always say."

"You know I can't," Caitir answered. She raised a brow at Aidryn. "No kiss for me, then?"

"You act so surprised," he said dryly, starting for the gate. "You can't have everyone doting on you."

"True to form." Caitir exchanged a knowing glance with Lira. "Do you think I'll ever be able to catch him off guard?"

Lira snorted. "Doubtful."

They were accustomed to Aidryn sticking close, and Lira knew he held a deeply protective affection for his younger sister. Caitir had made a game of trying to draw compliments and flattery out of Aidryn, which he playfully withheld. Lira thought their guarded sparring was strange; she and Talfryn had always been open with one another.

The girls linked arms and followed Aidryn through a towering, ornate archway of weathered stone and heavy, wrought-iron doors—the gateway from the Dome into the city proper. The path from the Dome to the gate was paved in mica, worn to a shine by centuries of foot traffic in and out of the city. Once through the gate, the streets changed to deterio-rated cobblestone, a foundation laid long before the Dome existed.

Walking in Iathium had always sent a thrill through Lira. It didn't matter that she traveled the familiar roads every day. Each building, each stone underfoot had a story. Although there was no way she could collect each one, she felt their weight, as well as the presence of those who had walked these streets before.

Lately, she had been too busy to walk with her friends like this. Lira's work in the archive and Caitir's duties at the Dome had long since broken their childhood ritual. Now that Lira had been anointed Defender, their meetings would be even more seldom.

She sighed quietly, a wave of sadness rippling through her. Although Lira had always been focused on becoming a histo-rian, she felt somehow shaken by how rapidly time had passed. The long, drawn-out days of adolescence and young adulthood had given way to responsibilities that would consume them from now on.

"I miss the old days," Caitir said, as if reading Lira's thoughts. "Pretending to serve the Raní was more fun than actually doing it."

"I don't know how you tolerate it. I need my solitude and quiet time to read."

Caitir lifted her hem off the ground as they stepped through a puddle of rainwater. "You spend more time with those books than you do with people."

"That's my favorite part," Aidryn piped up from behind them.

"Mine, too," Lira added.

Caitir laughed. "You're both mad."

The trio passed through a throng of street vendors hawking their wares outside the courtyard—artisans, clothiers, wood-carvers, bakers, and musicians competed for the attention of nobility exiting the Dome for the day. Booths and tents lined the cobblestone walkway that led into the heart of town. Lira's mouth began to water at the sight of one farmer's table, spread with an array of colorful, sweet berries and fresh vegetables.

Merchants always crammed the walkways leading to and from the Dome; it was their best chance to catch customers with plenty of coin. But today, the streets were especially noisy and crowded; the city was preparing for *Nami Mostari*, an annual festival celebrating the coming spring and the reign of Iathium's greatest ruler.

"How were lessons?" Lira asked over the din, sidestepping one merchant from Clan Beran who practically shoved a neck-lace of wooden beads in her face.

"Boring." Caitir fingered some colorful, silky ribbons hanging from one of the carts they passed. "Except for dancing —but that has a tangible reward."

Lira sometimes envied Caitir's private tutors and continued lessons that had extended well beyond Iathium's customary school years of ages eight to sixteen. But as the child of an ambassador and a high lady-in-waiting, Caitir had been afforded the best courtier training the city had to offer. Her mother had managed to secure her a handmaiden's post in

Raní Macha's private quarters. But it had all come with a steep price; Macha was notoriously difficult to deal with. The mere thought of the woman made Lira shudder.

"I passed the Rí in the corridor this morning," Caitir answered, eyes brightening. "I'm counting on him to recognize me at *Nami Mostari*. I've practiced the opening reel so many times, I could do it in my sleep."

Lira's stomach twisted at the memory of Eremon's electrifying touch. She tried to keep her expression impassive—and hoped it was convincing.

"He has ignored that tradition for the past seven years," Aidryn said. "Don't expect it to change this year just because you perfected your simper."

Until Eremon's ascension, it was custom for the Rí to choose a young, noble lady for the festival's first dance, named after Iathium's first supreme ruler. But he had yet to participate in the ritual, and he didn't seem bothered by disappointing anyone.

Caitir ran her fingertips through her hair. "This year is my best chance yet. Once I turn nineteen, all bets are off—Mother said so."

Lira's cheeks heated; at one year her junior, Caitir had always been too aware of the inevitable progression of time. Nineteen was still a marriageable age, though conventional wisdom considered it to be late. Eremon's refusal to marry had not only succeeded in aggravating his own mother's infamous nerves; it had also given opportunistic mothers like Aila Tarlach hope for an advantageous match.

"Caitir, you could barely pass for fifteen," Lira replied. "You're going to be just fine."

"Don't flatter her, Lira," Aidryn said with a grin. "She gets enough of that at home."

"And plenty of pressure to go along with it," Caitir added. "It rather negates the compliments."

Her brother gave her a little sideways glance; he wasn't quick enough to conceal the pained expression that crossed his face before Lira spotted it.

"I've always said you would make a wonderful dressmaker —that's a compliment," Aidryn said. "And I wish you hadn't stopped drawing and sewing."

His sister's steps faltered, and Lira slowed down to stay in pace with her. Aila had abruptly ended Caitir's sewing lessons the year before, and it had devastated her. But Caitir wouldn't discuss how she felt about it with Lira or Aidryn. It had been upsetting to them both to see her give up something she had loved so much.

Caitir looked rattled for a moment before she parroted her mother. "Dressmakers don't inherit thrones or estates."

"Says who?" Aidryn shot back. "Just marry up. Your husband doesn't have to be the Rí or one of his lords; there are plenty of nobles with sizable inheritances."

Caitir rolled her eyes. "I'm not going over this with you again, Aidryn. You know what Mother wants; I'm just doing my best to give it to her. It doesn't hurt that the Rí is ridiculously handsome."

Lira stumbled, slipping on a cobblestone as she struggled to regain her footing. Caitir tightened her grip on Lira's arm.

"Don't fall!" she cried. "You'll take me down with you."

Lira righted herself, flustered. "Clearly, my feet aren't working properly today." The statement sounded like a cross between a sputter and feigned laughter. "Proof that I should never walk down any aisle, anywhere. I'd probably get nervous and trip."

"What made you nervous just then, Lira?" Aidryn probed. His blue eyes sparked with a knowing that would have made Lira blush, if it hadn't annoyed her so much.

"D'you know those awful, killer hare drawings in the illuminated manuscripts?" she asked, hoping he'd take the bait.

The ancient drawings of murderous hares torturing and maiming unsuspecting humans were something of a running joke between Lira and Aidryn. In their younger years, they'd taken to slipping practice sketches of the offending scenes into one another's books, and the habit persisted—even after Aidryn began training as Defender.

Aidryn humored her, dropping the subject. "What about them?"

"Well..." Lira sighed. "I was thinking about how I have to sketch one tomorrow."

Caitir wrinkled her brow. "But I don't unders—"

"There's a nude man in it," Lira blurted.

Caitir crowed with laughter. "Lira, stop! That's the worst!"

"I know!" She forced a giggle. "And the most excruciating part is waiting for Irem's approval. He has to make sure I got all the—" she waggled her index finger before her, as if drawing—"you know. All the bits right."

"No!" Caitir squealed, doubling over with laughter. "Is the tome a copy for the archive, or will it go to some noble's home?"

"The original is falling apart," Lira answered quickly. "It can't be re-bound."

"Pity," Caitir said with a mischievous grin. "I'd have liked to know who ordered it."

Lira laughed along with her, until Aidryn caught her eye and shook his head. "Nice try," he mouthed.

She scowled at him briefly before looking back at Caitir, who was breathless with laughter, her cheeks rosy from the exertion of the walk. Lira had never seen her look so stunning.

"You're too hard on yourself, Caitir," Lira said, "truly. You'll find the best match out of us all."

"I don't know." Caitir shook her head but smiled anyway. "But I do think you should stop acting like a spinster who'd rather marry an old scroll than a handsome lord."

"I don't need a husband," Lira replied. "Besides, no man would want to compete with the archive for my affection."

As a member of the working nobility, Lira had the option of both continuing her work and having a family; but it was rare for young, married women to remain in their posts at the Dome. Instead, many left work to have families, then returned after their children had grown and left home. Lira wasn't ready to consider any ramifications that marriage and children might have on her job.

Caitir nudged her playfully. "You could always marry Lord Irem and inherit the library at his estate."

"What?" Lira cried.

Aidryn snorted. "She *would*, if she knew books were part of the agreement."

"I would *not*," Lira protested loudly, smiling in spite of herself.

Two women walking ahead of them glared disapprovingly over their shoulders at Lira, and she sucked in a breath, biting her lower lip to quiet her voice. Next to Caitir's finery, she and Aidryn looked like servants. Their ink-stained archival uniforms stood in stark contrast to the shimmering fabric of her friend's gown. Perhaps passersby shared the same opinion.

"I wouldn't," Lira repeated, more quietly this time. The last thing she wanted was to attract more undue attention.

Hurt flashed briefly in Caitir's eyes. "With my luck, I'll probably end up married off to some elderly lord."

Aidryn winced but gave a little shrug. "If he has resources and leaves well enough alone, you can do what you please."

"That doesn't sound like you." Caitir glared at him accusingly.

"It's not good advice, but you don't want that," he snapped. "You care too much about what Mother wants."

His sister laughed hollowly, waving a dismissive hand. "I

suppose an old man wouldn't mind my sewing and drawing, so long as I give him an heir."

Lira raised her eyebrows, desperate to revive their light-hearted banter. "Ah, so then *you* can buy me a library, Caitir, and I won't need a man to give me one."

"What makes you think a man would want to give you a library?" Aidryn asked.

Lira knew he was joking, but the jest stung. Impulsively, her mind flashed to an image of Eremon presenting her with an ornate library, complete with five stories and soaring spiral staircases. She imagined a glass oculus at the top that scattered shimmering cobalt light around the room. Now, her face was blazing.

"Nothing," Lira sputtered. "That's why I'm not in the market for one."

Caitir waggled her eyebrows. "A library, or a man?"

Lira stuck her nose in the air in mock offense. "If you don't know the answer to that, then you don't know me."

Again, Lira found herself thinking of the way Eremon had touched her during the anointing. It had been entrancing and intimate—something she'd never experienced with anyone, and had certainly not imagined would happen with *him*. She couldn't shake the way it had felt to have him so close to her.

I'm just flustered, she thought. *It was all so unexpected.*

Besides, Caitir had her heart set on catching Eremon's eye. And it was logical that the two might end up together; Caitir was beautiful, engaging, and strategically positioned for a smart match. With Caitir's feelings to consider, it would be foolish for Lira to start imagining Eremon as anything other than an acquaintance.

They stepped onto the Drochaid, a natural bridge that spanned the width of the Moravon River. Iathium was built on a plateau that straddled the river, which flowed north and spilled over jagged cliffs at the northwest corner of the city. The northern wall acted as a barrier between the city and the river's long, deadly drop into the gorge below. No matter what part of the city Lira was located in, she could always hear the faint rushing of the river below. On summer nights, she loved to open the shutters to her chamber and listen to the river and the sounds of the nocturnal birds that sang in her trees until the early morning hours.

The three of them crossed the bridge in silence, emerging into the market district, a peaceful, affluent area. It boasted quaint, neatly-kept shops, luxury vendors, and artisans who were fortunate enough to be sponsored by the Dome. Sunlight gilded the recently repaved cobblestone streets and flawless architecture, and Lira tilted her chin toward the warmth, willing it to lift her spirits. She was glad Caitir didn't seem to notice her unease.

Caitir stopped walking when they reached the corner nearest the stylist's shop. "Aidryn, will you be back to walk me home?"

"Not today. I'm shoeing Fannin before it gets dark." He tweaked Caitir's chin with his thumb. "Like you, he requires maintenance. I'll send Father."

His sister swatted his hand away. "I'll see you at home, then. Lira, please don't forget the flowers tomorrow."

Lira's mind had wandered to the anointing again. She'd never been close enough to see that Eremon's eyes were gray— almost silver, with flecks of shimmering teal. Their color reminded her of the fish that swam against the current in Beran's Gorge every autumn.

Caitir stepped closer, rested a hand on Lira's shoulder, and repeated, "Lira?"

Lira's gaze snapped to Caitir's. "Flowers?" she sputtered.

"For the *Nami Mostari* crowns. You've never forgotten." Caitir grasped Lira's hand now, bouncing on her toes. "Honestly, Lira, where is your mind today? You've been acting out of sorts."

Every year, the girls wove circlets of fresh flowers, which they carefully dried during the weeks before the two-day celebration. Lira had a knack for finding early blooms every year, so it had fallen to her to gather enough flowers for both of them.

It was a longstanding tradition for the young ladies of Iathium to wear similar crowns to the festival. When Eremon chose his dance partner—if he chose one this year—he would replace the crown with a circlet of fresh blooms.

"How stupid of me; of course, I'll bring the flowers." Lira squeezed Caitir's fingers. "And I'm fine; just a little tired, that's all."

"You're working too hard," Caitir said. "You need to make plans to enjoy the festival this year; otherwise, you're going to miss everything."

"I really should." Lira nodded toward the shop. "You'd better get inside."

Caitir nodded and crossed the street, her steps light as she dodged people and carts. She turned back once she'd reached the shop.

"I'm going to make sure you have fun this year," Caitir called. She raised the hem of her skirts to climb the stairs, then disappeared inside.

Aidryn jerked his chin in the direction of Lira's house. "Come on, I'll walk you home."

Lira wrapped her arms around her middle. "No. You're shoeing Fannin, and I need some quiet."

Aidryn scrutinized her, rubbing his neck. "What I said back there, about marriage and a library, and all that nonsense—did it upset you?"

"What? No," Lira replied with a shrug. "It was just a joke."

She hoped she was playing it off convincingly.

He took a step closer, as though he didn't believe her, and lowered his voice. "It seemed to bother you. If it did, I'm sorry."

"It didn't." Lira dropped her arms and instead clasped her hands behind her back, leaning nearer to him conspiratorially. "But if it had, I would pardon you."

He looked relieved for a moment but pressed on. "Are you going to tell me what has you tied up in knots today?"

She forced a smile. "I would like to know why you gave up your title."

Aidryn's eyes flicked toward the shop, flashing with panic. He took Lira's arm and steered her further away as he whispered, "So that's it. Couldn't you have said something back at the Dome?"

"No." Lira had to trot to keep up with his pace as they cleared another block. "Why didn't you tell me first? The least you could have done is warn me before Lord Irem sprang the news."

He crossed his arms as they walked. "I assumed you would be ecstatic."

"Not the way everything happened," she said. "Aidryn, there's more. I need to talk with you about it, but I've been asked not to."

"Then don't," he replied, holding up a hand as she opened her mouth again. "Keep it between your ears. When the time is right, we'll discuss everything with Lord Irem. Sooner, if we must—but let's try to avoid that."

Lira nodded, adding, "And Erem—"

Aidryn clapped a hand over her mouth before she could finish saying the Rí's name. "Are you daft, Lira?" He shook his head, releasing her to hiss, "Don't drop his title. By Nami, you know better."

"You're right," she said, voice low. She scanned the area around him before saying more. "He asked me to call him by his name, but perhaps I shouldn't say it in public. It's bad form."

Aidryn sighed. "It was bad form for *him* to invite that sort of familiarity. Be careful, Lira; you have to keep quiet about any contact you have with him."

"Why?"

"I can't—" He lowered his voice to a whisper, motioning for her to walk with him again. "All I know is that I have been told pieces of the story, and you have probably been told a few *different* pieces. And we've been asked not to put those pieces together."

"I can't understand why," she said angrily. "Don't you think it would be better to work together? I hate being left in the dark and expected to play along."

"Yes," he conceded. "I'm sure we'll talk more soon. For now, if anyone asks, I'm trading spices outside the city."

She nodded shakily and attempted to swallow the lump in her throat. "Then I suppose that's what I'll say."

Aidryn rolled his shoulders. "You can also tell them I needed more time outdoors. Hunching over books was starting to make me feel like an old man."

Lira massaged a knot in her neck. She'd already developed aches and pains from the long hours studying and transcribing, herself. "So you'd rather *I* hunch over them until I'm ancient?"

"At least until you *feel* ancient." He winked. "Which shouldn't take long."

The sun had dipped low in the west, casting an array of shadows and wide swaths of warm light across the aged buildings and cobblestone streets. Lira thought of Skelly and the summers she'd spent climbing trees in sunsets like this, happily listening to her clan's folklore, her bare feet dangling from her favorite perch.

At the time, she'd believed the stories to be fiction—vivid and engrossing and strangely alive, but fiction, nonetheless.

Skelly always had a way of sparking Lira's imagination until she could smell, touch, and taste elements of the dream worlds her grandmother created.

Iathium's histories had never stirred Lira in quite the same way, but she had come to believe that perhaps truth could never be as lovely as fiction. Da had gently separated her from Skelly's fantastical tales and instead nurtured her love of the city, grounding her in truth and instilling her passion for events that had shaped its past, present, and future.

Now, Lira questioned whether the spark of life in Skelly's tales might hold more truth than the archive did.

For a moment, she wondered what Skelly would say about the conversation she'd been part of today. But she shook off the thought; she wasn't ready to hear her grandmother's bemused *I-told-you-so*. First, it would be best to get proof that the histories had been tampered with. Then, she'd worry about how and what to say to Skelly.

Lira glanced back at Aidryn, who still walked by her side. His good-humored expression had given way to a weight that settled over his features and rounded his shoulders in a subtle, yet uncharacteristic hunch. It was rare for anything to rattle his normally buoyant personality.

"I'm sorry you're going," she ventured, sighing. "I thought I would be thrilled about—" She clamped her mouth shut again; it was imperative to avoid words like *anointing* and *Defender* right now.

And words like Eremon.

"What? About the...?" Aidryn pointed to his forehead, then reached out to tap hers.

Lira flinched; her cheeks burned. "Well, I—"

"Congratulations, by the way." He gave her a slight bow and smiled ruefully. "I only wish you were gloating about it right now. Finally, the greatest victory against your sworn rival, and you're not the least bit pleased."

Lira pushed at the ink-stained cuticle on her left thumb and shrugged. "I want to be pleased about it. But I have a feeling all these secrets are going to become difficult to bear before long."

She lowered her voice; there were fewer people around them now, and her words would be amplified on the quiet street. "I wonder why Lord Irem doesn't trust us."

Aidryn shrugged a shoulder. "Oh, he trusts us implicitly. But he was given specific instructions; and so, they trickle down."

They walked together in silence for another half-mile. Lira had never been banned from discussing work with Aidryn before; there weren't many other people who matched her zeal in a discussion about ancient irrigation methods, or who were willing to debate the accuracy of the weaponry illustrations in the oldest scrolls.

A swell of dread rose in her as her cottage came into view; she pushed it down deep. "And here, I thought I told you not to walk me home." She glowered at him playfully.

Aidryn smirked. "My first official offense."

"One among thousands, I'm sure," she said, rolling the edge of her linen apron between her fingertips. "How long will you be away?"

"A week, maybe two." He rubbed the back of his neck. "Most of the time, I'll be in the city, so if you're pining for me, I won't be far."

"Don't count on it." She elbowed him in the arm. "Go home to your pony. It'll be dark before he gets his shoes."

"That's Itelorian Stallion to you."

"Fine. Cross-bred racing pony." She shooed him away.

Aidryn shook his head as he started back down the street. "We'll see if he lets you go for a ride anytime soon."

Lira laughed as she called, "What makes you think I want to?" Once he was out of earshot, she muttered, "He's a pony."

The Tarlach family's estate was another mile from here, a

tower home built of ancient stone that occupied an entire city block. Lira imagined that the house, comparable to a small palace, had been situated on a sprawling, grassy plain before Iathium was constructed around it. Hundreds of archaic structures were enclosed by the city walls two thousand years ago during the first Rí's reign. They had been occupied by aristocratic families ever since.

Lira closed her eyes and heaved a sigh of relief. She took her time meandering toward the cottage, listening to the distant roar of the Moravon. The sound of the river calmed her, and she tried to let the tension melt from her shoulders as she walked.

Even though Eremon had explained why he'd chosen her as the new Defender, she still felt guilty for accepting a title that was rightfully Aidryn's. He had been her only real competition during their apprenticeship. Lira had outperformed all her peers except for him; the two were infamous among their classmates for their fierce rivalry. Now, they compared daily assignments, determining the winner of each round by an unspoken set of rules only they understood.

Her mind drifted back to what Eremon had said about the hidden histories. She didn't know what to make of any of it. Skelly's tales had mostly been fairy stories—children's tales about magic and mythical creatures that were meant to teach them basic life lessons.

Some of Skelly's stories painted Iathium in a terrible light. Lira had built her life in and around the city, dedicating everything to its service. Accepting those dark tales without sufficient evidence would strip that life of its meaning, or worse, redefine it.

What she did know was that the city-state's existence alone had allowed the outlying clans to become wealthy through commerce. And anyone could make a prosperous life for themselves inside Iathium's walls, as long as they were dedicated and persistent.

"Hard work yields prosperity," she whispered, echoing the words her father had spoken time and again. "Iathium shall prosper."

The familiar refrain of the city had carried her straight to the title she'd earned today. Despite her questions, Irem and Eremon—even Aidryn—*had* deemed her worthy. And perhaps that was enough.

CHAPTER 3

Lira shouldered the door of her stone cottage open to meet the scent of baked fish and fresh bread. Her stomach growled as she locked the door behind her.

This cottage was reminiscent of the old mountain style. Clan Mór's territory had once stretched all the way to Beran's Gorge, so Lira assumed one of her ancestors had built it here centuries ago. Her father must have chosen the home out of necessity rather than nostalgia, since he had adorned its interior with the rich colors and textures of Iathium rather than the clan he came from.

When Lira was a child, she'd begged her father to decorate the little house with the armor he built at the forge. He'd humored her, crafting a life-size suit of armor—complete with chain mail—that Lira and Talfryn displayed proudly in the living quarters. Even now, it remained in the corner of the small room. Talfryn and Lira took turns dismantling and cleaning it; between the two of them, they kept the armor shining like new.

Arlen's skill had been unparalleled, and he had even been commissioned to teach the other armorers his techniques. The work he'd left behind surrounded Lira, and there was a strange comfort in knowing her father had designed every piece of armor the Rí's sentries wore. Iathium's legions were nearly impenetrable because of it.

Da would be proud today, she thought, fingering the delicate shirt of mail. Her father's essence was just as alive to her every day as if he were standing beside her.

She remembered the last book burning Rí Corlan had held in the courtyard of the Dome when she was a child. Back then, she'd been small enough to ride on Arlen's shoulders. Her father had taken her to witness the massive bonfire; it had distressed Lira, who couldn't understand why perfectly good books should be used for kindling.

Arlen had explained that *these* books were treasonous—unsanctioned by the supreme ruler and, therefore, illegal. She could still smell the burning leather and parchment from the fire that had raged in the courtyard for three days.

"The Rí stands for truth, and nothing less," Arlen had said as his daughter clutched him. Her eyes filled with tears as the fire consumed each precious tome.

"Iathium is truth, and truth is freedom. Don't be afraid, little twig; we are being set free."

Her father had later warned her not to speak of the burning that summer, and every summer after that. For the memory had never faded, and she asked about it every year that followed.

"If you want to understand—if you want to protect truth—become a historian," he'd finally answered, grasping her shoulder firmly. *"Learn the true histories of this place and never stop teaching them."*

Now, more than a mere historian, she was Defender. For the first time since she'd been anointed, a thrill rose within her. Whatever these hidden histories were, she would help to expose them. And whatever the lies, she would help shatter them for her city.

She would help Eremon finish what their fathers had begun.

"Lira?"

Her brother's voice shook her from her trance.

"In here," she called, tearing her eyes away from the armor.

"I thought I heard the door." Talfryn looked around the corner from the kitchen, and his mouth stretched into a wide smile. "I made supper."

Lira crossed the room toward him. Despite the weight of her thoughts, she couldn't suppress the joy she felt in his presence. Talfryn's effervescence could dispel the tension from a room in seconds. It had always been that way, ever since he was a baby.

His spindly frame now towered over Lira. Talfryn might be three years younger, but he had surpassed her in height long ago. He had inherited their father's sharp features and high cheekbones, along with their mother's dark curls and emerald eyes.

"You hungry?" he asked.

Lira's stomach rumbled loudly. She giggled, patting her stomach. "There's your answer."

Talfryn laughed. "Come eat."

Lira followed him to the kitchen, dumping her satchel onto the worktable in the center of the room. Talfryn set to work, filling a dinner bowl for her. A fire crackled in the hearth, warming the soft soles of her leather slippers and the evening chill that had settled into her toes. She sighed and plopped down onto a stool, peeling off her shoes.

"You stink," Talfryn said as he set her bowl in front of her.

"It's Irem's incense."

He set a mug of water next to her bowl. "Smells different."

She shrugged, heaping a spoonful of food into her mouth. Talfryn moved to the basin against the wall, scrubbing the dishes and spoons he'd used.

As he worked, he glanced over his shoulder. "Don't forget, my training starts tomorrow."

Lira swallowed hard, her food suddenly losing its flavor. "I wish you'd wait one more year."

"Not this again." Talfryn sat across from her, his dark hair falling into his striking green eyes. "We've been over it; I'm ready to be a sentry."

"I know." She sighed. "But I don't have to like it."

"We're trading places, little twig." He grinned, reaching across the table to muss her curls. "I'll be the one keeping you safe for a change. You'll be proud of me."

Lira forced a smile, swatting his hand away. "I'm already proud of you, but I don't want you to go yet."

"You're at the Dome more than you're here; I'll probably see you there more often."

A pang of guilt twisted her stomach. That had always been true; she'd left Talfryn to fend for himself more often than she liked to admit. But he was a man now, and there was no use shaming herself.

"You're right," she ventured, squashing the urge to apologize. The anxiety that had been building since she left the chamber churned in her gut.

Lira took another bite, debating what to say next. Finally, she whispered, "Can you keep a secret?"

She knew the answer already. He had never let it slip that she'd taught him to read and write Athi as a child. If he could keep that secret, he could keep this one, too.

Her brother's eyes lit up. "Like a river rock."

Lira leaned closer, and he mirrored her excitedly. "I've been anointed as the next Defender."

"You're joking." Talfryn laughed, his eyes shining.

"You can't tell anyone; I've been sworn to secrecy."

"What about Aidryn Tarlach?"

"He gave up the title," Lira answered. Her stomach dropped at the admission.

Talfryn raised his brows. "Why would he do that?"

"Something about working with his father—I'm not really sure," she hedged.

He let out a long, low whistle. "So you're nobility now."

"Hardly. I'm not officially titled until Lord Irem leaves—whenever that might be."

"Did you meet Rí Eremon?"

Her cheeks reddened. "I did."

"That's incredible." Talfryn reached across the table to grasp her hand. "Leave it to you to steal my thunder, meeting him face-to-face first."

"No thunder here." She tried to laugh but averted her eyes, focusing instead on the fire that crackled in the hearth.

He squeezed her fingers. "You should be crowing from the rooftop. What is it?"

"I wish I could tell you," she whispered, "but even I don't have all the answers yet. Something's wrong, Tal. I want to be happy about this, but I learned things today that frightened me. I'm not sure what's going to happen."

"If anyone can sort it all out, Lira, it's you," he answered. "And if I can help you, you know where to find me. All you have to do is ask."

"If I think of something, I will," she said, "but right now, I hardly know myself."

Talfryn squeezed her hand, then rose. "Sleep on it," he said, echoing their mother's favored advice as he pushed the bench closer to the table. "Maybe by morning, you'll have it sorted."

"I wish it were that simple." Lira stood, reaching out to pat his shoulder. "Good night."

As she padded down the hall toward her chamber, she heard her brother whisper, "Well done."

LIRA DREW her thick curtains over the windows and changed into her shift. Then, she crawled under the quilt. But every time she closed her eyes, vivid images of the conversation with Eremon and Irem invaded her thoughts.

Sleepless hours passed. Lira lay awake, trying to fill in the gaping blanks in the story she'd been told today. She thought of her father and mother. Of her childhood retreat in the mountains. Tales she had tried so hard to forget over the past few years drifted into her consciousness, as sharp and clear as memories.

She didn't know what to believe. Her studies in the archive had produced a tightly-woven story about a pair of brothers—young rulers—from Iteloria who fell in love with Rodhlan and its people. One of those brothers, Riku, established Iathium and became the first Rí. But Rasu, his twin, envied him.

Rasu spent fifteen years quietly assembling an army. When he marched on Rodhlan, his warriors slaughtered any clanspeople who refused to take up arms against Riku. This period came to be known as the Felling of the Clans.

It took Rasu's army months to penetrate Iathium's walls. The first Dome was destroyed during the onslaught, and Rasu and his wife were murdered. But their teenage son, Nami, survived, killing his uncle before he could seize Iathium's throne.

Rí Nami went on to rule Rodhlan for a century, but he never forgave the clans whose people had turned against his parents and his city. He outlawed all written communications in their native languages, narrowing Rodhlan's records down to one common tongue: Athi. People of the clans were even barred from speaking their own languages inside the city walls.

Each time the clans attempted an uprising, Nami added a new decree against communication, for he had come to believe that treason began with the written word. Finally, even the city's citizens, save for the few historians at the Dome, were banned from writing or reading in Athi. Over time, that particular law had been allowed to lapse, though oral histories remained the preferred method of learning.

Nami's rage was legendary among the clans. Lira remembered Skelly telling wild tales about him—legends the great Battle for Iathium had spawned. It was curious, though, that her recollection of the stories felt like memories. Lira could almost see the events unfolding as she lay in the dark, and Skelly's words tumbled from her lips in a fevered whisper:

"In his rage, Nami the Furious split the sky above Iathium. The clouds broke open with a thunderous crack, so that even the ground beneath his feet quaked. He brought the hatred of a thousand cyclones down on Rodhlan, and the Great Clans were felled like a dying forest, cut down and brought low; yet their roots remained, ready to spring forth new life once more."

Years had passed since Lira had thought of Skelly's stories. She couldn't remember the last time she'd studied the heirlooms her grandmother had pressed into her reluctant hands at the end of every visit.

She rose from bed, lit her lantern, and padded across the room to the bureau that sat against the wall. It only took a moment of rummaging through one of the drawers to locate the soft leather pouch where she kept the trinkets.

Sinking back onto the bed, she opened the bag and spilled its contents onto the quilt. She surveyed the familiar items: six slick, colorful stones; a pair of glittering leaves that had been dipped in silver and dusted with gold; a large brass key; a smooth, gray pearl; and a heavy bronze pendant fashioned into a filigree tree.

The necklace felt warm to her fingertips, and she recoiled. She studied its intricate design carefully, then picked it up. She'd forgotten how its swirls and whorls seemed to move and flow like a stream rolling over stones. In the flickering lantern light, the pendant looked more alive than ever.

After the Felling, the remnants of the clans were driven back to their ancestral territories, and the great city-state in the heart of Rodhlan continued its unprecedented rise. Skelly had always told her that Iathium had been the end of magic; what magic, she couldn't begin to guess. Lira's father had strictly forbidden her from asking questions about it, and Skelly had grudgingly respected his wishes.

Iathium had been built of the few remaining unified clanspeople and Itelorian settlers who came at the Rí's call—courageous men, women, and children who braved the treacherous sand and mudflats that spanned the ocean from the islands to Rodhlan. The path only opened once every ten years, and to make the journey, travelers had to move swiftly. Those who weren't fast enough were lost to the high tides.

Exhaustion tugged at Lira, beckoning her to sink into her pillow. She lay down, clutching the pendant against her heart.

She slept fitfully through the night. The lantern burned low as memories flooded Lira's dreams, each more vivid than the last.

CHAPTER 4

Lira's final dream—no, nightmare—crashed over her like a wave and held her under.

She struggles to swim, but the tide rises higher as the undertow holds her firmly to the ocean floor. Her eyes burn as she blinks in the salt water, and her lungs fill with it. She tries to kick, to propel herself upward, but something binds her feet.

When she looks down, she sees them: shackles. Her ankles are enclosed in iron cuffs, and just before she blacks out, she sees the long line of people on either side of her, some still fighting against their own heavy chains, others already lifeless.

Lira's eyes flew open and she scrambled onto her hands and knees, coughing violently; her eyes and throat were on fire. She clutched at her throat, her eyes tearing to clear away the burn. It took a long time to right herself, but she was finally able to draw a deep breath, allowing the silence of her room to calm her racing heart. Shakily, she moved to sit on the edge of the bed, her nose and eyes stinging as if they had truly been filled with seawater.

Early-morning sunlight filtered into her room through cracks between the curtains. She pressed her palms to her eyes, groaning as she rolled toward the edge of the bed. Exhaustion weighed her limbs down as she sat up, swinging her legs over the side of the bed.

In the process, she knocked the pendant into the floor. When she picked it up, she could've sworn it had a heartbeat; it thrummed against her palm like a living creature. Mesmerized, she held it at eye level, watching it swing on its chain like a pendulum.

She unlatched the chain and put the necklace on, letting the heavy charm thump against her chest as she lowered her hands and gazed in the mirror. The pendant felt familiar and comforting around her neck, like an embrace from an old friend. Warmth flooded her body as she studied her reflection.

The only other time she'd worn this necklace was on her seventh birthday. Skelly had draped the heirloom reverently around her granddaughter's neck, infuriating Arlen. Da had furiously demanded that she take it off, then forbade Lira from wearing it again. Though she'd loved the gift at the time, Lira had hidden it away in her room, heartbroken.

She'd only *thought* it had suited her back then. Now, as she surveyed her reflection, it looked like a part of her.

Lira splashed her face with water from the basin, then ran her wet fingers through her curls. When she took one last glance in the mirror, she froze.

Her father's face stared out at her, his brown eyes a mirror of her own, his expression drawn and contemplative. She blinked hard once. Twice. And then there was her reflection once again: her mess of brown curls, the rumpled uniform, the dark circles under her eyes. Arlen Mór's face had haunted her dreams, too, but she hadn't expected him to follow her into waking.

"I'm losing my mind," she said, shuddering.

She checked the timepiece. The sand in the large hourglass, which measured time in twenty-four-hour increments, had already run out. Normally, the last grains were falling as she readied herself to leave. She was running later than usual, though the sun was still rising. Hastily, she tucked the pendant beneath her dress, grabbed her satchel, and bolted down the hall and out the door.

Lira practically ran all the way across the city, slowing only when she reached the Drochaid or crossed a crowded street. She was accustomed to skipping breakfast, but she felt hungrier and more frazzled than usual.

Her heart was hammering and her side cramped by the time she reached the Dome. She padded into the main archival chamber quietly, having gained control of her panting on the way down. The apprentices were already assembled at their desks, working through manuscripts.

"Good morning, Silira," Pedr, a boy of about fifteen, called.

"And to you," she acknowledged breathlessly, moving past the desks more quickly than usual. Normally, she didn't mind speaking with the apprentices in the morning, but today, she was too nervous to pause.

If there was ever a day when Aidryn would raise a ruckus in the quiet chamber, this would be it. She braced herself for the sound of his voice as she rounded the bottom of the staircase, but it never came. His desk was empty. A sick sensation crept into the pit of her stomach.

Lira felt the apprentices' eyes on her back as she ducked into the inner chamber, whose door was, thankfully, unlocked.

Irem was hunched over his desk, scratching with his quill when she entered. He looked up from his work and peered at Lira over the rims of his spectacles. "You're five minutes late."

"I'm sorry, sir. I slept poorly."

"You look like you didn't sleep at all," he mused, turning back to his work. "Up celebrating all night?"

"No, my lord. I was actually rather unsettled."

For a long moment, all she could hear was the soft

scratching of Irem's quill and the dull drip of melting candle wax. Her restless fingers found the hem of her apron, and she fussed with it until she could no longer bear her mentor's silence.

"Sir, I've never been late," she continued, her chin quivering. "Talfryn began his training with the sentries today."

"That's a pity," Irem replied, setting his quill aside. "He's so young."

They locked eyes for a long moment, until Lira felt near to bursting. But then Irem cracked a wry smile.

"You look ready to do penance, Silira."

"It's not that," she said. "I've also been feeling unsettled about the matter of the histories. I want to believe what you're telling me, but there are too many missing pieces. The histories I know feel complete; how do we know these records from Iteloria aren't full of lies?"

Irem handed her a heavy ring of small iron and brass keys.

"Pull one of the emerald leather-bounds," he said, nodding toward the locked bookcases across the room. "I want you to see for yourself."

Lira exhaled, trembling as she studied the keys in her palm; she dipped her chin and crossed the room reverently, her hands sweating as she fumbled for the right key. She opened the iron gate over one of the shelves and ran her fingers over the worn spines.

"I can't believe these exist," she said, studying the unfamiliar languages inscribed on the covers. "The scholars could've been executed for recording these."

Irem leaned heavily on his cane, crossing the room slowly to join her. "Rí Nami underestimated his council's first loyalties."

She whirled to face Irem. "The clanspeople he used to enforce his decrees?"

"That's right. They were quite resourceful; they sent the volumes to Iteloria with his ambassadors."

Lira sighed. "I still don't understand why you never told us any of this, not even that you suspected the histories could be flawed."

"What good would that have done?" he said, taking off his spectacles. "I was steeped in it, just as you and Aidryn and the apprentices were: indoctrinated and fully convinced that the records here were infallible. It took quite a bit of persuading, on Corlan's part, for me to consider housing these books. And even after that, you know how many years it took us to get them here."

"What changed your mind?" she asked, carefully removing an aged tome from the shelf. Its cracked leather binding was so dry, she feared it might shatter into pieces before she got it to the desk.

"Your grandmother," he answered. "Skelly secretly wrote to me for many years, requesting that we meet. It wasn't until after Corlan's death that I relented. I didn't feel that I could refuse her, since she had also lost her son."

Lira blanched, though the statement was more confirming than surprising. "Skelly was involved in this, too?"

"When she was a young woman, she helped a covert group of clanspeople keep these books hidden until they could be removed from the continent," he said. "They are in terrible condition, in part, because they were stored in the catacombs below Rodhlan for centuries."

"Someone should restore them," she mused. "They're falling apart."

"That is what I've decided you and I will be doing for the time being," Irem answered, carefully fitting the arms of his spectacles back over his ears.

"What about recording the oral histories, like Aidryn?"

"We should have everything we need here."

Lira pulled a stool over to her work area and sat before the tome, her fingers working uncertainly at the edges of its cover. *Onnen*—that was what Skelly had called this tongue. The letters resembled rigid trees; its vertical lines were crisp, with short branches protruding at odd angles.

"I think you will find, Silira," Irem said, pushing a fresh ink pot toward Lira, "that Onnen is very similar to Athi. While its sound is foreign to the ear, its written structure is similar to our own. You should pick up on it rather quickly."

Lira recoiled, her heart hammering at the mere mention of transcribing, let alone learning, one of the banned tongues. "You expect me to learn it? It's treasonous!"

He handed her a blank, newly bound manuscript. "Against whom? You're acting out Eremon's wishes."

Irem had a point. Still, the law hadn't been changed; she felt, somehow, as if they were all treading on dangerous ground. Perhaps she could ask Eremon if he intended to enact new decrees about the languages and written records—if she ever had the chance to.

"Fluency in the ancestral clan tongues is required in your new position," he continued. "You do realize that young Tarlach can speak and write two of the four languages, do you not?"

Lira's face burned as she shook her head. "Which ones?"

"His own clan's tongue, of course," Irem answered, "which is impressive, considering Clan Tarlach was scattered after the Felling."

"And the second?"

A sullen feeling crept up Lira's spine as Irem answered, "Onnen."

Aidryn had been learning the ancient tongues, all while keeping pace with her at transcription? If she was going to take his place, she wanted to master everything he had learned. Though the idea was fueled in part by their competition, it also made sense that the things Aidryn had learned would be what he and Irem had considered most relevant to the role.

"Why did he give this inheritance to me—really?" she asked. "I know there's more to this story than what you've told me."

"He believes he can be of more help to us elsewhere, and so do I."

Lira sighed. "The secrecy is—"

"Necessary for his safety, and yours. The less the two of you discuss, the better. Everything will coalesce in time."

She felt her shoulders hunch under the weight of secrets she had yet to learn. "I don't like this. It feels like we're a band of criminals, conspiring together—not scholars discussing books and stories."

"For the time being, we are exactly that: conspirators," Irem said. "Eremon is risking his throne to set things right. It's up to us to lie low and do as he asks until the time comes. Remember, there are many in power who don't respect his youth. It would be easy for them to unseat him, given the opportunity."

The hair on Lira's arms rose. "Maybe we shouldn't be doing this. It feels too dangerous."

"Then you need to understand what it means to be a Defender who reveals the truth," Irem replied severely. "Our leaders have long expected the archive to help spread their lies —and we have done so, more than willingly, for two thousand years. The title Defender of Histories is, in itself, deceptive; for why does the truth require defending?

"We have been taught to use the archive to reinforce the lies when they're challenged. Have you not perfectly executed your training over the last two days, as you faced down both your ruler and your mentor when your understanding of the truth was challenged?"

Lira had gone rigid. She tried to draw a steady breath, but her heart was pounding erratically, her body trembling. Under any other circumstance, she would have never argued with Irem—and certainly never with Eremon. But if Irem was correct, she had obediently defended the lies without curiosity, assuming instead that the authorities right in front of her were being dishonest.

Irem leaned nearer. "You're the right person for this role because you are passionate about truth, Silira. Once you learn how deeply Iathium's leaders have deceived the people, you won't be able to contain yourself. You will *want* everyone to know the truth, and that will be the well you draw your courage from."

"Can you swear to me these records are true?" she asked quietly.

"Yes."

For a moment, Lira looked from her mentor to the tome, and back again. The thought of putting pen to paper, of really transcribing a clan language, still terrified her. Everything about the unfolding situation felt wrong. But after what she'd learned, she knew she couldn't go back to defending the stories she knew so well.

Her father had died trying to retrieve this book that lay open before her. The least she could do was learn why.

She chewed her bottom lip, then finally nodded. "Where do I begin?"

Lira sank into her work. Copying the Onnen script was cumbersome at first, but after the first few hours, the letters began to flow easily from her quill. With the help of a lexicon Irem had left with her, she was soon able to identify certain words and phrases. She copied the letters feverishly, neglecting her hunger and ignoring the passing of time as if the inner chamber had swallowed her whole.

When Irem finally rose from his desk, stretching his legs and fumbling for his cane, Lira was still fully immersed in the Onnen manuscript. He spoke to her, but his words were lost in the haze as he left her alone in the chamber.

Hours may have passed after Irem departed; she wasn't certain. But a loud banging on the door shook her enough to check the timepiece that sat on his desk. It was already late in the evening.

"Yes?" she called, rubbing her bleary eyes.

"Have you been in there all day?" Caitir's voice called through the heavy door.

Lira pried herself away from the chair and unlocked the door, heaving it open. "I—I'm sorry. I'll be right out."

"You look awful," Caitir said, her expression pained. "I waited for you until sunset."

The flowers. Lira's heart sank. She pressed her hand to her eyes with a sigh. "Oh, no."

Caitir sighed. "I can't believe you forgot." She pouted, kicking her slippers off and massaging one of her heels. "But I suppose it doesn't really matter. We won't be able to weave the crowns together this year, anyway."

"Why not?"

"Mother has my schedule completely filled from now until the festival. She thinks new gowns and extra dancing lessons will give me a better chance with the Rí."

"Don't worry," Lira said, "I'll make them both."

Caitir shrugged. "It's just not the same."

Lira tried to think of something to say to make things right, but she checked herself; she'd have to be careful not to slip about the work she was doing. She drifted back over the chamber threshold, turning only to say, "It's late; who's walking you home?"

"Árchú is outside," Caitir answered.

The eldest Tarlach brother was something of a mystery to

Lira. Árchú was thirty-four, a former sentry, and had always had an intimidating air about him. Lira had seen him from time to time when she was a child, but their age difference had been such that he barely interacted with his own siblings, let alone her. These days, he came and went freely from the family estate, leaving the city for months at a time to negotiate trade agreements with the clans.

Lira took her keys from the desk and turned to find Caitir standing next to her, her eyes roving over the books that lay open there. She gripped the ring of keys so hard that her nail beds went white. "Caitir, you know you aren't allowed in here."

"I thought *you* weren't allowed in the chamber without Lord Irem," Caitir said accusingly.

"He made an exception," Lira hedged, resting a hand on her friend's arm. "Come on; I'll walk you to the stairs."

Caitir made no move to go. Lira followed her friend's gaze to the Onnen manuscript; she had deciphered its title, *The Seeing Forest*, an hour ago. She tried not to suck in a breath.

"What's that?" Caitir asked, nodding toward the book.

"The reason I've been in here all day," Lira answered, stepping between Caitir and the book. She closed it carefully.

"It's not written in Athi." Caitir leaned past Lira to get a better look, brushing her fingertips over a page of the original. "What language is that?"

"I'm not sure," Lira lied. "I'm just copying the letters, like the apprentices do."

"Don't lie to me." Caitir glared at Lira, crossing her arms. "You could just say the Defender told you to keep quiet. That's what Aidryn does."

Lira didn't bother trying to hide her annoyance. "Then there's your answer. But you need to swear you didn't come in here, and you never saw that book. Or, on my life, I will have Lord Irem report you to Raní Macha."

Caitir bristled, but she nodded. "I swear."

She held up a palm and they interlocked their fingers, resting their foreheads together. It was a ritual they'd acted out since childhood.

"Thank you," Lira exhaled, grasping Caitir's other hand and giving her a tug. "Now, come *on*. Handmaiden privileges don't extend to the chamber."

Caitir relented and headed back into the main archive. "I suppose I can see why you forgot about the flowers," she said, retrieving her slippers.

"You know I'd never do it on purpose." Lira fiddled with the hem of her apron. "The past few days have been strange. I suppose things will settle, but I can't predict when."

"Well, I want to hear all about it when Irem ends your vow of silence."

Lira smiled tightly as Caitir started up the staircase. "I can't make any promises."

Her friend paused on the steps, turning back to say, "You have to make me at least one promise: that you won't lock yourself away for *Nami Mostari*. This is the most important festival of my life thus far; I want you to be part of it."

"I promise. I'll do my best not to miss it," Lira said, gripping the ornate railing. "I'll see you soon."

Caitir looked satisfied as she began climbing again. As soon as she was out of sight, Lira ducked back into the chamber.

She sagged against the door, pushing it shut. Normally, she wouldn't be so worried about Caitir breaking protocol; but with the new volumes in hand, she was gravely concerned about Caitir's blatant defiance of the well-established rule. Her friend was capable of keeping secrets; she had kept plenty of Lira's when they were adolescents. But this secret could get Caitir closer to people in power, especially if she let it slip to her mother that she'd been inside the chamber and seen the text. Lira hoped their friendship would mean more to Caitir, in the end, than a power play at court.

"Perhaps that's that," she said to herself, trying to shake the feeling of foreboding that had taken root.

With a sigh, Lira returned to her work. She sat before the massive, emerald-colored volume and ran her fingers over the cover again. Her eyes locked on the author's name that had been carefully stamped into the aged leather, and she blinked: *Wilga Mór.*

It can't be.

"Skelly," she breathed.

She grabbed the lexicon, scanning one letter after another until she was convinced her interpretation was correct. In disbelief, she dropped it back onto the desk, resting her head in her hands.

Skelly was a walking library of clan lore, to be sure, but to have a volume in the Dome archive? Lira didn't know what to make of it. She chewed the inside of her cheek; her grandmother had never mentioned this. Surely Irem would have answers in the morning.

With renewed fervor, Lira resumed feverishly copying the Onnen manuscript—the one her *grandmother* had penned.

CHAPTER 5

Lira worked painstakingly through the night. By dawn, she could decipher many of the words and phrases in the old manuscript, but her finite understanding of the letters only got her so far. She could only dredge up a vague idea of its meaning. And she supposed that was fitting; as Lira grew older, communicating with Skelly had begun to feel like running a gauntlet of loaded riddles.

But unlike those exhausting interactions with her grandmother, this book enthralled her. Every page compelled her forward to the next, then the next, then the next.

Lira needed to know what, or who, this "Seeing Forest" was and what role it had played in getting these books across the sea. She had always taken it for granted that the clans obeyed the sanctions on their written languages simply because it was the law. What else had she accepted without question?

Her stomach dropped; who, if not the clans, might have attempted to record these stories in Athi?

She whirled to regard the new stacks once again. Hastily, she rose, toppling her stool as she rushed back to the stack. She fumbled with the keys as she unlocked door after door, revealing shelves full of similar texts. In all, she counted fifty-seven volumes of history with Skelly's name on them, followed by a title: *Witness Tree*.

She ran her trembling fingers over a green leather spine gilded with silver leaf. A memory slammed into her so hard, it nearly knocked her off her feet.

"But Da, why can't we see Skelly again?" Lira had been nine years old at the time.

"We can't speak of it, Silira. But your grandmother is a poor influence. Her ideas are..." Arlen had hesitated. *"They could endanger us all."*

A wave of emotion washed over Lira; as a young girl, she'd adored Skelly. But Arlen had worked painstakingly to ensure they spent less and less time together over the years. He'd led Lira to believe her grandmother had gone senile, her reasoning and good sense lost to age.

Time and again, Arlen had also implied that Skelly was treasonous, something Lira had grown terrified of after years of quietly speculating. He'd never told her exactly what he suspected, but now the scattered pieces were beginning to make sense.

There was a reason why her father had taken her to those book burnings—made sure she saw everything. And there was a reason he'd estranged himself and his family from Skelly and the rest of the clan.

Skelly had attempted to record the clan histories in Athi.

"That's what Corlan was burning," she said to herself.

Lira doubted the writer had ever been caught, but her father must have suspected what Skelly was trying to do. Or perhaps he knew for certain, and was so afraid of being associated with Skelly's defiance that he's distanced himself from the clan.

Although she felt ready to burst with questions, there was nothing more to be done until Irem arrived. She glanced at his timepiece and realized it was nearly dawn. So, Lira secured all the locks on the stacks again before righting her stool and sitting back down with the manuscript. If she went home now, she would sleep through the day.

Her stomach growled, and she wished for a stout cup of tea. Aidryn was known to bring her something from the upstairs kitchens occasionally, chastising her for working overnight while he leaned against Irem's desk, casually flipping through the books that were usually piled there.

Lira always accepted his offers grudgingly but was secretly fond of the banter they exchanged in the early mornings. Now, in the solitude of the inner chamber, she felt a pang of loneliness.

An hour more, and Lira completed the final pages of transcription. She gingerly turned to the back cover of the original; there, carefully sketched by a steady quill, was a perfect depiction of the pendant she wore.

It made sense; the necklace had belonged to Skelly before, and it had been significant to the elderly woman. Like the pendant, the drawing seemed almost to be in motion, and Lira studied it closely, drawing the necklace from beneath her gown to compare the two. Leaning over the manuscript, she turned the chain so the charm faced up, and laid it beside the sketch.

Suddenly, as if magnetized, the pendant snapped into place over the drawing. The chain went taut.

Lira tried to pry the pendant from the page, but she was immobilized, her fingers frozen around the charm. Roaring pressure exploded in her head, and she began to panic as darkness closed in around her. Her chest and throat tightened, clamping down on a scream.

A violent wind tore wildly through the room, scattering papers and documents, and lashing her hair against her face. The cacophony thundered in her head like a cyclone leveling a forest. Lira couldn't tell which was more consuming—the sound of roaring leaves in her ears, or her own screaming as it finally ripped from her throat.

Shadows formed behind her eyelids then, barely-visible images that conveyed movement and sound. They sharpened: *a circle of hooded figures; the clashing of swords; the smell of burning parchment and flesh. War and agony and death.*

The reek of old blood filled her nostrils, and she dropped to the cool floor and vomited.

As quickly as the chaos had begun, it was over. Lira blinked hot tears from her eyes, bracing her trembling body on all fours, afraid to make any sudden movements. Bile burned the back of her throat and the inside of her nose. A sob broke from between her lips. She pulled the bottom of her apron up to her face to wipe away the mess, whimpering.

A key turned in the lock, and Lira groaned as Eremon entered the chamber, Irem close behind.

"By Nami, Silira!" Eremon knelt beside her, his brow furrowed. "What happened?"

"I don't know," she whispered, her face burning. She crumpled the soiled apron in one hand and rested her back against the desk.

"That book. I..." She shook her head. "I must be ill."

That would explain why she'd slept in the day before—the strange dreams. Perhaps she had a fever. It wasn't unusual for her to experience fever dreams.

Can a person have fever daydreams? she thought absently, her mind in a fog.

Eremon placed a palm on her shoulder, pressing the back of his hand to her forehead. Lira struggled not to flinch away from him. Irem eyed them over his spectacles, his hand on the door.

"Sit with her, will you, until I can bring some cleaning cloths," Irem said, shuffling out of the room.

Lira scrambled to her knees. "But Lord—"

Irem pulled the door closed behind him, engaging the lock once again.

"Let me help you," Eremon said. His voice was gentle, but she couldn't look him in the eyes.

"I don't want to make you ill," she replied, pulling away. "I should see a healer."

"Nonsense. Come here." He motioned for her to lean forward, and she obliged him. He untied the linen apron strings for her, then rocked back on his heels as she pulled it over her head in disgust.

"Thank you," she whispered, using the soiled cloth to cover the mess on the floor.

"Do you need someplace to rest until you feel better?" Eremon asked, leaning against the leg of Irem's work desk. He crossed his legs casually.

"No, I—I'll be all right," Lira lied. "Truly."

She tried to smile reassuringly, but Eremon just raised an eyebrow and grinned.

"You have no talent for lies," he said.

"So I've been told." She rested her head against the opposite table leg with a shudder. "I apologize, my lord. I'm rarely ill; I should have gone home to sleep."

Eremon grimaced. "*My lord*. If we're going to be working together, you can't call me that." He noticed the open shelf on the restricted stack then, and seemed to latch on to what she'd just said. "You stayed here all night?"

Lira shrugged. "I was completing a transcription." She jerked her chin toward the desk.

"One of Wilga's books; no wonder."

"I never knew she'd written nearly sixty manuscripts."

Eremon's eyes drifted to the pendant around her neck, his gaze troubled. "She never told you?"

"No; and neither did Lord Irem." A wave of resentment toward the elderly Defender washed over her. "My father wasn't keen on her mythology. I was, until I was old enough to be discerning, of course. Now, I prefer facts and figures—primary source documents."

He scoffed softly. "You don't consider these primary source documents?"

"Well, I—"

"You just said you didn't fully understand what you transcribed," he said pointedly. "So how would you know whether she was the primary source, or not? How would you know whether you're looking at history or mythology?"

She shifted uncomfortably. "I suppose I wouldn't."

"I can teach you to read it. Quickly."

Her lips parted in surprise.

The lock disengaged, and they both jumped as Irem hobbled back into the chamber with an armload of hot cloths and a clean apron for Lira. Eremon leapt to his feet, smoothing his robes as he took the cloths from Irem and set them on the floor beside Lira.

"Lira, would you like something warm to drink?" he asked. "I'll have it sent down from the kitchens."

"Tea, I think," she answered weakly. "Black."

He nodded, lowering his voice as he turned to Irem. "When you sort out what's happened, will you send for me?"

Irem bowed. Eremon stole one last glance at Lira before he let himself out.

When the door clicked shut, Lira cleaned the tiles with one of the wet cloths Irem had brought, then washed her face and hands with another before donning the fresh apron. She turned to find her mentor standing over the two *Seeing Forest* manuscripts, studying them closely.

Irem ran his gnarled fingertips over the illustration of Skelly's pendant that had appeared in Lira's copy of the book. "How did you accomplish this? It's a perfect rendering."

Lira stepped back, shaking her head. "I don't know what

happened. One moment, I was comparing her drawing with this, and the next..." She held up the pendant, her face burning.

"Siren's snare, Silira," Irem cried, reaching for the bronze charm, "where did you get this?"

"From Skelly."

"Of all the times you could've chosen to wear that..." An expression Lira couldn't place flashed across the scholar's face. "This was the worst."

"What did I do wrong? It's just—"

"It's *just* nothing; that pendant is dangerous."

Lira ran her fingers over the tree's swirls, her frustration rising. "How could it be dangerous? It's a necklace."

"I have never seen you wearing it before," Irem said. "How long have you had it?"

"Twelve years, at least," Lira answered. "My father forbade me from wearing it."

"And you choose now, of all times, to defy his wishes. He was wrong about many things, but not about that charm." Irem sank onto a stool wearily, patting the seat beside him. "Everything is happening too quickly."

"Lord Irem, what do you mean?" Lira sat, palms sweating. "If I had truly known, I wouldn't have touched the necklace. No one ever told me anything about it."

The elderly man hesitated before answering. "Your magic is stirring too quickly. The transcription would have done the job, but you wearing that necklace spurred it on."

"*Magic*? Are you ill, too?" Lira laughed, but the pitch was high and forced. "Lord Irem, what kind of jest is this?"

His onyx eyes flashed. "This isn't a jest."

For a moment, the only sound in the chamber was the soft, slow drip of candle wax against the tiles. She took a deep breath. "I'm trying to understand, truly. But you taught us to reject any lore that bears no evidence—"

"Is this not evidence enough?" Irem motioned toward the fresh manuscript, exasperated.

"You *promised* to tell me the entire truth." Lira's voice broke. "What just happened?"

Irem's shoulders slumped. When he didn't immediately answer, she plowed ahead.

"This magic you speak of—it's just legend. No one has ever seen it." One look at Irem's expression made her mouth go dry. "*I* have never seen it," she added in a whisper.

Yet, she didn't need to see it; she'd felt it. She remembered how the chain had gone taut moments before, dragging her toward the book. Her ears still rang from the thunderous roaring, and her stomach still churned.

Irem sighed heavily. Dark eyes full of guilt met hers. "Forgive me, Lira; I believed you would embrace this more readily if the answers came to you slowly."

Suddenly, she felt ill again. "Embrace what?"

He heaved another sigh. "Your birthright; a role truer and infinitely more important than Defender of Histories."

She opened her mouth to ask another question but shut it again; she couldn't imagine what could be more important than the role she stood to inherit.

"Please," she begged again, "help me understand."

Irem picked up a dry quill and rolled it between his fingers.

"Eremon and I wanted to teach you without directly involving your grandmother," he answered. "We agreed that you would be more likely to trust us, but you were much more resistant than we expected. Now, I fear we've lost your trust entirely."

Oddly, Lira found herself trusting Irem more; she was not, however, willing to admit it yet.

"I hoped that giving you the Onnen book to transcribe would bring your power about gradually. It takes time to learn a language, you see; so, it should have been a slower manifestation, like—" He cut himself off, searching for his next words.

"What does language have to do with magic?"

"From what Eremon and I have discovered through our limited research, the written word appears to stir the magic," Irem replied. "Write the histories in your birth clan's tongue, and if you're meant to inherit power, it will arise within you. We thought your power would take root at whatever pace you began to understand the language. But I never considered the necklace playing a part in any of this. Not yet."

Lira's fingertips brushed the charm. "What is it about this necklace?"

"Certain objects can be laced with magic to bring about one's power. Your pendant is much more than an heirloom; it's imbued with the power of the Witness Tree."

The reverence in his voice set her hair on end. "The inscription on Skelly's books."

"Yes," Irem said. "Much like an ancient tree bears witness to thousands of years of history—wars, famines, times of plenty— the Witness Tree can peer into the entire span of Rodhlan's history. And perhaps, beyond that."

He closed his eyes and recited, "*The Witness Tree is wisdom herself. She uproots lies and restores her peoples' past. She is discernment made flesh. Her roots spread far and wide, gifting the clans with truth.*"

Lira thought she might truly be sick again as he uttered his next words: "You are the Anointed of Clan Mór, Silira, like your grandmother before you. A living vessel of our peoples' history. The Witness Tree of Rodhlan."

CHAPTER 6

"A living vessel of history," Lira breathed. "What does it mean?"

Irem's eyes shone. Now, he beheld her with the same reverence that had emanated from him at his first mention of Skelly's title. "It means you carry memories of Rodhlan's past inside of you—even more so, once you receive your birthright. You will be a repository of truth; no written record shall override your word.

"It is the role Skelly should have played all these years; the role that generations of Clan Mór's women have been preparing for, since the days of Nami the Furious."

The room vanished before Lira's eyes.

Lira stands in the courtyard beneath a great Dome—older than this Dome, yet somehow, more infinite. The air is thrumming with a terrible power that crackles and pops like the fireworks at summer solstice.

Suddenly, the Dome shatters with an earth-shaking boom. Glass shards spray in every direction, hurtling into people and homes near the heart of the city. There is screaming and blood—so much blood. A young man strides from the rubble into the middle of the court-

yard, barely a scratch on his tan skin. He has silken black hair, like Eremon's, but he doesn't look a day past fifteen.

His dark, angular eyes are wild. Veins of black power crackle between his fingers, charging the atmosphere around him with a low, lethal hum. The air smells sharp and fresh, like the mountain forests after a fearsome storm. A pounding pressure drowns out the cries of the surrounding city-dwellers.

Nami stops in the center of the courtyard, chest heaving.

"Clans of Rodhlan," he shouts, "my mother's blood is on your hands! Today I will claim the power you stole from her. I will sit on my father's throne, and as long as I live, you will suffer for your crimes!"

With an enraged cry, Nami raises his hands. Black lightning tears his palms open as it bursts upward, splitting the sky.

"Nami!" Lira screams. "Stop!"

Cries of horror rise from the people who have gathered in the city's center as Nami's lighting sparks and jumps from one cloud to the next above their heads. The sky darkens to a deep, bruised purple, shot through with a sickly green glow. Thunder explodes around them violently, shaking the ground beneath their feet.

The first bolt of black lightning bursts from the clouds to the ground with a piercing explosion. A pressure wave from the blast throws the crowd backward and the world slows, the smell of charred flesh filling the air.

With a cry, Lira found herself in the chamber again, white-knuckling the thick sleeves of Irem's cloak. Her heart pounded erratically, and her hands shook.

"What did you witness?" Irem asked gently, placing a hand on her shoulder.

Lira squeezed her eyes shut and took several shallow breaths before she answered, "Nami destroying the Dome, unleashing power on the clans. How is that possible?"

"A dark power we have yet to understand," Irem replied softly, taking Lira's arm.

He led her to a stool where she sat shakily, wrapping her arms around herself.

"Dark power—what dark power?" she asked tremulously.

"Magic Riku brought to Rodhlan, which was largely referenced in unfounded sources until recently." Irem pulled up his own stool and sat across from her, concern evident in his dark eyes. "Tell me more."

He listened patiently as Lira described the vision. Then, he asked, "Have you witnessed anything else?"

"Twice before," she said, her throat dry. "Once, the night I put on the necklace. And again, when my pendant paired with the book."

Lira explained what she'd seen in those visions, too. Irem didn't respond, but instead massaged his brow. The silence was unbearable.

"I don't want this, Lord Irem," she pleaded. "We have to contact Skelly; ask her to choose someone else."

Irem shook his head. "It isn't that simple."

"Why not? I don't want to be tormented by these visions. I have no desire to be a part of Clan Mór; I don't want anything from them. Not their magic, not their inheritance. Iathium is my home. I'm taking your place here in the archive, like I agreed to do. But I *never* agreed to being relentlessly tortured by memories that have nothing to do with me."

"No one suggested you move into the mountains or assimilate into the clan," Irem said. "There is nothing keeping you from fulfilling both roles right here in the city."

"Write to my grandmother; tell her to release me from this birthright," she begged. "Have Eremon seal the letter—whatever you have to do. She'll have no choice but to—"

"*You* have no choice," Irem said pointedly. "Moreover, she has no choice now."

Lira sat back, aghast. "I don't understand."

Her mentor closed his eyes, shaking his head. "Silira, the

seed was planted long ago. Your grandmother anointed you as an infant. Once these things take root, the course is set."

"But what does that mean?"

"The rules of ancestral magic dictate that once an anointed is chosen, the decision is fixed. They are the anointed for life, whether or not they choose to accept it. No one else can fill the role completely."

"That isn't right," she protested, her chin trembling. "Each person should be free to choose their own path."

"Is it right for a people to go without the heir they were promised?"

"My life wasn't hers to give. My path—"

"For all this talk of paths," Irem said, "tell me, Silira: have you ever had full control over your chosen path?"

"I—"

"Don't answer yet; think." Irem stroked his beard as he watched Lira carefully. "Wilga chose you, but your father ran from the whispers of magic. He thought he could protect you, so *he chose for you.*"

She blinked hard, trying to shake her father's image from her memory.

"Da wanted to seek his fortune in Iathium," she insisted. "He didn't want to live off the land like the clan, farming to survive. He'd mastered a lucrative trade. He..."

Though the explanations tumbled from her lips, she got the distinct impression that every one of them was a lie. She closed her mouth then, grasping for anything she might say or do to set her world right again.

"Your father left the clan because he feared your birthright," Irem said, heaving a sigh. "He learned his trade long after he arrived here.

"Your life in the archive has been a misguided attempt to fulfill your true destiny. He misdirected you to protect you. If only he had understood Corlan's plans sooner—he might have allowed you to learn the truth, to prepare for a future when the clans wield their magic freely once again."

A knot formed in Lira's stomach. "If I was misguided, why did you choose me to take your place?" She bit her lip, but the next question spilled out of its own accord: "Was I even qualified for this work, or was it all a ruse?"

"It was never a ruse," Irem said patiently. "Aidryn was next in line by right, but you were always our first choice—especially Eremon's. What better than to have the Witness Tree serving as Defender of Histories in Iathium? You have the power to shed light on the lies, to right the wrongs of the past."

"That's a heavier burden than any one person should have to bear," Lira said.

"You won't be alone," he said. "We will help you."

"But you haven't!" she cried. "All these years, you could have been teaching me the true histories—*if* the accounts have been tampered with, as you say."

Irem's shoulders drooped. "I've dealt with all of this in the worst way possible," he admitted. "When I first met your grandmother, I knew she was revered among the clans for her wisdom and her accounts of the mythology; but I was too indoctrinated in Iathium's rhetoric to accept the things she tried to tell me. I didn't begin to believe her version of history until Eremon's father approached me about the records. And even then, I promised myself I wouldn't embrace the stories until I saw the writings and experienced the magic for myself."

Lira felt a momentary pang of pity for Irem as grief etched itself into his expression. He bowed his head and continued, "Until these books were in my hands, I took pride in teaching you Iathium's histories to the smallest detail, and having a hand in your perfect mastery of them. The two greatest regrets of my life are aiding Nami's crusade to rewrite history and keeping you from fulfilling your true destiny."

"You paint my so-called destiny in broad strokes," Lira

said softly. "How could I be so instrumental in restoring truth—by translating these old books? What could possibly be more convincing than Eremon himself simply *telling* the truth? And where does this supposed magic play a part?"

"Because when you accept your full birthright, you will *be* the archive. And when you learn to wield your magic, you'll have the power to discern truth from fiction—and share that truth with others in ways that infinitely surpass this room full of dusty books.

"Eremon believes you can help him deliver the news to our people in a way they understand. I think, perhaps, they will accept it coming from us as a united front."

"What if I decide not to wield this power?" Lira asked bitterly, ignoring his plea. "I could sail to Iteloria, disappear forever. Let the people here sort it out for themselves."

Irem winced at her implication. "You may not embrace your birthright, but magic will be inside of you, regardless. If you don't accept the power you've inherited, you will never gain control over it. And if you never learn to control the magic, it will control you." He nodded pointedly at the pile of soiled linens where she'd been sick.

"If I learn to control my power, I'll be nothing but a means to an end." Lira stood abruptly. "I need to think."

She clenched her fists, her nails pressing hard into her palms as she rushed toward the door. If she stayed with Irem a moment longer, she feared she might lose control of her anger. Walking out of the conversation seemed a better alternative than shouting at her master.

Lira burst into the quiet archive, nearly trampling a bewildered Eremon in the process. His jaw dropped as she passed, her face flush with embarrassment.

"Lira—?"

"I'm sorry," she called over her shoulder as she careened

toward the staircase, tears sliding down her cheeks. "I need to clear my head."

She didn't fear his reprimand, but she couldn't look him in the eye, nor could she stop for a discussion. Raising her voice at Eremon would be infinitely worse than disrespecting the Defender, so she kept her head down and fled up the stairs before the bewildered young man could call after her.

As Lira emerged onto the main floor of the Dome, the sun hadn't yet risen. Torchlight illuminated the wide corridor, the fire's reflection playing off the endless panels of glass that stretched the length of the building and high overhead. She strode quietly toward Eremon's garden in the center of the Dome—a memorial once built for Nami's parents, who had perished in the destruction of the first Dome two thousand years ago.

So she'd been told.

Memories of the witnessing flashed before Lira's eyes, but she pushed them away. She didn't want to relive the horror of seeing Nami's power turned against his people. And she wasn't sure she wanted to know how his parents had truly been killed.

The air in the lush, expansive indoor garden was fresh and mildly humid as Lira entered. She took a deep breath to calm herself, savoring the earthy scent of greenery and freshly-turned soil. A clear stream meandered around the room's perimeter, burbling and splashing over smooth, colorful river rocks brought into the city from Clan Beran's territory.

Aside from the archive, this garden was Lira's favorite place in the Dome. When she'd read or transcribed as many pages as she could stand, she loved breaking from work to wander among the fountains and trees. There was something about the clean air and thriving flora that made her feel more awake and alive.

The first hint of dawn illuminated the clear glass panels that arced upward toward the magnificent oculus at the garden's heart. Daylight played upon the sleeping blooms that flanked the path, teasing them open to reveal a rainbow of colors. Though the entire Dome was made of glass, the garden was the only place where it was clear—where Lira could see the clouds above.

Lira crossed a small red bridge that stretched from one side of the garden to the other, spanning a reflecting pool filled with black and silver fish whose fins were as translucent as phantoms. Their movements were eerie and mesmerizing, and Lira found herself immobilized in the center of the bridge, following their every move.

"A gift from Clan Énna."

Lira gripped the railing, heart pounding as she whirled to face Eremon. "You frightened me."

"I'm sorry," he said, lowering his head to catch her gaze.

Lira trained her eyes on the fish again, heat rushing to her cheeks. His behavior toward her still felt too informal—too familiar. She had barely grown accustomed to being face-to-face with him. It felt like too great a leap to imagine him as anything but her ruler; but here he was, treating her like an old friend. Equally unsettling was the fact that she wanted him so close, when she knew she should not.

"Notoriously hard to catch, the little fiends," Eremon continued, motioning toward the fish. "Irem could tell you more about them than I can."

Gently, he laid a hand on her arm. She turned back toward him resignedly and was met with the mug of steaming tea he held out to her. "You left this behind."

Lira wasn't in the mood for tea any longer, but she took it anyway. "You didn't follow me up here for this."

"No, but it was a good excuse."

She swirled the hot liquid in her mug, watching the dregs rise with the motion, then sink back to the bottom. "What happened to waiting for Irem to send for you?"

He considered for a moment, gazing over the pond. "I decided not to wait," he finally admitted, drumming his fingertips lightly on the railing.

Lira sighed, following his attention to the fish. "Is it true that you and Irem chose me because—"

"Shh. The trees have ears, Silira." He lowered his voice, glancing around the garden before he spoke again. "Yes, that is true. But it's also because you're brilliant, and I've never met anyone else like you. You're perfect for this, in every possible way."

Lira blew a puff of air out from between her lips, stealing a glance at him. "That's very flattering."

"It's true."

Silence overtook them again as they studied the fish. Lira pushed off the railing and started back down the bridge, Eremon following a few paces behind.

She paused beside an elaborate arrangement of lush plants that bore blooms in eye-popping shades of blue and teal. "These are exquisite. I've never seen them before."

Lira reached for one of the flowers. When her fingers made contact with the velvety petals, she gasped as her vision shifted from the garden in the Dome to an unfamiliar beach with sand as white as the sky above it.

She blinked; as quickly as the vision had begun, it was over. A wave of dizziness washed over her, and Eremon grasped her elbow to steady her.

"Iteloria," she breathed, meeting his eyes. "I've heard stories, but..."

Eremon nodded. "My father said it's lovely." He studied her unabashedly as the room's spinning began to slow. "Fascinating. Are you all right?"

Lira shifted away from him, concentrating on the flowers instead. "What are they called?"

"Nea'la roses." He let go of her arm, cupping one of the

blooms in his palm. "They bloom once every decade. Emyr Tarlach brought them back after his last journey."

Her brow furrowed, a shadow crossing her face. "His daughter and I are friends. Speaking of flowers, I was supposed to gather them for *Nami Mostari*. You aren't one for tradition, I know, but we've always woven crowns together. It sounds silly."

"Not if it's important to you."

Lira shrugged. "I know she's disappointed in me."

"You can't please everyone." He flashed her a smile. "I should know."

They strode through the garden together in silence. When the morning bells in the courtyard began to chime, Eremon gave her a small bow and excused himself.

"I have audiences all day, but I hope you'll consider... well, all of it." His eyes shone hopefully.

"I will accept your offer to help me with the manuscripts in question," Lira answered carefully. "And I'll consider the rest."

He inclined his head, leaning toward her slightly. "Until then."

She mirrored his nod and stepped back as he turned to go. There was a nuance to his movement that made him seem reluctant to leave. Shaking off the thought, Lira turned her attention back to the roses, studying their velvety petals and considering Eremon's offer.

For the rest of the day, Lira and Irem went about their business as usual. Neither of them brought up the subject of her birthright again; the unspoken words were heavy enough.

Question upon question began to build in Lira's mind. She threw herself into transcribing another of Skelly's manuscripts, burrowing deep within the pages like a baby bird in its nest, eager for the next morsel of knowledge. The rewards came with each new word she deciphered.

And then, at the end of the day, she received a surprise: when she arrived home for the evening, a flat, woven basket bursting with flowers sat on her doorstep. The blooms had been gathered and carefully arranged, their long stems stretching out over one side. She crouched by the basket, savoring every color, until she spotted the bright teal bloom peeking out from between two pink roses.

Her hands trembled as she reached for it, lifting it gingerly by its stem. It was one of the nea'la roses she and Eremon had admired this morning.

Lira's heart raced as her fingers brushed a folded piece of paper tucked between the stems. She opened it, slowly unfolding the paper to read:

A twofold peace offering: one to accept, one to give. Use them well.

"Peace offering, indeed," she murmured. She couldn't help smiling.

Lira worked on the flower circlets until late into the night. She hung them up to dry. They were the most beautiful and intricate crowns she had ever made, yet the work had come as easily as breathing.

She set the rose and several white lilies aside, arranging them in a small earthenware vase on her bureau. Every time she glanced at the striking blue petals, she thought first of Eremon, and next of Caitir. It would be hard to wait for the next opening in her friend's busy schedule, but she would be patient; she wanted to see the smile on Caitir's face when she presented the crown.

Reluctantly, Lira changed into a nightdress, splashed her face with water from the basin in the corner of her room, then blew out her lamp. She climbed into bed but did not lie down; instead, she shimmied beneath the covers and drew her knees to her chest, bunching the quilt up around her.

Lira had debated whether to remove Skelly's pendant before bed. She hadn't been able to convince herself to take it off. Its presence offered a strange comfort, despite the havoc it had wrought today.

Her room was too quiet. The sounds of her work had been a pleasant distraction. Now, in the early-morning hours, it seemed as though the entire world had been plunged into a deep and terrifying silence.

The silence brought back the memory of that roaring chaos she'd experienced in the chamber earlier. Her visions played back through her head unbidden, and she began to shiver violently.

It's late, she thought. *I need to sleep so I can work tomorrow. But I don't want to close my eyes again.*

Alone in the cottage and with Talfryn gone, she had no one to talk to about the dreams and the visions. It had been years since she'd longed for her mother's comfort, but tonight, she wished she could crawl into bed beside her and never emerge.

Finally, Lira allowed herself to lie down and rest her head on the pillow. For a long while, she lay wide awake, her breaths coming too rapidly in the dark, the quilt clutched in her fists.

When she finally drifted off, her sleep felt less like rest and more like fitful dozing. Through the night, she tossed in her bed, and she couldn't help wondering whether she would ever sleep peacefully again.

CHAPTER 7

Golden beams streamed into the Dome's main floor as sunrise broke on the horizon. Lira followed the winding staircase down into the archival hall and made a beeline for the inner chamber.

She had awakened well before dawn and headed for the Dome as quickly as she could, despite her restlessness the night before. Somehow, she had made it through the night without terrifying dreams, so she counted that as a small victory.

When she entered the chamber, she found Irem hunched over his desk, arranging several stacks of bound parchment. He started when the door clicked shut; when he saw it was Lira, his shoulders sagged.

"I have some things to show you this morning," he began, handing her a heavy ledger.

Irem spent the next two hours showing Lira the systems he had put in place over the past five decades to ensure the archive operated smoothly. Lira's questions faded into afterthoughts as they pored over assignment records, attendance and financial ledgers, and the massive directory that outlined nearly every manuscript the archive held.

When the morning's training was complete, Irem removed his spectacles, rubbing his eyes. "It took me fifty years to develop and fine-tune my methods; now, you've learned them in mere hours."

Lira rose from her stool and stretched, grinning mischievously. "Will you be quizzing me tomorrow?" Her smile faded when his expression turned grave. "What is it?"

Irem heaved a sigh. "There won't be a tomorrow, Silira."

She searched her mentor's face for any hint of levity, but came up short. "What are you talking about?"

"I have urgent business in Rodhlan Ridge," he began, standing slowly and groping for the gnarled walking stick he'd leaned against the desk. "I'm going to ask your grandmother what she knows about the power's resurgence."

She pressed a hand to her stomach, but it didn't stop a nervous cramp from gripping her insides. "Why?"

"We've received reports of magic stirring from both within and outside Iathium, in city-dwellers and clanspeople alike," he answered, studying her face. "The records we have provide a working knowledge of everything, but Wilga will have a deeper understanding. While I'm with her, I'll be working to stir my own magic. I'm old; I need someone who can help me when it manifests."

Lira's eyes widened; she hadn't considered whether Irem might have inherited power from Clan Énna. "What will I be doing here in the meantime?"

"Eremon will work through the books with you. Follow his lead."

"But you'll return soon," she ventured hopefully. "I still have so much to learn from you."

He shook his head sadly. "Our time has run out. I've resigned; the archive is yours now."

"No." She backed toward the door, a sick sense of dread overtaking her. "No, no, I'm not ready! I need your help."

"I have no choice." Irem moved to the peg by the door, where he'd hung a heavy gray traveling cloak. Lira watched in dumbfounded shock as he shrugged it on.

"I can't manage all this alone!" she cried.

"You won't be alone," Irem said. "I trust Eremon to guide you. I have also left special instructions for Aidryn Tarlach to assist you with the apprentices when he is here."

"But what about the magic?"

Irem sighed sadly. "You may ask Eremon anything you want to know. Consult the books when he can't answer."

"No, Lord Irem, I need *you*," she cried, clutching the thick fabric of his cloak sleeve, desperation overriding her anger. "Stay here, just one more day. I need more time with you; I don't want you to go."

He heaved a sigh. "Silira..."

"What if you don't return?" She studied his familiar, weathered features—the laugh lines around his eyes, the spectacles perched on the bridge of his nose—and committed each to memory. "You're like a grandfather to me. I can't lose you like I lost Da. I don't think I could bear it."

"Silira, every day that passes carries the risk of death, especially at my age," he said gently. "That is precisely why I must go.

"There is a darkness at play here that I have never seen. We have precious little information about it in our books. It's moving rapidly; who knows whether I can find the answers I need in time."

Lira recoiled. "Darkness, like the magic you spoke of yesterday? Riku's magic? Is it somehow linked to the clans' powers?"

Her mentor nodded gravely. "I fear there is some sort of interplay between the dark magic and the clans' powers—

perhaps some unwritten law of balance. Where one exists, so must the other."

"Who possesses the dark power? Is someone wielding it?"

"We're not sure of the full impact," Irem hedged. "My travels will reveal more answers than I can find here in this archive. For now, I can tell you that I believe there are those among us who do wield it."

She sucked in a breath as he continued, "We have also learned that a group of clan descendants is operating in secret within the city, using the written word to help manifest the clans' powers."

He drew a worn, folded piece of parchment from his coat pocket and handed it to Lira. A line of verse had been scrawled on it in messy Athi:

> *Our Rhona fair, to Rodhlan green*
> *Four magicks she did give,*
> *To peoples she did love*
> *As long as Goddess she did live.*
> *But Rasu in his raging might*
> *Beseeched them, seeking power;*
> *When they refused, he envied—*
> *And turning, did devour.*

"What does it mean? Who wrote this?" Lira demanded.

Even as the question left her lips, she felt foolish for asking it. From the trajectory of their conversation so far, she thought she might know.

"It's a bit of ancient mythology," he answered resignedly. "Have Eremon recount the full tale for you."

"I don't recognize this handwriting," she pressed. "It doesn't belong to any of our scholars. Is someone from one of the clans teaching the common folk to write? Is that how this is happening—they're learning a bit of lore, writing it down, and their magic is returning?"

"Yes," Irem said. "I fear the situation may decline rapidly."

Lira pinched the corners of the paper. "Decline, how?"

"You don't truly need me to answer that," Irem replied. "Magic-wielders in the city are in grave danger, both from their own power and the powers-that-be."

"Can't Eremon protect them? He's the supreme ruler."

"You know as well as I that Eremon is on a tight leash," he said. "A ruler anointed so young doesn't stand a chance of making independent decisions until all his advisers are dead."

Lira swallowed hard at his frankness, her heart pounding. "Is this happening because I copied the book?"

"In part."

She tried to ignore the shame that rose in her gut. "This isn't my fault," she protested weakly.

"No, it isn't. It's mine. I gave you orders; you merely did your job. Now, though, I'll ask you not to transcribe any further texts until you hear from me. I've instructed Eremon to avoid writing, as well. You may read, but let that be the end of it. Do not write down any of the clan histories. Do you swear?"

"I swear." Lira's chin trembled. "Now, swear to me you'll return."

"I cannot promise you that," he replied sadly. "I'm old, and a storm is brewing. I'll count myself lucky if I reach the Ridge at all."

Something inside Lira shattered, and she closed the distance between herself and the elderly man, embracing him gently.

"I don't want you to go," she cried. "I can't do this alone."

"You can," he whispered, stroking her hair. "You must."

Irem pulled away, patting her cheek affectionately. "You are not a child any longer. It's time for you to step into your true power. Embrace who you are meant to be."

He raised his hand, placing his fingertips on her forehead. "Witness," he said.

The contact sent a jolt through her; she gasped and closed her eyes, spilling tears down her cheeks. Suddenly, she could see the pattern that opened the hidden stairwell below the chamber. She saw Eremon emerging as he had on the day of the anointing, as if witnessing the scene all over again. But as soon as Irem withdrew, it was over.

Blinking hard through her tears, she choked, "What was that?"

"One of the many benefits of your magic," Irem said. "You have much to learn; I'm sorry I can't teach you more." He moved toward the door, but paused. "I will miss you, Silira."

The former Defender withdrew and let himself out of the chamber. Lira engaged the lock behind him, her entire body trembling. She sank to the stone floor and sobbed until she gasped for breath. When her tears felt like they'd run dry, she rested her head wearily against the leg of Irem's desk until her lashes fluttered shut.

HOURS MAY HAVE PASSED before she moved from the floor; Lira didn't know. She could hear the archival staff moving about in the main hall outside; she ignored several knocks at the door, hoping to collect herself before she allowed anyone inside.

The only thing that roused her from her daze was the scratching of parchment on the floor beside her as it slid through the gap under the door. She snatched it up, swiping her hand across her nose as she sniffed. A message was scrawled across it in familiar handwriting.

I know you're in there.

Lira growled; this was the worst possible day for Aidryn to be back. He couldn't see her like this. If he started asking ques-

tions, she might cry again. While she craved his companionship—and even his help—it wouldn't do for her to appear so
vulnerable.

She carried the paper to her desk and grabbed a quill.

Go away.

She shoved the paper back under the door and received a
prompt reply:

As you wish, Mistress.

Lira broke a sweat. She scribbled:

Calling me that is forbidden and punishable by dismemberment.

She sent it back to him. A very long moment passed before
the parchment returned, sliding slowly from beneath the door.
Aidryn had sketched an image from one of the ancient illuminated manuscripts at the bottom of the parchment: a depiction
of two human-sized hares brandishing broadswords and tying a
grown man to a tree. Naked.

Lira blushed and laughed in spite of herself, choking on a
half-sob as she replied:

Dismemberment and torture by gigantic, deadly hares. Go away.

She sent the note back under the door and returned to the
desk, sorting mindlessly through the stacks of ledgers Irem had
left lying there. The lock rattled, and she whirled as the door
creaked open and Aidryn stepped inside, shutting it swiftly
behind him.

"How did you—that was locked!"

Aidryn strode across the chamber toward her with a shrug.
"It opened for me. Maybe the lock didn't engage."

"No, I'm sure I—" She shook her head, waving him off. "I
told you to go away."

She pressed her palms to his chest and pushed, steering
him back toward the door, but he planted his feet and resisted
her efforts. "Silira Mór, Defender of Histories, is it? Sounds a
bit... battle-ready. Fierce."

He reached out to place a palm on her head for emphasis.

"A short warrior, perhaps." She knocked his arm aside, punching his shoulder halfheartedly. He chuckled, releasing her. "But a warrior nonetheless."

Lira scowled. "Get out."

Aidryn stilled, drumming his fingers on Irem's desk—Lira's desk now, she realized. "What's the matter?"

She glared at him. "I'm not in the mood for your nonsense."

For the first time, he looked out of place here. He'd discarded his usual uniform in favor of a cream tunic and leather jerkin, and his hair had grown longer than she'd seem him wear it before—just barely touching his collar. He looked sun-kissed and a bit windblown, and the heady scent of spring had followed him into the chamber.

"No, I mean it." He studied her face, his voice softening almost imperceptibly. "What's wrong? You've been crying again."

Lira turned away from him, busying herself with items on the desk. She carefully arranged the quill, ink pot, and stack of books to her liking before she replied, "I don't want to talk about it."

"But—"

Lira's shoulders slumped, but she kept her back to him. "You know once I start crying, it's hard for me to stop. I've stopped now, so leave it be."

Aidryn sidestepped her, moving into her field of vision. "Maybe I can help."

Lira almost crumpled again. "How could you possibly help me? You have no idea what's happened."

"I know you weren't expecting Irem to leave today. No one was," he offered, dragging a stool over to the desk. They sat, facing one another. "Did he tell you where he's gone?"

Lira shrugged a shoulder, thumping a fleck of leather binding off the desk. "Secret romances, political intrigues, his traveling puppet show—the usual business."

Aidryn smile was pinched. "All those conversations we're not supposed to have, then."

"Right, now that we've been abandoned." It was difficult not to feel bitter toward Irem, though she suspected he would never leave this way unless circumstances were serious. She pushed her hair out of her face. "So, everyone knows Lord Irem left?"

He nodded pointedly. "They're waiting for orders from you."

Lira sagged, rubbing her eyes. "I can't go out there like this."

"Then send the assignment record with me. I'll take care of it."

She shrugged, pushing the document toward him. "You can tell them to carry on as usual. I'll figure out what to do later."

Aidryn took the record from the desk and stood. "Anything else?"

"No. I just need to get sorted," she answered softly.

He moved toward the door, a shadow crossing his face as he studied her again. "All right. You know where to find me if you need anything."

She nodded, pressing her lips together as he left. For a long while, she was immobilized, curled over the desk with her face in her hands. The silence in the room roared in her ears until it was broken by a rhythmic tapping from beneath the tiles.

CHAPTER 8

Lira opened the floor, rubbing furiously at her face as if it would somehow conceal the evidence of her tears. Eremon bounded up the steps barefoot, a parchment scroll in his hand and a warm smile on his face.

"May I be the first to congratulate you?" When he saw her expression, his smile faded.

Lira shook her head, backing away a few steps. "Don't congratulate me. I've already failed; I can't do this."

Eremon let the scroll fall to the ground as he rushed toward Lira, gathering her in his arms and pulling her close. She tensed at the contact, then allowed herself to yield to him, resting her cheek on his chest as her silent tears fell. To her surprise, his warmth was a welcome comfort, the embrace easy and familiar. It negated the sense of impropriety that might have risen in her otherwise.

"This isn't how ascension is supposed to feel, is it?" he asked, cupping the back of her head in his palm.

She shook her head. His fingers wandered into her curls as he continued. "The day my father's body was returned to Iathium was the hardest day of my life. I was twelve years old—

who expects to rule a continent at that age? But there wasn't time to grieve; there was only time to act.

"I owned my role because I had been prepared for it, as you have been prepared." He squeezed her, then released her. "You were made for this work; I have no doubt of it."

She tried to force a tight-lipped smile, but found herself lacking the will to follow through. Eremon, Irem, and even Aidryn seemed to believe her fully capable of stepping into the Defender role with ease, as if she had been created for this sole purpose. If her only concerns were historical records and apprentices, she would have agreed; but her world and the landscape of the role had shifted dramatically in mere days. What had felt so familiar and desirable before had suddenly become unknown territory, and she had been thrust into it without the preparation she craved.

Eremon went back for the scroll he'd dropped by the stairs, then handed it to Lira. It had been sealed with his emblem. "Go on, open it."

Lira ran her fingertips over the seal before she broke it and unfurled the scroll, spreading it across the desk. It was a document naming her *Lady Silira Mór, Defender of Histories*. Eremon and Irem had already signed it, and there was a space left for her own signature. Silently, she dipped her quill in the ink pot and signed her name to the document.

The ink dried on the scroll's crisp surface. Tiny black veins spread from the curves and angles of each letter and bled into the surrounding parchment.

She studied her signature as cold dread seeped into the pit of her stomach. Weight settled on her shoulders, bearing down as she struggled to make eye contact with Eremon once again.

"Now we begin," Lira whispered.

A chill swept over her skin. While she was accustomed to feeling invigorated and energized by the prospect of studying a new tome, this work filled her with dread. It felt like she was standing on the edge of a precipice, a yawning, dark vault looming below.

He squeezed her shoulder before taking a seat. "We have a few hours yet for lessons; let's make them count."

She sat beside him, taking a few deep breaths. "First, I have questions."

"Go ahead."

"The written word triggers this power. How?"

Eremon brushed his palm lightly across the cover of a tome Lira had brought to the desk. "From what I've gathered so far, writing the histories in our ancestors' languages—even just a piece of a story—works like striking a flint to kindling. It's the reason Rí Nami banned the clans from writing their languages. What he didn't understand is that each clan has its own modality for magical inheritance."

Lira eyed the assortment of quills she'd arranged on the desk earlier. "So not all the clans pass their power down through writing."

"All of them *can*," he answered, "but it's not the favored route of each group. Your ancestors, for example, not only transfer power through written stories, but through physical touch."

Eremon flexed his fingers. Lira couldn't help running her thumbs across the pads of her own.

"In the beginning," he continued, "all the clanspeople were simply born with an equal measure of power. Along the way, some of the leaders set up barriers to entry, if you will—criteria for receiving their full magical inheritance. Rí Nami ruled for a hundred years; the people tried to outwit him by changing the rule of arbitrary inheritance to something more deliberate in order to hide their true power.

"Anointed ones were chosen to receive more. Magic must be expended, you see; so when the old alliance agreed to change the rules, it became necessary to pour more magic into chosen members of each generation."

"So the rules of this magic are more fluid than binding."

A shadow crossed his face, and he leaned forward slightly. "That depends on who you ask."

Lira lowered her voice. "Who was part of that alliance?"

"Select members of each clan, long ago; Nami called them The Seeing Forest."

Now, it was Lira who ran her fingertips over the cover of the book. "We were taught that he banned the languages to prevent treason."

"It's a partial truth. He was also trying to keep the clans from altering the natural order his mother set in motion."

Lira chewed her lip and stood, picking up both new and old copies of *The Seeing Forest*. She carried them to the stacks and slid them onto the shelves. As she worked, she could feel his gaze on her. Her ears heated, followed by her cheeks.

"So he wasn't trying to prevent power from manifesting in the first place?" she asked over her shoulder, selecting another manuscript from the bookcase. She dallied at the shelf, waiting for her blazing cheeks to cool before turning around again.

"No; he didn't want the power tied to specific actions like writing. He wanted it to flow freely."

She returned to her stool at the desk, careful not to brush against Eremon—they had been sitting so near to one another before.

"Skelly called him Nami the Furious. Why would he have wanted each child of the clans to inherit their full power, if he hated them so?" Lira paused for a moment, recalling something Eremon had said moments earlier. "And what did his mother have to do with any of it?"

Eremon's features softened, as if he was reliving a memory. "She was the goddess Rhona, who gave Rodhlan its power."

"That verse Irem showed me—her name was in it. But gods

and goddesses, immortal, all-powerful beings... it's all just mythology, isn't it?" She had a feeling she wasn't going to like his answer.

Eremon closed the distance she'd tried to create, leaning toward her as if sharing a closely held secret with a dear friend.

Perhaps he is my friend, she thought, all too aware of the scent of his robes—vanilla and warm spices. *But perhaps he is also too close.*

"Rhona was a mortal goddess," he finally answered, his tone measured. "No one knows where she originated, but she found her way to this land. As I understand it, she fell in love with the clans and granted them magical powers.

"To Clan Mór she gave the power to guard knowledge and tend the earth; to Clan Beran, the ability to defend the land and heal its people; and to Clan Énna, the power to master the waters and judge rightly.

"I know little of Clan Tarlach's power; in times past, their anointed was called the Key Keeper, and they had extraordinary abilities to manipulate metal. I have heard a tale or two about a Tarlach who could speak to animals, as well."

Lira traced a fingertip over the rings on the wooden table-top. "I remember Skelly's stories about these powers—she claimed she had a magic garden. Da said the soil in the mountains has always been rich, that there was nothing extraordinary about her climbing roses." She shook her head, pausing for a moment before she added, "All of this still seems too outlandish."

Eremon leaned nearer still, his voice lowering to almost a whisper. "But it *feels* true, doesn't it?"

She closed her eyes, nodding; the magnetic warmth emanating from him made her want to touch him again. "Is that how my power helps me to discern?"

"Yes. Follow what your soul is saying. This magic is energy;

it can be given, taken, manipulated. It is very much alive, and it will speak to you, if you allow it to."

Lira focused deep inside herself; this time, she felt a subtle tug at the back of her mind, as if some force within her was nodding its approval. She was struggling to keep her questions linear, so she asked the next one that came to mind: "Irem said he believes dark magic is rising alongside the clans'. How is that possible? Where did it come from?"

"That's where he and I disagree," Eremon said. "I believe the dark magic has remained all along—wielded in secret. My father gave me these histories before he died, and now, I'm going to give them to you."

Eremon took a breath, his gaze flicking to the candles that burned in the chandelier above them. Lira caught herself studying the silvery gray of his irises, how the candlelight reflected in them... and she forced her attention to her hands before he began speaking again.

"The dark power Irem told you about came from Iteloria, my ancestors' homeland. The first Rí was also a mortal god. His name—"

"Riku was a god?" she blurted. "Irem told me the dark magic was his, but not that he was a god."

I knew Riku came from Iteloria, she thought, *but I never thought about the dark magic being tied to the land. And gods? I don't know if I can accept that, but I'll hear him out.*

Eremon nodded. "As well as his twin, Rasu the Vile, yes. Mortal gods. Riku married Rhona, and Nami was their son."

Lira's mouth fell open. "Wait... the god and goddess married? Rhona is never mentioned by name in the texts; only in passing."

She remembered touching the diadem all those years ago. *But I know her face. I know her face and the way the sunlight caught her auburn hair.*

"That was part of Nami's plot to conceal her existence."

She recoiled. "Why would he erase his own mother from the histories?"

"Because he blamed the clans for her death and deemed them unworthy of worshiping her. He hated them for joining forces with Rasu and stole back the magic his mother had given them.

"*That* was an ability he inherited from his uncle. They could siphon magic from others, take it into their own bodies, and twist it into something vile."

"Corrupt it with the darkness," Lira whispered.

"A long line of his successors did the same. Each time Rhona's gifts resurfaced among the clans, there would be a slaughter. They made themselves more and more powerful, passing the warped magic from one generation to the next for centuries."

"What happens to a bloodline with a mix of magic like that?"

His throat bobbed as he glanced at her from beneath heavy black lashes. "My ancestors remained as strong as gods for generations. Rather than weakening over time, the power appears to accumulate." His voice dropped to a whisper. "I have their power within me, Lira."

She studied him warily, searching for any sign of the darkness he claimed to possess. For a moment, she followed that thread of power in herself, waiting for a sign that being here in Eremon's presence was dangerous or threatening—but all she could feel was the safety and comfort she had come to expect from him.

"No one would ever suspect it," she ventured. "What does it feel like, to have inherited a magic like that?"

Eremon rolled his sleeves up to his elbows. "It doesn't feel dark or dangerous—more restless, like a sort of nervous energy that keeps me awake at night. I can't remember the last time I slept more than two or three hours in one stretch.

"My healer has been working with me to channel the feeling, but it hasn't helped much. We've added drills to my training regimen, and I've studied how to discharge the power properly."

He studied Lira's face unabashedly. "I can sense when others possess power long before they know themselves. Perhaps it has something to do with the way my ancestors consumed magic. It's like a craving that will never be satisfied. Father taught me never to wield it, and I never will. I don't trust myself with it."

Lira flushed, rolling the edge of her apron between her fingers; she wasn't sure how to respond.

"You know I have part of your clan's magic in my veins, don't you, Lira?" Eremon continued, resting his fingertips on her hand and stilling her nervous fidgeting. "Your power calls to me, and mine to yours. It feels a bit like a reverberating lute string or a low hum."

He drew back again. Lira trained her eyes on the tiles, trying to imagine the sensation. She swallowed hard, lacing her fingers tightly in her lap. Suddenly, she couldn't look back up.

"Could you tell me something else?" she asked.

"Of course."

"The other night, I dreamed I was drowning in the ocean, chained to a long line of people. It was so real—I even woke with the taste of seawater in my mouth." She shook her head. "What—"

"A memory from your clan." He clenched his fists. "Chained together and left on the sandbar for high tide to claim them. It's one of the many ways Nami murdered the people he'd drained of their power."

Lira swallowed the bile that tried to force its way up her throat. She wanted to feel shocked, but it was like she had already lived it. Survived it. "What finally ended it all?"

"Several centuries passed with no hint of clan magic. My

forefathers grew confident the clans' powers would never return. Iathium eventually left the clans to their own devices, and later opened free trade. It was as if the past had truly been rewritten.

"That became the Rodhlan we live in now, where clanspeople move freely about the continent, doing business and trade with Iathium and one another. They're free to come and go as they please, even move into the city and seek their fortunes here, like your family did."

She sat in quiet thought before she replied. "If their magic is stirring now, what will you do? Will you let it take root again? Will you rein them in, once this power is no longer a whisper?"

Eremon set his jaw. "I want all of us to exist in peace."

He traced his finger along the wood grain of the desk. "The problem is, if the magic manifests strongly in the clans' territories, they could unite—build armies to march against Iathium. I fear they'll seek retribution for the past."

"Why would they? Today's clans haven't known a day of war. They're prosperous because of Iathium."

"That's where you're wrong," Eremon said, a muscle in his jaw twitching. "When their magic returns in full force—when they realize their true potential—that's when they'll know how much was stolen from them."

Lira rubbed her temple. "So you want to reveal the true histories to the entire continent and allow the clans to wield their magic, all while keeping the peace." She shook her head. "What if they turn on you?"

"I'd have no choice but to defend my city. My people are innocent; they've done nothing wrong. But we must avoid war at all costs. I've assembled a secret council of special ambassadors to go to the clans and begin preemptive peace negotiations."

All his talk of avoiding war, of sending ambassadors to the clans, reminded her of Irem's statement about needing the clans to trust *her*. Lira wasn't certain exactly where she fit into Eremon's plan.

They want to use my magic to help them avoid war, not just uncover the truth, she thought. *I have a right to know what he has in mind.*

"Where do my powers come in?" she asked.

Eremon winced. "I haven't quite worked that part out," he answered. "I know we'll need you to help us communicate the problem of the histories—"

"The disaster," she cut in.

"Yes." he sighed. "I try to believe everything will unfold as it should, but I haven't decided where I need you most. For now, continue studying Skelly's manuscripts. Absorb as much information as you can over the next few weeks."

"I haven't mastered Onnen," Lira said. "I don't know how long it will take me to get through the books, but it's not going to be fast."

"You and I can fix that. Remember, I promised to teach you."

"How?"

He reached for her, but hesitated. "May I?"

Lira nodded. They turned to face one another on the stools, knees touching. For a moment, her gaze lingered on his lips. They looked soft and full, and she swallowed hard before forcing herself to meet his eyes again.

She shivered when she noticed Eremon's gaze drop to her mouth, too—brief and fleeting. He touched her forehead gently, his fingertips warm against her skin. For a moment, she thought she felt the hum he'd talked about—the shared magic that bound them in some strange way.

"Will it hurt?" she asked.

"It won't."

She flinched, drawing back. "Is it dark magic?"

"No." He laughed softly. "It's something Irem taught me—a

sort of transfer, as I understand it." He knitted his brow, drawing back slightly. "Don't tell me you're afraid of me now."

Lira's cheeks burned. "I'm not afraid."

Quite the contrary.

"All right, then." He touched her forehead again. "Close your eyes."

Lira squeezed her eyes shut as she felt a jolt similar to the one that had coursed through her at Irem's touch. This was stronger, though; she felt rooted to her stool, to Eremon himself, as if his fingertips had fused to her skin. Whispers and images began pouring into her mind, filling her senses as her clan's native language flooded her consciousness.

When Eremon finally broke their connection, Lira was panting; beads of sweat dripped down her forehead.

"Well?" he asked hopefully.

With a trembling hand, Lira gave him the keys to the restricted stack. "There's only one way to find out."

CHAPTER 9

Over the next two weeks, Lira took every opportunity she had to steal away to the inner chamber, immersing herself completely in Skelly's manuscripts. Her mastery of Onnen felt as natural as if it were her first language, and she flew through the books at breakneck speed, filling each volume with bookmarks as she gathered bits and pieces of information about dark magic and mortal gods.

She rapidly grew accustomed to managing the daily operations of the archive, doling out assignments and mentoring her apprentices. Aidryn disappeared again as abruptly as he'd returned, and Lira often found herself wishing he could help her shoulder the burden so she could spend more time studying.

Eremon visited the chamber often to talk through the histories. Lira had found an unexpected friend in him, and she relished the time they spent working together. Their companionship quickly became effortless, and on the days he didn't show, it was difficult for her not to feel disappointed. Those days, she doubled down on her work, poring over the manuscripts feverishly to keep herself occupied.

Lira spent less time at home than she ever had; when she was there, she thought about Talfryn. She wondered how he was holding up to training, but even more, the idea of war troubled her deeply. Even the youngest sentries were traditionally sent into battle, fully trained or not.

There was no true comfort for Lira's anxiety. She was thankful Talfryn wasn't home to tempt her, for she might have been compelled to tell him everything she knew—to beg him to flee the city until things were set right. But her brother's loyalty to Iathium rivaled her own, and deep down, she knew he'd never leave his post.

On the day before *Nami Mostari*, Eremon came to the chamber again. When he knocked, Lira was poring over a scroll about the giving and taking of magic. She opened the stairs absently, and he joined her at the desk, sinking down onto his stool.

"This is much more complicated than I realized," Lira said, returning to her parchment. "Listen to this: *'A person may freely give or take magic that is rightfully offered to them, and the power will be at peace in their body. Magic wrongfully taken goes to war with its host and returns to its rightful place tenfold.'*"

Eremon nodded, pressing his lips together. "And can magic wrongfully taken be freely returned to its rightful place?"

"I'm not sure," she said. "Why?" She studied his face; dark circles had formed under his eyes.

"I want to know whether I can freely give back this stolen power." He flexed his fingers. "Whether the clans' power can be separated from my ancestors'."

She furrowed her brow, shaking her head. "But you didn't take it; and there's Rhona's power to account for. Wouldn't your bloodline have inherited some measure of that?"

"That's the power to transfer. It came from her, and the clans inherited it. My ability to give you Onnen was part of her gift to me. But she created the powers the clans possessed from her own imagination. In other words, she didn't exactly have those same powers. Each thread of magic from the four clans in my body was, I presume, stolen by my forefathers."

"So you want to know if those magical threads can be separated, then transferred."

"Yes. But now, it's like..." He swallowed hard and began again. "It's like the powers are trying to escape from my body. I can't explain it better than that.

"It's wearing on me. If I could be rid of it, I would be doing myself *and* the clans a service."

A service, how? she thought. *How would it help to unleash magic on them when they have never wielded it? When most have no idea it exists?*

Despite her questions, she worried for him. She couldn't imagine the thought of being saddled with so much power.

He must truly be suffering.

"I'll keep looking, see what I can find," she promised. "Is there anything else I can do to help you?"

"No. I'll just be glad when this blasted festival is over."

"I'm looking forward to it, myself," Lira said. "It'll be a welcome distraction."

"Enjoying it is one thing," Eremon said, cracking a half-smile. "Listening to your mother and her committee plan it day after day is nauseating."

Lira giggled.

"You know you'll have a seat at the high table this year, Lady Silira."

She froze, and her heart began to race. Drawing attention to herself was the last thing she wanted to do—ever. "Oh, I didn't think about that. My mind has been here." Lira motioned toward the books.

"So has mine." His eyes flicked to her face before he looked down at his clasped hands. "You're a noble now. That has its advantages."

"Like making small talk with stuffed shirts I've never met?" She wrinkled her nose.

"I'll make sure you sit beside the stuffiest shirts at court." He winked at her, making his way back to the stairwell. "Thank you for your hard work. I'll see you tomorrow."

"Goodbye," she called after him.

The stairwell had barely shut when the chamber door behind her creaked open, and she nearly jumped out of her skin. "Aidryn!"

He entered the room with a spring in his step. "You should learn to engage that lock properly, Defender."

She rolled her eyes. "What do you want?"

"Caitir's in the courtyard. She said you kicked her out of here a few weeks ago, so she asked me to come fetch you this time." The corner of his mouth turned up in a crooked grin. "So? Are you coming?"

"Is it already that late? I was working on—" She cut her eyes toward the documents on the desk. "I'm not quite finished for the day."

"*Nami Mostari* begins tomorrow. Can it wait until morning?"

"Not really, but..." Lira sighed, glancing at the books again. "Let's go."

"LADY SILIRA MÓR, DEFENDER OF HISTORIES," Caitir trilled as she embraced Lira in the courtyard. "Why didn't you just tell me? You know I can keep a secret."

"You certainly cannot." Lira laughed, returning the hug. "It wasn't my place to tell; Lord Irem was still in the role then, anyway."

Caitir pointed accusingly at Aidryn, but her tone was light. "And you knew the whole time. I hope whatever Father has you doing is worth giving up a place among the nobility. I'm not sure if I can forgive you just now."

"If you can't manage to get the Rí's attention from your vantage point, I don't know what to say to you," he answered dryly.

Lira glanced over Caitir's shoulder at Aidryn, who flashed her an affectionate smile. Caitir looped her arm through Lira's as they began the long trek across town.

"Have you met the Rí yet?" she asked expectantly. "What's he like?"

The sea foam-green gems that dangled from Caitir's earrings caught the afternoon sunlight. They matched the gown she was wearing: a flowing, floor-length masterpiece with a scoop-neck, snug-fitting sleeves, and a short train. She had slipped on the wrist loop to keep the rich fabric from dragging on the street.

Lira schooled her expression into indifference and forced herself to keep walking. "He's... very polite. A bit disarming. Not at all what I expected."

"It sounds like you really *know* him," Caitir breathed with an urgency that almost made Lira squirm. "I thought he might have simply anointed you, but—"

"He's friends with Lord Irem," Lira hedged, "so I've seen him here and there."

Caitir whirled toward Aidryn, scrutinizing her brother as if seeing him for the first time. "So you *would* have crossed paths with him when you were in training," she accused. "And you never introduced us."

Aidryn's expression darkened. "He is a private person, Caitir," he scolded. "Not only did I have little interaction with him; I deliberately avoided being in his presence out of respect."

Lira flinched at the sharpness of his reply; she had a habit of stepping in to smooth things over when she sensed tension between them.

"Caitir," she ventured, noting several passersby who were near enough to hear their conversation, "I understand the Rí tends to spend time in the archives irregularly. His schedule is unpredictable."

"Isn't there a chance you could introduce us, Lira?" Caitir pleaded. "If I could just speak to him, I'm certain—"

"You know there's not," Aidryn cut in firmly, with a meaningful glance at Lira. He lowered his voice. "Don't make things uncomfortable for Lira. She needs time to adjust to the role, and even then, the moment would still have to present itself. Lira would risk her post by forcing you in front of the Rí."

Caitir's eyes flicked downward, and she pressed her lips together for a moment before she spoke again. "You're right; I wouldn't want to overstep my welcome."

There was a pained edge to her voice that made Lira pause. She wanted to find some way to make Caitir happy; her friend looked so disappointed. Lira hoped Aidryn would talk more to Caitir later; but if Aila Tarlach ever found out Lira was so close to Eremon, she would double the pressure she was already putting on her daughter to get near him.

"I'm sure something could work out," Lira said reassuringly, though she carefully avoided making any promises. "I'm so new to all of this; perhaps it will all be easier to navigate in time."

"Will you tell me more about him soon?" Caitir asked hopefully. "I mean, as you get to know him."

"If there's more to tell," Lira hedged, "but now that Lord Irem is gone, the Rí has no real reason to spend much time in the archive."

The words stung as they left her lips. Lira felt Aidryn's gaze on her again, and her face began to burn. She hoped it wasn't noticeable in the late afternoon sunlight. Aidryn had always been able to tell when she was lying; she just hoped he wouldn't point it out this time.

Aidryn kicked a pebble down the street, his mouth pressed into a thin line. "Caitir," he finally said, "it's not good for you to focus on one man. I wish you would at least look at some of the others who want your attention."

She scoffed. "Like who, the Énna boys you've been running the streets with?"

Aidryn cracked his knuckles and shrugged. "Aeron won't leave me alone about you."

Caitir's steps faltered. "He's a *sentry*," she sputtered.

"Sentries were good enough for you last summer," Aidryn replied, glancing sidelong at her with a smirk.

Lira raised an eyebrow and attempted to make eye contact with Caitir. Infuriatingly, Caitir wouldn't look at her.

"What did I miss last summer?" Lira pressed.

Now Caitir's cheeks blazed red, but she ignored Lira. Instead, she kept her attention on her brother.

"Last summer, I wasn't being stuffed right under the Raní's nose like a silk handkerchief." Caitir stopped walking for a moment, reaching down to yank off her slippers. "These bloody shoes are blistering my feet," she grumbled.

Lira rarely saw Caitir express agitation about being so close to Eremon's mother. She could imagine that it would be frustrating to try so hard, for so long, and never be able to get as close to Eremon as Aila wanted her to be. A wave of shame crashed into her; she hated covering up the truth and having the truth withheld from her. Hated that it had to affect her friends. Hated that lies already tainted the friendship that was growing between her and Eremon.

"Why don't we go to the cottage," Lira said softly. "I have a gift for you there."

Caitir beamed for a brief moment, but then her expression

fell. "I want to, but I need to go home and soak my feet. Can it wait until tomorrow?"

"Of cour—"

"I'll walk Lira home and bring it back for you," Aidryn offered.

Lira's shoulders sagged. *Now he's going to hound me.*

Caitir beamed with relief. "Perfect."

They took her as far as the estate grounds, then set off again in the direction of Lira's home. Aidryn walked at a fast clip, so that Lira had to trot to catch up with him. They were several blocks away before he spoke again.

"If you're going to lie to Caitir, at least have the decency to sound convincing."

"I don't know what you're talking about."

"I've known you for most of my life, Lira." He shook his head, smiling ruefully. "When you lie, your voice rises by half an octave."

She sighed. "You know how your mother is. If she believes there's even the tiniest chance—"

"Oh, I agree. Mother doesn't need any encouragement. But you need a story that will hold up better against the rumors. You know they've already heard them."

"What rumors?"

"It's all over court that Eremon goes into the archive nearly every day now. Why would that be, I wonder?"

Her stomach knotted. "I thought he was being discreet."

"There's no such thing as discreet for—listen." He stopped her with a hand on her shoulder, squaring with her. His deep blue eyes bored into hers, flashing with concern.

"It's your business, Lira," he said, "but Caitir is not in the best spirits right now, and I don't think she would take well to finding out you're getting so close to him, especially since you weren't honest about it."

Lira shrugged away from his touch. "What was I supposed

to do when she pressured me like that? If you were me, would you have been honest?"

The corner of his mouth twitched.

"Oh, that's right. You *weren't*," she snapped. "So stop acting like you have the moral high ground."

Lira stalked ahead of him, chin held high, and was satisfied that he hung back several paces behind her until they reached the cottage. She didn't bother waiting for him to catch up as she unlocked the door and slipped inside.

Once in the cottage, she headed straight to her room, unclipping Caitir's crown from the twine line she'd hung it on. The flowers had dried beautifully; she took a moment to inspect her work before turning to find Aidryn in the doorway to her room.

"That's a nea'la rose," he murmured, his gaze trained on the remaining blooms that still hung where she'd dried them.

Lira's eyes flew to the teal bloom she'd dried alongside the wreaths after it had begun to droop in its vase. Her cheeks burned as she fumbled for an answer. She finally settled on, "You're right."

"Where did it come from?" he asked, his words deliberate and slow.

There was no use lying, so she straightened as she answered, "You know where it came from."

They stared one another down for a long moment before she sighed resignedly. "He's my friend, Aidryn. You know how often he comes to the archive; you told me yourself."

Aidryn's brow furrowed. He looked up at the ceiling for a long moment before he finally made eye contact with Lira again. "I don't think you realize what you've gotten yourself into."

She twirled the stem between her fingertips nervously. "Why would you say that?"

"You know why." He took a step nearer, as if daring her to

tell him everything. "Just know that if your involvement with him breaks Caitir, we could both lose her. You have been her only true friend over the years, Lira—the only one who has never tried to undermine or sabotage her. But in her mind, that's exactly what you're doing by lying about this."

Lira leaned in, willing him to feel the full force of the anger rising inside her. "It isn't undermining or sabotaging if Eremon chooses me for a companion over her. You're intelligent enough to know that; stop trying to manipulate me into staying away from him to protect her feelings."

Aidryn edged nearer; Lira's first instinct was to back away, but she held her ground as he leveled with her. "I've spent years trying to be a voice of reason for Caitir, to keep her grounded. But she has become so singularly focused on the throne that whoever stands in her way will suffer for it," he snarled, his breath hot on her cheek. "Now, I'm dangerously close to losing what little influence I've had over her.

"I don't want to see my sister spiral any further into the disaster I fear she's becoming," he said, "and I don't want to see her wrath turned on you. So forgive me if I can't be happy about your new *companion*."

Lira's breath caught in her throat. She hadn't considered how he might respond to learning about Eremon, but it was infuriating that he believed he had a say in the matter.

"That isn't fair, Aidryn," she said. "It's not my fault she's under pressure. Besides, I can't *order* him to stay away from me."

"You do have a choice, though," he said, his eyes flicking to the rose again. "You aren't obligated to get any closer."

"No, I'm not obligated," she snapped. "But if I want to get closer, you said it yourself: it's my business."

They glared at one another for a long moment before Aidryn set his jaw and bit out a clipped, "Let's go." He turned on his heel and stalked toward the door.

Lira followed him out of the house, circlet in hand, as they made their way back to his family's estate. She wanted to rage at him for ruining the afternoon; instead, she mulled over their argument while he brooded two steps ahead of her. By the time they reached Caitir, Lira's frustration had cooled, but she made up her mind not to speak to Aidryn again, at least until he apologized for overreacting.

When they arrived, Lira held out the crown to her friend.

"It's perfect," Caitir cried, trying it on. "Your most beautiful work! Where did you find these flowers?"

"I wanted them to be perfect this year," Lira answered with a shrug.

"Well, you certainly worked your magic on them." Caitir embraced Lira. Relief flooded her when Caitir didn't ask any more questions about where the blooms had come from.

In a moment that mirrored their embrace in the courtyard, Lira peered over Caitir's shoulder to find Aidryn watching her with a scrutinizing gaze, his eyes narrow and accusing. She quickly glanced down, pulling away from his sister.

"I'm glad you're happy," Lira said. "I'll see you tomorrow?"

"Stay for supper," Caitir said. "There's plenty to share."

Lira's stomach growled, but she ignored it; she didn't think she could eat and visit while Aidryn glared at her from across the table. "I wish I could, but I need to go home tonight."

"If you must." Caitir sighed, willing a smile to her face. "I can't wait for tomorrow. I'll see you at the festival!"

"Until then," Lira said, stepping away from the door. She raised a hand toward the siblings; Caitir waved, but Aidryn stared, unmoving, until Lira whirled to step back into the street. She felt his gaze burning into her back, so she walked as quickly as she could until she'd rounded the corner. Then, she took a moment to press her back to the cool stone wall and take a few slow breaths.

When Lira arrived home, she cooked dinner for herself in silence, brooding over the afternoon's events. Despite the almost overwhelming temptation to go back to the archive, Lira forced herself to eat. Afterward, she carefully dismantled her father's armor, waxing and buffing each piece meticulously before spreading it across the worktable in the kitchen. The manual labor was a welcome outlet for the tension that had settled into her muscles.

When the plate was polished, she took the chain mail down to inspect it and was dismayed to find rust forming on some of the rings. She dipped into her father's sand barrel, shoveling several heaping scoops into an old sack she'd found in his tool shed. Sitting on a work stool by the back door, she heaved the chain mail into the sack and shook it, her frustration melting away with the movement. She repeated the process until the rust was gone, then hung the mail in the entryway again.

When they were children, Talfryn had often complained about how small Arlen had made the shirt of mail. At the time, women weren't permitted to enlist as sentries, so their father had humored Lira by constructing the mail and plate to fit a female's body. Now, she wondered if his foresight had something to do with her magic.

By the time she finished working, the moon was high. Gnawing anxiety about *Nami Mostari* replaced her anger; she had managed not to over-analyze her new rank for a little while, but keeping herself busy only went so far.

Before Lira lay down for the night, she carefully hid the dried rose behind the leather pouch of heirlooms in her bureau. She sighed sadly, pushing the drawer shut to conceal the bloom from further prying eyes.

CHAPTER 10

Iathium was brimming with excitement the next morning. Citizens, artisans, and shopkeepers set up their booths and prepared their shops and homes for the week's festivities. Lira abandoned her usual work uniform, instead choosing a simple brown dress whose sleeves stretched to her elbows, its hem brushing the ground. She carried her circlet of flowers gingerly as she walked.

Most mornings, she kept her head down and rushed across town to the archive. She wasn't fond of making eye contact with passersby and preferred to draw as little notice as possible. This morning, however, she couldn't help slowing down a bit to greet her neighbors, savor the bustle, and enjoy the light-hearted spirit the festival brought with it. As she meandered through the streets, she took her time to stop by artisans' table and enjoy the smell of the spices wafting on the air.

One of the vendors who had set up shop was offering small bowls of rice tossed with grilled fish and sweet onions. Lira bought a bowl for herself and ate the firm, savory fish happily as she walked.

She had almost reached the Drochaid when Caitir called

her name. Her friend had already donned her circlet and was draped in cascades of soft ivory charmeuse and chiffon. The dress was airy and graceful; the long, sheer bell sleeves started below her bare shoulders and were long enough to brush the ground. Her neckline plunged so low, it left little to the imagination.

"Caitir, you look like a bride," Lira breathed, admiring the luxurious fabric.

"Mother had gowns made especially for each day of the festival this year." Caitir's gaze roved over Lira from head to toes. "Do you want to borrow one of them?"

Lira shrugged; she shouldn't feel stung by Caitir's implication, but she found herself bristling. "This one is fine."

Caitir linked arms with Lira and pulled her away from the bridge, toward one of her favorite dressmakers' shops. "You're nobility now; it really won't do."

"Didn't you have something else to do this morning?" Lira asked, grimacing as they neared the storefront. Caitir was right, but she didn't want to admit it.

"I thought I might lurk in the garden, catch a glimpse of the Rí. But I can help you look for a gown instead."

Lira bit the inside of her cheek. "All right. But let's make it quick; I don't want you to be scolded for changing your plans."

"It's a holiday," her friend said. "Mother will be more lenient today." Her words were slower—quieter—as they wandered toward the shops.

They stopped by Caitir's favorite shop, owned by a dressmaker named Lisette. Lira browsed the hanging garments, running her fingertips over the richly textured fabrics. The dressmaker hovered over her anxiously as she looked, but nothing in the shop appealed to her enough to justify the cost.

Caitir stayed near the front window, glancing out every few minutes as Lira looked. Less than fifteen minutes passed before Lira crossed the shop to her friend.

"Let's go," she said, nodding toward the door. "I haven't found anything yet."

Caitir nodded and followed her back out into the street, eyes darting as they eased into the crowd.

"Maybe you shouldn't press your luck," Lira ventured. "If you're worried about being caught out, you should probably go where you're supposed to be."

Caitir sighed, nodding. "I should." She kissed Lira's cheek. "See you tonight!"

Lira waved as her friend disappeared down the block, then continued her meandering. Along the road, visiting vendors had pitched tents and set up booths to hawk their wares during *Nami Mostari*. Lira recognized some of the merchants' clothing as native to Clans Énna and Mór. She snaked through the crowd toward a large tent at the end of the street and ducked inside; it was packed full of clothing and jewelry, and she marveled at how the vendor could have possibly carted it all in from outside the city.

The noon sun had risen in the sky before Lira finally settled on two new gowns for the occasion. The first was an airy dress the color of midnight, covered with intricate needlework from bottom to top—branches, vines, lush leaves, and flowers that had been carefully stitched into the bodice and skirt from silken thread. Its sleeves ended at her elbows and opened into sheer bells that fell nearly to the floor.

Lira's second gown was a deep emerald embellished with threads of bronze—the traditional colors of Clan Mór. She wondered briefly if wearing it might attract undue notice but shrugged the thought away; her new status wouldn't go unnoticed during the festivities. Though the thought of being an object of discussion made her cringe, skipping the parties didn't seem like a good solution. Besides, Caitir had insisted she come, and Eremon would be expecting her.

~

LIRA SPENT most of the day alone in the archive, struggling to focus on her notes. She thought about Eremon's request from the day before, and scoured the manuscripts for answers. So far, there were no records that detailed whether a person who harbored stolen magic could return it freely.

It seemed simple enough; if magic could be freely given at all, it stood to reason that someone should be able to return power to its rightful owner. Still, she couldn't nail anything down.

As the day went on, it grew harder and harder to concentrate. Lira checked the timepiece periodically until evening fell; finally, she gave up trying to read and changed into the midnight gown. She finger-combed her curls, letting them tumble down her back, and tucked her pendant beneath the low neckline of her dress.

A few moments later, she emerged into the courtyard. Paper lanterns were strung from one end to the other, setting everyone aglow with warm candlelight. Musicians played a lilting tune. Tables had been set up on one side of the courtyard for feasting, with the high table erected on the platform on the northwestern end of the Dome, near the royal family's quarters.

The courtyard was teeming with people—mostly members of court and workers from the Dome. Because the grounds around the Dome were meager in comparison to the building's size, few lay citizens were allowed near the royal feast. But festivities were spread throughout the city; after this meal and the dancing ended, attendees would flood into the streets to continue celebrating and indulging.

Lira wove through the crowd toward the platform, scanning for Caitir and Aidryn. She found them near the platform, where Caitir was holding vigil until Eremon appeared.

"You're finally here!" Caitir squealed, grabbing Lira's hands. "Where did you get your gown? I've never seen anything like it."

Aidryn's eyes drifted to the dress. He worked his jaw but said nothing.

"From one of the merchants," Lira answered. "It's inspired by a fashion that was popular during Nami's reign." She fingered the delicate needlework. "It was common to weave intricate little flowers and vines into layers of sheer fabric that overlaid a fitted bodice like this one."

"Fascinating. I suppose our noted scholar is allowed to wear an outdated style if it pleases her." Caitir winked. "Then again, none of my gowns has an interesting story attached."

Members of the high court began to file onto the platform, taking their places at the high table. Lira adjusted the sleeves and smoothed her skirt, pressing her palms to her bodice as she scanned the faces who claimed their seats at the table.

Aidryn touched her elbow lightly, leaning in to whisper, "The ancient rag suits you, if I say so myself."

Lira relaxed. "No one asked for your opinion." She flashed him a grateful smile. He rubbed the back of his neck and glanced toward the platform, then mumbled something about finding his father before he strode off across the courtyard.

Only a few empty spots were left at the table before Lira finally moved toward it, promising to fill Caitir in on every detail. She surveyed the table, unsure of where she should sit. That was the downside to waiting; she hadn't wanted to be alone at the table, waiting anxiously to see who might take a seat next to her. Yet, now she didn't want to sit beside anyone she didn't already know. It didn't help that her list of options was incredibly short.

Eremon's mother had taken a place beside her son at the head of the high table. The Raní was a regal, formidable woman, worthy of the title in every sense. She would retain it until Eremon married; then, the title and crown would pass to his wife. If he never married, he would name an heir to assume the title and throne after his death.

Eremon had never shown an interest in choosing a bride, but he also hadn't named an heir. As with all other traditions, he was dragging his feet for as long as he could, to the ire of his council. Whispers around court indicated that, over time, his mother had grown more agitated by this particular delay. Lira had heard that, though Macha wanted to control Eremon's marital decisions, she was also terrified he wouldn't continue the bloodline.

Macha was dressed in red, gold, and ivory robes that cascaded down her slight frame like a gentle waterfall. The folds of ivory silk tumbled down from beneath a blood-red satin tunic that was adorned with a wide, gold belt. Her fingertips peeked out from beneath the wide sleeves, and her silver hair was held back with a comb made of solid gold.

Lira caught Macha's attention as she moved toward an empty seat, and she shrank from the woman's exacting gaze, and the chair she'd intended on occupying. She kept moving backward until she bumped into someone with an unladylike, "Oof!"

Whirling, she found herself chest-level with Emyr Tarlach, Aidryn and Caitir's father, who grinned and offered her his arm. "Care for an escort?

"I'm sorry," she stammered, blushing. "I'm more out of my element than I'd like to admit."

He chuckled. "You're not alone."

Several members of court looked over curiously, watching her as she took Emyr's outstretched arm and walked with him to the high table.

"It's the armorer's daughter," she heard someone whisper.

"The new Defender of Histories," said another.

"There's an empty place beside me, if you don't mind the company," Emyr said, pulling her chair out for her.

"Thank you," she said, relief washing over her.

"Caitir has spoken about only two things for the past few weeks: this festival, and your new title." Emyr smiled as he joined her, blue eyes twinkling.

"May I offer you my most heartfelt congratulations? You've worked very hard; I couldn't be prouder if you were my own daughter."

Lira smiled. "That means so much, Lord Tarlach. But I—I'm sorry you're not congratulating Aidryn instead."

"Things always work out as they should, Silira." Emyr winked, then turned his attention to the head of the table.

Eremon was standing, a goblet of mead in his hand. He stared straight down the table, directly at Lira. For a moment, time slowed; the commotion around her narrowed to the connection between the two of them. A little shiver ran up her spine as she flushed, grinning.

Eremon raised a hand, silencing the chatter.

"My friends, it is an honor to dine with you as we celebrate our city's founding. Familiar faces and new ones"—he locked eyes with Lira again, raising his glass to her— "I'm glad all of you are here. *Nami Mostari!*"

Everyone at the table followed suit, toasting Eremon and his forefathers. He smiled broadly, stealing another glance at Lira before he set his cup on the table and moved to take his seat.

Lira felt it before it happened, like a ripple in the atmosphere. Her eyes snapped to Eremon. There was a collective gasp as he doubled over the table, bracing himself there as his face contorted in pain. Sweat beaded on his forehead, and he dragged a hand over his face, fighting to catch his breath.

A long moment passed before he looked up again at those assembled for the meal; wincing, he raised himself to his full height. "If you'll excuse me..." He waved a hand toward his guests. "Carry on."

Eremon turned and moved toward the Dome, unsteady on his feet. Two of his councilmen rushed to escort him. Lira craned her neck, her gaze fixed on them until Macha moved to block her view. Her glare was enough to make Lira want to crawl beneath the table.

Eremon's mother raised her own goblet then, proposing the traditional toast to the city, to the rulers who had gone before, a tradition her son had blatantly ignored. She noticed a handful of advisors nodding in approval while others shifted uncomfortably in their seats.

Lira sat in dazed silence as the lords and ladies around her repeated the toast. Her eyes remained fixed on where Eremon had disappeared inside the Dome.

"I heard the Rí complaining of a splitting headache this morning," she heard one lord say. "No doubt he's gone to the healer. He'll be back in no time; nothing keeps him down for long."

"I don't know if he is just lazy, or if he means to rewrite the traditions of this entire city."

"Speaking of traditions, will he choose a dance partner this year?" a lady asked.

"Not likely," another chimed in.

"Rumor has it he's *very* interested in the histories."

Lira felt eyes on her; her face was blazing, but she kept her attention trained on the empty plate in front of her. She eavesdropped as the gossiping council members drunkenly debated whether historians knew how to dance, and took wagers on whether or not Eremon would try to find out.

Lira fell into reluctant conversation with the other nobles seated around her: five other ambassadors, counting Emyr. Their faces were vaguely familiar, but Lira was too distracted to remember all their names. She sat on pins and needles, involving herself in the exchange as little as possible as she waited for Eremon to emerge from the Dome.

Finally, Eremon returned to the table during the main course, and Lira nearly slid out of her chair with relief. He chanced a glance in her direction; she furrowed her brow, tilting her head questioningly as he sat. Her face warmed as he offered her an almost imperceptible, but reassuring, nod.

Her attention snapped back to her dinner mates when one of the ambassadors, a slight, balding man of middle age, exclaimed, "I say, that's an artifact from Clan Mór!"

All eyes in close proximity snapped to Lira—or rather, the pendant that had worked its way to the outside of her gown. She clutched it, hesitant to make a scene by hiding it again. "What do you mean?"

"I'm the ambassador to Rodhlan Ridge," the man continued excitedly, flapping his hand in the general direction of the necklace. "I've seen artwork, depictions of that symbol."

"Calm yourself, Gaib," Emyr said, his eyes sliding to the pendant. "Silira has family in the Ridge. Have you never seen jewelry depicting the tree?"

"Never," Gaib said reverently. "It is magnificent. May I?" He held his empty palms toward her expectantly.

Lira shook her head. "I'm sorry; it was a gift from my grandmother. I don't part with it."

"I understand," Gail said, nodding reverently. "Neither would I. With the clan's recent aversion to outsiders—well, they're becoming more like Clan Beran every year."

Lira tucked his implications away for later, though it was curious that her clan had self-isolated. Still, she didn't want to reveal how out of touch she was with its goings-on, so she asked, "Are you a cousin of mine, Gaib?"

The ambassador shook his head. "No, my lady; but I sincerely wish I was."

Gaib launched into stories about his adventures in the Ridge, regaling the other ambassadors with outlandish tales of his encounters with the members of Clan Mór.

Lira ignored him, letting her eyes drift back to Eremon. He looked better than before as he spoke and laughed with his guests. When she was satisfied that he had recovered, the knot in her stomach finally loosened, and she, too, was able to savor her food.

CHAPTER II

Lira joined Caitir and Aidryn in the courtyard after the meal ended; her friends had eaten their fill of hors d'oeuvres and were sipping on mead when she caught up with them.

"What was it like?" Caitir asked, lacing her fingers through Lira's.

"Delicious," Lira answered. "Your father offered me a seat with the ambassadors; they're an interesting breed."

Caitir rolled her eyes. "There were two empty chairs closer to the Raní."

"There was no way I was sitting near her," Lira said. "The way she looked at me—"

"Is the way she looks at everyone," Caitir finished. She stood on her tiptoes, scanning the platform for a glimpse of Eremon.

Aidryn turned to Lira. "You were wise to keep your distance," he said. He lowered his voice, leaning closer. "What happened up there?"

"No idea," she whispered. "He looked terrible. They rushed him into the Dome, but he seemed better when he returned."

"He isn't well," Aidryn said.

Lira glanced toward the platform to find Macha peering in her direction. They locked eyes briefly before Lira averted hers again, heart pounding.

"What do you think's happening?" she asked Aidryn.

"It's all part of the intrigue, isn't it?" He handed Lira his goblet of mead, and she took a long swig, its sweet warmth blooming in her belly. "Meet me in the archive at dawn; I think it's time to talk about what we know."

A hush fell over the courtyard as the music ended, and Eremon stepped onto the platform. In his hands, he held a crown of teal roses, silken ribbons streaming from it. When the crowd saw the wreath and realized what his intentions were, they began to buzz and chatter.

Caitir sucked in a breath and clutched Lira's arm. "He's finally going to choose a partner!" she whispered excitedly.

Lira bit back a whimper, choosing instead to squeeze Caitir's arm.

Aidryn tipped his chin, his eyes narrowing as he took in what Eremon was holding. "Lira, perhaps we should have that talk now."

"Hush," she hissed, fixing her gaze on Eremon. He had already made eye contact with her; she grew lightheaded, as if she was free-falling from the top of the Dome.

"Father's roses from Iteloria." Caitir tightened her grip on Lira, letting out a squeak. "It can only mean one thing."

"Caitir," Aidryn warned, "it can mean a great many things."

"Wish me luck, brother," she breathed.

Lira was the only one who heard him quietly reply, "I wish I could."

The crowd grew rapt and silent, fixing their attention on Eremon, eager to know his next move. His satin robes shone in the candlelight, his black boots perfectly polished. He stood tall, his jaw set, his gaze steely as he scanned the crowd—a stark contrast to the tender, scholarly young man Lira had come to admire; here, he was unbreakable. Here, he was a god.

Eremon raised the wreath to the sky; his voice boomed across the courtyard. "Begin!"

The musicians struck a chord, and the crowd receded to make room for the nobles and high-born young women to step forward. Caitir rushed into the fray, Lira trailing behind her. Everyone formed two lines and began the intricate folk dance that opened every *Nami Mostari*.

Lira followed along half a step behind, trying her best to mimic Caitir's movements until she fell into the rhythm of the dance. They'd practiced these steps over and over when they were children, but it had been years since Lira had even thought about dancing, much less practiced.

"It's just like old times," Caitir called over the music. She clasped Lira's hands as they spun, the picture of radiance as her golden hair whipped around her face, her pale cheeks rosy with the exertion. She threw her head back and laughed, and Lira finally relaxed, laughing along with her friend.

The world spun around Lira as she and Caitir wove and dipped between dancers, clapping and whirling. She heard the collective gasp as Eremon finally stepped down from the platform, crown in hand, and moved in her direction.

Panic rose in Lira's throat as Caitir let out an excited cry, squeezing her hands. For a moment, her friend's cheeks were rosy, her eyes alight with expectation until Eremon gave her a slight, dismissive bow and reached for Lira.

She couldn't think about the consequences now; she would sort it out later. Here, in front of her Rí and a courtyard teeming with nobles, she couldn't afford to stumble. *I am their equal now. I am Defender of Histories.*

Lira met Eremon's eyes, sinking into a bow. He caught her elbow and gently drew her back to standing; without breaking her gaze, he reached up to remove the crown of flowers she had made and replaced it with his own. Pitching the dried circlet to the ground, he snaked his arm around her waist, pulling her close. She closed her eyes, letting herself relax into him as his breath tickled her cheek.

Lira forgot everything else as Eremon swept her into the dance. His touch was electrifying, his movements fluid and confident as he locked eyes with her. She matched pace with her sovereign, praying she wouldn't trip over her feet. Her heartbeat pounded in her ears—exertion, and something more. When he flashed her a broad grin, she lost her footing, but he held her up, unfazed by her lack of grace.

The music sped to a feverish tempo as the crowd danced. Eremon gripped Lira tightly, as if he couldn't hold her close enough. Delight filled her as they spun together, the world blurring around them.

For a moment, title and rank melted away and they poured themselves into the dance, laughing and twirling, two dear friends sharing a celebration of the city with their people. Lira shrieked as Eremon grasped her waist and lifted her before leading her back into the reel.

Too soon, the music slowed. Eremon followed the tempo, pulling Lira against him once more, rich laughter rumbling deep in his chest. She tipped her head back to regard him, a warm smile spreading across her lips as he pressed her knuckles to his mouth.

Eremon leaned in to brush his lips against her ear. "You're beautiful," he whispered, squeezing her hand before he stepped back to survey her again. "Thank you for the dance."

Lira was glowing as she dipped a curtsy. He took one step back, then two, then backed all the way to the stage, tearing his eyes from her only when it was time to ascend the stairs.

It was customary after the first dance for him to watch the proceedings from the stage, but Lira found herself wishing she could join him. She felt vulnerable now in the cool evening air, suddenly keenly aware of the attention they'd drawn. From his place on the platform, he flashed her a radiant grin and a wink before signaling the crowd to begin the next dance.

The crowd around Lira buzzed; she could feel their eyes on her as they reluctantly moved into position with their partners once again. Her face burned; she wasn't accustomed to anyone noticing her. She backed out of the crowd in search of a quiet place to collect herself.

Eremon had chosen her. Of all the people he could have chosen—after all these years of *refusing* to choose—he had chosen Lira. She could still feel the brush of his lips against her ear, the feeling of his kiss on her hand. Another deep blush crept up her neck and washed over her face.

She scanned the crowd for Aidryn and Caitir; she felt too exposed, standing here alone on the outskirts of the crowd. The other dancers were overly generous with their curiosity, craning their necks to gawk mercilessly in her direction.

"Who do you think you are?"

By the time Lira registered the voice that came from behind her, a slender hand had clamped down on her shoulder, whirling her around. She found herself face-to-face with a livid Aila Tarlach.

Lira pulled away. "I beg your—"

"You know how hard we have worked to get Caitir in front of that boy." Aila's calm, smooth voice was unnerving; Lira found herself wishing she sounded as angry as she looked. "And yet, you don't care."

Caitir stood four paces behind her mother, staring at the ground, her face blotched and eyes red-rimmed. In the lantern light, Lira thought she could make out a red welt on her friend's cheek. Her heart sank.

"I do care," Lira said, her eyes trained on Caitir.

This time, her friend looked up. "Then how could you do this to me?" she cried.

"I know you're disappointed. I can explain."

"You lied about him," Caitir said, her voice wavering, "because you didn't want me to know you were in love with him."

It was all Lira could do not to crumple, but she knew the women could read it all over her face.

"In my position, there are times when I have to protect sensitive information," she hedged carefully. "Eremon's presence at the archive has been part of that."

Caitir shook her head. "It doesn't matter now. I was going to lose either way, and all of this has been for nothing."

"This isn't a competition!" Lira protested.

"Where the Rí is involved, it is always a competition," Aila said sharply. "There are many losers, and only one winner. It wasn't supposed to be *you*."

The words stung. Though Lira knew she had hurt Caitir with her secrets, she suddenly felt betrayed by a family she had trusted since childhood.

"I was never part of this game. Eremon is my friend, but I didn't—"

"*Enough*." Caitir's voice was quiet, accusing. "You've stolen everything from me, and I will never forgive you, Lira."

Her friend whirled, disappearing into the crowd before Lira could respond. Aila still stood before her, a chill rippling from her body. Lira shivered and took a step back.

"I am not finished with you yet," Aila said, catching Lira's arm in a hard grip. She leaned in closer until their noses were nearly touching.

"You are *quite* finished," Lira said, easily prying Aila's hand off and stepping back. It was the first time she'd ever felt grateful that her father had made her grapple with Talfryn growing up. "Don't come near me again."

Aila closed the distance between them again, this time

raising her hand to strike. Lira caught her wrist; a jolt passed between them, knocking Lira to her knees.

"What was that?" Lira cried.

But Aila was gone.

Lira's left palm felt as if she'd doused it in fire; the burning traveled up her arm and into her shoulder. She turned her hand over to find it bloody and raw.

Someone hauled her to her feet then, and she found herself face-to-face with Aidryn. He didn't look her in the eye, but he tore the sleeve of her gown, peeling it away from her arm.

"Stop!" she cried as he ripped the sleeve completely away from the bodice.

"You need to see Eremon's healer, now," he said, grasping her free hand. "Come on."

"Where are you taking me?"

"The Dome," he answered. "We'll have Ljós summoned to the archive."

"I'm fine," she lied, her voice rasping. Her arm was blazing. "I can go myself."

Aidryn ignored her, pulling her along as he hastened toward the Dome. "You should've listened to me," he growled.

"So you're withdrawing your friendship, too." She shouldn't have been surprised.

He finally looked back at her. "Never. But you've started an avalanche I can't stop. Meet me back here at dawn; I'll tell you more then."

Aidryn left Lira on the archive steps, rushing away to find the healer.

～

WHEN LJÓS BERAN ARRIVED—WITHOUT Aidryn—he applied a sweet-smelling salve to Lira's palm and arm, soothing her nerves with his gentle reassurance that the burning would be gone by morning. His accent was thick and guttural, reminding Lira of her stepfather, Artur.

"What happened to me?" she asked as he wrapped a linen bandage around her hand.

She noticed the healer's eyes were a deep amber color, flecked with gold. He secured the wrap before he said, "That is not a question I can answer, on pain of death. But your friend—he will be able to tell you more."

Lira sagged. "You're sworn to secrecy, too?"

"A quandary you understand." It sounded more like a question than a statement. "But perhaps we will see one another again soon, when the gags are not so tight."

He worked another wrap up her arm to hold the salve in place. "Until then, you should stay clear of the person who did this. The Rí will want your help locating her."

"He won't have any trouble," Lira said. "She's the Raní's lady-in-waiting."

Ljós's expression darkened. "I see." He stood, surveying his handiwork again. "I will tell him."

"Ljós—" The healer paused. Lira searched his face before she asked, "What happened to the Rí tonight?"

He dipped his head, packing the salve and bandages in a soft leather satchel adorned with wooden beads and fragments of bone. "I cannot answer that, either," he said.

"Am I not part of what's happening?" she groaned. "What sense does it make to uncover one of my eyes, while insisting the other remain closed? How can I truly help if so much is kept secret?"

"You must ask him in the morning," the healer said, gathering his things. He inclined his head. "Good night, Lady Silira—heir of the mountains, child of the fortress, keeper of truth."

The hair on the back of her neck rose at his mention of Clan Beran's daunting Fortress Halgeir, but she ignored the urge to correct him. Instead, she stopped his leaving with a hand on his arm.

"Will he be all right?" she asked quietly.

When he looked back at her, the expression of pity on his face turned her stomach. "You must discern that for yourself. Good night." He shouldered his satchel and moved away swiftly, his soft leather boots padding on the glistening tiles.

Rising on shaky legs, Lira descended the archive stairs. She locked herself in the inner chamber, removing her ruined gown and changing back into the simple brown dress she'd been wearing that morning. She sank onto her stool, wincing as she gingerly fingered the bandage on her hand.

Lira understood the unfathomable amount of time, money, and emotion Aila and Emyr had invested in advancing their daughter in society. Although Caitir and Aila hadn't yet achieved noble rankings of their own, Emyr was an ambassador. That, along with Aila's service to Macha, had given Caitir every opportunity to maneuver herself closer to Eremon.

She dreaded seeing Aidryn again in the morning.

Squeezing her eyes shut, Lira willed herself to remember the details of her dance with Eremon instead. She'd never imagined being this close to him. It had been enough to be his friend—to have found common ground with a man who was powerful, yet tender; handsome, yet intelligent. Hadn't it?

But it *wasn't* enough. What had happened tonight—the way he'd looked at her, the way she'd felt when he held her close— was undeniable. Despite her better judgment, she'd dropped her guard with Eremon, and had fallen in love with him without considering the repercussions.

She loved him; she'd known, but she had carefully repeated to herself that it was only friendship, only *care*. But care wasn't a strong enough word for the rush that coursed through her whenever their eyes met. It didn't adequately describe the longing she felt for him to spend every moment of the day with her in the chamber, poring over books at her side.

Until Eremon anointed her, she had deemed the archive her life's purpose. The anointing should have reinforced that; but she had allowed Eremon to distract her. Worse, she had *wanted* him to. Because of their dance, to the outside world, her accomplishments as Defender would forever be overshadowed by the bond she'd forged with him.

All she'd ever wanted was to be renowned as a scholar, to pass her love of the histories to others. But from now on, she would be whispered about: the Rí's lover, the armorer's daughter, the unworthy girl from the mountains who had stolen Eremon's attention from women more suited to a throne than she.

Regret gripped her; no one would remember her as Defender of Histories. The shifting in her world was happening too quickly. There was no way to set things right again. No way to repair the damage she'd done to her friendship with Caitir and Aidryn.

Until now, Lira's life had been ordered, predictable, satisfying. She was proud of her achievements; she loved the life she'd built for herself, and she loved her friends. The question she'd failed to ask was whether she loved Eremon enough to give it all up; now, the answer didn't matter.

Lira took a shaky breath and let her eyes fall to the stacks across the room. Her life might be fraying, but there was still one thing she could control.

She rushed to the stacks, chose one of Skelly's manuscripts, and threw herself into reading it.

CHAPTER 12

Lira didn't emerge from the archive until after midnight, when the commotion outside had finally quieted. The courtyard was empty as she ventured across it, and she slowed when she glimpsed remnants of Eremon's wreath, scattered and trampled into the ground.

In her shock at Aila's outburst, she hadn't realized that she'd lost it.

The wreath's scraps lay in a little grove of trees, not far from the Dome's eastern entrance. She sank to her knees in the grass, gathering blue petals into her palms. With a sigh, she closed her eyes; she remembered Eremon standing before her hours earlier, his gray eyes tender as he lowered the roses onto her head. Every detail of the arrangement had been etched into her mind, and she let her memories recreate its beauty, bloom by bloom.

When she opened her eyes, the disparate pieces of the wreath were hovering in midair, illuminated by glowing emerald light. One by one, the torn petals knit themselves together before her, as if the blooms had never been touched, much less trampled. She reached up and plucked the wreath from the air, gasping at the jolt of pure energy she felt as it made contact with her fingers. It reminded her of what had passed between her and Eremon at their last meeting in the archive.

So this is what magic is supposed to feel like—not like a violent illness or a roaring cyclone, but a quiet, humming power.

A power that was as dangerous and unpredictable as it was lovely.

"Incredible."

Lira's eyes snapped up to meet Eremon's; he knelt before her in wonder, marveling at the flowers.

She nodded, a lump forming in her throat. "I—I'm not sure how it happened," she stammered, finding that she could not hold eye contact with him. "I don't know if I could do it again, even if I wanted to."

As the words left her mouth, she realized she hated the feeling of using her power. Hated its unpredictability, her inability to control it or bend it to her will. Most of all, she hated how little she truly understood about magic, and perhaps that was why she felt so averse to it.

They sat in silence for a long moment, inspecting the wreath together. Eremon finally edged closer, reaching up to stroke her cheek. Lira stilled, her heartbeat pounding in her ears as she willed herself to hold his gaze.

"I knew you were here," he began. "I could feel it."

Her lip trembled. A tear slipped down her cheek, and Eremon brushed it away with his thumb. She held still, as if the slightest movement might shatter the moment.

"What can I do?" He reached for her hand hesitantly; she caught it in hers, intertwining their fingers. A look of surprise crossed his face, but he relaxed, rubbing the back of her hand with his thumb.

Lira shook her head, pressing her eyes shut. "There is nothing anyone can do. Caitir was like a sister to me. Aidryn told me to be careful; he suspected she might react badly. In the moment, I didn't care. But I also didn't think—"

"About how people would talk?"

Her face burned. She couldn't look at him. Yet she didn't release her grip on his fingers as she smoothed the wreath's ribbons with her free hand.

"About any of it," she whispered, looking at the grass.

"I had the sentries escort Aila Tarlach from the grounds," Eremon said tentatively. "She won't be allowed to return to *Nami Mostari.*"

"Caitir will never forgive me," Lira said, her voice breaking.

"Why do you need her forgiveness?" He reached for her again, his fingertips grazing her jawline to guide her gaze back to his. "What have you done wrong?"

"She has always been infatuated with you." Her voice dropped to a whisper as she struggled to stop crying. "I feel like I've shattered her dreams."

Eremon laughed softly. "They're only dreams, Lira. They aren't real." His eyes flicked to the wreath in her hand, and he took it from her. "But this—this is real."

He touched her cheek again. Lira's breathing hitched; there was an intensity, a purposefulness in his eyes as he moved nearer.

She swallowed hard. "I'm honored, Eremon," she said. "You're a wonderful friend... and I love—loved dancing with you tonight. But you're the Rí and I'm—"

"A titled member of my court," he said, his gaze roaming over her face. "Since we were young, I've watched you go about your duties with unparalleled dedication and integrity. You're intelligent and driven and wise beyond your years."

Tears fell freely from Lira's eyes now as Eremon continued. "I have loved you for a very long time, Lira."

The world slowed around her as she fought to steady her

breathing. He pressed his forehead to hers; his fingers trailed around the back of her neck and into her hair.

She trembled, afraid to move as he pulled back to survey her face. He was radiant, his expression an earnest plea as he offered her the wreath again. "May I?"

Lira nodded, dipping her head. She was afraid to speak. The night was still; even the trees' peaceful rustling seemed to quiet as Eremon moved closer again. He set the crown atop her curls, pressing a kiss to her forehead and cradling her face in his hands.

"And... may I kiss you?" he asked, his voice barely a whisper.

She licked her lips, her heart hammering as she breathed, "Yes."

Eremon leaned in again and kissed her mouth lightly. Lira returned the kiss, wrapping her arms around his neck to pull him closer. The familiar scent of his robes enveloped her— incense and spices, roses and—

"Marry me, Lira. I can give you everything," he whispered against her lips. "You can keep the archive. If we could rule together—"

Lira pulled away and pressed a palm to his chest, still dazed by the kiss. "What?"

"Yes," he said, his brow furrowing. He leaned in to kiss her again. "Think of it: Defender of Histories *and* my wife. We could make things right together."

"I care for you very much," Lira hedged, brushing her fingertips over his cheek. There was the lie again: *care*. She prayed he wouldn't notice how clammy her hands had become.

"Perhaps this is more sudden for you than it is for me," Eremon fumbled, rocking back onto his heels. "Did I assume wrongly that you would say yes?"

Lira's mind raced. She hadn't expected one dance and one kiss to turn into a marriage proposal.

Squeezing her eyes shut, she shook her head. "I want to say yes. But the crown..."

It wasn't just the prospect of ruling Iathium that bothered her. There was still so much more to learn about her magic and his. Her clan. The resurrected powers. What they might be up against. But... perhaps they could do that together.

Eremon kissed her again, questioning silently: *Then why not?*

"It's so soon. I need some time to think about it," Lira said. "And I want us to spend more quiet time together like this, without an audience."

Eremon's gaze was heavy, his disappointment palpable. It tempted her to change her answer, but instead, she brushed another kiss to his mouth and whispered, "Just a little while. I promise."

He pulled her into his warm embrace and whispered into her hair, "As my Defender wishes. But while you wait, will you protect something for me?"

Lira tilted her face toward him. "Anything you ask."

Eremon held out a hand, summoning a cobalt glow in his palm. Lira's stomach lurched when a golden ring appeared there, inlaid with a smooth stone in the same color as his magic. The aged band was etched with ancient markings she didn't recognize.

"This has been in my bloodline for two thousand years," Eremon said, placing the ring into Lira's hand and closing her fingers over it. "It's yours now."

Lira looked at her closed fist, then back to Eremon. Her lips parted in protest, but he spoke first.

"I'm not pressing you for an answer," he said hastily, "but I want you to keep it. No matter what you decide, whatever happens, I would never give it to another."

"Thank you, Eremon," she whispered, her cheeks burning as she inspected the artifact. For that's what it was: a piece of history she had been gifted. And who better to guard it than the Defender?

But something he'd said tugged at her, and she asked, "Why do you need me to protect this? What did you mean by that?"

Eremon looked to the sky for a moment and swallowed hard, as if he wasn't sure how to begin. His shoulders hunched for a split second; Lira could almost feel his shame as he said, "It's no secret there are members of court, my mother included, who see me as immature and incapable of ruling well. If I have no children, they will attempt to choose an heir for me, rather than letting me decide. Without the ring, they don't truly have that power."

All the words he didn't say hit Lira like a bludgeon. "Why have I never heard of this ring?"

"Every ruler before my time had children to pass it to quietly," he answered slowly, "and their children after them. If this bloodline ends with me, I want the ring in safe hands."

"Does possessing the ring make me your heir, or simply a custodian?" Lira asked, shivering as she pulled away from him. "And who would ever allow *me* to name an heir?"

His expression grew distant as he answered, "Custodian, unless you choose to wear it." He ran his fingers through the grass. "As a ruler, planning for my own demise is a necessary evil. It's something I've had to do since I took the throne."

Lira squeezed her eyes shut, remembering the lonely boy who had locked eyes with her so many years before. She shook her head; the idea that he'd had to imagine his own death at such a young age was unfathomable to her.

"When I was fifteen," he continued, "I drafted a decree that named the Defender of Histories as Crown Regent if I die before I produce an heir."

"Lord Irem," Lira said softly.

It made sense; Irem had always commanded deep respect at court. As his successor, it fell to Lira to shoulder his mantel.

Now, she fully understood why Eremon had jumped at the chance to anoint her: he loved her. Regardless of whether she returned his feelings, he would be putting the throne into the hands of the one he loved. The realization nearly overwhelmed her with its gravity.

"I—I don't know what to say," she stammered.

"This ring is many things," Eremon said earnestly, plucking it from where it hung on her chain. "It's a method of naming heirs and a sacred key. It protects its wearer. And, it is a repository of hidden memories, passed down by my ancestors for generations. Perhaps it will help us complete the histories as we seek to reveal the entire truth to our people."

Lira grasped his hands; there was a heaviness to his gaze—a *need*—she wasn't ready to explore. "You know I will help you however I can. I'll keep it safe; you have my word."

"If you decide..." He swallowed hard, his voice catching. "If you decide to accept my offer, please, wear it as your answer."

"I promise." Lira unlatched her chain, sliding Eremon's ring onto it to hang beside her pendant.

She leaned closer and kissed him again, savoring the softness of his lips. Eremon deepened the kiss, resting one hand on the small of her back as he brushed his fingertips along her jawline and into her curls. And that need she'd seen in his eyes —she felt it in his kiss, his touch. Felt it, and fervently returned it.

When Eremon finally broke away, they were both breathless. "I could make you happy, Lira; I can give you everything you desire."

"You already make me happy," she answered, returning his smile. "But I don't want the world; just you."

She grasped the ring on its chain, pressing a kiss to his jaw. He enveloped her hands in his own, pulling back to study her. His eyes flicked to where she held the ring.

"Keep it hidden until you decide." His voice was a hush,

thick with longing. "But I pray you won't keep it hidden for long."

Lira tentatively placed a palm on his cheek, then brushed a loose strand of hair behind his ear. Resting her forehead against his, she whispered, "Thank you for giving me time to make my choice."

<h1 style="text-align:center">CHAPTER 13</h1>

Lira and Eremon lingered together in the courtyard until the sky began to lighten with the coming dawn. As they watched the sunrise, Eremon crafted a lush, perfect blue rose for her using the thread of Clan Mór's magic he possessed. Though she knew he carried some of her ancestors' power within him, it was still a shock to watch him use it.

Eremon wouldn't consider letting her walk home alone, so he summoned Talfryn to escort her. She hadn't spoken to her brother since he'd moved into the barracks.

The Dome's sentries rose before the sun, but Talfryn was still bleary-eyed as he followed Eremon across the courtyard to meet Lira. He wore a green knit tunic that emphasized his emerald eyes, and his brown curls were mussed in a way that reminded her of the early mornings they'd spent together as children.

She threw her arms around Talfryn, squeezing him tight.

"I've missed you, Tal," she said, stepping back to survey him. "You look well."

"I am well," he answered, looking cautiously between Lira

and Eremon. "You—you've…" Talfryn pressed his lips together. "I beg your pardon, my Rí; I'm not sure what to say."

Lira suddenly felt exposed and embarrassed. The thought of Talfryn jumping to conclusions—

Eremon grinned conspiratorially. "I apologize for summoning you at this hour, but your sister shouldn't walk home alone. If I could take her myself, I would, but…"

"Oh, I understand—it's perfectly fine, calling on me," Talfryn said. "I'm at your service, of course." He looked to Lira for reassurance, as if afraid he'd done something wrong. As if he was only her younger brother again, not a sentry in training.

Lira smiled. "I'm glad you thought to summon Talfryn, my Rí," she added. "We haven't seen one another since he moved to the barracks."

Eremon inclined his head—first to Lira, then to Talfryn. "See your sister home safely," he said. Talfryn bowed his head reverently, hand over his heart.

The Rí turned to Lira, pressing his lips to her fingers. "I would say good night, but—good morning. I'll see you soon."

"Goodbye," Lira said meekly, watching him stride back toward the Dome.

Talfryn looked from Eremon back to Lira, half-shrugging in resigned amusement. "This is the most interesting summons I've ever received."

Lira and Talfryn linked arms and started for the gate that led to the city. "It isn't what it looks like; last night was a disaster."

"Oh, I know. I was called to escort one Aila Tarlach off the grounds for threatening the Rí's *lover*. Some new member of the nobility, it seems." He glanced sidelong at her. "She was the subject of quite a few rumors before the night was over."

Lira's cheeks burned. "Who might that be?"

Talfryn elbowed her. "I wonder what her brother thinks about all this," he teased.

Lira dipped her head. "I think she's probably a bit worried about how he might react—and she hopes he'll check with her before believing any outlandish stories."

Her brother's dimples deepened with his grin. "So I take it the *entire* night wasn't disastrous."

She wrinkled her nose at him. "For Nami's *sake*, Talfryn."

He turned to face her, walking backward as he asked, "How did all this happen right under my nose? You're even more of a mystery now than you were when I lived at home."

"I... it's a long story."

"You were with him all night, by the look of it. What's your diplomatic response to my assumption?"

Lira didn't have one. Instead, she exclaimed, "Talfryn!"

He threw up his hands. "I'm just anticipating the gossip. People are already talking, and it's only going to get worse. I suggest you prepare a few inconspicuous answers."

She groaned. "I'll think of something, I hope."

They reached the cottage before Lira realized how far they'd walked, and Talfryn led her to the door.

"Lira..." He studied her face; his expression was difficult to read. "This is just a lowly sentry's opinion, but I think if you're offered the chance to marry him, you should take it."

His words sent a jolt through her; Talfryn had an uncanny way of guessing things he hadn't been told.

"It's not just a sentry's opinion," she whispered, taking his hand. "It's my brother's."

There was an unfamiliar intensity in Talfryn's green eyes as he leaned in to peck his sister on the cheek. "There's no one I'd rather see ruling beside him. No one I'd bow to but you."

Lira bit her lip, holding in the words that threatened to spill out—that she *did* have the chance, but she'd chosen to consider it first. That she knew she and Eremon would make a formidable pair, but it terrified her for that very reason.

"Tal, don't say that."

"Why not?" he asked. "It's true."

The responsibility she'd hold for the wellbeing of her people, both inside and outside the city, was heavy on her shoulders. She hadn't been crowned, yet she could already feel the weight of it. Again, her heart sank; if she married Eremon, she would be Defender of Histories, the Witness Tree, and Raní. No one in Rodhlan's history had ever held so many titles.

Instead of saying anything else about it, she squeezed Talfryn's shoulder. "I'll see you soon, Tal."

"I love you, Lira," he said, backing away from the door.

She pressed her fingertips to her heart and raised her hand in farewell as he stepped onto the cobblestones and turned to cross the city alone.

LIRA SAT ALONE in her kitchen as the morning dawned, listlessly stirring the hot tea she'd brewed to keep herself awake; it was no use going to sleep now. Memories of the previous evening whirled in her brain like a never-ending cyclone.

The fear that had taken hold of her at nighttime now crept into the day. Her stomach had clenched into a hard knot once Talfryn left her at the cottage, and she had not been able to right herself since. The memory of Caitir's betrayed expression, of Aila's rage—and the power she had used to burn Lira—replayed in her mind over and over.

Talfryn's words had sunken deep into her soul. Whatever she chose to do—accept or refuse Eremon's offer—her life would be changed forever. She could never go back to being the invisible historian, hidden away safely in the archive. And she could never go back to her friends.

Iathium would always whisper about what she had once been—what she *could* have been, had she not thrown away the opportunity. *There's nothing I despise more than wasted potential.*

That was something she'd heard Aidryn repeat for years. She certainly didn't want to waste hers.

According to Irem and Eremon, Lira held vast potential, far beyond her opportunity to marry a Rí. Would it truly be a waste, then, if she were to refuse a throne? What would it mean for her to fully embrace her birthright outside the constructs of her life in the city? She had never considered shedding Iathium's trappings in favor of Clan Mór's; she had also never imagined Eremon offering her a throne, and she wasn't sure which notion frightened her more.

For a moment, Lira's mind drifted to Skelly's mountains, and she found herself wondering whether her clan would even accept her. Would she be disgraced as the woman who refused the Rí's hand, or lauded as some sort of prodigal? The idea of leaving Iathium, at least for a little while, was tempting; she could seek solitude in the mountains, disappear for a while.

Still, accepting Eremon's proposal might be their best chance to defeat whatever darkness was rising. The idea of sharing power with him, of using it for the good of the clans instead of for their harm, felt right. Frightening, but *right*. And it wasn't just a notion; it was a very real opportunity, ripe for the taking. It had been offered freely to her by a man she'd grown to love. Who loved her.

She sighed, brushing her fingertips over her lips.

The rose Eremon had made for her caught her eye; it now rested in a small earthen vase on the worktable, and she leaned forward to smell it. Its light fragrance reminded her of the whirling dance and the kisses they'd shared. It was almost enough to push the memory of Caitir's devastation out of her mind. Almost.

A heavy, insistent knock rattled the front door, and she jumped, sloshing her hot tea onto her nightdress. Lira hissed, though the thin fabric cooled quickly, and wrapped her dressing gown around herself as she padded to the door. She peered cautiously out the window, and her stomach dropped when she spotted Aidryn standing on the stoop.

"Oh no," she groaned, resting her hand on the latch; she'd forgotten all about meeting him at the archive.

For a moment, she stalled, but he knocked again. Taking a deep breath, she opened the door. There was a look of shuttered anger on Aidryn's face, and something else—hurt, or shame, or pity—or a combination of them all.

"Aidryn," she began as he shouldered his way inside, "I'm not exactly presentable."

Aidryn took in her dressing gown, the nightclothes peeking out from underneath; for a moment, he seemed embarrassed.

"You never bothered meeting me like we agreed, so I came looking for you," he mumbled, clearly uncomfortable.

Lira half-shrugged, anxiously wrapping the fabric more tightly around herself. "I know; I'm sorry—so much has happened." The excuse sounded feeble without context.

"So I've heard." He rubbed the back of his neck before finally looking her in the eye. "This is a terrible time to be distracted, Lira—especially by him."

"He isn't a distraction," she argued. "He can help us."

Aidryn leaned against the door's thick, wooden frame, resting his head on it as he closed his eyes. "It has been agony to keep my distance, to trust Irem and Eremon to open your eyes to this new world. I thought I was making the right choice by stepping aside and allowing them to lead the way."

He opened his eyes again, an unspoken plea flickering in their cerulean depths. "Now, well..." He pushed off the frame, pacing before her in the entryway. "I find myself so far from your notice that I can hardly secure an audience."

They had always been able to speak freely with one another, each unafraid of risking the other's ire. It wasn't unusual for them to banter and bicker, but something about the edge in his voice cut Lira too deeply this time, and the stinging hurt quickly gave way to anger.

"Aidryn, that's unfair," Lira said shakily. "I've done the best I could to navigate this without Irem's guidance. And I won't let you insult Eremon—he has offered me help that no one else could, or would."

"I won't deny that, Lira, but I warned you not to entangle yourself with him," Aidryn replied, his voice raw. "Now, it's too late."

She paled. "What are you talking about?"

"I heard this morning—how Talfryn had to walk you home from the Dome before sunrise because you'd been with Eremon all night." He rubbed the back of his neck again, looking everywhere except directly at her.

"How dare you." Lira seethed. "We spent the night talking in the courtyard; you're inventing a scandal that doesn't exist."

"Lira, there *is* a scandal!" he exclaimed, finally meeting her eyes. "Do you even know what the courtiers are saying about you?"

She stilled. Aidryn had never been riled enough to raise his voice at her before. The frantic, panicked look in his eyes took her aback nearly as much as his anger did.

"What are they saying?" she asked quietly, though she didn't truly want to know.

"That the new Defender of Histories knows no discretion," he answered, his voice laced with disdain. "She locks herself away with the Rí in the inner chamber for hours on end and hasn't deigned to work with her apprentices for weeks."

Lira blanched. "We've been studying tomes, trying to decipher this magic no one is supposed to be talking about."

"It wouldn't surprise me if that were true," Aidryn pressed, unruffled by her mention of the power. He turned and strode toward the kitchen, Lira on his heels.

"*If* that were true?" she cried. "It is true! Aidryn, what is wrong with you? You *know* me!"

He looked up at the dark-stained beams that reinforced the ceiling, swallowing hard before he answered her.

"I thought I did," he said mournfully. "But it isn't like you to—"

"To what, Aidryn? To study?" Lira's voice rose; she huffed a disbelieving laugh. "Why does Eremon's presence suddenly make my normal behavior a scandal? If you and I were the ones locking ourselves away, no one would think twice about it."

She couldn't decipher the stricken expression on his face as he answered, "The court doesn't know you as I do. They don't understand your propensity for regular self-isolation—or your enjoyment of reading the histories, for that matter."

"But you do," Lira pressed, "so what is this about? Is it because Eremon hasn't hidden his feelings for me?"

"Stop pretending like you don't understand your actions' implications at court," he answered, agitated. "He's making a spectacle of you; members of his council are petitioning to have you removed from the archive."

After the dance with Eremon, she knew—she *knew*—that this path would ultimately divert her from the course she'd determined for herself so long ago. Lira knew her work would be redefined and reframed if she chose to marry him, but she hadn't considered *this* possibility. The thought of losing her position made her feel nauseous.

"They can't do that," she whimpered.

"They likely won't succeed," he agreed, "but they'll make their point about where his loyalties lie. They'll stand back and let him prove that he thinks with his emotions—that he's still too young to rule in absolution.

"His mother and half the council have stunted his political power since Corlan was killed, and this situation is not helping him. Lira, I know it isn't your intent, but you're hurting his authority by going along with all this."

"His mother wants him to make a match," she protested. "Why am I not good enough for her? For the council?"

"Because you're too intelligent," Aidryn answered without hesitation. "They want him matched with someone who won't challenge them while they lead him about by the nose— someone who is well-versed in court niceties but knows little else."

Ah, there it was. Caitir had been trained to please the court but had no instinct for politics and no interest in the histories. Lira had never held a candle to Caitir in poise or grace, and Aidryn had borne witness to her at her most ungraceful.

"Perhaps *you* can't imagine why he would choose someone like me over Caitir," she accused. "To you, I'm still that shy, bookish child you grew up with."

It was a small comfort that Talfryn, of all people, had encouraged her to embrace the chance to be with Eremon. He was her *actual* brother, for Nami's sake.

"Lira, you're far from the child I knew," Aidryn answered softly, leaning heavily on the mantelpiece over the hearth. His eyes were filled with a deep sorrow she wasn't ready to explore. "This truly isn't about Caitir, though I wish..." He sighed.

Lira moved toward him, resting a tentative hand on his shoulder. A look of surprise crossed his face at the contact, and he turned to face her again.

"I—I didn't expect him to want me, Aidryn," she said pleadingly, letting her hand drop to her side. "I didn't expect to want him."

Aidryn took a step closer, reaching for one of the dark curls that fell over her shoulder. "Perhaps I've never said it aloud, but..." He twirled the end of the curl between his fingers but dropped it quickly, as though he'd forgotten himself for a moment. "I care about what happens to you, more than you know."

"I don't want to lose you the way I lost Caitir," she admitted.

"You won't. You're my dearest friend," he whispered. "And I don't want to lose you; that's why I've been so harsh. I can't predict what's going to happen. It feels as though everything I've fought to save has slipped through my fingers."

Defeat flashed in Aidryn's cerulean eyes; Lira knew he was thinking of his sister. She wondered how completely her friend had been shattered the night before—and, for a moment, she wondered why Aidryn was here with her instead of comforting Caitir.

"Lira," he lamented, "I shouldn't have been so cryptic before; we should have told one another everything weeks ago." His desperation was so palpable, Lira's eyes welled with tears.

"Perhaps," she ventured weakly, "but we were doing our best to obey orders."

"Damn the orders," Aidryn growled, shattering the quiet moment. He raked a hand through his hair and stoked the fire, shoulders tense. "We both know the ancestral powers are alive and well. But here is what no one will say: Eremon is dangerously close to losing control of his magic."

Lira remembered how Eremon had described the sensation of a body that held more power than it had ever been meant to contain, and she shivered. "I knew he was struggling—"

"More than that; he's going to get you killed."

Lira tried to hide her shock. "He would never harm me," she protested, though her own power recoiled within her as the words left her lips.

"It wouldn't be intentional," Aidryn said quietly, more to the crackling fire than to her. "Not even his healer has been able to untangle the mess of power he's carrying."

"He's trying to protect me," she insisted. "I know his heart, and what he wants to do for our people." She stepped closer, tilting her head imploringly in an attempt to draw his attention. "He is a good man, Aidryn."

Something about Aidryn's resigned expression made her feel broken and vulnerable, though she couldn't pinpoint why.

"I know he's a good man, and I wish he wasn't; it would make all of this much easier," he said. "But he's putting you in harm's way. His power is warped. He doesn't know how to protect you from it, and neither do I."

Lira clutched her pendant anxiously. Her mouth was suddenly dry, her thoughts scattered. And though she gripped the heavy charm, she'd neglected to cover Eremon's ring, whose stone now glinted in the morning light. Lira realized her mistake the moment Aidryn squinted down at the chain.

"*Lira*," he breathed, paling. "Please tell me I'm mistaken. It can't be."

"It is," she admitted, hiding it behind her gown again. "But I haven't given him an answer."

"He must think it will make you immune," he mused, covering his mouth with a shaking hand, his eyes shining with tears. "Of course, he does."

"Protective magic," she mused.

"Yes, but it was crafted to protect the wearer from pure dark magic, not this monstrosity he's fighting," Aidryn answered, his voice breaking.

Lira swallowed hard, hoping she didn't betray the fear that was rooting deep within her. While she wanted to ask him questions—to delve deeper into everything that was happening around them—she felt too rattled and unsteady to try.

Aidryn wore the same look as he did when deconstructing complicated historical accounts, as if he'd almost fit all the puzzle pieces together in his mind. "You say you haven't answered him?" he asked, his expression achingly hopeful.

"I have not," Lira answered carefully, "though he asked me to guard it, whatever I decide."

"Lira, listen to me," Aidryn pleaded. "Give up the ring—leave the post. End this before it goes too far."

Lira started to shake her head, but he stepped nearer and gently cupped her face in his hands, brushing a thumb over her cheek.

"I can take you to your grandmother, get you out of Iathium," he whispered. "You'll be safer away from here." His gaze roved over her face with a devastated intimacy that made her heart clench, his voice dropping until it was barely audible. "Come with me—let me protect you. *Please.*"

Aidryn had never reached for her like this before; she wanted his touch to feel foreign and unwelcome. Instead, she felt a thrill of curiosity. Lira drew a shuddering breath, expecting him to close the remaining distance between them.

She caught herself wondering what it would feel like to kiss him, and whether he might truly persuade her to abandon the idea of marrying Eremon. He smelled of the meadowlands and fresh spring air—of freedom. Suddenly, she yearned to ride across the continent with him, far from this place.

His breath was warm on her face. If she leaned only a bit closer...

Lira stopped the thoughts in their tracks; it felt wrong to explore them while she wore Eremon's ring around her neck.

Her expression must have betrayed her, because Aidryn sagged wearily and released her. "But you're not going to do that, are you?"

She didn't answer—couldn't. Instead, she fingered the golden band, refusing to meet his eyes. Tears clouded her vision and slid down her cheeks.

"You're so stubborn, Silira," he growled, "but it *is* your choice. Run headlong into disaster if you wish; don't listen to someone who—"

"Stop this, Aidryn; I am not your enemy," she said, her voice a low warning.

"You have no idea how much easier it would be if you were." Aidryn sighed, then stalked away, leaving Lira alone by the hearth. The door lock engaged as he let himself out.

Lira slumped on her knees before the fire, a jumble of emotions warring within her. Her thoughts raced out of control; she dwelt on what Aidryn had told her about Eremon's magic, about the council's wish to make her disappear. She wondered what the nobles would be capable of if she did marry him and something terrible happened. Would they have her deposed, exiled, or worse?

Then, there was Aidryn. Lira didn't know what had come over her. Rocking back and drawing her knees to her chest, she stared into the flames and tried to forget the unexpected longing she'd felt to run with him. It had been as fleeting as a breath, but it had been real.

Surely it was natural to fear taking on the responsibility of a throne. She couldn't be the first woman to balk at that kind of power. Her father had once told her that she could fear, yet still act with courage; and it would take tremendous courage to help Eremon set things right in Rodhlan.

It frightened Lira to think of what might happen as they uncovered the true histories and helped their people embrace their rightful magic. She had been given a tremendous opportunity, and if she wasted that potential, she would never forgive herself.

Lira remained before the fire for a long while, allowing its crackling to soothe her. When the morning sun rose a little higher in the sky, she rose with it to prepare for the day ahead. Pulling her gown tight, she leaned across the table and plucked the rose from its container, twirling its stem between her fingers.

A strange popping sounded in her ears, and Lira's gaze flew first toward the hearth; nothing was amiss with the fire. The popping continued until something singed her fingers. With a yelp, she let go of the rose's stem—the source of the sound, she realized with a gasp. Instead of falling to the table, the flower levitated, hovering just at face-level with Lira.

The deep blue rose crackled from stem to bloom with an energy Lira had felt when Aila had burned her the night before. *Aila.* She'd been so caught up in Eremon's romance and Aidryn's panic that she'd neglected to ask either of them about the burn she'd received.

The rose's edges glowed faintly, and it hummed with the unusual power. She reached out to touch it, but it crackled again, jolting her fingertips. Her hand flew to her mouth as she watched tiny veins of black lightning consume the rose until it was reduced to a pile of ash on the stone floor.

CHAPTER 14

A shock of shimmering green cut through the crowd on the Drochaid as Lira pushed her way through the throng, heart hammering as she ran for the Dome. Her fingertips still stung where the electrified rose had burned her. She shuddered at the memory of the pain, of the flower turning to ashes before her eyes.

Those black veins of power had left a charge in the air like what she'd felt emanating from Aila the night before. It was furious and alive, writhing within her consciousness. She had hoped getting outside the cottage would lift the crushing weight from her chest, but the darkness only seemed to grow more insistent, more palpable. Even the sky seemed uncharacteristically gray.

No doubt, Aila was somehow connected to the dark magic. Was that part of what Aidryn had wanted to tell her?

It made sense; he'd wanted to discuss their secrets at dawn. His mother's touch had burned Lira's skin; perhaps Aidryn had been preparing to tell her about Aila's dark power. Instead, he'd become fixated on dividing Lira and Eremon.

Distracted indeed, she thought. *He's the one who can't focus.*

She had always admired Aidryn's reasonable, measured disposition and sharp wit. Despite their zealous competition, he had always made it clear that he held her in the highest regard. She couldn't deny that his disapproval stung, but she supposed it was easier for him to find fault with her now that he blamed her for Caitir's distress.

Lira shoved away the memory of his cerulean eyes—the way he'd looked at her. She could understand why he wanted her to run; it seemed out of character for Lira to choose Eremon's offer, yet it was exactly the kind of decision she would make out of loyalty to her city. The notion of marrying the Rí had always seemed silly to her—because why would he pay her any mind? She'd never even deigned to imagine herself by his side; the thought of Eremon arm-in-arm with an archivist was absurd.

Now that the choice was hers, it seemed clear: accept Eremon's offer of love. Work with him to save Rodhlan's people from war. Preserve Iathium for the coming generations of magic-wielders and clanspeople who would dwell there together. Unite two descendants of the gods and the clans to usher in this new era.

Perhaps her misgivings about marriage had been trite. She had seen the darkness for herself now; Iathium needed all the strength it could muster in order to defeat it. If she could help advance that strength, what was she waiting for?

Lira swallowed hard, clutching the ring again before she concealed her necklace beneath her gown. Trepidation gnawed at her stomach. Her heartbeat pounded in her ears, knees weakening as she stepped onto the grounds of the Dome.

All eyes turned to Lira as she crossed the courtyard. Instead of following her usual entryway, she headed toward the western towers, where the royal family's quarters lay. She tuned out the whispers that followed her, moving near the door she'd seen Eremon enter the night before.

Each step forward brought a new wave of anxiety, but Lira kept moving. When she was within reach of the door, she was thwarted by two sentries who crossed their spears before her, blocking her path.

A low, metallic voice reverberated from one of the sentries. "Lira, what are you doing?"

She jumped; peering at the helm of the sentry who had spoken, she caught a glimpse of Talfryn's green eyes staring back at her. The man who accompanied him was much older; no doubt, this was part of her brother's training rotation.

Lira hesitated, yet she had already come this far. "I need to speak to the Rí."

The other man snorted; Talfryn shook his head, holding the spear steady. "No one may enter, on orders from Raní Macha."

"It's urgent, Talfryn."

From behind Lira, a rich, velvety voice crooned, "The boy is much smarter than his sister."

The hairs on Lira's neck stood on end. She turned slowly to find herself face-to-face with Macha, who offered Talfryn an appreciative nod. "Well done, men."

Talfryn and his companion offered her a respectful bow, but Lira could see the panic in her brother's eyes. She sucked in a breath and dipped low, bowing before Eremon's mother. The rich, silken layers of the Raní's robes rustled in the breeze, the perfume she'd doused herself in overwhelming Lira's senses.

"You forget yourself, Silira Mór," Macha crooned, lingering above Lira. "It is a pity that mere sentries must set the example for titled nobility."

Macha snapped her fingers, signaling Lira to stand. Lira obeyed grudgingly, resenting her legs for following the command like an obedient pup.

Eremon would never stand for this.

Lira willed herself to meet the Raní's eyes. Macha moved so close to Lira that their noses almost touched.

"Don't fool yourself into thinking your title or that dance will get you into my son's bedchamber," she growled, raking her eyes over Lira from head to toe. "Remember your place, clan filth, and get out of my sight."

Macha's insult reverberated through Lira like a blade striking steel plate.

Lira bristled, fighting to keep her voice steady as she whispered, "*Sura masi.*"

A storm roiled in Macha's eyes as Lira dipped again and spun on her heel, clenching and releasing her fists as she stalked toward the other side of the Dome. Lira's body trembled; she was both horrified and empowered by what had just flown from her mouth: "*I live to serve,*" the archaic sealing vow Eremon had taken upon his ascension.

It was also a vow reserved for the Rí's marriage rites.

Lira quickened her pace.

Even after Lira had locked herself inside the inner chamber, she still felt Macha's malice as if it had followed her into the depths of the archive itself.

Lira's encounter with Macha left her rattled, distracting her through her studies in the chamber, as well as her interactions with the young apprentices. After Aidryn's censure, she made doubly sure to be present with them today.

She missed sitting among them, so teaching them—guiding them through the steps of proper transcription and manuscript illumination—should have been a welcome change from being secluded in the chamber. But today, the last place she wanted to be was among her charges, especially when there was still so much research to complete.

Worse, the apprentices were more interested in Lira's dance with Eremon the night before, and the ensuing conflict with Aila and Caitir. Their whispers were unbearable, and Lira's voice wavered as she raised it to speak.

"Silence, if you please," she said.

For a moment, her charges' voices died down. She turned back to assisting Pedr, a young man who had been childhood friends with Talfryn, and Revna, a girl of fifteen and her newest archival apprentice. Revna reported directly to Pedr, but the young man had expressed to Lira that Revna was struggling with her letters. Lira surmised that it wasn't so much Revna's lack of skill as it was Pedr's struggle to convey clear instructions.

"Pedr, note how I explain each step," Lira began. "Revna, please mimic my actions."

Slowly and deliberately, Lira dipped her quill into her ink and made a show of scraping the excess back into the pot.

"Take care not to leave too much ink on the quill," she began, placing the quill's sharp tip on the parchment. "Then, you—"

"Lady Defender," Revna interrupted, making no attempt to pick up her own quill, "when will Master Tarlach return permanently?"

"I can't answer that," Lira said, lifting her quill and moving it away from the manuscript. "You should ask him the next time he's here."

"That's a pity; I do so enjoy his tutelage," she said, her voice taking on a strange tone that Lira couldn't quite pinpoint.

Lira lifted an eyebrow. "Please, pick up your quill and continue."

The apprentice ignored her, biting her lip. "Lady Silira, may I ask you something?"

Attempting to keep herself composed, Lira said, "That depends on the question."

Revna leaned closer, though her voice rose loud enough for

everyone in the archive to hear. "I tire of quill work. Would you give us lessons in seduction instead?"

The other apprentices froze. Lira stilled, the quill slipping from her fingers. Ink splattered onto the tabletop. Slowly, she turned to look at Revna straight-on.

"This is an *archive*," Lira bit out. "You are here to train as an artisan, not a courtesan. Hold your tongue."

"Of course," Revna continued smoothly, "I never thought you to have any talent outside of this place. I suppose I wanted to learn a more enjoyable way to achieve an unearned title."

"Revna!" Pedr hissed, his eyes wide.

The room had grown deathly silent; everyone's attention was now completely trained on Lira. Her heart pounded; her first instinct was to slap Revna's mouth, the way Irem might have struck Lira if she'd spoken to him with such disrespect. But she was painfully aware that now, more than ever, every move she made would be scrutinized.

So instead of striking—or pouring the contents of her ink pot down Revna's uniform—she said sharply, "If you continue to push me, I will end your apprenticeship posthaste."

"As quickly as the council will end your tenure as Defender," Revna shot back.

Lira stood abruptly, face blazing. The stool she'd been sitting on toppled over backward, clattering loudly onto the tiles. She opened her mouth to banish Revna from the archive, but the smug expression on the apprentice's face faded abruptly, replaced by wide-eyed horror.

"If you wish to behave as a courtier," Eremon's voice said from behind Lira, "you can join the other simpering fools up there." He pointed toward the stairs.

Trembling, Revna averted her eyes and dropped to the floor, bowing her head low. "Forgive me, my Rí. I—"

"If you want to be treated like a piece of meat, leave the archive. We've no energy for that here," Eremon said softly.

"Silira gained my deepest respect through her dedication and work ethic. I suggest you learn to emulate that. You will find the rest of your existence far more satisfying."

"Yes, my Rí," Revna mumbled, still hiding her face.

"Lady Defender," Eremon asked, "may I have a word?"

Lira gave him a curt nod, then turned back to the apprentices. She fought to keep her voice steady as a smile threatened to creep across her lips. "Carry on. Pedr, Revna—please continue where we left off."

She followed Eremon to the chamber, careful to stay three steps behind her sovereign. Though she knew the apprentices would talk more than they already were, she barred the door once they were inside. They couldn't risk prying eyes or eavesdropping ears—not now.

"I'm sorry," Eremon whispered, his expression pained. "It seems I have caused trouble for you."

"Prevented trouble, more like." Lira took a seat at her desk and offered him the spare stool. "You saved me from knocking Revna's teeth out."

"You would never." He chuckled. "You'd be too worried about splattering blood on the manuscripts."

Lira laughed softly. "You're not wrong."

Eremon reached for her, brushing his knuckles over her jawline. "I know," he whispered, leaning forward to kiss her.

A rush of pleasure coursed through her, and she grasped the lapels of his robe, deepening the kiss. *This*—this was what he was offering her, and so much more. Lira wanted every moment with him to feel this way, and she *did* want to run—away from the memory of the burning rose. She kissed him harder, intending to delay her questions a moment longer.

"I saw you near the western towers," Eremon whispered against her lips. "What happened?"

"Your mother." Lira sighed, breaking away reluctantly. "That's what happened."

He looked ashamed. "I'm sorry. If I had gotten to you in time, I would have escorted you inside myself."

"I know." Lira bit her lip. "I'm afraid I might have started a war."

Eremon laughed self-consciously. "My mother is at war with everyone. But there's something else." He slid a finger under Lira's chin and tipped her face up, meeting her eyes as he kissed her again. "What is it?"

"Your—th—the darkness," Lira stammered, finally giving in to the inevitable. "I've seen it."

His expression darkened. "Tell me," he said, leaning an elbow on the desk. "What did you see?"

"The rose you created—it burned up. The magic was black —it blistered my fingers when I touched it."

She showed him her fingertips; he gingerly took her hand in his, kissing each one. Her voice dropped to a whisper.

"I suppose it looked something like black lightning—sparking, burning." Lira shook her head. "It's like nothing I've ever seen. The sensation never left; I still feel it, even now."

Eremon knitted his brow. "It's heavy today; I've felt it building since this morning, like the atmosphere is charged." He averted his gaze, taking a sudden interest in the swirl of mosaic tile on the floor. "Lira..."

"Yes?"

"I'm not sure how to begin." Pain flickered across his face as he massaged one of his temples. "Will you promise me something?"

"Anything."

"Promise you won't run from me."

"I swear it."

Desperation etched itself into his expression as he held out one of his hands. When Eremon closed his eyes, black sparks began to pop and hiss in his palm. He winced, gritting his teeth in pain.

When the magic dissipated, beads of sweat glistened on his forehead; he panted, spent from the effort. His palm was blistered and bloody as he lowered his hand into his lap.

After a long moment, he finally dared to open his eyes. Lira's own eyes went wide with horror.

"The dark magic is yours," she whispered.

A pained expression crossed his face as he nodded. "It is."

Lira reached for him, grasping his uninjured hand. "How long has this been happening?"

"It started after Irem left."

"Does this have anything to do with what happened to you last night?" Lira shuddered at the memory of Eremon bracing himself over the table in pain—and the fact that she already knew the answer.

He squeezed his eyes shut. "Yes."

"Why didn't you tell me?" Lira asked, her voice trembling. "You said your magic was causing you *discomfort*, but this—"

For a moment, he looked like the lost boy she remembered from the courtyard so many years ago. "I didn't want to worry you," he said.

"You didn't want it to be *real*." Lira pressed a palm to her forehead. "Eremon, we could have been researching this together."

"I've been scouring the archive when you're not here," he confessed, "to search for answers. I have yet to find anything that describes this."

Lira stood abruptly. "Eremon..." She turned to him with a heavy sigh. "You can't risk yourself to protect my feelings. This is what I'm here for; to help you find answers."

She gently held his face and scrutinized him, taking note of the dark circles under his eyes. "You haven't been sleeping at all, have you?"

"Not much," he admitted.

"I'm afraid for you," she said, kissing the top of his head. "You should have come to me before."

He wrapped an arm around her waist and rested his head against her belly. "I know. I'm sorry."

They let several silent minutes pass. The only sounds in the chamber were the flickering candles and the ticking of the timepiece on Lira's desk. Lira stroked his hair absently; he'd tied back the silken strands with a leather band at the nape of his neck, and she let his soft tresses slip between her fingers over and over.

"Did either of your parents have this power?" she finally asked.

"Father did," Eremon said. "I remember hearing him talk about feeling it beneath his skin. But he was gone long before my magic emerged—and I was never allowed to see him wield his."

Lira ran her fingertips across his forehead to brush away strands of hair that had fallen loose, resting her palm on his cheek. His eyelids drifted shut as he leaned into her touch.

"My father, my grandfather, my great-grandfather—they self-limited their use of this power. They favored peace over magic, so they suppressed their own. Instead of giving it back to the clans, they held it inside their bodies with incredible restraint. And meanwhile, it built and pressurized."

"So the suppression made the magic more potent?"

"And deadly," Eremon whispered. "Magic is rebellious that way; it's meant to be expended and regenerated."

He opened his eyes, studying her expression for any hint of fear. "I thought someone else must be tampering with the darkness until I realized it was coming from me. It's as if the power is starting to discharge on its own. It feels like it's overpowering the other strands of magic in my veins."

The memory of the burning rose invaded Lira's senses; she

shook her head to clear it. "Who else knows about your magic, Eremon? About the sparks?"

"Ljós."

The healer who had treated Lira's wounds the night before. She realized with a start that he must possess Clan Beran's healing powers.

"And your mother?"

He shook his head. "I think she suspects something, but she doesn't know exactly what is happening. If she did, she would seize the throne for herself."

Lira blanched. "How could she?"

"She has enough support in court to do it. The council respects her; she is still loved by the people." He sighed heavily, his expression strained. "I think, given the right circumstances, she can do whatever she wishes."

Lira recalled what Aidryn had said about the council's quest to prove Eremon was unfit to rule. She wondered whether she should have fought back so hard against Aidryn's warnings. Regardless, she knew what she needed to do.

Wordlessly, Lira inspected Eremon's burned palm, stroking the back of his hand gingerly. "You should let Ljós heal your hand, then rest. Leave the research to me."

Eremon smiled wearily. "Perhaps."

She followed him to the staircase, where he kissed her tenderly, cradling her face in his good hand and searching her expression. "Are you afraid of me now?"

Lira shook her head, meeting his eyes. "Never."

"And my magic?"

Her throat bobbed. "We'll find a way to fix this, whatever it takes."

Eremon squeezed her hand. "Dance with me again tonight?"

"Of course."

He smiled sadly as he started down the steps. Lira tapped

the tiles; as they closed, she collapsed at the desk again, bracing her head in her hands. She fought to steady her ragged breathing; the terror of what was unfolding threatened to overwhelm her, but now wasn't the time to feel. Now was the time to uncover the truth.

CHAPTER 15

Night had fallen and the revelries outside were in full force by the time Lira's research yielded anything useful. She was flipping furiously through yet another manuscript on the history of Iteloria when she spotted a description of the mortal gods' black lightning:

Although they could never fully wield the external magic they absorbed, the Tai'Ceru bolstered their own inborn power with what they took from others. Over time, the dark magic corrupted the stolen powers, then turned on its hosts, devouring them alive.

Those who wished to rid themselves of magical corruption, made a drawing salve from crushed nea'la roses. They applied the salve to their feet after opening the skin of the heels, allowing the corruption to flow freely from their bodies. This technique was practiced using wooden bowls, and the contaminated blood was burned along with the bowls that collected it.

"The roses," Lira cried, slamming the book shut.

She rushed to the door, eager to find Eremon. But when she tried to heave it open, it wouldn't budge. No matter how hard she rattled the latch, it wouldn't give way. The lock seemed to have fused into place. With a shout, she slammed her palm against the door, pain reverberating up her arm.

Lira snatched her keys from where they lay on the desk and clipped them to her belt, then skidded toward the tiles that opened the floor and pressed them in. A relieved sigh whooshed from her lips as the tiles gave way to the open stairwell. She lit a lantern, descending the stairs as fast as her feet would move.

She had never explored the catacombs beneath the Dome. There was only one path forward for what seemed like a mile before it split into four separate tunnels. Pausing, she closed her eyes to visualize where beneath the Dome she might be by now.

When she rested her hand against the smooth stone wall, she caught movement out of the corner of her eye. Her attention snapped to a figure that passed her on foot and continued down the tunnel on the far right. She could just make out a flash of red silk and the black hair that tumbled over his shoulders—

"Eremon!" she called, scurrying after him.

He didn't acknowledge her presence; just continued moving down the dark corridor as if he hadn't seen or heard her. Perplexed, she moved faster, hoping to catch up. It was alarming to see him rushing straight into darkness with no lantern; something must be terribly wrong.

Lira followed Eremon, calling after him every time she got near enough for him to hear, but each time, he didn't answer. Finally, she lost sight of him. Frustrated and panicked, she pressed forward, climbing up a steep stone incline until she reached what felt like a ceiling of large, smooth rocks above her: a dead end.

"Where are you?" she panted. "What's happening?"

Her body began to tremble as it did after a witnessing, and she realized what had happened: she'd been following a memory of Eremon down this path. She hadn't accessed memories from something outside herself since that first day with Skelly's book, and it was a mercy this vision hadn't made her ill.

A pulsing blue light caught her attention, and she glanced down to find it emanating from the ring. Lira used the light to inspect the rocks above her head and was surprised to find a marking etched into one of them: Eremon's seal.

The light in the ring pulsed insistently as she drew it nearer to the seal, until she finally pressed the gem against it. Bright, blue light blasted into the cavern; this magic felt cold, and it smelled of saltwater and sand. There was something silky and graceful about it as it wrapped itself around Lira, then dissipated into the pathway behind her.

The smooth rocks gave way with a low groan, and she moved upward, emerging into a secluded part of Eremon's garden. Outside in the courtyard, the rollicking music was loud enough to drown out the racket she'd made to get here.

Lira made her way slowly across the stream that burbled along the garden's outer wall, stepping lightly. Carefully, she plotted a path through the lush greenery until she reached the main walkway. There was no one in the garden as she moved toward the exit into the Dome, so she sped up, walking as quickly as she dared.

Just as she was about to cross the threshold, Aidryn stepped into her path, blocking her way. He held out his palms. "Stop, Lira."

"Let me pass!" Lira tried to push past him, but he blocked her again.

"No." His voice was low as he drove her deeper into the garden. "Something's wrong out there. I don't want you to get hurt."

"I have to get to Eremon. It's urgent; you have to help me!"

"I don't know what's about to happen out there, but you

mustn't go." Aidryn held something before her—her key ring. He jangled them before her.

"*Tarlach*," Lira breathed as the realization washed over her. "You're the Key Keeper." His clan's anointed, born with an extra measure of magic.

Suddenly, Aidryn's recent uninvited entries into the locked inner chamber made sense. She wanted to slap the smirk from his face.

"Yes; my power is awake," Aidryn said, closing his hand over the keys; they disappeared. "Like yours."

Lira regarded him with horror. "You locked me in!"

She had been so absorbed in the stirrings of her own magic, and so preoccupied with Eremon, that she'd never considered Aidryn's ancestral power. She cursed herself for her naïveté, and cursed Aidryn for turning it on her.

"Lira, listen."

"No, Aidryn, *you* listen to me," she said, her voice steely. "*I* have Eremon's favor. *I* am Defender of Histories. And you will let me pass."

He didn't move. Instead, he extended his hand to her, his expression pleading.

"Come with me," he begged again. "We're running out of time."

"I can't," she cried, trying again to push past him.

Aidryn caught her by the shoulders, and when she dared to meet his eyes, his gaze was full of pity. "He's dying, Lira."

The soft words descended like a heavy shroud. She shook her head slowly. "No."

But fear washed over her at the tug in the back of her mind, and at Aidryn's measured tone. She scanned his face for any hint that he might be lying, but she could find none; only the fearful sincerity of the friend she'd known for so many years.

"I—I've found the cure," she stammered. "In the archive."

"Nothing can cure this."

"Yes, it can, but you have to let me go."

"*Please*, Lira," he said, his eyes welling with tears. "Don't."

"I have to." Her chin trembled. "I wish I could make you understand."

Aidryn sighed, dropping his hands resignedly. "So do I." He jerked his head toward the garden's exit. "Go. If you change your mind, I'll do what I can to help you, whatever that's worth."

"And if I don't change my mind?"

He shook his head sadly. "Then there's nothing I can do."

For a moment, Lira hesitated; then, she stepped past him and broke into a trot, crossing through the Dome and into the courtyard.

Lira made her way through the crowd that had gathered outside for another night of feasting and dancing. She wove between revelers, her slight form making quick work of the masses. When she spotted a flash of golden silk, she nearly wept with relief; Eremon was standing on the ground before the platform, chatting and laughing with three of his council members.

His eyes sparkled as they met Lira's, and he immediately broke from the conversation, taking her hand in his and pressing a kiss to it. "I've been waiting for you."

Lira took his arm and they moved toward the whirling throng to join the dance. She caught a brief glimpse of a defeated-looking Aidryn standing several yards away, but averted her eyes, focusing instead on the man before her.

"Did you rest this afternoon?" Lira asked.

Eremon shrugged. "I tried."

"So, no?"

He shook his head. "I had a terrible headache. It took Ljós hours to find a remedy that would alleviate it."

"But it worked?" she pressed.

Eremon tightened his hold on her. "Well enough."

Lira frowned, unsatisfied with his answer. "Speaking of remedies, I think I've found something."

"What?" He studied her face. "What is it?"

"Bring Ljós to the archive as quickly as you can."

"Tonight?"

"Now."

"Lira, you're incredible," he said, daring to press his lips to her forehead, to the shock of the other dancers nearby. She felt his lips curve into a smile against her skin. "Stay in my arms just a little longer. After this dance, we'll go."

Warmth washed over Lira as he let him hold her under the lanterns. But she moved too stiffly and gripped him too hard; her fingertips dug into his arms. Aidryn's words reverberated through her, stoking the panic she'd been feeling since the morning.

A low rumble of thunder echoed in the distance as a light, misty rain began to fall. The heavy darkness Lira had felt this morning pressed harder on the courtyard and the revelers continued their celebration, unfazed by the charge in the atmosphere.

Lira rose on tiptoe to whisper, in a trembling voice, "We shouldn't wait any longer."

Eremon's gray eyes met hers. His brow furrowed as he took in her expression. He laced their fingers together, pressing his lips to hers brazenly. Lira wanted to return the kiss—to press herself into him and wind her arms around his neck. Instead, she went rigid.

"It's time to go, Eremon," she whispered against his mouth, keenly aware of the lull in the courtyard—aware of the hundreds of eyes now trained on them.

"You're right," he said. "I—"

Suddenly, Eremon's muscles tensed beneath his tunic—tensed, and then froze. He worked his mouth to speak, but no words came. Terror filled his eyes as he stood, unable to move, as if rooted to the ground.

"Eremon?"

The Rí's tender grasp on her body tightened to a death grip as he squeezed his eyes shut, beads of sweat sliding down his forehead as he hissed in pain.

"What's wrong?" Lira cried, panic overtaking her as his fingers dug into her sides. She yelped as she struggled to pry his hands from her body. "Eremon! Eremon, please..."

Eremon lurched forward, seizing as he collapsed, pulling Lira down with him. Her head cracked hard against the ground, and the world swirled above her as the crowd around them closed in, jockeying for the first look at their fallen ruler as he lay curled on his side, his face contorted in agony.

Lira scrambled to her knees and leaned over his body, "You're going to be fine, it's—going to be fine. Just hold on." She reached for him, stroking his forehead soothingly. "Please hold on."

Eremon inched toward the sound of her voice, opening his mouth to call her name; instead, an agonized scream erupted from his lips. His body writhed with each torturous wave of pain.

Lira trembled as she watched in horror. "Help!" she screamed. "Bring Ljós Beran!"

The teeming mob pressed in against Lira and Eremon, their cries of terror drowning out Lira's pleas for help. Someone wedged between her and Eremon, shoving her to the side. She landed hard and rallied, clawing her way back in his direction. Bodies closed in on her, and she was swept farther and farther from Eremon as he lay suffering in the center of the courtyard.

Lira found herself curled on the ground beneath the horde of onlookers as they stampeded toward Eremon. They trampled her, swarming hungrily over their sovereign like buzzards over carrion.

Eremon groaned as a bolt of lightning split the sky. Lira raised her head to survey the scene, and suddenly, she despised the spectators with more fury than she'd ever felt toward anyone or anything. She hated them for their eagerness to watch her beloved suffer; she hated them for their failure to help him; and most of all, she hated them for separating her from Eremon when he needed her most. When she alone knew what to do.

Lira dug her fingers into the grass, near bursting with rage. Her fists closed over the damp, mossy growth. Beneath her fingertips, the earth began to thrum, beating a rhythm that matched the pounding of her heart. A glowing wave of emerald green blasted from her fists across the courtyard with a great boom that drowned out the thunder overhead.

Onlookers whirled toward her as the ground beneath their feet exploded. Two walls of giant, gnarled thorns burst from the broken soil, scattering the teeming crowd and launching several of those nearest Eremon into the air. Their bodies crunched sickeningly on the ground as they landed. Men and women screamed in horror as the thorns tore at their clothes and their skin, leaving jagged gashes in their wake.

Lira knew she should be horrified at the magnitude of this unbound power, but all she could focus on was Eremon. The walls of thorns, each one at least ten feet high, cleared a path straight to him. She began to crawl in his direction, her arms and legs moving instinctively. Spectators who had managed to rally near the thorns scattered at her approach, crying out in terror as she collapsed at his side again, spent.

He had quieted for a moment and was deathly pale; Lira sucked in a breath at the sight of him.

"Eremon," she whispered, "I'm here. I'm here." His hands found their way to hers, gripping them weakly.

A chorus of cries for help rose from the crowd. They

pressed themselves as close to the thorns as they dared, like terrified onlookers fascinated by a rabid beast.

I am the beast. Lira's heart sank at the sight of the bloodied throng.

"Raní!" one woman screamed. "Sentries!"

"No—" Eremon gasped. "No, no..." His hands clamped down on Lira's as his eyes rolled back, his chest arching violently upward.

"Get away from him, Lira!"

Her attention snapped to the source of the frantic voice. Aidryn stood on the other side of the thorns, his palms bleeding as he gripped the thick, twisted branches. Working his boot into a sturdy bend in a branch, he began to scale the wall. Members of the crowd tried to grab his boots, his ankles, his trousers to pull him back down; but he kicked them away, piercing his thigh on a long thorn as he continued hauling himself upward.

"Stay back!" Aidryn cried again.

Lira bared her teeth angrily; if her desperation to reach Eremon had yielded these massive thorn walls, no one else would stand between them. Not Aidryn, not the sentries, not Macha—*no* one.

She turned her attention back to Eremon, stroking his face and resting her head on his chest as the pain subsided again and his body sagged with exhaustion. "Eremon, I..."

"The ring," he rasped wearily. "Lira—"

Of course.

With trembling fingers, Lira unhooked her chain and slipped the ring from it. She grasped his hand, but he roared again. His back arched so sharply, it looked like his spine might snap.

Wails of terror rose from the crowd. Men and women followed Aidryn's lead, climbing the thorn walls to get a better view of the spectacle unfolding below.

Eremon cried out again as tiny veins of black magic began sparking on the surface of his skin. Lira scrambled backward, sobbing his name as she watched him burn—as *everyone* stood by and watched him burn. She wanted to reach for him again, but the heat from the sparks scorched the grass around him in a wide swath. It was as hot as standing before a bonfire.

When the surge of magic passed, she scrambled back to him, took his hand and slipped the ring over his fingertip—but he squeezed his fingers into a fist, shaking his head almost imperceptibly.

"What are you doing?" she cried. "Let me save you!"

"The ring won't stop this," he whispered, his voice thick with exhaustion. "I want to see you wear it before I die."

"You're not going to die." Lira's tears flowed hot and fast, blurring the sight of his lovely face.

"It was meant to protect you—in every way," he said. "Please, Lira."

The sound of steel blades hacking at the sturdy thorns gave her pause, and she turned to see a company of sentries outside each wall. The men chopped at the overgrowth, cutting a slow path toward Eremon.

Thunder rumbled; clouds roiled in the sky as the full weight of darkness pressed upon the crowd. Sentries, nobles, and lay people looked fearfully overhead, as if the charged atmosphere had finally impressed dread upon them.

The earth trembled as Eremon choked on an agonized shout. A bolt of black lightning erupted from his chest and electrified the sky, crackling across the churning clouds. Lira screamed as his body went limp, his head lolling to the side when the magic's torture finally ended. The horrified crowd fell into a shocked hush, unable to make sense of what they had just witnessed.

The quiet in the courtyard was almost worse than the chaos

as Lira gently stroked Eremon's cheeks. She could feel the warmth—the *life*—rushing out of him.

"Eremon," she pleaded, kissing his forehead. "Please, stay, *please*."

He opened his eyes; they lingered on the sky for a moment, unfocused. Then, he blinked wearily, meeting Lira's gaze.

"It's all over," he whispered, his chest heaving. "It's gone."

"Shhh," Lira soothed, kissing his lips as tears streamed down her face. "You have to save your strength for... for the healer."

Eremon raised his hand, brushing his thumb along her mouth wordlessly. Along the towering thorn walls, shimmering nea'la roses budded, then opened into bright blooms that glowed like the gemstone in his ring.

"You're going to live," Lira cried. "Hold on, Eremon. Stay with me. Marry me."

Eremon's eyes shimmered as he fought for breath; a tear slipped down his cheek. "The ring?"

"Yes—my answer." She help it up for him to see. "My promise."

Panic filled his eyes. "Put it on," he gasped. "Please."

Lira never tore her gaze from Eremon's face, slipping the ring on and holding her hand up for him to see. He grasped it, rubbing a thumb over the stone. "My Lira. My Raní."

"Now, stay with me," she whispered.

Eremon groaned; Lira began to sob as he used the last of his flagging strength to draw her in for another kiss. She lingered there, her lips brushing his as he stroked her cheek. He reached for her hand, and they laced their fingers together.

"Eremon, please," she begged, kissing him again. "I love you."

His chest rose and fell with a final breath; then, he was gone.

CHAPTER 16

Lira wailed, cradling Eremon's head in her lap as the light faded from his eyes. Her tears wet his brow as she brushed his hair out of his face and leaned down to press her lips to him again.

"I'm sorry," she cried. "I was too late. I'm sorry."

For a moment, everything was deathly quiet, save for the ominous electricity that crackled in the atmosphere. The sentries who had been cutting their way through the thorn walls stood immobilized with sorrow. One by one, voices rose as word spread to the outer edges of the mob. Like a wave, their cries traveled back to Lira, cutting into her consciousness.

"The armorer's daughter!"

"Defender of Histories!"

"Sentries!"

Lira felt a strong grip on her shoulders and turned to face a grief-stricken Aidryn. "You have to run!"

She blinked, barely registering his words.

He shook her, rattling her back to awareness. "Get up, Lira! They think you killed him!"

"I did." Her voice was heavy with desolation. "I failed him."

"Listen to me," Aidryn hissed as the sentries broke through the final branches on one side of the wall, "You're the heir now, but you have to *say it!*"

One armored sentry reached Aidryn, seizing him and yanking him to his feet as another pressed the tip of his sword to Lira's throat. She stilled, holding her breath; a warm trickle of blood slid down her neck where the blade made contact.

A general Lira didn't recognize approached, sword in hand. "Dispatch her, sentry."

"General Peros—" Cold dread filled the pit of Lira's stomach as the familiar voice registered.

"That's an order!"

"She's my sister." Grief saturated Talfryn's every word as he stalled. The blade quivered in his grip, the slight movement slicing a shallow gash in Lira's throat.

"Do it, Talfryn," she whispered. "Obey your general."

Talfryn withdrew his sword, swinging it above his head; Lira squeezed her eyes shut, bracing herself for a pain that never came. She opened her eyes again when she heard steel pierce the ground, and found her brother kneeling before her, the point of his blade driven deep into the dirt.

Her heart sank further. "No," she moaned, shaking her head as fresh tears spilled over her cheeks.

"I told you, Lira," Talfryn said, raising his head to meet her eyes. "There's no one I'd bow to but you."

"Insubordinate traitor!" the general roared, advancing from behind as Talfryn held his position.

Peros drove his blade into the slit between Talfryn's chest and shoulder plates, pushing it clean through. Her brother screamed in agony as the general tore the sword from his shoulder. Talfryn collapsed in a heap, soaking the grass with blood.

General Peros leaned down and pulled the helmet from Talfryn's head, slinging it to the ground. Grasping a handful of his hair, the general yanked him to his knees, forcing him to look at his sister. Sorrow and pain twisted Talfryn's face, but there was something else there, too—resolve. Not fear, but a gritty determination beyond his sixteen years.

Icy horror seeped into Lira's bones. "Tal!" she shrieked, lunging toward her brother. Two more sentries restrained her, but she cried out, fighting them with all her strength as Talfryn's green eyes met hers once more. "No!"

The general's lips twisted into a sneer as he bellowed, "A traitor's fate!"

He raised his sword, but paused, his eyes trained on the platform at the other end of the courtyard.

Macha was looking down on them, clothed in crimson silk. Her expression was stricken, but she seemed oddly calm as her eyes fell on her son's body. Only when her gaze shifted to Lira, then Talfryn, did she speak.

"Lock him up," she barked to Peros, who lowered his blade grudgingly. "We shall make an example of him. See to it that his mother is brought into the city for the execution."

Unbridled hatred surged through Lira as she pushed herself up on all fours, her trembling limbs threatening to collapse beneath her.

"No," she cried as Peros handed Talfryn off to another sentry, who led him toward the towers.

Talfryn managed one panicked glance over his shoulder at Lira before he disappeared from her view.

Macha raised her hands, and the crowd grew rapt.

"The Rí has fallen," she began. "What you have witnessed today is the result of a naïve child tampering with dark magic and vying for a throne."

The mob roared again. Lira's ears pounded, her hearing muted by the bedlam that surrounded her. She cut her gaze toward Aidryn, who was still detained by a sentry on the edge of the crowd. His eyes were wild, and his mouth moved frantically, wordlessly. Lira squinted, training her gaze on his lips;

she didn't understand. Almost imperceptibly, she shook her head.

Aidryn's voice broke through the avalanche of sound as he demanded again, "Say it!"

The two sentries caught Lira in their bone-crushing grip and dragged her toward Macha. Aidryn's lips were still uttering something unintelligible as the sentries dumped her at the base of the platform.

"Rise," Macha commanded, her voice as sharp as flint.

Lira was immobilized. Macha jerked her chin at one of the sentries, who yanked Lira back up by her arm. Her knees knocked beneath her as she struggled to remain upright.

Macha raised her voice. "This sorceress has resurrected a dark magic Rodhlan hasn't seen in two thousand years—the magic that killed my only son."

Murmurs of assent swept the mob as their dowager sovereign continued. "She has single-handedly destroyed the peace my bloodline worked so hard to establish. And now, our beloved supreme leader is dead by her hand, and I must now resurrect a power long suppressed."

The murmurs became a rumble that grew into an all-out roar. Macha raised her hands again; the roar subsided immediately, unquestioningly.

"This wretch was your Defender of Histories," Macha cried. "Do you want a clan witch tampering with our sacred records?"

"No!" the crowd jeered.

"Silira Mór," Macha boomed, "I hereby strip you of your title, your properties, and your citizenship. You are nothing. You are no one." Lira hung her head as she sobbed, enraged and humiliated. She longed for the Raní to end this now, to call for her head.

But Macha raised her voice louder still. "Let this serve as a warning to you all: traitors to my crown will be shown no mercy!"

The cool, midnight breeze ruffled Macha's featherlight robes; the reek of her perfume wafted toward Lira, sparking pain behind her eyes.

"Who is your sovereign?" Macha bellowed.

"Raní Macha!" shouted the mob.

Macha moved to the edge of the platform, where Lira's thorn walls ended; slowly, she reached for the needle-sharp point of the nearest thorn. She pressed the tip of her finger to the point, drawing a drop of blood, and fixed her steely gaze on Lira. Both walls exploded then, disintegrating into a fine dust that dispersed across the courtyard. The masses covered their faces and eyes as debris rained down.

"Bow to your sovereign!"

Macha's voice rattled the glass panes of the Dome, reverberating into the ground and back up through Lira's feet. She tried to get back up onto her hands and knees, but a sentry ground his boot into her back, stomping her down. The young man pressed his boot into her harder, and she coughed and choked on the dust.

Despite the pain, an afterimage of Aidryn's lips had burned itself into her brain. Over and over, they repeated the same phrase—something that was beginning to look familiar.

She coughed as the air was shoved out of her, and still, that phrase played on Aidryn's lips: *Sura masi.*

"Say it!" he had begged.

Sura masi.

From overhead, Macha's voice echoed once more. "Long has my bloodline suppressed our magic, fearing to wield it for the good of the people. Now, I swear on my son's life that I will use his throne to defeat the darkness the clans have resurrected. My people, I am honored to serve Iathium in Rí Eremon's stead!"

The crowd roared.

You're the heir. The heir. The heir.

The earth trembled with the people's response. Lira lay unmoving beneath the sentry's boot, her mind racing. Eremon had told her—but what had he told her? She couldn't think.

The mob was quiet again. Macha cupped her palms and lifted them toward the sky. She tipped her head back and began to chant in a language Lira didn't recognize. Cobalt blue light filled the woman's open hands.

A closer, fainter flash caught Lira's eye, and she looked to the ring. Its stone pulsed with a dim light.

Macha was trying to claim it.

If this bloodline ends with me, I want the ring in safe hands.

Wind whipped Macha's robes as she chanted, swirling around her like a small cyclone. The golden band on Lira's finger began to burn.

It was meant to protect you in every way.

From her vantage point on the ground, she managed to find Aidryn once more. His eyes flashed, and she could have sworn she heard his voice echo through her mind: *You are both Witness Tree and Eremon's rightful heir. A double inheritance. Don't let her take the ring; say the vow and save yourself.*

She blinked at him once, twice—four times, to the cadence of the sealing vow. He sagged imperceptibly, as if realizing she finally understood.

Lira's heartbeat pounded in her ears. She dug her fingers into the earth again, pressing her forehead into the cool grass as she whispered, "*Sura masi.*"

A rolling boom began under Lira's prone body and spread like a wave across the courtyard, toward where Eremon lay. Her sentries stumbled back in alarm, drawing their swords. The teeming crowd cried out in panic. Lira raised her face toward the platform in time to see Macha blanch with horror.

"No!" Macha moaned, her gaze flashing to her empty hands before resting on Eremon.

Macha vanished into a cloud of crimson vapor and reappeared at Eremon's side a split-second later. She began a desperate search his of robes, running her hands along the silken folds of fabric. A relentless tremor took hold of her hands—her entire body—as she inspected his singed tunic over and over.

Lira pushed herself onto her knees, turning to watch in terror as Eremon's skin began to shine with an otherworldly glow. Sparkling colors played across his pallor as the rumble reached his body, and the magic muted itself for a moment before bursting from him in a cascade of light. Four bright beams of power coursed from his body in shades of emerald green, crimson, gold, and violet.

A shaft of emerald magic blasted into Lira, smashing her body against the platform. She reeled with the impact. Her skin shimmered with the pulsing magic as it synced with her heartbeat; then, the color faded as it soaked into her pores.

The mob had no time to react before the lights cut into them, too, showering bystanders and court members alike with the same luminous sheen. Clan descendants received their stolen magic with terror—crimson for Tarlach, gold for Beran, violet for Énna. Lira scanned the crowd for other descendants of her clan, but found none nearby.

People scattered, trampling one another as screams filled the courtyard. They bottlenecked at the gate, crushing against each other like a stampede of terrified cattle. Some collapsed as sparks of magic burst haphazardly from their skin.

A line from one of Skelly's manuscripts played across Lira's mind as the chaos unfolded: *Magic wrongfully taken goes to war with its host and returns to its rightful place tenfold.*

So much unchecked power, and so many unprepared hosts. This horror was what Eremon and Irem had been trying to avoid.

Lira noticed with a start that her sentries had fled. She pushed herself to her feet and scanned the pandemonium for

Aidryn, but he was nowhere to be found. Her muscles felt refreshed, as if the magic had strengthened her. If she ran right this minute, while the courtyard was still in complete disarray, perhaps she could get herself out of the city.

The mob began to move again as people poured into the street outside. Lira hesitated; this crowd knew her face now. Panicked or not, they would turn on her in a heartbeat.

I have no choice.

She ducked her head and moved to slip into the crowd, only to find herself nose-to-nose with Macha. The Raní's face was contorted with hatred, but her voice was flat and lifeless as she growled, "You."

Before Lira could think, Macha's hand was covering her face. Pain seared into her eyes, nose, and mouth, so consuming she couldn't scream. Her vision shifted into white light as her consciousness dimmed.

But then, cobalt light burst from the ring and shattered Macha's spell, forcing her backward. For a moment, Lira and Macha stared at one another, dazed. And then General Peros stepped between them, raising his steel gauntlet and striking Lira across the face with it.

The last thing she remembered was searing pain.

CHAPTER 17

The general jostled Lira's body roughly as they descended into the catacombs beneath the western side of the Dome, where the dungeons lay. Like the archive shelves, the dank cells had been fashioned out of solid stone. Hulking iron doors sealed prisoners tightly inside, and the only light that filtered through the slits in the doors was the dim flickering of torches on the wall.

The first thing Lira noticed as she began to awaken was Peros's foul, gamey stench. He smelled of rotting meat, and the reek churned her stomach. The farther they descended into the dungeon—the stronger the odors of mold and refuse grew— the sicker she felt. By the time the general had manhandled her into a cell of her own, bile was rising in her throat.

Peros slammed the iron door with a reverberating boom and locked Lira inside as she retched. She remained on all fours, gasping for breath, limbs trembling, tears searing her eyes until she got her bearings enough to lean against the stone wall with a guttural groan.

Lira touched her nose gingerly, wincing with pain. Sticky, clotted blood covered her face, and one of her eyes was nearly swollen shut. If she didn't move—if she just remained here against this wall, perhaps numbness would settle in. Refusing meals would speed the process, and maybe she would die here before Macha could execute her in some excruciating public display.

If Macha had wanted Lira dead in the courtyard, the deed would have already been done. Lira's mind raced; the Raní would likely take her time devising how to best dispose of her for dramatic—and memorable—effect. It had been decades since anyone had been publicly executed in Iathium; Rí Corlan's father had put an end to those deaths, and his son and grandson had upheld his decree. But it was no secret among the nobility that the Raní approved of spectacle. If Macha truly believed Eremon to be dead at Lira's hands, there was little hope of escape.

Talfryn would soon be killed as an example, too, for his brazen public display of loyalty to Lira over Macha—and to ensure no one else followed suit.

Where had they taken him?

"Talfryn?" she called—softly at first.

No one answered.

"Talfryn!"

Her desperate plea reverberated inside her cell, echoing down the dark corridors. There was no response.

"What have I done?" she cried.

Lira thought of the quiet determination she had seen in her brother when he had knelt before her. She wished she'd had time to tell him she was proud of the man he'd become. Would she be left here long enough to forget his beautiful, joyful face? How long would he be allowed to live before he met his fate—if he was still alive at all?

Next, her thoughts drifted to Aidryn. He had been right; she should have fled with him when she had the chance. She'd been so naïve to think she could help Eremon; she hadn't even accepted his proposal properly before it was too late. Her acceptance had been a desperate attempt to keep him alive, but like everything else she'd tried to do, it had been futile.

Lira ran a finger over the gemstone and wondered why Macha had not taken it from her. She hadn't touched Skelly's pendant, either.

Somehow, Aidryn had known that repeating the sealing vow would finalize Eremon's intention to make her heir and release the ancestral magic that had been trapped in his body. Would Aidryn be seized next? The thought of Macha attempting to lock him up was absurd, though; how would Iathium contain the Key Keeper?

Lira couldn't imagine the chaos aboveground now. What would happen to all those people who had received such a powerful measure of magic, so suddenly? And what lengths would Macha go to in order to rein them all in? The longer she sat with her churning thoughts, the more hopeless she felt.

She wished General Peros would return with his sword, take her head, and have it done.

HOURS DRAGGED by until the perpetual darkness distorted Lira's perception of time. She guessed it had been near midnight when Peros left her, but hours or days may have passed; it didn't matter. Her life had been completely obliterated: the man she loved, her family, her friends, her home, her future.

It didn't matter that she had been loyal to Eremon's bloodline all her life. No one cared that she had given up her clan for Iathium. She had sacrificed relationships, a birthright, her ancestral lands, and even her own common sense in favor of an illusion. Her life had been dedicated to learning and preserving a history full of lies.

Macha was right—Lira *was* no one. She had nothing left, though she'd had very little to begin with.

Lira lay down, her limbs aching, and stared into the yawning darkness above her. When she blinked, a dull glimmer of green coated her vision; she blinked again, and it was gone. Again, she squeezed her eyes shut, and when she opened them, the emerald flare overpowered her sight like a brilliant, bright explosion. She gasped; her body went rigid as she fought against the vision that overtook her.

The axe comes down hard, and hot blood splatters her face. Her pinched scream is drowned out by the roaring crowd that fills the courtyard and presses in on her. This is Iathium, but it's an Iathium she has never seen for herself. Under any other circumstance, she would be marveling at the ancient fashions and comparing the buildings and homes to what now stands—but she doesn't want to see any of it. Especially not the young man who was just executed.

She tries to shut her eyes, so she won't have to watch the executioner hold the man's head high. But she finds herself frozen in place, forced to watch as his body bleeds out on the scaffold. Her feet are fused to the ground—she can neither turn away nor run. So she remains where she is, sobbing bitterly.

The nightmare went on for hours. Each scene played out before her, vivid and raw. She was plunged into more visions of tortures and executions, many from centuries long past. With each shift in her sight, she entered a new scene, but the pattern was always the same: a son or daughter of the clans put on unjust trial by the ruler of their time, and then sentenced to a horrific fate.

Lira was frozen in place, forced to stare into the eyes of each victim as they died. She could do nothing to free herself from the string of visions, each more gruesome than the last.

Finally, she saw herself kneeling before a steely-eyed Eremon.

Eremon is as handsome as ever, but cruel. Cold. Not the

charming young man Lira remembers. She falls to her knees before him as he motions for Peros to hand over his sword. Something like joy flickers across his expression for a split second before he raises the sword to strike her down himself.

Immobilized on the cold stone, Lira began to shriek—a panic-stricken, unnerving sound that reverberated around her and filled every cell in the dungeon. The prisoners down the corridor protested loudly. But locked in her vision, they were the bloodthirsty mob that gorged itself on her suffering.

The lock on the iron door disengaged with a loud groan as it creaked open. Suddenly, the trance loosened its hold on Lira's consciousness and she came to, trembling and gasping for air. A massive shadow with heavy footfalls entered her cell, and she found the strength to scramble against the far wall.

Lira shook her head frantically, weeping as she covered her face with her arms. "Don't take me to her, don't—"

But a warm hand grasped one of her fists reassuringly as the door clicked shut again. "Hush, Witness Tree! I am here to help you."

Lira opened her eyes to see Ljós Beran, his amber eyes luminous even in the dark. Lowering her arms, she reached out to grasp the sleeves of his gray robe in earnest.

"I couldn't help him," she rasped, the words searing her raw throat.

Ljós shushed her, pressing a thumb to her forehead; an intoxicating, calming sensation washed over her body as her ragged breathing slowed. She sagged into his touch.

"Where is Talfryn?" Her speech began to slur, her tongue slackening in her mouth. "Is my brother dead?"

The healer caught her as she slumped, positioning her head carefully on his thigh as he helped her lie back down.

"Don't talk," he whispered, his warm fingers playing across her face and head. "He lives. I healed him as best I could before I came to you. They are holding him in the barracks."

Lira offered one slow, groggy nod and closed her eyes, allowing relief and exhaustion to drag her down.

"No," Ljós said. "Stay awake—listen. I am under orders to heal you before you're presented to the Raní."

Lira knew she should feel panicked, but her body and mind felt calm, relaxed. Her thoughts wandered idly, tripping over the meager features of the cell, the iron door, the healer, and the otherworldly warmth he emitted. His accent was thick—similar to her stepfather's—and he wore the traditional long, braided beard of Artur's clan.

"They'll hear you, child of Beran," she drawled. "You must be careful, son of..." She lolled her head drunkenly. "... whomever you are."

"Shh. I have muffled their ears." Ljós gently closed her eyelids again, his fingertips fluttering against her skin. "I know your mother, Silira—daughter of Arlen, granddaughter of Wilga. I served your stepfather at Fortress Halgeir until young Eremon became ill."

Behind her eyelids, Lira sensed a faint glow, but she kept them closed. "I found a cure just before he died: the roses, the blood." Her chin began to tremble again, tears rolling down either side of her face. "It was too late. I failed him."

The light dimmed, and Ljós stroked her hair. "I know that remedy, little scholar. It may have prolonged his life for a time, but he still would have suffered greatly. The only cure would have been for him to begin wielding his power long ago. After he grew ill, he could not control the magic even when he tried; so he chose not to use it. It is not your fault."

"I loved him. Maybe—" She sniffed, swiping at her nose, and was surprised to find that it no longer hurt. "Maybe we could have helped him if—"

"Quiet, little girl," he chided softly, patting her shoulder comfortingly. "We must keep moving ahead. Think of what you will do with your future."

She sat up and turned to him. "I have no future. And now, my past doesn't matter."

"But it does. You gave Eremon a chance to love completely," Ljós replied sternly. "To know what it was to value another person over a throne. An entire continent over his great city."

"He loved Rodhlan before he ever knew me," she protested quietly, her gaze dropping to the floor.

"Do not argue. He loved and trusted you enough to make you his heir. To give Iathium to a child of the clans: a daughter of Mór and Beran alike.

"You will give the clans hope that their glory might be restored. You are a symbol. Something worth fighting for."

She sniffed. "The clans don't want me."

"Don't underestimate yourself, Silira. We have been waiting for someone like you." Ljós released her and met her eyes. "Now. What will you do with your future?"

A half-laugh, half-sob broke from between her lips. "I'll die on display." Lira tried to breathe deeply to calm herself, but a louder, shuddering cry overtook her instead. "And Eremon is dead, and they're going to kill my brother, and next—"

"Listen to me!" Ljós grasped her shoulders, his eyes shining. "As long as you're wearing that ring, the Rani cannot take your life. Your death would not benefit her. That ring contains magic that will protect you and no one else."

Lira sagged in his grip. "So the ring protected him until he gave it away?"

"Stop trying to make this tragedy your fault," the healer scolded, giving her shoulders a firm squeeze. "You're behaving like a child, Silira. Nothing we did could have stopped what happened today. But the peoples of this continent believe in you, and you must rise for them. Eremon risked the future of his bloodline by giving you that ring—show him you are worthy of it.

"You must use its power to name an heir, whether you have

a child of your own or choose a successor from outside your bloodline. But if you die without an heir, the ring will vanish, and with it the divine sovereignty Eremon granted to you. Macha will want to get that ring onto her own finger, but she cannot harm you in the process. For her to claim the ring, you would have to die by your own hand—the protective magic is that binding."

Her eyes widened. "What's stopping her from making me name her as heir?" She imagined Macha lining her remaining family and friends up before her, threatening to slit their throats if Lira didn't give her the throne.

"Your aversion to her," he said. "The ring's discernment is molded by its bearer; if there is someone from whom your magic recoils, then the ring can sense that. By default, it will not go to that person willingly.

"The only time the ring becomes impressionable is if its wearer takes their own life. And in that case, its power would be at risk."

"You speak of this ring as if it's sentient," Lira said. "Why?"

"It was forged by the god Riku to protect his wife, Rhona, from his dark twin," the healer answered. "Would you like to hear the story?"

"Do you have time to tell it?" Lira whispered. "I don't want to be alone."

Ljós inclined his head. "The ring was meant to shield Rhona, who was vulnerable to the twins' dark magic. Though Riku never harmed her himself, he was unwilling to risk it— and he knew that Rasu's power was warped beyond comparison."

"Rasu the Vile," Lira whispered. She scooted back against the wall, leaning her head back and shutting her eyes as he continued.

"Riku devised a way to make the ring's magic go beyond simply protecting Rhona from his brother. He designed the first

Dome to extend the spell he had placed on the ring to everyone inside. And the oculus—cobalt like the gemstone, in those days—could theoretically be used to project the power outward, to cover the entire city."

Shimmering pictures of the first Dome form in Lira's mind—memories of a past long gone. The glass oculus is, indeed, a striking blue—and the Dome's towers are overlaid with pure gold. She marvels at its opulence; in the centuries since, the buildings in Iathium have become more practical and less grand. The Dome that stands now could never compare to Riku's.

"In order to protect Iathium," the healer continued, "the ring's bearer had to travel to the oculus and place the stone in its center.

"On the day Rasu's army—made of clanspeople and Itelorians he'd assembled—finally breached Iathium's walls, Riku took the ring back from Rhona. In preparation for the possibility of invasion, his sentries had built scaffolding in the Dome's central garden that rose all the way to the oculus.

"Riku scaled the scaffolding with ease, confident that once he reached the top, he could save the city from his brother with as little bloodshed as possible. But when he got there, Rasu was waiting for him. He'd allowed a decoy to lead his army to the wall, while he wormed his way into the Dome through the catacombs below it.

"Riku was caught off guard, and he froze; when Rasu charged him on the top of the scaffolding, he lost the ring. It tumbled to the garden below as the brothers brawled.

"Fear got the best of Riku; he was defeated in his mind long before Rasu bested him. Rasu stole his brother's power, draining him dry before throwing him over the edge of the scaffolding. Riku fell two hundred feet to his death.

"Rasu shattered the oculus. Great cracks ran down the sides of the Dome from its center. It is said the breaking was so powerful, it could be heard all the way in Rodhlan Ridge."

Lira's backside ached from sitting on the stone floor for so long. She shifted, curling her legs to the side to reduce the pressure.

"Then, Rasu descended, drunk with power, to find Rhona and Nami—who was fifteen at the time—waiting for him, grief-stricken and enraged. Rhona had retrieved the ring, and she was able to deflect Rasu's magic for a short time. But soon, the dark power began to overwhelm her. With his brother's magic now inside him, Rasu was twice as powerful as before.

"Rasu hit Rhona with blasts of his power—again and again. Each time, Nami tried to defend her, but she pushed him back until finally, she was too weak to protect him any longer."

A tall, imposing woman shields her son—Nami. The mortal goddess meets Rasu's black power with a terrifying blast of her own —a spectrum of color and wind and light. Rhona's tan skin has an otherworldly sheen that dulls with each blast from Rasu.

"But Rhona knew the unique mix of magic Nami had inherited—half darkness, mixed with his mother's array of elemental magic and powers of innate wisdom. She had faith her son would be stronger than Rasu, given a fighting chance.

"So, she held Rasu at bay long enough to slip the ring onto Nami's finger. And then, she threw herself in front of her son as Rasu burned into her with a killing blow. She was reduced to ashes before Nami's eyes."

Rhona takes a final blast of dark magic straight to her heart. Her mouth opens wide in a soundless scream, but the power overtakes her in seconds.

Though Lira wanted to turn away from the images that played through her mind, she watched it all unfold. Tears streamed down her cheeks at the vision of a young man—not much younger than Talfryn—crumpling in grief at his mother's loss.

"But then, Nami's fury erupted," Ljós breathed, reaching

out to grasp Lira's fingers. "When Rasu turned his power on the boy, Nami was untouchable.

"First, Nami killed his uncle and claimed his power—and Riku's. Next, he turned his anger and grief on the clans; their conspiracies, to his mind, had resulted in his parents' deaths. Mortal gods, they were—but first, they were a mother and a father. A husband and a wife. Their loss cut Nami to the core.

"Nami released a quake of power that shattered what remained of the Dome into millions of shards—shards that rained down on the city."

Lira winced, the smell of blood saturating her senses.

"In his rage, Nami the Furious split the sky above Iathium. The clouds broke open—"

"—with a thunderous crack, so that even the ground beneath his feet quaked," Lira continued, opening her eyes to the darkness once more.

Together, they recited: "He brought the hatred of a thousand cyclones down on Rodhlan, and the Great Clans were felled like a dying forest, cut down and brought low; yet their roots remained, ready to spring forth new life once more."

A heavy silence fell over the cell for a long moment before Lira whispered, "Skelly always told me that last bit, but the rest was new. Coming from her, that ending always sounded hopeful. But in context, it's more ominous."

"It depends on who's telling the story, doesn't it?" Ljós said.

Lira drew her knees to her chest, her feet slipping on the mildewed straw that covered the floor. "So Nami was truly the start of the corrupted power in Eremon's bloodline."

"Indeed. Some of the rulers who followed brought wives here from Iteloria; others intermarried with clanspeople, corrupting the power further. Eremon would have been the first in a long line of his predecessors to marry a woman who did not possess some measure of dark magic."

"Thus, diluting the power in his bloodline," Lira mused.

She didn't want to think about what could have happened to any children they might have had together.

"He did it for the clans," Ljós said. "For you. He was ready to stop the amassing of dark magic—and the theft of the clans' power—with his rule. And if you loved him—if you want to honor his memory—you'll remember that. You will do your part to keep evil from ruling Rodhlan."

He rose to his feet, and Lira followed. Her legs were weak, and she swayed beneath the weight of everything he'd told her. "What do I do now?" she whispered.

"Mourn," the healer answered. "Weep when you must. But do not lose hope.

"There is much locked away in your mind—much that you can learn. Tap into it; use your people's memories to learn your magic. Everything you need is inside of you; but you must call to it."

Lira took an unsteady breath. "And how will I do that?"

Ljós grasped the iron door, but hesitated as he turned back to her. "We are arranging for your release, but I cannot say when that will happen. It could be weeks, months—but someone will come for you."

"What about Talfryn?"

"Aidryn Tarlach and a small group of sentries are making plans to free him. For now, keep yourself alive."

She nearly sobbed with relief. Without another glance at her, Ljós left the cell, locking the heavy door behind him. Lira sat again, closed her eyes, and let the darkness envelop her.

CHAPTER 18

Lira dozed fitfully in the cold cell that night. Over and over, exhaustion dragged her down like a riptide, only to shatter as the realization of what had happened—what was still happening—burst into her consciousness. Each time her body began to relax, she would jolt awake with a start. And each time the overwhelming shock washed over her, she trembled against the wall, adrenaline pumping.

She cursed Ljós for healing her wounds; the physical pain had almost been a distraction from the grief. She tried to call up her clan's memories as the healer had instructed. But when she closed her eyes, the memory of Eremon's final moments flashed mercilessly before her.

Several days passed before Lira finally gave up trying to rest. For the first time since the healer had visited, she began paying attention to the stirrings in the cells around her. The man in the cell nearest her passed the time by talking and laughing bitterly to himself; another across the corridor spent his days trying to engage anyone who would respond to him in conversation.

There was a keening woman further down the hall whose wailing rose and fell at all hours through the days and nights.

Groans and cries rose from the other prisoners. Some begged for freedom; others for death. Yet others called out for their meals, as if they expected a regular patrol to care for their needs on demand.

Few sentries walked the halls of the dungeon. Lira wondered if, perhaps, it was because the prisoners were so well-contained. There was barely enough light coming in through the slits in the doors for fellow inmates to conspire, let alone attempt an escape. Whenever the unexpected clanging of armor did echo through the dungeon corridors, Lira sat up in anticipation, only to sag against the wall again as the noise dissipated.

She wondered whether she'd ever see the sunlight again, and the dread that overtook her the first time the thought crossed her mind was so overwhelming, she forced herself to suppress it. Someone would come for her; Ljós had promised.

But if no one ever came—she tried to shake the thought away, but it rooted into her mind. It choked her; her stomach ached, her breath coming in short gasps as her chest tightened. There was a power here, invading the space as it pressed against Lira, as if searching for a way to slither beneath her skin. She shuddered, clutching the pendant as her own magic withdrew deeper inside of her. Rhona's ring began to pulse, its cobalt light filling the cell.

As if disgusted, the power recoiled; Lira could just make out a mist of shimmering, shifting energy that hovered before her. It glowed emerald for a moment before flaring into a bright burst of light; then, it was gone.

The ring stopped pulsing, and she was plunged into darkness again. But as her eyes adjusted, she could make out a length of thick, smooth vine that lay corded along the cell floor. She followed the vine up to where it had been looped around one of the short bars at the top of the door.

Hands trembling, she picked the vine up, studying it closely.

The power that had formed it was long gone, and while it had momentarily resembled hers in color, it had felt nothing like the magic she harbored.

Lira's gaze fell to the end of the vine that lay on the floor, and she gasped, dropping it.

The vine had been fashioned into a noose.

She pressed a trembling hand to her mouth, taking one step back, then another. Ljós had warned Lira that death by her own hand would be the only way for Macha to seize the ring. Was this some strange trick of the Raní's power?

Suddenly, the lock disengaged and the iron door before her swung open. She retreated into the shadows, trembling.

A young sentry, not much taller than she, stood in the doorway dressed in full regalia, one hand on the hilt of his sword as he looked between the noose that dangled from the bars and a wild-eyed Lira, who had flattened her body against the far wall of the cell.

For a moment, she wondered whether she could create thorns again, the way she had in the courtyard. Thorns to keep him away from her, to seal her in—

The sentry unsheathed his sword and gripped the vine, slicing it loose with a clean swipe before he stalked into the cell, blade at the ready, and slammed the door shut behind him. He sheathed his sword again and shoved a fistful of vine toward Lira's face. She cowered, whimpering as she turned her head away from the sentry.

"You dishonor Eremon's memory," he snarled, pulling his helmet from his head, "you ungrateful wretch."

"I dishonor no one," she said quietly.

The sentry inched closer to Lira; his black eyes shone with something like panic as he took in her appearance.

"How do you explain the noose, then?" he asked angrily. "Did you forget the healer's words?"

"I didn't—"

"You've lost hope." His whisper was almost unintelligible as he set his helmet down. "After everything we've fought for."

Her gaze snapped to the sentry, whose chest rose and fell with a cadence that revealed the distress his smooth, deliberate movements concealed. Although his frame was small, he bore the weight of his armor and weaponry with graceful ease. His tan skin, curly, jet-black hair, and finely chiseled features were vaguely familiar, and Lira struggled to recall where she had seen him before.

The sentry glared at her, then down at the vine. Both fists curled around it as he surveyed Lira's craftsmanship. His knuckles tensed, and the vine exploded into a spray of seawater that showered the floor of the cell, splashing Lira's face. She blinked hard against the burning salt.

"Clan Énna," Lira stammered, wonder momentarily overtaking the fear. "Did Ljós send you?"

"I'm taking you to the Raní," he said curtly, offering to help her up.

Lira swallowed hard, her tongue suddenly like sandpaper in her mouth. She shook her head frantically. "No—please—"

The sentry grabbed her arm and wrenched her into a standing position.

"Get up," he seethed, his breath hot on her face. "I have orders to follow."

Lira reeled as he released her, her arm throbbing where his fingers had dug into her skin.

"I'd rather die than go to her." She bunched her matted curls into a fist and lifted her hair, exposing her neck. "So have it done; you seem eager to cause me harm."

He huffed a shallow laugh. "You're a sorry excuse for an heir, Silira. Talfryn is like a brother to me. For his sake, I won't kill you here. But I want you to prove that you're worth the price he's paid for you."

At the mention of her brother's name, she nearly collapsed.

For the first time in weeks, she felt a jolt of hope. "Talfryn's still alive?"

"He is," he replied, producing a pair of iron restraints. "I am only here because he and Tarlach asked for my help. I'm doing it for them, not for you."

Lira tried to hold steady, meeting his hard glare with her own. "I told Tal to kill me, but he wouldn't."

The sentry was so uncomfortably close, but Lira didn't shrink away. They shared their next breaths as a long moment passed. "Perhaps he should have, before he had a chance to entangle me in this part of the mess."

"It would have been the better option," the sentry replied.

Lira squeezed her eyes shut and let him clamp the restraints onto her wrists.

"You'll do well to steel yourself," he answered, heading for the door. He placed his hand on the latch, but paused for a moment, glancing back over his shoulder and lowering his voice. "Macha is endlessly ruthless and morbidly creative. I can't say I care for you, but I like your brother. I love my city and I loved Eremon. So for all that, I'm sorry for what you're about to endure."

"I don't think I will survive it," she said listlessly, pressing herself back against the stone wall again. "But perhaps that's what I deserve."

A brief flash of pity crossed his face. "Whatever she has planned for you will be enough terror to last a lifetime. Just stay alive tonight."

His gaze fell to her ring, then back to her face. "Ljós prepared you, did he not?"

"He told me what they desire," Lira answered. "But the noose wasn't—"

"It doesn't matter," the sentry answered. "I don't want your explanation."

He motioned for Lira to join him, but she shrank farther,

shaking her head. Her breaths came in frantic gasps. "I can't face this."

"You will," the sentry replied, pulling her toward him by the restraints. "I've been ordered to deliver you alive. I'll not die for you." He opened the iron door and pushed Lira out into the corridor ahead of him. "Come on."

The sentry prodded her forward as they began the long trek up the rising, spiraling hallway. Lira tried to move quickly—the feeling of his gaze on her back was unnerving—but she found herself already out of breath and trembling from the uphill climb. She'd barely moved in her cell except to take care of her most basic needs, and her limbs protested the sudden exertion.

For a long while, the only sound was the clanking of the sentry's armor, his sword hilt tapping against the polished silver plate. Lira's attention narrowed to the feeling of the floor beneath her feet as she moved. The walkway wasn't a spiral stair; rather, it was a stone path so worn and smooth it was almost slick.

They climbed for half an hour before the spiral path opened and leveled into a long, narrow corridor that resembled the one she'd taken from beneath the archive to the garden. By now, they were walking side by side, and the sentry had long since stopped driving her forward.

Against her better judgment, Lira broke the silence. "You never told me your name."

She expected him to dismiss her, but he replied, "Faolan."

"Ah." Ahead of them, at the end of the corridor, Lira could just make out the late afternoon sunlight filtering into the darkness. It had been so long since she'd seen the sun; despite what was coming, she felt a tiny twinge of relief.

Ever so slightly, she tipped her head in Faolan's direction. "Faolan, you said my brother paid a price. What was it?"

Faolan pressed his lips together, his expression darkening. His brows knitted in concentration for a moment before he said, "That is not my story to share. Besides, he'll want to be the one who tells you everything. You know how he is."

Whatever that price was, it must have been terrible for Faolan to refuse her request. No matter what happened, she would think of her brother—and of Aidryn—and try to make it out alive. She ran her thumb over the smooth stone of Eremon's ring, and her voice cracked as she asked, "What will happen at my hearing?"

The sentry glanced sidelong at her. "It's not a hearing."

Her heart pounded. "Then what is it?"

Faolan sighed. "You'll find out sooner than you'd like."

CHAPTER 19

Finally, Lira and Faolan reached an entrance to the Dome's interior. She squinted against the sunlight that filtered through the glass. It had been so long since she'd seen light that her eyes ached; she could barely hold them open. Faolan took her by the elbow, leading the way as her vision slowly adjusted.

When she could see normally again, she took in her surroundings; they were deep within a part of the Dome where she had never set foot: the ruling family's quarters.

Gleaming marble floors veined with silver and gold stretched as far as she could see. Plush crimson and gold upholstery covered the gilded furniture. It was deathly silent, save for the careful footfalls of the servants who tried to remain unnoticed as they moved about, their curious eyes darting to Lira as Faolan led her down the wide hallway.

"Just so you aren't surprised," he said through barely-moving lips, "I'm going to be a bit rough with you."

Lira offered a nearly imperceptible nod. "A valid excuse to manhandle me—"

"Indeed—"

"—though I'm hardly surprised," she finished, her voice almost inaudible. Faolan's wry expression told her he'd heard well enough.

They followed a long, narrow glass archway that stretched from the Dome to one of the tall towers. Faolan gripped her upper arm as they entered the ground floor of the tower, hauling her across the perimeter of the room. He shoved her unceremoniously through a small archway that led to a narrow, spiral staircase. They climbed the stairs wordlessly until they reached the highest level, where the stairwell opened into an ornate parlor of white, crimson, and gold—much like the area of the Dome they'd just passed through.

Lira's breath caught in her throat when they halted before Macha, who sat expectantly on a chaise, hands folded, back ramrod straight. Her hard, gray eyes glinted with malice as she took Lira in, and her lips curled into a sneer.

"Filth," she snarled. "It suits you."

Lira's cheeks heated, and she dropped her gaze as she bowed.

Macha's eyes darted to Faolan, and she simpered at him with a practiced, sensuous smile.

"Well done, little wolf," she purred, rising from her perch to stand before him. "You may unlock her restraints."

Faolan released Lira's arm and bowed deeply. "It is my honor, my Raní."

"You are dismissed, sentry."

He inclined his head, pivoting before Lira could catch his eye. She listened helplessly to the echo of his footsteps as he descended the stairs.

Macha took Lira's chin in her hands, inspecting her closely. "How did you manage to ensnare my son?" she asked, her voice soft—curious. Almost kind.

A shiver snaked down Lira's spine. "There was no snare,"

she answered. "Perhaps that is why he fell in love with me—and I him."

"What a boring tale." Macha released Lira and sat down on the chaise again. "He wasn't content to produce heirs for me—that was the least he could've done."

"You might have gotten those heirs, had you not interfered with him."

"And taint the bloodline with clan filth? Stupid boy," she said, her steely eyes flashing with loss for a moment before she added, "It's better this way."

"How could you say that about your child?" Lira blurted. Her outburst echoed through the opulent room.

Macha massaged her temples, exasperated. "You will find that it's unwise to form attachments to others in the pursuit of power. A throne doesn't take kindly to affection or empathy—precisely why you were so ill-suited all along."

"Eremon was kind. I would have carried that legacy forward. And I think empathy suits the throne more than you'd like to admit."

Macha pursed her lips. "Whatever idea you have about that ring, it won't turn out the way you think. You have no support in Iathium."

Lira's power recoiled at Macha's words. She shook her head. "My magic leads me to truth, and there is none in you."

Macha hummed dismissively. "Let us talk of magic." She reached to pat the cushion beside her, but retracted her hand abruptly, as if remembering Lira was too filthy to sit. "Did you know my son believed he was hiding the extent of his power from me?"

I believed he was hiding it, too. "I never asked him what you knew," she answered carefully.

Distance registered in Macha's gaze, as though she was recalling a memory she had almost enjoyed. "Eremon couldn't continue to hide it because he drew half of it from me. Even after all his father's efforts to help him suppress the stolen magic, he failed."

It felt horribly intimate and decidedly wrong for Macha to confide in her this way.

"Why are you telling me this?" Lira asked.

Macha swept a palm over her robes. "Because of my son's failure to manage his magic, I am poised to rule," she said. "Despite Corlan's attempts to keep me from full power, I finally find myself rising to the throne."

It was widely known that Macha had attempted to be made her husband's heir. Infamously, she had mourned more openly at her failure to wrest the throne from Eremon than she had over her husband's loss—and had secured enough support from his council to act as Crown Regent in Eremon's stead until he came of age.

"But this time, no one will stand in my way. Not a figure-head husband or son, not a council, and certainly not a wretched librarian."

"*Archivist.*"

Macha's lips curled. "Did you know that the mortal god Rasu had descendants of his own? Or was that detail left out of my son's books—the ones your fathers perished to retrieve?"

Lira felt the blood drain from her face. Macha almost smiled as she leaned forward.

"I'll tell you a secret," she whispered. "I am one of Rasu's many descendants. There are members of my court who are as well, including one of my handmaidens.

"She was poised to marry Eremon and continue my ances-tor's bloodline. But he paid her no attention because of *you.*"

Her eyes shone with emotion for a moment. "I wasted a measure of power on her to ensure his offspring's glory; now, I shall have to kill her to take it back."

"Can't you steal magic without killing?" Lira asked.

"Yes; but the ambitious always find a way to take what they

believe is theirs. Because the girl is ambitious, she must die. And her mother along with her."

"That's heartless."

"Holding a throne demands heartlessness."

"Your son had a heart—"

"Indeed. And now he is dead." Her eyes flicked to the curtain. "I have spent the past weeks thinking about how best to punish you for my losses.

"I've contemplated many ways to make you suffer," she continued, motioning for Lira to follow her toward a chamber door just off the parlor, "but I don't want to look at your pathetic face any longer than I must. After much deliberation, I've finally settled on the most fitting fate."

Lira's blood pounded in her ears as cold dread settled in her bones. She tried to keep her knees from knocking together as she kept her eyes trained on Macha.

This is it. It's over. It's—

Macha reached for the door, but her hand paused on the gilded knob. "My attendants will bathe and prepare you for what is to come," she crooned. "A fitting end for a would-be bride, I think."

"Despite what you may think, I am not your enemy," Lira bit out shakily. "All I wanted was to work in the archive—to serve Iathium well."

Macha pushed the door open, but paused long enough to glance over her shoulder and reply, "And you failed."

She motioned for Lira to enter the antechamber within. Lira's entire body trembled as she forced herself to take one step, then another toward the door. Her teeth chattered and her shoulders drew up as she struggled to control her breathing. The feral panic blooming in her gut threatened to swallow her whole, but she moved forward despite it. She had no other choice.

Heavy crimson curtains divided the antechamber from the

main rooms, and Macha led Lira toward a large bathing room to the left of the curtains. Four ladies-in-waiting met them in the doorway, the sleeves of their flowing silver robes rolled to their elbows, faces covered with gossamer veils. Their hair was concealed beneath headdresses that matched their wispy robes.

As one, the four young women dropped to their knees reverently, touching their foreheads to the floor before the Raní's feet. Macha preened before them.

"You have your orders," she said, bidding them to rise again. "Complete them, then bring the girl to the antechamber. You are not to interact. Do your work, then leave her to me."

Macha produced a small key and unlocked the restraints on Lira's wrists, then presented the restraints and the key to one of the handmaidens, who stretched out her flawless hands to receive them.

"In case she resists," Macha said. The maid nodded obediently, the movement pious in her sovereign's presence.

Macha departed with a small, but ominous, click of the bathing room door. Immediately, the attendants began moving silently about the room; two of them drew a hot bath, perfuming the water with expensive oils while the other two began to undress Lira. They peeled her dingy clothes from her trembling body, whisking them away.

Her cheeks heated as she stood before them, completely exposed. She was thankful for the anonymity their veils provided. But being undressed by Macha's handmaidens was the least of her worries, so she tried not to think about it as she allowed them to assist her into the steaming bath.

The more the attendants fussed over her—scrubbing the grime from every inch of her body, combing and lathering her hair, grooming her nails—the more apprehensive she became.

Lira mulled over what Faolan had said—how he had urged her not to give in. What options could she possibly have, besides doing what was expected of her? There would be no escape from the tower; this much, Lira knew.

Lira's stomach churned as the young women helped her out of the now-squalid bath water and wrapped her in a plush robe. She allowed them to fuss over her hair and dress her in silken robes as her racing thoughts immobilized her. The hand-maidens perfumed her body and applied cosmetic creams and powders to her face.

When Lira caught a glimpse of her reflection in the mirror, she looked almost unrecognizable. Luminous.

She was careful not to look at herself again.

When the maidens' work was complete, one of them took Lira's hand, leading her back into the antechamber where Macha waited in silence. Without a word, the four young women filed out into the parlor. When the door clicked behind them, Lira's knees gave way and she slammed onto the marble floor before Eremon's mother.

"Such a clumsy young heir," she said. "Rise, girl."

Lira obeyed, then dared to meet Macha's hate-filled eyes.

"You wanted to marry my son, did you not?"

"Yes." Lira's voice was tremulous and strained.

"But accepting his offer was against your better judgment."

She closed her eyes, vulnerable beneath Macha's keen discernment. "It took time for me to decide. I'd always wanted the archive. But he promised I could continue my work. And when he was dying—" her words caught on a sob—"he begged me to wear the ring for him. I would have given him *anything* in that moment."

Macha clicked her tongue, turning away from Lira. For a moment, it appeared the Rani was composing herself.

"So you did not know to say the vow," she said, more to the red curtain than to Lira. "I will find the wretch who helped you, and he will suffer for it."

"Then I will pray he escapes first."

Macha allowed a heavy silence to envelop the antechamber for a moment before she said, "I vaguely recall denying you access to our living quarters once. I understand you never set foot in the western side of the Dome, much less my son's chamber or his bed—the one place you most wanted to see, no doubt."

Lira's face heated. "It's true that have never been to the royal chambers. But you have no understanding of our relationship. We were friends first, and I valued him as a person; not for his power."

A knowing smirk twisted Macha's lips. "As a parting gift, I have decided that you shall spend your final night here." She gestured toward the crimson curtain. "Not in the dungeon, and not on the executioner's block. But in the comfort of the late Rí's bedchamber."

The words hit her like a physical blow.

"It seems fitting that you should end your life in the place where you most wanted to spend it. I have supplied you with more than adequate means to take your own life with as little inconvenience to my household as possible."

There it was—just as Faolan had warned.

Macha went on, running her smooth fingers over the red curtain. "If you fail to follow my instructions, your brother will die—along with all your subordinates."

"No!" Lira cried. "Please, my Rání—show them mercy."

"My attendants have already prepared your body for the burial my son would have desired for you, so try not to undo their handiwork. They'll collect it at sunrise."

Lira wrapped her arms around her middle, sinking to her knees as hot tears slid down her cheeks.

Macha paused at the chamber door, her gaze raking Lira from bottom to top. Her lip curled. "You're ruining your makeup, my dear."

The lock engaged loudly behind her.

Lira's tears flowed freely as she turned in place, truly taking in everything around her for the first time. This was where Eremon had lived. Where he had dreamed. Where he had planned to share his life with her.

Faolan said not to give in. He had ordered her to disobey. Lira sighed, grasping the heavy curtain; how was she to resist Macha's wishes if that meant her brother—and her friends— would die?

She prayed Aidryn and his family had cleared the city before they were seized, too.

Lifting the curtain, she stepped into Eremon's bedchamber. Golden sunset streamed into the room, illuminating everything inside. Her eyes snapped to Eremon's bed before she could stop them.

Lira's horrified shriek pierced the silence. There, on the massive canopy bed, the late Rí's body lay in state.

CHAPTER 20

Lira's hand flew to her mouth, her eyes fixed on Eremon. He was dressed in ceremonial robes of azure and gold silk, his hair carefully tied at the nape of his neck. His skin had taken on an unearthly sheen, and it bore no evidence of his torturous death.

In death, Eremon looked almost as beautiful as he had while he lived, but his powerful charisma and youthful energy had faded with him. Heart aching, Lira lay her hand on one of his; it was as cold as stone. Her ring pulsed dully, like a fading heartbeat—as if it *knew* he was truly gone.

The full weight of his absence crashed into her. She missed his affection, his companionship, his presence. The darkness and isolation of the dungeon had provided a strange sort of hiding place from the truth. But now, here it was—undeniable and unbearable.

"Forgive me," she wept, kneeling to rest her forehead on the mattress. "I failed you."

Lira held vigil at Eremon's bedside until the night sky began to lighten, and her throbbing knees had gone numb beneath her.

Lira lifted her head to gaze at a small glass table that sat beneath the window on the other side of the chamber. She squinted, unable to make out much more than the glint of vials and bowls upon its mirrored surface.

There it is.

Lira stepped closer to investigate. Upon the table sat an assortment of crystal vials, a decanter of noxious amber liquid, a decorative bowl brimming with tablets of some kind, and a small velvet bag tied with a drawstring. A miniature scroll lay among the selection of poisons, and she plucked it up.

Her stomach clenched as she skimmed a poem crafted by a master calligrapher, the swirling whorls of its letters an enchantment in their own right.

She blinked the haze from her eyes to read:

> *To calm thyself before thy doom,*
> *Take a vial of red or blue.*
> *To slumber deep and never wake,*
> *Seven tablets you must take.*
> *Drink deeply, dear, for when you do,*
> *Swiftest death will come for you.*

Below the poem was an additional, hastily scrawled line of verse:

> *If you're uncertain what you need,*
> *Look no further than the seeds.*

The handwriting was painfully familiar, but Lira's mind was so clouded she couldn't place it.

In the silence, she contemplated her choices. What would it be like, to choose a poison and simply die beside Eremon? Deep down, she knew it wouldn't spare her friends; Macha's ruthlessness would claim them, too.

She reached for the velvet bag and dumped its contents into her palm. Six iridescent seeds pulsed and glowed against her skin, illuminating it with an emerald sheen. In answer, the pendant around her neck began to thrum with power.

These seeds were laced with *her* magic.

Lira turned the scroll over and over, looking for any hint of how she should use the seeds; but there was none.

She moved to the window and looked out over Iathium. Her eyes skimmed the courtyard; three times the usual number of sentries patrolled its perimeter. The gates that led from the Dome into the city were shut and locked, no longer welcoming citizens to come and go as they wished. And in the distance, on the other side of the northern wall, a violet glow illuminated the clouds.

She wondered what chaos had erupted in the streets these past few weeks. While she was imprisoned, she'd heard nothing from the outside—and she hadn't asked. Now, her heart sank as she considered the terror Macha was sure to bring down on those who had inherited the ancient powers.

Rodhlan was poised to repeat its own history; tens of thousands of people, if not more, would die by order of the Raní before this was over. Lira chewed the inside of her cheek; the histories were inside her, Irem had said. How was she supposed to access those memories? Beyond that, how would she ever share them?

If she hadn't allowed herself to fall in love with Eremon, to accept his ring, perhaps she truly could have impacted the continent for the better. Now, she doubted she'd ever be able to set foot inside the archive again.

Her gaze drifted to the south; in the gray light of the coming dawn, she could just make out Clan Mór's mountain range. For the first time since she was a child, she longed for Skelly's embrace, for her stories. Would Skelly even want to see her again? Would her family accept her?

If she had created that vine in the dungeon, perhaps she could grow something tall—perhaps a tree or a collection of sturdy vines—to climb down from the tower. She weighed the seeds in her hand, considering. Who had left them here for her?

Lira's pulse quickened as she palmed the windowpane, searching around its frame for a latch, but there was none. She shoved the poisons off the little table and picked it up, swinging it at the window with all her might. Glass shattered everywhere with a crash, but she was dismayed to find that the window had not broken; only the mirrored surface of the table, whose shards now reflected the peach-and-blue glow of the coming dawn.

She panted, her body drained from the sudden exertion and the jarring impact. Studying Eremon's ring, she wondered for a fleeting moment if, perhaps, it might be a key out—just as it had been a key into the garden. But after a sweep of the chambers, she found nothing.

The first light of morning appeared then as the sun rose from behind Rodhlan Ridge. A wide, golden beam cut across the chamber, illuminating the curtain into the antechamber. Lira blinked twice as the heavy, crimson fabric parted down the center and eight of Macha's handmaidens filed into the chamber.

She froze, clutching the bag of seeds as the attendants regarded her, seemingly emotionless. They stood shoulder-to-shoulder before her with such quiet poise that their presence was unnerving.

Their matching robes shimmered in the morning sun as they stared Lira down. She pressed her back against the cold marble wall, willing her expression into a stoic mask. Raising her chin, she returned the stare.

For a long moment, the chamber was deathly silent; then, a small sob escaped one of the maidens. Her veil fluttered with the slight movement before her shoulders began to shake, and she took two steps forward before collapsing to her knees.

One of the other young women snapped a finger, and two of their company stepped forward, scooping the girl up by her arms and dragging her toward the center of the room. Lira retreated, backing away from them as the crying girl began to shake her head frantically. The veil seemed to ripple in slow motion as they released her to the floor, her knees slamming into the pile of broken glass and shattered poison vials. Blood seeped through the fabric, oozing from the cuts on the girl's knees and shins as she whimpered.

"Avert your eyes," said a familiar voice from the other side of the crimson curtain.

Lira felt faint when Macha emerged into the chamber. Her eyes went wild when she saw Lira, and her lips parted as thought she might scream.

Immediately, the handmaidens dropped to their knees and bowed their heads. The Raní briefly locked her gaze with Lira's.

"For your defiance, Heir of Iathium," Macha crooned, offering a mocking bow to cover the panic on her face, "they must all pay a price."

Macha knelt beside the sobbing girl, ripping off her veil. Silky red tresses spilled over the maiden's shoulders, her face blotched with tears as she hurled a gaze full of loathing at Lira.

Lira's heart sank as she realized exactly what price the handmaidens would be forced to pay for her resistance. The deaths weren't only reserved for her friends.

"No!" she cried.

The older woman inclined her head toward the girl on the floor, her velvety voice as smooth as her robes. "Make your choice or I shall make it for you."

There were few choices of poisons left to be made; the broken vials' contents had destroyed most of the tablets. Lira watched in horror as, hands trembling, the girl scraped a handful of the remaining poison tablets into a palm. She stared down at them, as if she couldn't quite comprehend what to do next.

"Now, girl."

The echoes of the girl's sobs filled the room as she forced the tablets into her mouth and tilted her head back, squeezing her eyes shut. Her body slumped to the floor seconds later, tears leaking from beneath her closed eyelids as she died in the pile of glass.

Lira hit her knees.

"Ladies?" Macha called, her voice as smooth and cool as polished marble. "Step forward."

The other maidens turned around again, but started at the sight of their friend, dead in the center of the room. Despite Macha's beckoning, they did not move from where they stood.

"We will obey our Raní's orders," one of the maidens said, her voice an eerie monotone. "Our lives for the prisoner's failure to comply."

"*I* will not die today," a lilting voice declared from beneath one of the veils.

Lira raised her head at the sound of that voice. Her eyes met the shimmering veil of the young woman who now approached. The handmaiden moved smoothly across the room toward the Raní, whose face darkened with rage.

"You will obey," Macha warned, an edge to her voice that did not befit her carefully-cultivated demeanor.

"I live to serve, heir of Rasu. But I do not serve to die."

As the maiden forced the last word out through gritted teeth, she lunged at Macha. Lira shrieked as the horrible, familiar black lightning buzzed and popped between the girl's fingers.

Macha flailed and struggled. She arched involuntarily into the handmaiden's touch; the lightning was magnetizing, holding Macha in place until its brutal work was done. When the Raní finally went limp, the handmaiden's power fizzled out. Thick, pounding silence overtook the room as the body crumpled unceremoniously onto the floor.

The handmaiden flexed her fingers before abruptly turning her attention to the horrified ladies, who were frozen in place near the curtain, clutching one another.

"Run!" she hissed. "Save yourselves!"

None of the maidens spared a glance back as they scrambled toward the antechamber.

When silence had again fallen, the remaining handmaiden turned to Lira, reaching up to remove her veil. Familiar blue eyes peered out first, then a thick golden braid tumbled from the veil's confines.

"Lira," Caitir breathed, eyes shining as she reached a hand toward her friend.

Lira rose to her feet slowly, warily. "You killed her."

"Don't be silly; I'm not powerful enough to kill her."

Caitir's attention drifted to the bag of seeds in Lira's hand before she looked up again. Ever so slowly, she moved closer.

"I've come to get you out," she said in a low, soothing voice.

Lira backed away a step. "That measure of power Macha told me about—she gave it to you."

A small nod. "That's right." Another step forward. "You shouldn't be afraid of us, Lira."

Lira stepped back again. "You never told me you had dark magic."

"We all do what's best for ourselves in the end, don't we? You did," Caitir said, moving closer.

"We?"

Her friend faltered. "Mother and I."

"What about your father and brothers?" Lira asked.

Caitir shrugged slowly. The movement was graceful and smooth. "They know partial truths."

Lira's eyes narrowed. "I don't believe that."

"I promise, I will explain everything. But first, you need to come with me." Her tone took on a pleading edge. "It's only a matter of time before we're caught."

Lira considered. It was true she hadn't the faintest idea how else she'd get out of the tower alive. And the healer *had* said someone would come for her.

The clatter of armor in the winding stairwell reached their ears. "Hurry!" Caitir pleaded, only a step away from Lira now, hand outstretched. "I can get us out!"

The sentries were getting closer. "How?"

"It's called *turas*—magic—I'll explain later."

In Lira's moment of hesitation, Caitir lunged, looping an arm around her waist as she produced a small golden key. She grabbed Lira's tree pendant and pressed her key against it.

An inky void swallowed them whole as pendant met key. Caitir shrieked and Lira's stomach churned as they hurtled through the darkness, clutching one another. It felt as though they had both been engulfed by that burning, black power Caitir wielded. The magic popped and sparked around them, the smell of singed fabric and hair filling Lira's nostrils.

As suddenly as it had begun, the *turas* was over, and the girls found themselves tangled together in the courtyard of the Tarlach estate. Caitir pushed herself to her hands and knees, arms trembling.

Lira's entire body ached, her head swimming as she blinked to clear her vision. She wanted to rise, but her limbs protested; it felt like an impossible weight had settled over her entire body. Her lips parted, but all she managed was a low moan. Resignedly, she let her body relax into the soft grass.

She heard footsteps and the swish of heavy fabric against the cobblestones as someone approached.

"Good girl," a familiar voice cooed. "I knew you'd bring her to me."

CHAPTER 21

Aila Tarlach knelt in the grass and brushed Lira's tousled curls from her forehead with slow, soothing strokes before pressing a kiss to her brow.

"You're quite a sight," Aila crooned. "Let's get you inside."

"Why didn't you tell me?" Lira slurred.

Something flashed in Aila's eyes—something that, perhaps, had always lingered under the surface. With a sly smile, she tilted her head, stroking Lira's hair again.

"Do you believe you're entitled to all knowledge, little scholar?"

Aila stood, her gown swaying with the movement. "Árchú!" she called.

Lira wanted to flee, but her body still felt like dead weight. Terror filled her at the thought of Macha's kin taking her anywhere.

"Take her upstairs," was all Aila said as the burly Árchú—Caitir's eldest brother—approached. He scooped Lira up effortlessly.

The sudden movement triggered an intense wave of nausea she could barely suppress. She tensed in Árchú's arms, too nauseous to fight back as he carried her through the small courtyard and into the house.

He jostled her roughly as they ascended the stairs toward the chambers on the second level. The thick fabric of his jerkin chafed her cheek, and the pads of her fingertips met a leather square sewn onto the breast of his garment. Stamped deep into the soft leather was the image of a key.

Vivid images began to flash before her eyes, unbidden: *A processional led by eight massive, gray horses. Rí Corlan's body lying in state within a glass casing, his folded hands grasping an ancient golden key. A stone sepulcher attended at every corner by hooded, cloaked figures who sit as if frozen in eternal mourning. A young Eremon, tears streaming down his cheeks.*

Lira gasped, stiffening in the man's arms. She felt her eyes open, yet her sight was not her own. Her body writhed against the magic.

"Mother, her eyes!" Caitir cried. "What's happening?"

"Get her onto the bed," Aila ordered. "And bind her."

Árchú's grip on Lira tightened as her back arched violently. She felt herself being lowered onto something soft, then released.

Lira began to regain consciousness while he bound her ankles and wrists, tying tight knots in the rough rope. The circular room was built of ancient stone, with an arched ceiling made of centuries-old wood. Morning sunlight filtered in through the narrow windows that lined the outer wall.

Aila wasted no time hovering over Lira and grasping her chin. She forced Lira to look at her.

"What did you witness?" Aila's voice was edged with hunger.

Lira tried to shake her head; instead, her eyes rolled back again. Aila's palm met her cheek with a loud crack, the sting jolting Lira into awareness.

"Tell me!"

"Nothing," she rasped, trying to hide the tremor in her voice.

Aila assessed her with an exacting gaze. "No wonder Eremon kept you as his pet. You're more powerful than I expected."

Her dark eyes were cold and emotionless. Caitir stood four paces behind her mother, her gaze carefully trained on the bedpost.

"Caitir," Lira pleaded, "help me. We can end this now."

Caitir's eyes drifted lower—to the wooden floorboards. "Just give her what she wants," she whispered resignedly.

Lira's heart sank. "Caitir," she pleaded, "why are you doing this? We were friends, you and I—we—" Tears clouded her vision.

"Don't, Lira." Caitir murmured, shaking her head. "It'll be easier if you don't fight it."

Lira tried to focus on Aila once more, struggling to contain the rising panic in her voice. "What is it that you want?"

"Witness Tree of Rodhlan," Aila breathed, each syllable slithering over her tongue like the warning hiss of a coiled viper. "I want this rare power of yours."

She sat on the edge of the mattress next to where Lira lay, the gesture's intimacy in stark contrast to her intent. Lira fought back memories of all the childhood nights when Aila had tucked her into bed beside Caitir—nights when Lira had wished she was truly Caitir's sister.

"I thought of you all as family," Lira whispered, training her gaze on Caitir. "Was I ever anything to you?"

Aila's eyes fell to the ring. "You were useful when it counted —let's see if that holds true."

A heavy, oppressive power settled over the room. Lira felt the pressure in the air change, as if the very atmosphere wrapped itself around her head and squeezed. Her ears popped. In response to the surge of magic, her ring heated, spreading a warmth over her body that was almost calming.

Then came the familiar emerald glow that emanated from the filigree tree around her neck. Magic pulsed with each beat of Lira's heart.

Caitir's eyes widened as the powers mingled in a blaze around Lira. Aila watched with a wry, knowing smile.

"You see, my dear?" she asked her daughter. "You shouldn't feel ashamed of our secrets. Silira has been keeping plenty of her own."

The girls locked eyes again. This time, Caitir didn't hide her contempt.

"Caitir, help me," Lira pleaded.

"Friends don't lie to one another," Caitir replied, her tone eerily steady. "They don't destroy one another's lives."

"So you say," Lira was surprised at the edge in her own voice. "So you *do*."

"You've never trusted me in your precious archive," Caitir pressed. "You think you're better than *everyone*. I let you think I couldn't read, just to see how you'd treat me—and I was right."

"You said you couldn't—that you didn't care about it," Lira cried. Her own tone made her cringe as it rose higher, more desperate.

Caitir laughed airily. "Did you really believe that, Lira? Why would I *choose* to be inferior to you in any way?"

"She always was too honor-bound and idealistic to question anyone's word," Aila added. "Too immersed in the past to see what was happening before her eyes."

The statement's sheer truth felt like a blow to the gut.

"Caitir—" She tried to laugh, but it fell flat. "This is like one of those silly quarrels we got into as children. It doesn't make sense."

Caitir barreled on, ignoring Lira. "You were always closer to

Aidryn than you were to me. I had to beg for your attention. Even your own brother got your scraps, at best."

"That's not true." But there *was* just enough truth in the statements that they struck right where they were meant to. Lira curled in on herself in shame.

"You broke my heart, sneaking around with Eremon. Did you think we wouldn't figure that out? And Aidryn was crushed. Why else do you think he's been avoiding you?"

Lira tried to recite the truths in her mind, but Caitir's words sank deeper.

"Did you know that I'm descended from a god, Lira?" Caitir raised her chin. "What can you do, with that fragmented magic of yours? I can grow beyond ruler to become a mortal goddess. But what will you become?"

Lira's sight winked out for a moment, leaving only the emerald glow in its wake. As quickly as it had left her, it returned. The room came into focus again, sharper and more vivid than ever. And Lira didn't hesitate when she whispered, "Witness Tree."

Caitir gave her a curt nod. "We'll see."

Black veins of power crackled between the Aila's fingertips as she reached for Eremon's ring. Her pale hands were stronger than they looked as her fingers locked on it. She began pouring her power into the band, immobilizing Lira.

Lira felt herself weaken with each moment. A defiant scream ripped from her throat at the thought of escaping one prison, only to be bound again by those she'd once considered her closest friends. Her chosen family.

The realization stung more than the scorching power.

"Quiet, or I will burn your tongue out myself!" Aila shouted through gritted teeth.

The power in Lira's ring flared, sending a shudder through Aila as she doubled down.

"Caitir!" Aila cried. "Help me!"

Caitir strode forward and reached for Lira's pendant then, closing her fingers around it. Her look of triumph was immediately replaced by one of horror—at the exact moment the reek of burning flesh reached Lira's nostrils.

When Caitir withdrew her trembling hand, her fingers and palm were covered in bleeding blisters. Her eyes went wide with horror.

Aila grabbed her daughter's wrist in a tight grip. "Stupid, careless wretch!"

Caitir began to sob, the initial shock of her injury giving way to rage. "I hate you," she shrieked at Lira. "You ruined everything!"

The chamber door banged open then. Aila let go of Lira's hand, and the pulsing power retreated.

Silence fell over the room—except for Caitir's cries—as Aidryn stepped inside, surveying the women before him. His gaze rested on Lira, and his lip curled into a sneer.

"What a mess you are," he drawled.

Tears pooled in Lira's eyes.

Aidryn then looked to Aila and Caitir. "I told you not to do anything stupid," he snapped. "Now you've ruined your hand."

"She will be fine." But Aila's gaze drifted to her daughter's palm, suddenly doubtful.

Aidryn adjusted the sword that hung at his hip—something Lira had never seen him wear. "You should have consulted me; I could've helped you avoid this. You'd already have the ring by now, if you'd bothered to ask."

"Why?"

"Because the ring is a key." He sat on the foot of the bed.

Aila's eyes widened. "How long have you known this?"

He shrugged. "Not long. But I know the spells Eremon put on this ring. I think I can unravel them, if you give me time."

"I will give you all the time you need, but you will answer for this power you've hidden."

"You knew I had it all along, Aila," he replied, turning his attention back to Lira. "And now it serves your purpose."

"You snake!" Lira snarled, heaving herself forward to spit in Aidryn's face.

"Temper," he murmured, dragging his wrist across his cheek. "Is that all you can manage, with the power you possess?"

Aidryn leaned over her, bracing one arm by her side as he traced her jaw with his fingertips. She averted her eyes, tears sliding down her cheeks. "I thought you were smarter than this," he whispered.

Pressing against her chin, he turned her face toward his again, his expression unreadable. Lira could hardly tell him from the man who had begged her to run with him. Maybe he'd only meant to capture her like Caitir had.

"If you had paid attention to something other than your precious Eremon, you might have figured this out already." Aidryn's fingers drifted to the pendant, which had come to rest over her sternum. "Or maybe you wouldn't have. Perhaps your intelligence only applies to books."

When his fingertips made contact with the pendant, the bronze singed his skin, too, and he jerked his hand away with a hiss.

"I warned you, but you're so stubborn, Silira." His breath was hot on her face; for a disarming moment, his tone softened to that plea from the cottage. "Why couldn't you listen?"

"Please," she whispered. "Just let me go. I'll disappear; I'll never set foot in Iathium again."

Aidryn huffed a laugh. "Oh, you'll disappear, that's certain."

Lira tried to recoil further as he leaned in, invading her space. His gaze fell on her lips; he never looked away from her face as he called to Aila and Caitir. "Leave us for a moment; we have one final score to settle before you tear her apart."

Lira lost control then, and a loud sob broke from her. She

bit her lip and tried to take hold of the power inside her. Surely, she could figure out how to use it against him—against them all.

"Of course, Aidryn; it's so little to ask," Caitir said, eyes gleaming maliciously. "Help her understand how we suffer at her hands."

"Indeed," he said quietly, tucking a curl behind Lira's ear. "She has haunted us all."

There was a hint of tenderness in his gaze that gave Lira pause. For a moment, he had been so frighteningly convincing, she'd believed him to be her enemy. But he couldn't keep up the charade, nor could he fully harden the familiar kindness she had known for so long.

Lira hoped she was right—that the affirming tug in the back of her mind wouldn't lead her astray.

Aila raised her chin and glanced between her children, clearly reluctant to let Lira out of her sight. "It is too much to ask," she said.

"What is too much," Aidryn said, glancing over his shoulder at Aila, "is allowing your daughter's hand to scar. After all the work you've done to keep her glowing like a newborn star, would you let this clan filth ruin her perfect skin?"

Caitir looked like she might faint as horror washed over Aila's expression. "We'll have her hand anointed and bound," she said. "Settle your score before we return."

She left the room in a rustle of skirts, Caitir on her heels. The door slammed, locks rattling as the sound reverberated through the chamber. Aidryn lifted his hand, and the locks engaged on their own. The keys appeared in his palm a split second later, then vanished once more.

"Please, Aidryn—" Lira began, her voice wavering. She flinched when he reached for the ropes that restrained her.

He withdrew at her discomfort, searching her face as he said, "I want to release you; may I?"

Lira could only nod, her face crumpling as he raised his trembling hands over the ropes that bound her and murmured a spell that severed them. Once she was free, he made a show of dropping his blade to the floor; it skittered halfway across the chamber and Lira sat up, eyeing it.

Slowly, Lira pushed herself to the bed's edge. Her limbs ached, and she sucked in a sharp breath at the pain that gripped her back. Her wrists and ankles were rope-burned and bruised, blood blisters already forming in dark rings around them.

She was keenly aware of the scant nightgown she'd been dressed in the night before. Although it was long, the fabric was thin, her skin pebbling in the cool morning air. She wrapped her arms tightly around herself and averted her eyes; she didn't know what to say to him, or how to begin.

As if mirroring her thoughts, Aidryn turned and crossed to a wardrobe against the far wall. He rifled through it for a moment before producing a worn-out jerkin and tossing it to her. She thought he seemed reluctant to look at her; he kept his back turned while she slipped the jerkin over her gown.

Lira licked her dry, cracked lips and said tremulously, "Are we now to settle our score, Aidryn?"

Aidryn returned to the bedside then; he dropped to his knees before Lira, his face contorted with grief, tears welling in his eyes.

"There is no score, Lira, but please, forgive me for what I said and implied." His words tumbled out in a breathless rush. "Nothing else would have convinced them to leave, but what I said—" he stopped for a moment to bite back a sob—"I can still taste the filth of it. I would never—not in this lifetime or any other—do *anything* to hurt you. I hope you can still trust me."

Relief rushed over Lira; she *had* been right about him, but she wasn't ready to show her hand. "You let me believe you would harm me in the worst way possible."

"To spare us both the damage their magic would do otherwise," he replied. "You and I both know we're at a disadvantage here; our power is untested against theirs.

"Forgive me, Lira, *please*," he begged, his chin quivering. "I need you to trust that I'm the Aidryn you've always known."

She pressed her lips together reluctantly, wracking her thoughts for a solution. "When you asked me to come with you, back at the cottage," she began, "was that so you could bring me here?"

"Never," he whispered vehemently. "I asked you to run with me because I care for you."

Lira considered his words, knowing he spoke true, for warmth filled her at his answer. Still, she feared her own perception. "Why didn't you warn me about Aila?" she demanded. "Caitir?"

Aidryn sighed. "I pretended to be on their side to gain information, and to hide the fact that my magic was emerging again. It's part of why I left the archive; my power was interfering with my work, and I couldn't risk blurting the truth to you before it was time."

He rubbed the back of his neck, giving the details a moment to sink in. When he looked at Lira again, his gaze was sorrowful. "I hoped you could use the seeds to escape the tower on your own. But if not, I knew Caitir would bring you here."

Lira's eyes widened in surprise. "The seeds were from *you*?" She thought she'd recognized the handwriting.

"Yes. I had Faolan sneak them in."

Something else he'd said struck a chord in her and sparked her curiosity. "What did you mean about your magic emerging *again*?"

"May I share my memory with you?" he asked.

Lira didn't want to continue denying him forgiveness when

she knew his sincerity, down to her bones. When their time was quickly running out. She nodded her consent and whispered, "If you think we have the time."

He released a ragged sigh before moving slowly toward her and taking her face tenderly in his hands.

"Silira," he whispered, "witness."

Lira was overtaken by a rush of memories—Aidryn's memories, long suppressed. They weren't vivid, as the other memories she'd witnessed until now; instead, they were hazy and dark with neglect, having been buried so deeply within him for so many years.

A child lies supine, chained to a crude wooden table in the center of a windowless chamber. He looks about eight years old, and he is eerily calm. A younger Aila stands over him, holding hands with a tiny Caitir, who surveys the scene with rapt curiosity.

"Will she be safe?" Aidryn asks in a small voice. "Will my magic make her well?"

"Yes," his mother replies coolly.

"Promise?" His lower lip trembles—the first real sign of fear he's shown since he agreed to save his sister's life.

"She will be well enough to become Raní someday."

He squeezes his eyes shut with a shuddering breath. "Then do it. I want this to be over."

Aila hoists Caitir up onto the table. The little girl lies down beside her brother, wrapping her arms around him tightly.

"Are you afraid?" she whispers timidly as her mother positions her onto her back beside him.

Panic swells in him, but he shakes his head, and she tightens her grip on his hand. Aila raises her hands above them. A bright crimson glow radiates from her palms, and she places them on Aidryn, chanting the siphoning spell.

As she draws her hands upward, Aidryn screams; his back arches violently away from the table. A tower of crimson light bursts from his chest and into his mother's hands, who unceremoniously slams it down onto Caitir. The little girl loses consciousness, her tiny body sprawled lifelessly on the table.

When Aila's task is complete, she checks Aidryn's pulse. A serpentine grin spreads across her mouth. Satisfied, she severs his chains with a flick of her wrist, gathers her daughter into her arms, and leaves her son to regain consciousness alone in the dungeon room.

He whimpers with pain as the darkness envelops him, merciless cold seeping into his bones. The empty place in his chest throbs as he cries himself to sleep on the table, freezing and utterly exhausted.

Lira's sight returned abruptly as Aidryn let go of her face. A stillness settled over her as she studied the tears that now slipped down his cheeks. She could still feel the little boy's terror in the dark, quiet dungeon—the stripped sort of emptiness left behind in the wake of Aila's plundering.

"Did it work?" Lira whispered, lowering herself onto the floor to face him.

"Only elements of it," he whispered, surprise in his expression as he registered her proximity. "But I will always be the Key Keeper; my stepmother couldn't take that from me."

His words stunned her. "Stepmother?"

"My mother died giving birth to me," he answered. "I was born of two Tarlach descendants; Caitir was not. I suppose that made all the difference."

"Aidryn, how much of your life has been a lie?" she breathed.

He offered half a shrug, and she could tell he was trying to appear indifferent as he answered, "Almost as much as yours."

Timidly, Lira reached for his hand and grasped it tightly. "I forgive you," she finally said.

Aidryn gave her fingers a gentle squeeze. "I'm sorry I frightened you. It was the only way to get rid of them. I would never hurt you." His voice broke. "I swear on my life."

Lira met his gaze. "On your horse's life," she whispered.

"Yes, curse that pony."

She almost smiled.

He swallowed hard, now weighing something in his free hand; Lira peered closer to see the velvet bag of seeds she'd found in the tower chamber.

"I'm glad you brought these," Aidryn said, placing the bag into her hand and helping her stand. "Let me show you how they work."

CHAPTER 22

Warily, Lira followed Aidryn to a window that overlooked the grounds below, and he braced his hands on the stone sill.

"Envision roots springing from the ground, winding into a great tree," he said. "Then take a seed from the bag. When it begins to glow, drop it just there." He pointed straight down.

"What will happen?" Lira asked.

Aidryn glanced over his shoulder at the chamber door. "With luck, we'll have a tree to climb down."

Lira nodded and closed her eyes, visualizing a sprawling network of strong roots beneath the estate. She imagined not just one tree, but an entire forest springing up around the tower home. When Lira opened her eyes, emerald light sparked in her palms; Aidryn drew one seed from the velvet bag. A tendril of her magic reached for the seed, plucking it from Aidryn's hand.

The iridescent seed hovered above Lira's palm, its glow pulsing and brightening with each passing second. It began to sprout before their eyes.

"Now, Lira," Aidryn whispered, his voice edged with panic.

Lira leaned out the window and dropped the seed. It tumbled down, a trail of her magic following it as it penetrated the soil. Emerald light pierced the ground, spreading to illuminate the lush grass.

A deep rumbling rose from the earth and the ground began to quake. The house shook violently as hundreds of enormous roots rippled up from beneath the soil, splitting its foundation. Lira stumbled backward into Aidryn, and he reached out to steady her as they gaped at the magic unfolding before them.

The roots rose, winding together into tree trunks as they climbed the sides of the house. Large branches burst from the trunks, splitting and multiplying as the trees grew larger and taller.

The stones that held the large house together began to loosen and shift, some cracking and falling away completely as the trees squeezed the structure. Leaves bloomed on every branch and twig until the entire Tarlach home had been swallowed up by a veritable forest.

From outside the chamber door, Lira could hear Aila fighting to regain entry. Her shrieks of outrage sent a chill up Lira's spine, and she broke into a cold sweat, knees nearly buckling as Aidryn hoisted himself up and over the sill, testing the nearest branch with his boot. He stepped carefully into the tree. Once he had found his footing, he turned back toward Lira, reaching one arm toward her.

"Come on!" he ordered. "Climb!"

She hesitated, hands shaking. Suddenly, she was keenly aware of her physical weakness.

"I can't," she whimpered.

"I won't let you fall." He leaned closer, hand outstretched. "I swear—on Fannin's life, if that makes you feel better."

"Pony doesn't stand a chance," she muttered.

Lira sat on the sill, trying not to lose her nerve with every crash against the chamber door. Aidryn must have enchanted the locks—but they wouldn't hold for long if his battering ram of a brother burst straight through the wood.

She reached for Aidryn's arm and gripped it; he braced her as she lowered herself onto the branch nearest his. He was surprisingly strong, for someone who'd spent nearly as much time poring over books and scrolls as she had.

Her heart pounded, palms sweating as she found a foothold in the giant tree.

"Help, help, help," she chanted, struggling to keep what little composure she still possessed as they moved slowly downward. She yelped when her bare foot slipped, but Aidryn held fast, snaking his arm around her waist and holding her close as they descended.

Once she got her bearings and began climbing down on her own, Aidryn moved downward through the branches ahead of her, agile and swift. Shifting to an adjacent trunk, he shimmied down, leaping the last few feet to the ground. He landed on his feet and turned to Lira, holding his arms out to her.

"Jump!"

A loud crash sounded from overhead, and they looked up to see Aila at the tower window, red-faced and seething.

"Traitor!" Caitir screamed at Aidryn.

Neither woman made a move to climb down; instead, Aila whirled back toward the chamber, calling for Árchú.

"Now, Lira," Aidryn urged.

Lira let go of the tree and tumbled toward the ground, bracing herself for impact—but Aidryn caught her easily. Aidryn's sharp whistle pierced Lira's ears as he sprinted toward the gates of the estate, hauling her along.

The sound of splintering wood echoed from behind them, coming from the direction of the stables. She heard the thundering of hooves on cobblestones, growing closer and closer.

Then, Aidryn's massive gray stallion galloped into view, his white mane whipping behind him.

"Can you seal them inside somehow?" Aidryn asked through gritted teeth. Fannin was only a few yards away now.

"I don't know!" Lira answered, wild-eyed. She tightened her grip around his neck.

A door leading into the courtyard burst open, and Árchú stalked out, his battle axe in one hand, a hatchet in the other. Aila followed close behind, magic roiling around her fingertips.

"I will kill you both!" Aila screamed as Árchú raised the hatchet, hurling it toward Aidryn, who stumbled as he dodged it. The blade buried itself deep in the ground where he'd been moments before.

"Try!" he begged, regaining his footing.

Lira fished for another seed and threw it toward the house, furrowing her brow. *Trees to enclose them. Massive, hulking, ancient trees with bark as hard as stone—*

The earth quaked just as Fannin reached them; Aidryn threw Lira astride the horse and climbed up behind her, kicking him into a full gallop. Somehow, the stallion managed to keep a steady footing as the ground rumbled and groaned beneath his hooves.

Lira stole a wide-eyed glimpse over her shoulder. Behind them, gargantuan trees burst from the earth, swallowing the Tarlach estate whole. As Fannin careened into the street, Lira thought she could hear screaming and the collapse of stones upon stones over the groans of the expanding forest.

Clutching Fannin's mane fearfully, Lira turned her head. "I have heirlooms from the four clans at the cottage!"

"You what?"

"You said—" She tightened her grip as Fannin jostled them. "We need items!"

Aidryn changed direction, steering Fannin through the market in the direction of Lira's cottage. On a normal day, they would have had difficulty navigating the streets at this pace. But Lira noticed that today, there was almost no one outside. The streets that were usually buzzing with activity were quiet and still, as if some dreaded plague had invaded the city.

They slowed as they approached the little stone cottage; a lump formed in Lira's throat at the reminder of her last days here. Aidryn steered Fannin toward a little alleyway a block behind the house, but paused at the sound of a low whistle.

Lira tensed, but Aidryn braced a hand on her waist, clicking his tongue at Fannin. The stallion pivoted to face a sentry in full regalia, who stood on the walkway that led to the cottage. Her vantage point was different, but Lira recognized the man's height and build. She squinted to make out his features beneath his helmet.

Aidryn dipped his chin in greeting. "Faolan."

"Tarlach." His eyes flicked to Lira. "And you." A curt nod. "Good."

Faolan jerked his chin toward the cottage, turning on his heel to stalk toward it. Aidryn urged Fannin forward. No one spoke as they drew closer to the house.

When they arrived, Aidryn dismounted, then helped Lira to the ground. "We're lucky Faolan's on this rotation." He put a hand on the small of her back, nudging her toward the front door. "Get what you need; I'll be right behind you."

The young men clasped forearms, speaking in hushed tones as Lira made for the cottage.

She slipped into Talfryn's bedchamber, where she found a worn pair of leggings and a blue tunic. Disgusted, she surveyed the now-filthy gown Macha had dressed her in the night before. With a cry of rage, she peeled it off, popping some of the seams in the process, and threw it at the corner of the room as hard as she could. Then, she slipped into her brother's clothes, belted the tunic at the waist, and bolted for her chamber to collect her boots, satchel, and pouch.

Lira met Aidryn in the hallway, strapping the pouch to her belt. Aidryn handed her the shirt of chainmail—he'd dismantled her father's armor while she changed. She put it on, letting its weight settle over her, and wished she had a shirt of mail for him, too.

A loud whistle sounded from outside. Aidryn tensed; Lira could've sworn she saw his hair stand on end.

"Come on."

Her stomach lurched as he grabbed her hand and they bolted for the door. When they reached Fannin, Aidryn gave her a boost.

"Pull your hood up," he ordered.

She obliged, pulling the heavy mail over her head.

Faolan was waiting on the cobblestone street, holding a lighted torch in one hand, an inconspicuous parcel in the other.

"Get her to the north wall," the sentry urged. "Aeron's waiting."

Aidryn spurred Fannin into a full gallop toward the wall that separated Iathium from the roaring falls that tumbled into Beran's Gorge. They had only ridden half a mile when a shuddering explosion warped the world around them. Despite Aidryn shielding her back, Lira could feel the heat from it—could hear the resounding shatter of windowpanes nearby. She tried to turn around to get a glimpse of its source.

"Don't look back," Aidryn called over Fannin's hoofbeats and the wind that rushed around them as they rode. "He's buying us time."

Somewhere deep in her gut, Lira knew Faolan's diversion had once been her beloved home. Despite the fresh grief that flooded her senses, she didn't look back.

CHAPTER 23

The roar of the falls filled the air by the time Aidryn and Lira reached Iathium's northern wall, but they could still hear the unmistakable battle horn as it sounded the alarm from the other side of the city. Sentries would flood the streets soon, some to investigate the source of the blast, others to pursue Lira—if they weren't already on her trail.

The midmorning sun was high; there was no doubt the sentries had discovered her escape and the attack on Macha by now.

A young man with a deep tan and curly, raven hair like Faolan's was waiting near the wall, crouched by a cluster of boulders near the entrance to the falls. He snapped a wary stare in their direction at the sound of Fannin's hoofbeats. Rising, he strode purposefully in their direction, one hand resting on the pommel of the dagger that hung from his low-slung belt. He wore a tunic the color of the stones he'd just abandoned, and his mud-caked boots were scuffed and unkempt.

"You've done it, then," Aeron said by way of greeting. His

lilting accent had a cheerful ring to it—a stark contrast to the grim expression on his face. "Good work."

As Aidryn dismounted, Aeron strode to the stallion's side, extending a hand to Lira. She let him help her to the ground. To her surprise, he knelt and pressed an earnest kiss to her fingers.

"*Sura masi*," he said, hazel eyes shining, "heir of Iathium. Heir of *Rodhlan*."

"Oh..." Lira gaped. She cast a panicked look toward Aidryn, then patted Aeron awkwardly on the shoulder. "Please get up."

"Stop being so dramatic, Aeron." Aidryn took Lira by the elbow and steered her toward the ornamental stone archway that led to the falls. "Let's move."

"What about Fannin?" Lira asked. The stallion stood stock-still, right where they'd left him.

"He'll come for us when we've cleared the gorge," Aidryn said, waving a dismissive hand toward the horse.

"Cleared the gorge? That doesn't make sense!"

Lira trotted behind the men as they approached the falls. Mist sprayed her face as she dared to peer into the yawning abyss. Her father had always said the drop was over four hundred feet.

"Aidryn, you've lost your mind!" she shouted, her palms already slick with sweat. "I'm not clearing any gorge; find an alternative."

"Our only alternative is being impaled by sentries," Aidryn said, his voice raised above the din. "Besides, Aeron's been practicing."

"Practicing how?" Lira didn't attempt to hide her panic.

"Water magic," Aeron said mysteriously, waggling his fingers.

Another Énna, then. Lira could've sworn she saw violet waves crashing in his eyes as he grinned mischievously. He cocked his head toward Aidryn. "Ready?"

Aidryn's gaze slid to Lira for a moment before he nodded curtly and followed Aeron several yards upstream to the river's edge. Both men crouched, dipping their fingertips into the rushing current. Time seemed to slow; Lira could see a violet glow pulsing from Aeron's fingertips—the glow, she realized, that she had seen from the tower.

Aeron's magic spread quickly, just beneath the surface of the water; sunlight illuminated the sparkling power that pushed upstream against the current. Beads of sweat glistened on his forehead.

The water began to churn around his fingertips, forming a small whirlpool; large, violet bubbles pressed against the water's surface on its perimeter, but did not rise. Lira pressed her lips together to keep her questions from tumbling out. She wished she had a quill and parchment to record what she was seeing.

Aidryn shifted uncomfortably, casting a nervous glance in her direction before closing his eyes. He began to sing a low, imploring melody in a language she'd never heard. The sound was almost mournful, beseeching—a siren's song meant to lure out someone... or something. The hair on Lira's arms rose, gooseflesh covering her skin as Aidryn quietly murmured the verses.

Movement in the center of the river caught her eye; slowly, something white rose from beneath the water. It moved closer, unhindered by the raging current, until it broke the surface. She gasped.

It was a luminous horse, so bright it was painful to look at. If Aidryn's song had been the bait, this horse was a snare. Lira mentally rifled through Skelly's old stories—there was a name for this sort of creature, this shape-shifting beast that dragged men, women, and children alike into a watery grave—

"A kelpie," she breathed, her voice barely a whisper. Her eyes widened in wonder.

The water-horse tossed its head, ghostly and entrancing, its silvery mane billowing and drifting around its face. Lira didn't move, didn't breathe as the kelpie glided toward Aidryn, dipping its head low. It gently pressed its forehead to Aidryn's, who kept perfectly still as he continued to sing. After a long moment, it shifted its focus to Aeron; the kelpie drifted to his side and playfully nudged him with its muzzle.

Lira's brows knitted as Aeron huffed a laugh, pulling one hand from the water and drying it on his trousers. He fished in his pocket for a moment, the kelpie waiting impatiently beside him, and produced two sugar cubes. The water-horse made to snatch both, but Aeron managed to hang onto one, holding it teasingly in his fist as the beast attempted to nose his fingers open.

With a start, Lira noticed that Aidryn had waded into the rapids. As he inched closer to the kelpie, still singing under his breath, she saw that he held a bridle in his hand, reins slung over one shoulder.

Aeron rose then, stroking the kelpie's mane with one hand while he teased it with the treat. When Aidryn finally reached the kelpie's side, angling his shoulder near the beast's jaw, Aeron opened his fist, yielding the sugar cube. Aidryn gently lowered the bridle's crownpiece over the kelpie's ears and slipped the bit between its lips.

The kelpie bowed low then so Aidryn could mount it. Lira pressed trembling fingertips to her lips in astonishment as the kelpie again rose to its full height and looked pointedly at her. Following the beast's gaze, Aeron also turned to her, extending a hand.

"Your turn," he whispered.

She took a step backward. "I…"

"As long as you have a bridle," Aeron soothed, "you're safe. He won't harm you."

A glance toward Aidryn, then Aeron, and back again. She

took another step back. "How—" Her words caught in her throat. *How do I know I can trust you?* But now, it was too late for that question. She drew a shuddering breath.

Aeron's eyes flicked to the wall. "Come on."

Despite the roaring of the river and the crashing falls, Lira heard it, too—scores of footfalls approaching the northern wall. The clink of armor and weaponry. The sentries couldn't be more than a city block or two from the archway.

"Lira..." Aidryn murmured in warning. The current rushed around the kelpie's muscular legs.

She moved toward Aeron as quickly as she dared. His shoulders sagged with relief at her approach.

Aeron gripped her waist and hoisted her onto the kelpie, where she settled in front of Aidryn, her back flush against his chest. He looped an arm around her waist and offered her a section of bridle. She wrapped her trembling fingers around it.

"Whatever you do, don't let go," he said.

Lira nodded mutely, heart hammering; she wasn't sure she wanted to know what was about to happen.

"Call the herd," Aeron said, patting the kelpie's flank. He crouched near the large boulders at the water's edge as the beast carried Lira and Aidryn toward the center of the river. Then, he plunged his hands back into the water.

The kelpie's movements were eerily smooth as it drifted away from shore. Soon, the water was up to Lira's waist, and she shuddered, pressing against Aidryn for warmth. But she quickly forgot the cold as four dozen sentries streamed through the archway, spears at the ready.

One sentry raised his voice, pointing his sword toward Aidryn and Lira. "Raní Macha's orders: Return to the Dome at once."

Aidryn straightened behind Lira; she could almost see him throw his shoulders back, leveling a challenging stare at the man.

"*Sanosajo!*" Aidryn shouted. The front line of sentries assumed a fighting stance, spears poised to fly, but stumbled as the ground shook beneath their feet.

Suddenly, a spear of Aeron's magic burst from where he had concealed himself. It launched itself upstream, against the current, and bloomed into a sparkling shower of violet light. A herd of at least thirty kelpies emerged from beneath the gurgling water then, moving toward the shore, and the sentries stopped in their tracks. Some of the men blanched with terror; others stared in dumbfounded wonder.

"*Ano je,*" Aidryn commanded coolly. He steered his kelpie toward the mouth of the falls as a haunting melody drowned the river's roar. The water-horses were... singing.

The song was lilting and magnetic, like the one Aidryn had used to call the kelpie they now sat astride. It bewitched the sentries. Absence filled their eyes as the otherworldly voices drew them in. Wood and steel clattered to the ground as their fingers went slack around their weapons. One by one, the sentries began to venture toward the kelpies, who called to them from the water's edge.

Lira stared, transfixed with horror as the men began to mount the water-horses; they sat tall on the kelpies' backs like a spectral cavalry, vacant eyes shining beneath their helms. Those who didn't find a mount waded in the water up to their necks, vying for a closer look at the majestic creatures.

Aidryn surveyed them, then clicked his tongue.

As one, the herd of water-horses stopped singing and moved into the center of the river until their riders were waist-deep in water. The sentries blinked from their mounts, and comprehension filled their eyes. Almost as one, they began to struggle, but they were stuck fast to the kelpies they sat astride. Even their hands stuck where they held on.

They could not flee.

The men began to cry out, terrified, a split second before

the kelpies dragged them under. Those who had not mounted steeds of their own were pulled into the teeming chaos below. She could hear their screaming from beneath the water's surface as the river bubbled and churned violently.

Lira trembled with horror as a grim-faced Aidryn urged their kelpie forward. She shifted her weight on the water-horse to ensure she wasn't stuck, too, sliding over its side in the process. Aidryn caught her and hauled her upright again.

"It's the bridle," he reassured her. "She's ours to command."

Lira nodded tensely, white-knuckling her section of the reins as the kelpie moved them closer and closer to the water-fall. When they reached the mouth of the falls, the beast paused, unyielding against the sheer power of the crashing water. Lira bit down on her terror, afraid to make a sound.

Aidryn leaned past Lira to stroke the kelpie's withers. "*Anosaje*," he murmured. Then, to Lira, "Hold on." His arm tightened around her waist, and she noticed he was trembling, too.

The world around them seemed to slow as the kelpie galloped forward at full speed and leapt over the mouth of the falls. A scream ripped from Lira's throat as wind and spray whipped at her hair, her face. They were in free fall, hurtling toward certain death at the bottom of the gorge. Behind her, Aidryn was shouting, too, and holding her so fiercely she thought he might shatter her ribs before the impact could.

Their descent slowed, and the kelpie found its footing, easing into a rolling gallop. Lira cracked one eye, then opened both wide as she realized the waterfall had risen to meet the kelpie's hooves and they were no longer falling, but riding down a steep slope of water toward the bottom of the gorge. Aidryn huffed a disbelieving laugh, then threw his head back with a triumphant whoop.

The kelpie moved at breakneck speed, drawing its legs up and gliding into the water at the bottom of the gorge like a phantom swan. Walls of water rose on either side of Lira and Aidryn, then settled as they floated downstream on the water-horse's back. When the pounding of her heart finally slowed, Lira allowed a rush of freedom to fill her—freedom and wonder at what they'd just done.

But then she remembered the terrified sentries who had gone under with the kelpies. They were merely men who had been following orders, and now they were dead because of her. The thoughts ate away at her until finally, she twisted to look at Aidryn.

"Those men back there..." She couldn't bring herself to say it.

Aidryn's expression darkened, his jaw tightening as he fixed his gaze ahead. "We had no other choice. It bought us a chance to escape without pursuit."

"You and Aeron have been planning this," Lira pressed.

He nodded. "Yes."

"For how long?"

"Since the day you and I fought about Eremon—when I asked you to come with me."

Lira sucked in a breath. "And here we are now, despite my resistance."

"We'd started experimenting outside the wall before that," Aidryn offered, not commenting on her remark. "But that was the day I realized we'd need a real escape route."

Lira sighed heavily, facing forward again. She ran her fingers through the kelpie's mane as she ventured, "That day at the cottage—"

"I had my reasons," he cut in, "for everything I said and did. But... I could have handled myself better."

They were silent for the next few miles as the kelpie swam down Beran's Gorge. The afternoon sun barely penetrated the depths of the canyon that ran northeast, toward Rodhlan Ridge. It was cool and dim as they drifted further from Iathium.

Lira took to quietly braiding the water-horse's mane, gently separating and weaving sections of its silky hair.

"I was jealous of him, Lira," Aidryn blurted.

Lira's fingers stilled, her ears burning fiercely. She didn't reply, so Aidryn plowed ahead.

"I understand his reasoning," he said, "for wanting to marry you. Making the Witness Tree both Defender of Histories and Raní would have made the two of you a formidable team."

"Aidryn, it doesn't matter now," Lira whispered. She didn't want to dig too deeply into what had happened to Eremon, or to her as a result—not now. "I should have listened to you."

"I wish you had." He sighed. "I suppose, in the end, we still ran together, didn't we?"

"Yes."

Lira allowed herself to rest against him, remembering that faint scent of freedom that had tempted her. She supposed they were free, though not in the way he'd wanted; and for how long, neither of them could say. Sooner or later, Iathium would come for them.

For now, she wanted to hear more of his story—the parts she didn't know.

"Will you tell me more about your magic?" she asked.

"My mother was the Anointed of Clan Tarlach," he began in a gentle voice, "and my magic manifested early. Father said her full measure of power transferred to me as she was dying."

Lira sucked in a breath.

"I've recalled memories from as far back as two years old, I think," Aidryn continued. "I stole the housekeeper's key ring once, and that's how Aila found out about me. She waited for quite a long time before she attempted to give the magic to Caitir; but she is exceedingly patient."

A chill settled into Lira's bones as she considered not only Aila's failure to give Caitir Aidryn's full power, but her failure to get her daughter onto the throne.

"I can't imagine her wrath, because her patience hasn't been rewarded."

She thought she felt Aidryn shudder behind her. "Indeed, it has not."

Lira feared she might spiral into despair if she didn't keep talking. "Tell me of Caitir's power, then. I saw her use the dark magic in the tower, but what of your magic?"

"Caitir can speak to the horses, as I can. But she never inherited the clan's metalworking abilities, that I know of, or the Key Keeper's power."

"How much of your power did you have left after that?"

"Only a kernel. But I learned how to keep it secret and let the injury heal—well, tried to, at least. Once Irem found out about it, he put me to work transcribing the few Tarlach scrolls he could dredge up, and a measure of the power returned."

"So it was some sort of magical wound?"

He nodded. "I don't know if it will ever fully heal."

She wanted to comfort him, but she wasn't sure what to do or say. Instead, she plowed forward. "When did you find out about my power?"

"I've known about your heritage for years, Lira. Aila has known, too. She always encouraged Caitir to"—he gritted his teeth— "*keep you around* because she knew who, and what, you are."

Aidryn urged the kelpie to move faster. "I've spent the past few years trying to learn what my stepmother's connections are and why she was so interested in our power."

"Macha said Aila is a descendant of Rasu the Vile," Lira offered. "Caitir too, then."

"Yes. I became a scholar, in part, because of Aila. She always spoke of magic, of her bloodline and yours. I wanted access to the archive to see what else I could learn. Imagine my surprise at the lack of magical records." He smiled ruefully. "Ultimately, I stayed and advanced because of you."

Lira bit her lip. "What would you have been, if it weren't for me?"

He released a long breath. "A farrier, I think. I'd be content to live in solitude, with nothing but a pasture full of horses and a mountain of books to occupy my time."

"You're a lot like me, I think," she ventured. "I'd love nothing more than to pore over books all day for the rest of my life, but I'll probably never set foot in the archive again."

"You would've been safe there, at least for a while," Aidryn said.

"I wish I could go back," she whispered.

The water-horse's back was unnervingly cold, and the chilled water lapped around them gently as they moved downstream. Lira allowed herself to sink into Aidryn's warmth—the only thing that kept her teeth from chattering uncontrollably. Despite their nearness, it was a long moment before they spoke again.

The silence grew more palpable until Aidryn broke it.

"After I left the archive, I started working with Aeron and Faolan. We were part of an underground movement to reawaken the clans' magic—we distributed fragments of the true histories for the people to copy by hand.

"But when the healer sent word about what was happening to Eremon, we started evacuating them. We got over five hundred people out of Iathium before *Nami Mostari*."

Over five hundred in mere weeks. How many more did they manage to move after the festival?

"That's why you were so angry about me and Eremon," Lira ventured. "It took your focus away from getting people out."

"In part," he admitted, "but also because Eremon drew too much attention to you. If he'd stuck to our plan to teach you quietly, you would have been safe in the archive for the foreseeable future. But he allowed his emotions to override his common sense. He made a spectacle of you both—"

"That's enough," Lira snapped. She felt the kelpie tense beneath her and lowered her voice. "Whatever your opinion of him, he was good and kind. He loved me." Her voice wavered. "And I loved him."

"I know," Aidryn whispered, "and I'm truly sorry." He shook his head. "By the time I tried to intervene, it was too late."

She bristled. "You really had no business getting involved."

"Didn't I?" He leaned around her side to glare at her incredulously, but she turned her head away. "Your birthright was a target on your back from day one. Eremon wooing you, proposing to you, making you his heir—" A bitter laugh escaped his lips.

"Aidryn, let it rest. I've had enough shame to last a lifetime." Lira couldn't listen to another diatribe about Eremon; for, however tender Aidryn tried to be, his vitriol toward the Rí was palpable. A swell of anger hit her then, and she wished she had something to throw into the river.

Perhaps she could throw *him*.

Aidryn sighed heavily. "Did you know you're the face of the rebellion that's brewing?"

"What?" she asked, incredulous. "The council would never honor this—" She held up the ring. "They didn't respect Eremon then, so why would they now?"

"His actions must have carried some weight," he answered. "They're hanging people from the city gates who dare to speak your name."

Lira blanched; the fragile tether of peace she'd been holding onto snapped, and she felt like she was falling into oblivion with no end in sight.

"Why are you telling me this?" she whispered fearfully.

"Because you need to know what's coming," he answered. "No doubt, your clan will march on the city in due course. Whether or not you embrace their ways, you represent hope for them now. You're the lowly scholar with the most powerful birthright on the continent and the ring of the last Rí on your finger.

"You're the *heir of all things*—that's what they're calling you. They will fight for you, Lira. I will fight for you. There will be war in Rodhlan in your name."

She couldn't reply; bile had risen in her throat, and she was too busy trying to fight it back down.

"Why are you surprised?" he asked—not cruelly, but his words cut deep. "You know as well as I that the people will look to a daughter of the clans to right Iathium's wrongs. The scene is set. And you walked right into the role they're expecting you to play.

"I should've found a good reason to get you out of the city before the festival," he lamented. "By the time I got the nerve to ask, it was too late—I'd already lost you."

Lira blinked away stinging tears. "You didn't understand what I was doing, Aidryn."

"I swear, I did—I do. But that doesn't change the fact that it set us on this course."

It hurt to think her actions had influenced his path so much. "You didn't have to be a part of this."

"I chose to be! I wanted to help. If I could have kept you out of the courtyard that night—"

"If you hadn't locked me in the archive, he might still be alive. I was trying to save him, and you delayed me."

He flinched at her remark, but retorted, "Do you really want to debate about delays when you were gallivanting with him instead of doing your job? You might not realize it, but *studying the histories* is a euphemism in Iathium now. He made a mockery of you."

Lira stilled. Rage roiled in her veins, but she kept her voice a mask of calm. "I think we're finished here."

"*I* was trying to protect you," Aidryn snapped.

"You were trying to control the situation, and I suppose

can't fault you for that. But I still believe I could have helped him."

"Nothing and no one could have stopped that power from erupting," he replied firmly. "I wish you would accept that. Maybe then you'd stop looking for someone to blame."

Lira heaved a sigh, massaging around the braids she'd woven into the kelpie's mane. "We're talking in circles. Maybe we should stop for now."

The dismissal stung her own ears as much as it must have stung Aidryn's, and she considered taking it back, but decided to let it lie. She didn't want to open her mouth and say something worse.

Wordlessly, Aidryn urged the kelpie to move faster downriver toward the yawning mouth of the gorge, and neither of them spoke for a long while after.

CHAPTER 24

As Lira and Aidryn moved downstream, they found themselves vigilant to every sound that echoed through the gorge, every minute shift in the world around them. It was hard to guess when troops from the city might catch up. As if they'd wordlessly agreed to keep watch, they each scanned their respective sides of the gorge wall for prying eyes.

The kelpie seemed to know silence was of the utmost importance, too. It glided soundlessly, effortlessly down the deep, clear stream. She and Aidryn were immersed to their waists in water, their tunics soaked through.

Lira had long since put some distance between herself and Aidryn, abandoning the warmth she'd enjoyed earlier in favor of giving him the cold shoulder. As evening began to fall in the gorge, she grew chilled to the bone.

Aidryn sat behind her, brooding, one hand on the reins, the other on his thigh. Lira didn't know what to do or say; at first, she made up her mind to send him on his way once they reached land. But as the river grew shallower, the canyon walls shorter, the more that felt like a terrible idea.

"Lira," Aidryn whispered, "if you want to alert the whole of Iathium to our location, feel free to keep letting your teeth clack together like that."

With a start, she realized her teeth *had* been chattering loudly. In fact, her entire body was violently shivering. "May I lean against you?" she said in a thin voice.

Without a word, he opened his arm to her, and she shimmied back against his chest. He wrapped his arm around her tightly. Although they were both wet and cold, being nearer was comforting.

Lira ruminated over the words they'd exchanged, gnawing guilt creeping into her gut as she replayed the conversation in her mind. What he'd said to her was inexcusable, but what he'd done to get her out of Iathium... what he'd given up...

Her anger had overridden her common sense. No matter what he thought of Eremon, Aidryn had rescued her, giving up everything in the process. She didn't know what to say to make things right, so she said nothing; besides, apologizing could bolster his belief that he had been right about something that was none of his concern.

Apologizing might also force her to see her time with Eremon as a mistake, and she couldn't bear to frame it that way.

It was sunset by the time the kelpie reached the shallows at the far end of Beran's Gorge, where the water lapped against a shore of smooth, gemstone-colored pebbles. The sky was clear overhead, the setting sun casting a spectrum of color across the horizon.

The lower the sun sank, the more uneasy Lira became. There were no settlements for miles, and the trek into the Rodhlan Ridge would take two more days on foot. They had no tent, nor provisions; it made little sense to separate now, no matter how angry they were at one another.

When the kelpie rose from the water, its white coat glowing faintly in the dusk, the cool air hit in full force. Lira's teeth began to chatter again as she turned to glance over her shoulder.

"Aidryn?" she whispered.

His attention shot to her. "Yes?" He was shivering, too.

"It's two more days' journey until we get to the Ridge," Lira said, her eyes scanning the ridge that loomed in the distance. "Which way do we go from here?"

"Let's make a wide swing eastward and come in on the edge of the Cove, then up the mountainside."

The kelpie stopped in the shallows, the crystal-clear water lapping at its pearl-white hooves. Aidryn dismounted, his boots splashing in the ankle-deep water, and looked up to Lira, extending his free hand toward her. She hesitated, but accepted his outstretched hand.

"You can let go of the reins, but hold onto me," he instructed.

Lira grasped his hand hard as she let go of the reins and slid over the kelpie's side. Her legs were stiff and wobbly from the ride, but Aidryn's grip steadied her as she found her footing on the smooth stones. She made to release his hand, but he squeezed hers in warning. "Don't let go of me until we're out of the water, on the shore."

With a tense nod, Lira squeezed his hand harder. Slowly, carefully, Aidryn slipped the bridle from the kelpie's head, maneuvering Lira behind him as they backed away from the water-horse. He held the bridle at eye level with the beast as they inched onto the pebbled beach. Once they were out of the water, he slung the bridle over his shoulder.

The kelpie bowed low then, and Aidryn returned the bow reverently.

"Thank you," he whispered, resting his palm over his heart as the beast disappeared beneath the surface once more. The only sign of its movements was the faint, white glow beneath the water as it swam back toward the gorge once again.

"I'll never be able to repay you," Lira said, hugging herself against the chill air.

Aidryn shrugged. "I would never expect a friend to repay me."

"And... am I still your friend, after all this?" she ventured.

He squeezed her fingers with an exasperated sigh before he let go. "Don't ask stupid questions. Come on."

Lira gawked at his back as he stalked up the bank. From where they stood, the red and gray walls of the gorge were still at least twenty feet high. She had to jog to catch up to him, and was panting by the time she reached his side.

"After the way you spoke to me, I'm not sure it is a stupid question."

"You weren't exactly—"

"I had every right to be—"

A twig snapped overhead; they paused, still as deer in a clearing, until they were sure there was no one patrolling above the gorge walls. Lira's eyes sparked as she shifted her full focus back to Aidryn, lowering her voice.

"Whatever your opinion of Eremon and me—"

"I understand," Aidryn interrupted. "It would be easy for a man like him to want you. You're more than worthy of him, but it doesn't change the fact that he endangered you.

"I wanted to protect you," he said, his voice tinged with pain. The sound of it gave Lira pause. "I wanted to see you safe in the archive, not thrown into the dungeon, and not running across the continent like a criminal."

Lira tried to laugh. "But I am a criminal." The words felt like lies on her tongue.

Aidryn's eyes glistened with tears. "You should have your nose stuck in those dusty old books right now, not—" His voice broke. "Not this."

Lira felt her eyes prick, too. "He never meant for harm to come to me," she whispered.

"I know."

The way he looked at her—the depth of the pity in his expression...

Lira shivered, breaking his gaze. "It's cold. Let's keep moving."

The smooth stones squeaked beneath their boots as they hiked toward a steep path that had been carved into the gorge wall. During daylight, it was frequented by travelers going to and from Clan Beran's settlement, which was north of the river, deep inside an offshoot of the gorge the kelpie had passed hours earlier.

"Should we have gone to Fortress Halgeir?" Aidryn asked, as if reading Lira's thoughts. "Surely the overlord's wife would welcome her own child."

"No," she said, climbing up onto the walkway. "And Artur would sooner send us straight back to the Dome. He won't risk his clan, from what I remember of him." She moved slowly and steadily up the path; the stone had been rubbed slick from centuries of wear.

"Artur always said Talfryn and I were too loyal to Iathium. Anyone who isn't expressly loyal to the overlord is considered a threat—child, stepchild, or no."

"Delightful man," Aidryn mused.

"Mmm. They were right; I *was* too loyal to Iathium, to a fault. But even if I'd known what I know now..." She sighed. "I still wouldn't have gone to Beran. I suppose I'd be with Skelly instead."

Add that to my long list of failures.

"With any luck, Irem will still be there when we arrive at Clan Mór," Aidryn said.

"You've had word from Irem?" she pressed. She pushed her body to keep climbing. "I didn't expect him to write."

A muscle in Aidryn's jaw ticked. "His letter was cryptic. From what I understand, he wasn't given access to Skelly."

"Why?"

"He said the master was indisposed—on a journey into the city, ironically. But no one else dared let him speak with her."

With a sinking feeling, she realized her uncle Gerallt would've been the first to hear of her downfall. She tried to smother the panic that rose with the thought.

"Gerallt still makes deliveries himself," she panted. "Weapons and armor."

The path was so steep, they were practically crawling now. Lira's clothes and boots were still soaked, and the wet leather was slick against the stones. They grew silent, focusing on their movements up the incline and speaking only when they paused to catch their breath.

"If he's master now, why would he bother?" Aidryn asked when the ground finally began to level out.

She shrugged. "He's not one to give up control. Perhaps his business with the Dome is more important to him than over-seeing the clan."

"That's not how Irem's letter made it sound."

Lira caught herself as her foot slipped on the walkway again. "How did he make it sound?"

"I don't want to misinterpret, but..." Aidryn chewed his lip. "I think Gerallt is ruling the clan like a lord."

"Ruling the clan, yet doing business at the Dome," Lira mused. "Should we even be heading toward the mountains?"

"If we're not going to Halgeir, what choice do we have? Clan Énna's settlement is near the western coast now; we could go to them, but that's another four days' journey, at least. Besides, the only Énnas I know are in the city right now."

"But in the Ridge, there's familiar territory," Lira added. "There's my family. There's Skelly."

"Your birthright."

Lira's stomach clenched as she paused to look down at him,

nodding once. "I think going into the Ridge is a calculated risk. If you don't want to come with me..."

"We'll go together."

Lira dipped her head in agreement and began moving again, her pace slowing as exhaustion threatened to flatten her.

"Do you think Irem is in danger?" she whispered. "Or Skelly?"

Aidryn's eyes slid to her. "I don't know."

She knew he was lying, but she was too tired to press him—or perhaps she'd known the real answer before she asked.

They kept moving until they reached the top of the gorge wall, which opened into a wide, airy meadow that stretched for miles. The rolling meadowlands began outside the city walls and covered one-third of Rodhlan, stretching all the way to the mountain range and the western seaside cliffs of the continent. While the land was mostly bare, it was dotted with sparse clusters of willow trees and a scattering of large boulders.

Before they emerged into the meadow, they crouched on the walkway, careful to remain out of sight.

"If we're seen," Aidryn whispered, "I want you to try something. Listen closely."

Lira nodded mutely, her legs trembling from the climb.

"You can make plants and trees do anything you want—even become weapons. It's a matter of imagining what you want to create, like you did this morning. Think of it like... reaching out with your mind and your magic to touch the objects you want to manipulate, then creating a picture in your mind of what you want."

"How would I turn a tree into a weapon?"

"Make a javelin out of a heavy branch. Fashion a bow and arrows. Harden the leaves so they become impenetrable. We could try that for shelter."

"Or armor," she mused.

"Exactly."

She nodded, wrapping her arms around herself. The chain-mail had long since grown heavy and cold. "I don't suppose you have any warming magic hidden away."

"No," he chuckled, "but the next best thing is waiting by the willows."

Lira squinted in the dusk. Ahead of them, standing patiently near a copse of trees, was Fannin. The gray stallion's white tail swished as he regarded them.

"How..." Lira breathed.

"Don't you remember," Aidryn whispered, "that pony is incredibly fast."

"And smart," she supplied. Aidryn grinned proudly, jerking his chin toward the horse as he rose, stepping from the stone walkway onto the soft meadow grass. Fannin dipped his head as they strode toward him, scanning the area for pursuers.

As they drew closer, Lira sighed with relief at the sight of the heavy saddlebag slung over Fannin, bulging with what she hoped were provisions. A heavy blanket was strapped beneath his saddle. Her fingers tingled with the anticipation of touching it, of wrapping it around herself to shield from the night air.

Aidryn saw her gazing longingly at the saddlebag and blanket as they reached Fannin's side. "Aeron packed food and water. Let's pray it's enough for the rest of the journey."

He helped Lira climb astride the stallion, then climbed on behind her, gripping the reins. "Let's get to Acton's Cove before we stop for the night."

"But that's another day's ride from here," Lira said, shivering.

Aidryn eyed her, slipping one arm around her waist. "Not for Fannin." A grin tugged at the corner of his mouth. "I suggest you hold on."

Lira barely had time to grip the stallion's saddle before Aidryn clicked his tongue and Fannin was galloping toward the mountain range. What began as a steady, rolling run quickly became the famed speed of the purebred Itelorian bloodline.

Her eyes watered as Fannin's gray mane lashed her cheeks, the evening wind whipping so hard she could barely draw a breath. She tucked her chin, hiding her face from the onslaught.

Fannin tore across the meadow like a bolt of lightning, his hooves barely touching the ground as he effortlessly covered one mile after another. Lira found herself gripping the arm Aidryn had wrapped around her, fingers digging into him as she clamped her legs around the horse.

The stallion kept his breakneck pace until they reached the tree line that separated the meadow from Acton's Cove.

It was after midnight, and Lira couldn't remember the last time she'd truly slept. Fannin's gentle trot was as smooth as the kelpie's swim downriver, and Lira felt her eyelids drooping, head bobbing with exhaustion.

"Keep to the tree line," she slurred sleepily. "The archers…"

Aidryn nodded his understanding; Clan Mór's night watchers would be able to spot them in the clearing, but they stood a better chance of avoiding them among the trees.

Lira finally slumped back against Aidryn and drifted into a deep sleep. How much longer it took them to reach their campsite, she couldn't say; but she slept until he roused her enough to help her from the horse. He supported her weight as he led her through a thicket to a low overhang of rock. She shivered, pulling her knees to her chest as he helped her sit; he disappeared for a moment, then returned with a change of clothes.

"Aeron put clothes in the saddlebag, too," he said, nudging Lira. Her eyelids drooped sleepily, eyes glazed as he closed her hands over the roll of clothing. "Come on; change out of your wet things. Then you can sleep all you like."

He patted her shoulder, then stepped out from under the overhang. Blinking hard in the darkness, she fumbled to unbuckle her belt and wriggle out of the heavy mail shirt. She set them aside, teeth chattering, then peeled off her soggy clothes one piece at a time.

The dry tunic and pants Aidryn had brought were over-sized, but she was thankful for the hardy material as she wrapped herself in them. Her shivering began to subside as she hugged herself and lay on the soft grass, curling onto her side.

As if beckoned, Aidryn crept back into the shelter. Lira cracked one eye open to see him unfolding the heavy blanket she'd seen beneath Fannin's saddle. Closing her eye again, she allowed him to cocoon her in its warmth. He tucked it around her gently, then coaxed her to rest her head on a second roll of dry clothes.

"Sleep now," he murmured. "I'll keep watch."

"Thank you," she whispered, pulling the blanket tight before slumber claimed her again.

CHAPTER 25

Lira woke with a start, heart hammering, chest tight. She sat bolt upright, her vision going black for a moment at the sudden movement. Her body felt shaky and weighted with fatigue.

She glanced down, noticing the roll of dry clothes that had been placed under her head sometime during the night.

"Aidryn?" she whispered, clutching the clothes to her chest as she crawled toward the mouth of the overhang.

What if something happened to him while I was sleeping?

Her back was stiff, but the soft earth beneath her had been a vast improvement from the dungeon floor. She shuddered at the thought as she snatched up her boots and peeked outside.

Aidryn leaned against the stone wall, eating from a block of cheese. Lira's stomach growled at the sight of it—loudly enough, apparently, that he snapped to attention, scanning the trees around them before his eyes fell on Lira. A relieved smile spread across his face at the sight of her.

"Morning," he said, breaking off a piece of cheese and tossing it to her. Her sluggish fingers barely caught it, fumbling to keep it from falling into the dirt. He chuckled, popping a piece of dried meat into his mouth.

"It's too early for that," she grumbled, taking a bite.

The flavor was overwhelming, but she savored the food, chewing slowly. She hadn't eaten good food since *Nami Mostari.* It was all she could do to keep from greedily shoving every bit into her mouth.

Her eyes latched onto the square of butcher paper spread on the ground beside Aidryn, where he'd arranged the meat, bread, and cheese.

"Take as much as you like." He nudged the spread toward her.

She extended the roll of clothes toward him. "Why didn't you change into these? It was too cold not to."

He shrugged, taking them. "Being cold kept me awake to keep watch. We need to move soon. It won't be long before the sentries make it out here."

Lira nodded slowly, choosing a piece of meat. Aidryn was as stubborn as she was, if not more so. She knew he could've stayed awake simply because he wanted to. The unspoken words that hung between them—that he'd cared more for her comfort than his own—grew heavier the longer she considered them.

"I'm sorry to have dragged you into all this," she said quietly.

"Don't apologize again," he said. "This is where I want to be."

Lira's food suddenly lost its flavor, and she struggled to swallow the meat she'd been chewing. A tear trickled down her cheek, and she sniffed, attempting to take a bite of bread.

Aidryn took a swig from a flask of water, then handed it to Lira. "If we can get into the settlement without a problem, we can ask your uncle for asylum. His army is much smaller than

Macha's, but they have the advantage of knowing the territory here."

Lira took a drink. "And the best of Da and Gerallt's armor and weaponry at their disposal. They've always kept a cache in a storehouse on the valley's edge—weaponry, chain mail, plate. Everything."

She forced herself to keep eating, remembering the lay of the village in the valley high above and wondering whether Skelly would be glad to see her. What she would say about the chaos that had unfolded these past weeks?

As she ruminated, Aidryn grew still—as quiet and motionless as a deer in a thicket.

"What's—"

He held up a hand, silencing her. Lira strained her ears, listening; then, she heard it. Felt it.

A pulsing hum seemed to be emitting from the earth around them. It was barely audible, and it was accompanied by a low rumble. She pressed her fingertips into the soil, searching for the magical thread that would lead her back to the source. The strange force called to her—rooted her. Her vision blurred.

"Lira..."

But Lira stared straight ahead, her sight winking out. She felt Aidryn's fingers close over hers and tensed at his touch. Sweat beaded on her forehead despite the cool morning air. She gritted her teeth; her breath came in short, shallow bursts, and she was already winded when she began to speak.

"Riders at dawn. The mistress returns."

Her voice was strained, as if her throat were closing around the words.

Aidryn laced his fingers through hers and tugged. "Lira, lift your hands."

She raised her hands from the earth and lunged toward him, clamping her palms onto either side of his face. Somewhere in the back of her mind, she knew she was forcing him into her vision, though she didn't know how to regain control over her actions.

A dark tower room surrounds them, its stale air thick with refuse. Shafts of light pierce through narrow slats in an aged ceiling. Gnarled hands grip a splintered throne.

A valley yawns open in the heart of snowy mountains, sprawling and empty and young. Lush grass covers the land like a thick, soft blanket and the sky overhead is a brilliant midnight blue dotted with blinking stars. The land below is teeming with insects that dart and flicker with a cerulean glow.

In the center of the valley stands a copse of frozen willows covered in leaves of iridescent crystal. The gemstones stir in the breeze, tapping together in a disjointed cadence. The blue fireflies flit in from the meadow and converge on the willows, gathering beneath the shelter of the crystal leaves. Their light pulses from within the copse like a luminous heartbeat.

From every direction on the edges of the valley come hooded figures; some are riders whose mounts approach the willows warily. Others come on foot, moving gracefully through the tall grasses. They greet one another with terse nods, never lowering their hoods.

One figure—slight, perhaps a female beneath the heavy green cloak—walks directly into the cluster of trees, disappearing beneath the crystals. As the other figures arrive, they clasp hands to form a large circle around the copse.

Daylight rushed into Lira's consciousness once again as the vision dissolved. She and Aidryn found themselves grasping one another's shoulders, their foreheads pressed together. Panting, he jerked away.

"What was that?"

"I don't know."

Aidryn's expression clouded. "Was that your valley?"

"No. I've never seen that place before."

"Something strange is going on. Keep your fingers out of the soil for now, will you?"

He pushed himself to stand, striding toward Fannin and opening the saddle bag. His legs were trembling.

"It's not just the soil," she answered. "I've had visions while sleeping, studying manuscripts—even in the catacombs."

Aidryn unrolled the bundle, then peeled off his soggy tunic and chucked it into the grass.

Lira quickly averted her eyes, her cheeks heating. What little she'd glimpsed of his bare chest had been jarring. He was a stark contrast to the gangly boy who had run shirtless through the Tarlach home so many years ago, and he definitely didn't look like a scholar who hunched over books all day. Instead, he was built like a warrior, though leaner than the men of Clan Beran, whom she'd glimpsed in their training exercises while visiting their fortress.

She decided she probably shouldn't dwell on comparisons, or anyone's muscles.

"What was the common thread every other time you've had a vision?" he called as he rifled through the saddle bag.

She twirled a blade of grass between her fingers, careful not to look up. "The places and objects were imbued with magic, or heavy with memory."

"Well, this place is teeming with it," he said. "We need to be careful."

Aidryn pulled the fresh tunic over his head, then held up a pair of trousers, raising an eyebrow. "Do you mind?"

Lira's face blazed as she scooted out from under the overhang so he could change. Fannin was standing stock-still just outside the entrance, and he glanced at her, swishing his tail once in greeting. She inclined her head and stepped nearer, running her fingertips through his mane as she whispered to him. He nuzzled her cheek with his velvety nose, and she smiled.

"You're going to spoil him," Aidryn said from behind her. He had bundled the wet clothes, re-wrapped their food, and was opening the saddlebag to stuff everything inside. Taking the blanket roll from her, he secured it with a long leather strap.

"You're just afraid he'll like me more than you." She swung herself astride the stallion, patting his withers.

"He already does," Aidryn said, climbing up behind her. He handed her the reins. "Lead the way."

Lira sucked in a breath before clicking her tongue and nudging Fannin into a walk. She felt awkward and nervous; it had been years since she'd ridden into the mountains, and she prayed the trail into Mór's Valley hadn't changed since her last visit.

Her palms were soaked by the time they reached the mouth of the trail. When she spotted the old landmark—a massive boulder covered in moss—her shoulders sagged with relief. Fresh, frigid water from the mountain streams that converged there bubbled and gurgled around it, flowing into a wider stream that sliced Acton's Cove in half and flowed back down into the Moravon.

Fannin made quick work of the trek. Even the hardiest mountain horses couldn't make it up into the valley without stopping for rest and water more than once, but Fannin kept moving steadily and swiftly, his magnificent form navigating the winding roads and sharp inclines with otherworldly ease. The ride was smooth, his hoof beats quiet on the trail.

The closer they grew to Clan Mór's settlement, the harder Lira's heart hammered. She wondered whether she'd recognize anyone, or whether anyone would recognize her. She had been an awkward adolescent on her last visit.

"They'll be glad to see you back," Aidryn murmured, as if reading Lira's thoughts.

She cast a glance over her shoulder at him. "Maybe. I hope."

"You're not going to like this idea," he said, "but you should think of your position as leverage in any negotiations with the council. You're important to the clan, but also to Iathium. If you play your hand well, you can bend their ears."

Lira shuddered. "I'm no good at bending ears."

"You didn't get anointed Defender for being a fast reader. Irem admired your grit and your ability to read a room—he called it diplomatic prowess."

She snorted.

"That's part of the reason I decided not to challenge you for the role," he admitted. "I've no patience for playing politics. I had to wear a mask for my family; I couldn't keep up with more than one."

"I don't know how you did it for so long," she said.

She felt him shift as he shrugged. "I worry about Father. Macha will have all of their heads for what's happened."

Lira flinched at the absence of Macha's title. Aidryn must have sensed this, because he added, "She is not *my* Raní, Silira."

THE AIR WAS COOL, and the dense woods blocked the sun as Aidryn and Lira ascended the mountain. Though it was late afternoon, it felt like dusk beneath the thick canopy of leaves.

This path was achingly familiar to Lira, and she began to spot unusual trees she recognized from childhood—trees that marked the path to the village. Their trunks had been trained from saplings to bend into unnatural crooks. Lira remembered sitting on them with her cousins, Ellwyn and Artagán, as a child, telling jokes and stories, merrily swinging their feet over the sides of the thick branches.

She coaxed Fannin into a slower, quieter walk as they neared a long archway of trees whose branches had been woven together overhead. The archway was covered with white blooms—a favorite flower of her mother's. They brushed against the arch, and she reached out to capture one of the flowers in her palm, closing her eyes as she inhaled its sweet fragrance.

The archway of trees stretched for nearly a mile before it opened into a large grove of massive oaks just ahead of the valley. Lira's heart rose, then sank; this was a homecoming filled with trepidation instead of a happy reunion with her family. There was little comfort in the familiarity of the terrain; not even in the childhood memories that flooded her as she remembered Skelly telling her stories among these very trees.

As they entered the grove, there was a palpable shift in the atmosphere. Lira clutched the reins in a knot, unwittingly drawing them up to her chest. Aidryn lay one hand on her arm and held out the other. Wordlessly, she put the reins into his waiting palm and found the saddle horn, squeezing it tightly as he urged an ever-reluctant Fannin forward.

They made it to the center of the grove before six archers dropped from above, landing in perfect formation before them. Their weapons were trained on Lira before she could open her mouth. She went rigid in the saddle, frantically scanning what she could see of their hooded faces.

The middle archer stepped forward without lowering his weapon. "Who approaches?" he barked in Onnen.

Lira swallowed the lump in her throat before replying in her clan's tongue, "Granddaughter of Wilga Mór, niece of your Master Gerallt."

"Lira!"

Her eyes snapped to a female archer on the far left of the group, who threw her bow to the ground and bounded toward Fannin. The young woman's hood fell back to reveal a plait of red-gold hair and a pair of sparkling hazel eyes.

A sob broke from Lira's throat as she gasped, "Ellwyn!"

Hesitantly, the other archers lowered their weapons. Lira's

cousin was grinning broadly when she reached the stallion, and she clasped Lira's hands in her own. "You look exactly the same! What were you thinking, staying away so long?"

Lira leapt down from Fannin's back and embraced Ellwyn so hard they stumbled.

"I've missed you," she cried, her eyes rimmed with tears.

Ellwyn looked to Aidryn for a moment, then back at Lira. "Where is Talfryn? Is he alive?"

Lira opened her mouth to answer, but the words caught in her throat and she shook her head, glancing back at Aidryn. Her chin trembled.

"He is, but I couldn't get both of them out at once," Aidryn said. "We have friends in the city who are working to free him from the barracks as quickly as possible."

The center archer strode forward, throwing his hood back; it was Ellwyn's twin brother, Artagán. He had the same hazel eyes as his sister, yet stood a head taller. His long auburn hair fell over his shoulders, and he was heavily armed; besides his bow, he wore a shirt of mail like Lira's, overlaid with a leather bandolier that held six throwing knives. Daggers were strapped to his thighs, and Lira guessed even more blades were concealed inside his boots.

"Artagán." Lira said, wiping away a tear as she reached to rest a hand on his shoulder. "What are they feeding you? You're as tall as a tree."

Artagán took a step back, freeing himself from her touch, and she recoiled in surprise. His face was a mask of wariness as he regarded Lira, then glanced up to where Aidryn still sat astride the stallion. "You shouldn't be here."

Though his words stung, Lira could read something more in his expression—pity, or perhaps some semblance of relief.

"This is Aidryn Tarlach," she said, "my companion from the city. He rescued me."

Artagán studied Aidryn again, then turned to the other archers. "Back to your posts," he ordered.

The archers reluctantly obeyed, making no attempt to hide their fascination and surprise as they eyed Lira and Aidryn. They scaled the trees effortlessly, disappearing again into the thick leaves overhead.

"Ellwyn, your bow," Artagán chided, jerking his chin toward the weapon his sister had discarded on the ground.

His twin looped an arm around Lira's shoulders, hugging her tight. "Right," she replied, unruffled, before jogging over to fetch it.

Artagán trained his attention on Aidryn. "Dismount, Tarlach."

Aidryn's expression darkened; Fannin stomped the ground, sensing the rising tension. Artagán's eyes flicked to the stallion.

"Why?" Aidryn gripped the reins so hard, his knuckles turned white. The hairs on the back of Lira's neck rose at the sound of her friend speaking easily in Onnen, and she fought back her rising panic as the two young men sized one another up.

"Master's orders," the archer replied. "Outsiders' mounts are to be boarded in his stable."

Aidryn set his jaw. "I'll decide on my horse's lodging."

Artagán clenched his fists. "You would intrude on our lands and disregard our law?"

"Relax, cousin. He coddles his pony." Lira cut in coolly, flashing a disarming smile. "The last I was aware, Clan Mór was still welcoming to outsiders and family alike."

"That was before one of our own endangered the settlement," Artagán said, glaring pointedly at Lira, who tried not to shrink beneath his gaze. "Now, dismount or I'll call my archers back down."

Aidryn swung a leg over Fannin and jumped down. He grabbed the bridle angrily and stalked over to Artagán until he was nearly nose-to-nose with the archer. "We didn't come here for trouble."

"We seek asylum," Lira put in, praying Aidryn would shut his mouth long enough for them to get it.

"Asylum isn't mine to give," Artagán said. "That's up to the council."

"Then take us to the council," Lira said, looking from Aidryn to her cousin and back again. "We mean no harm. Truly."

"Of course, you mean no harm," Ellwyn said, hugging Lira's shoulders again. "Artagán, stop playing rooster and let's get them to Papa. The sooner they have asylum, the sooner we can eat."

Lira giggled, sniffling. "Still thinking with your stomach, El?"

"Always." Ellwyn grinned, winking. She tugged Lira toward the valley's edge. "Come on."

Artagán leered at Aidryn before he turned to stalk toward the settlement. Ellwyn and Lira followed, exchanging a terse glance. Aidryn led Fannin through the grove behind them, one hand on the hilt of his sword as the group emerged into the rolling valley.

CHAPTER 26

The village was larger than Lira remembered, yet somehow, it felt vacant. Too quiet. A marketplace of sorts had begun to take shape in its center, and outlying homes—cabins and earthen, dome-shaped huts— dotted the landscape in abundance.

Lira scanned their surroundings as they trekked across the open field and into the square. The hair on her arms rose as she noted that the clanspeople seemed to have retreated inside their homes and shops. This wasn't the welcoming place she remembered from her youth.

What had once been a central storehouse and communal wellspring had become a small center of commerce. The black-smith had moved his workshop from the valley's edge into the square. There were booths and displays boasting woven cloth, handmade soaps, ribbons, dry goods, tools, and clothing.

The group moved through the village without speaking; any noise they made would be amplified in the looming silence. Fannin's hoof beats were exceptionally loud, even on the packed dirt road that ran through the marketplace. The weight of hundreds of eyes pressed in on Lira, as if even the people living on the farthest edges of the valley were peering through shuttered windows at the party.

She swallowed hard, her heart pounding. Despite her many visits here, this place felt strangely unfamiliar, like a trap laid open for unsuspecting prey. Though she didn't know what to expect, she was beginning to fear that Artagán's resentment was shared among the clan.

When they emerged on the other side of the marketplace, Lira's legs almost gave out beneath her; a wooden fortress had been built in the heart of the valley, its looming keep jutting up from the center. Her mouth went dry. If memory served, Skelly's familiar dome-shaped cottage would either have been demolished to make room for this fortress... or the fortress was simply built around it. As they drew closer, she could make out the scaffolding still lining the western wall of the fort; tools had been left lying on the ground, as if progress had suddenly halted.

A moat had been dug around the fortress and was one-quarter full of muddy rainwater. The trench was still fresh, and the smell of the recently-turned earth clung to Lira's nostrils. Everything here was so lush and fertile, it made her feel awake and alive—even the dirt. Her magic stirred, as if recognizing its home, and she wondered for a moment why she had ever become so enamored with Iathium.

"How long since the master built the fort?" Lira asked.

Artagán's head snapped around, and he shot her a nasty glare. In spite of her brother's obvious disapproval, Ellwyn answered, "The keep was built three years ago; we raised the walls last month after we heard... well." She pressed her lips together and looked at the ground.

Lira's cheeks began to burn. She hadn't had time to consider whether everything that had happened in the city would endanger the clan. "What do you mean, 'we?'"

"Everyone in the valley pitched in to raise the fort," Ellwyn answered nonchalantly.

"The master won't wait for Iathium to level this place—the walls are a precaution," Artagán added.

"Yet there are still outlying cottages and properties that are unprotected," Aidryn cut in. "How is that?"

Artagán grunted, but didn't answer. Ellwyn filled his silence with, "Because Papa ordered everyone to move inside for now, until the threat has passed."

The eerie silence—the stillness of the valley outside the fortress—all of it suddenly made sense to Lira. There was no life outside the fortress today because there were no people outside it, either, save for themselves and the archers. She thought again about the discarded tools outside the wall. The valley must have been put on high alert, the clanspeople ushered inside the fortress, because Gerallt expected her arrival. Perhaps he'd received word from Iathium.

Lira wanted to stop right there—turn around and leave Clan Mór in peace. She'd vowed to Faolan that no one else would die on her behalf; yet here she was, exposing her clan to a danger far greater than they'd faced in centuries.

The thought of this peaceful place being ransacked because of her mere presence became a weight that bore down on her. But she remembered her grandmother and the birthright Eremon had wanted her to claim.

"Ellwyn," she began reluctantly, "what's happened to Skelly?"

Artagán answered for his sister. "We don't speak of it."

"Why? What could possibly—"

"Much has changed, cousin," he answered coolly, not bothering to look at her. "This place—it's not what you remember. I'll leave it at that."

Don't ask questions, he meant. Lira glowered at the back of his head.

Aidryn sensed her agitation; for a moment, Lira allowed him a brief glimpse of the disappointment in her eyes before she stared straight ahead again. He reached for her, brushing his knuckles lightly against her fingers before he, too, turned his attention back to the massive fortress.

Artagán wasn't the same lighthearted young man she'd grown up with. He carried himself with purpose and authority now, the good humor she remembered replaced by the weight of protecting the clan. But no matter how things had changed, they were still cousins; they still had that common ground, those shared memories. How could he turn his back on that? Still, he was already holding her at arm's length; perhaps it might be best to take a diplomatic approach.

"With all respect, Artagán," Lira prodded hopefully, "I need to know what has changed. I can't observe protocol if I don't know what it is."

Her heart sank as Artagán barely spared her a half-glance over his shoulder. "Forgive me; we weren't expecting a visit from the ambassador of—who, exactly, *do* you represent, Silira?"

Lira bared her teeth at him angrily, but a sharp look from Aidryn stopped the growl that rose in her throat. Diplomatic tactics, apparently, had no effect on the hardened archer who now led them across the lowered drawbridge.

When they reached the other side, Artagán held out a hand, signaling a halt. The others obliged; he stalked toward Lira, pushing between Ellwyn and Aidryn. She shrank as he glared down at her.

"You may be my cousin by blood," he began, "and you may stand to inherit more power and wealth than you deserve. But don't let it go to your head.

"To the clan, you're just a deserter; a traitor to Clan Mór and Iathium alike. You chose the enemy over your family, and we will never forget it."

He turned on his heel and cut through the small crowd that had gathered at the mouth of the fortress gate to gawk at Lira, Aidryn, and Fannin. Lira's face burned, her eyes stinging with tears. She struggled to control her ragged breathing, and she backed away a step, ready to run in the other direction.

As Artagán disappeared into the fortress ahead of them, Lira felt a tentative touch, a brush against her fingertips. Ellwyn still stood by her side, pity in her eyes as she laced her fingers through Lira's.

Her eyes welled with tears, too, as she whispered. "Ignore him. It's good to have you home."

A sob broke from Lira's lips at that; but no matter how Ellwyn tried to soothe and smooth over her brother's words, Artagán had been right. Lira was no one—no city, no clan, no credible claim to anything but ring on her finger and the birthright Skelly had promised her long ago.

If there is still a birthright to inherit.

Lira wanted to sag to the ground, to beg Artagán to help her make things right. Ellwyn must have sensed her thoughts, for she squeezed one of Lira's hands, and Aidryn took hold of the other.

"Stay on your feet, Lira, and never bow to anyone," he said in a low voice. "I won't leave your side."

At that, she found her footing again and straightened her spine, looking him full in the eyes. She said nothing, but gave him a curt nod before they turned their attention back to the fortress. Lira blinked back her tears and tilted her head up, surveying the massive wall before her.

The size of the fort was staggering. She couldn't picture this clan packed into the walls of a fortress, however large it might be. Each family in the valley had always owned their own parcel of land, and plenty of it. No matter how rich or poor, everyone living among Clan Mór had more than their share of everything, from food to livestock to acreage. What would they do, confined inside this fortress? What would they become?

On the other side of the heavy iron gates, the ground was nothing but tarry, packed mud—and the stench that rose from it made Lira gag. The entire place reeked; it was teeming with people, livestock, and refuse. A makeshift market had been erected in the center, a smaller, more crowded version of the marketplace they'd just passed through.

Archers stared down from their posts near the top of the walls, while clanspeople on the ground gawked at the outsiders. Ellwyn flashed easy, reassuring smiles at the people, who went back to their business as they passed.

Lira made eye contact with a few of the villagers; they were filthy, their cheeks sunken, eyes vacant. She couldn't bear to hold anyone's gaze, so she stared at the mud that now caked her boots.

She bit the inside of her cheek and took shallow breaths, careful not to inhale too much of the foul-smelling air. The dungeon had been a living nightmare, but this fortress was almost worse—perhaps because these people didn't realize they were prisoners.

Lira squeezed Aidryn's hand so tightly that his head snapped toward her in alarm. His expression was grim as he seemed to read the questions in her eyes: *What is Gerallt doing? Was this why Irem was so cryptic? Where's Skelly?*

He replied with a subtle shake of his head.

Lira counted her paces as they continued their trek across the fortress grounds. Twenty-five, twenty-six, twenty-seven—

They halted at the keep's stone threshold; Aidryn looked at Fannin's reins, at the great hall that lay before them, then back to Fannin again. Ellwyn let go of Lira's hand and stepped forward.

"I'll stay here with him," she offered, reaching for the reins.

He hesitated, then relinquished them. "Thank you," he said. With a half-smile, Ellwyn inclined her head.

Aidryn chanced another look at his horse before heaving a sigh and stepping inside the great hall with Lira. The floor of the great hall was covered with a thick layer of fresh straw, and their footfalls upon it caught the attention of four large hounds. Growling, the dogs bounded over to them; baring their teeth. Lira froze, stiffening as one of the hounds crouched low, ears laid flat as it moved closer to her.

Aidryn clicked his tongue at the dogs. "*Tanaphe*," he murmured. They scattered, returning to their places by the fire.

Lira exhaled shakily and followed Aidryn into the great hall. Once inside, she wrinkled her nose at the stench of animal excrement and moldy straw that covered the floor. This sort of filth had never been the norm in her clan; then again, neither were the conditions outside the keep.

She wasn't sure what she had expected, but she felt suddenly overwhelmed by the wrongness of this room. At first glance, it had appeared welcoming and abundant, but it quickly became apparent that the façade was fragile at best.

Coming here had been a mistake.

There was a high table before the hearth, and three long, lower tables that branched out from it. Unfinished platters adorned the tabletops and benches were pushed out from beneath it at odd angles, as if a meal had recently been shared here, then abandoned abruptly.

"My brother's daughter, come to beg for asylum."

The booming voice jolted Lira, and she whirled to face Gerallt Mór. Her uncle seemed larger somehow, his hulking figure more intimidating than she remembered.

"Tell me, little fugitive," he said, "what right do you have to trespass here?"

Gerallt wore heavy firs draped over his shoulders, their opulence—and his round, ruddy face—in stark contrast to the squalor she'd seen outside. His gray hair was cropped close, and he'd grown a long beard in the years since she had last seen him. He peered at her with steely green eyes, his hand moving to the hilt of the sword that hung from a thick leather belt he'd slung across his hips.

"I—" Lira balked, then swallowed hard. "I come peacefully, uncle."

He paced toward his niece, each step slow. Deliberate. Lira backed into a table, spilling a half-full goblet of mead. She nearly gagged when its fermented tang reached her nose. It smelled old, like it had been improperly prepared, then over-sweetened with too much honey to hide the fact that it was spoiled. Lira wondered whether Gerallt fed his dinner guests ruined food, as well.

"We know all about you, Silira—disgraced Defender of Histories, mistress of Eremon, heir of Iathium," he said.

Aidryn bristled. Lira ground her teeth at Gerallt. "I was not his *mistress*. And I stand to inherit nothing."

"Yet the people shout your name in the streets," he said. "Is that nothing?"

She didn't know what to say.

"Stop patronizing her," Aidryn said. "You're going to want her as an ally."

Gerallt's attention snapped to him. "And you are?"

"Aidryn Tarlach."

Gerallt raised an eyebrow. "The Key Keeper," he mused. "I've heard talk of you."

His gaze flicked between Lira and Aidryn. "How many in Iathium would have my niece on the throne?"

Lira's cheeks burned. "No one, uncle."

"*Lira*," Aidryn snapped, casting her an exasperated glare before he turned back to Gerallt. "Her supporters grow in number by the day."

Gerallt propped his boot onto a bench and draped a

forearm across his knee. "Talfryn was imprisoned for swearing fealty to her. Do you suppose any of his sentry friends will follow suit?"

"Some already have," Aidryn answered, "but I couldn't say how many."

Lira bristled, annoyed at him for giving Gerallt so much information. Aidryn lay a reassuring hand on her shoulder, but she avoided his gaze. She prayed that none of their friends would suffer the same fate.

"Pity," Gerallt said. "Your brother would've made a fine archer here. Better than an ornament rotting on Iathium's gates."

Artagán offered a curt nod of agreement as Lira's stomach lurched. She was dangerously close to losing control of her emotions and her faculties if she stayed here much longer.

"We have questions," Aidryn said, taking a step closer to Lira. She straightened slightly, struggling to remain calm. "We need to know—"

"In the morning," Gerallt said, waving them off. "I've just returned from a hunt; I am too weary to call the council. Let me sleep, and we'll speak tomorrow."

"We need to know what happened to Irem Énna," Aidryn pressed.

"Came and left weeks ago," the master said dismissively. "Come before the council tomorrow. We will decide your fate, and perhaps by then I'll have some recollection of your companion's visit."

"This can't wait until tomorrow." Lira drew herself up to her full height. *No one dismisses me.* "Macha's army will be in pursuit. It won't be long until they reach us."

"But that is quite a journey," he chuckled. "They won't arrive for days, if they come at all.

"Now—you'll stay someplace familiar tonight. Someplace that feels like home." He led them toward the exit once more, to where Ellwyn waited with Fannin. "I want you to stay in my mother's cottage."

"Skelly," Lira breathed, her heart lurching. "We'll stay with her?"

Gerallt pursed his lips, his mustache twitching with the movement, and picked up a goblet from the table nearest him. Golden mead sloshed over the edge as he raised it to his lips.

"She is... indisposed," he spoke into the goblet, taking a long swig.

"What does that mean?" Lira's voice rose with panic. "How is she?"

"Tomorrow," he said, waving his free hand and turning to go. His hounds returned at his summons, barring Aidryn and Lira's re-entry into the great hall.

Lira bristled, clenching her fists at her sides as her uncle strode in the opposite direction, keeping his back to them.

Before he disappeared down the long hallway, Gerallt turned to her again, almost as an afterthought. "I'm throwing a feast tomorrow night—here. Perhaps you'll have time to reminisce between now and then."

"So you're granting us asylum?"

"A place to stay for the night. The rest is up to the council."

Gerallt strode away then, quickly swallowed up by the shadows. Lira was torn between feeling relieved and angry at his departure—and apparently, so was Aidryn.

"He doesn't seem the least bit worried about Macha," he whispered.

Lira shook her head. "Something's not right. It makes me want to leave now."

"We have to risk staying," Aidryn whispered. "For Skelly."

Lira nodded almost imperceptibly as they approached Ellwyn and Fannin. Her cousin grinned warmly, while Fannin tossed his mane and stomped his hooves impatiently.

"Will you take us to Skelly's?" Lira asked.

Ellwyn blanched for a moment, but nodded, handing the reins back to Aidryn and leading them away from the keep. She half-glanced over her shoulder at them, hesitated, then looked back again.

"I'm forbidden from talking about it," she began in a low voice as they walked. "But life here is very different now, Lira. The people you grew up with—" she chewed the inside of her lip, considering her next words— "they're not the people you knew. This is not the place you remember."

"And Skelly?"

"She is..." Ellwyn faltered. "Alive."

"Alive and *well*?"

Her cousin went stone-faced as she answered with a clipped, "Alive."

Lira's stomach clenched. "Tell me, Ellwyn," she begged, grasping a fistful of the young woman's sleeve.

Her cousin gently extracted her sleeve from Lira's grip. "I can't," she whispered. "because I don't understand what's happened."

Ellwyn pressed on ahead of them, moving past the keep and weaving through the crowd. Lira and Aidryn glanced to one another, then followed, trotting to catch up with her.

They walked for half a mile before the familiar earthen hut came into view; it was unchanged, despite the keep around it. Even the grass was still lush, as if Gerallt hadn't the heart to let it be trampled into the packed, gray mud that covered the rest of the grounds. Lira felt a lump rise in her throat as she surveyed the cozy little hut she'd visited so many times over the years.

By the time they reached the front door, her hands were trembling.

Ellwyn adjusted her bow and quiver, holding an expectant hand out for Fannin's reins. "I don't expect you'll want him boarded—"

"No," Aidryn answered, his response a barely-contained clip. "I want him here."

"I've got first watch out here, so I won't be going far," she offered. "He'll be safe with me."

"We're under house arrest?" Lira asked, bristling.

Ellwyn shifted uncomfortably. "I suggest you sleep while you can. Now, hand over the reins. I can't be seen lingering with you."

Aidryn glowered at her, but he released them and went to work removing the saddlebag.

"He likes carrots," he said, glancing nervously at Fannin's face. He stroked the stallion's soft forelock, then hefted the leather bag from his back.

Ellwyn gave him a pinched smile. "Then he shall have them."

CHAPTER 27

With trembling hands, Lira turned the knob and opened Skelly's door, stepping tentatively over the threshold. Her lip quivered as she took in the sight; the hut was exactly as she remembered it.

Although it was small, it was inviting and cozy. Trinkets and statuettes covered every available surface, and wherever there was room for a shelf—whether hung on the wall or wedged between sitting cushions on the floor—there it would be, filled to the brim with keepsakes.

Straight ahead was a fireplace and a short worktable; two familiar stools sat before the cold hearth. Lira brushed her fingertips over the leather seat of one—the one she'd always occupied while she listened to Skelly's stories, a mug of stew in her chilly hands. Her empty stomach growled at the memory.

"Watch your language." Aidryn grinned.

"I can't be held responsible for what my stomach says."

Aidryn laughed lightly, but a pang of guilt coursed through her at their joking. In a way, it felt familiar and easy to jab one another like this. But it was also a bittersweet reminder of their days in the archive.

She sighed and picked up a small music box that sat on the mantel above her and wound it up, then began to move around the space, winding other mechanical trinkets as she went—clocks, more music boxes, and the like. They created a cacophony of sound that was as chaotic as it was soothing.

Aidryn screwed up his brow at her, but Lira only offered him half a shrug. "It was too quiet."

"I know," he said. "The noise was always distracting, but she insisted on keeping them wound."

Lira whirled on him. "*What* did you say?"

The blood drained from Aidryn's face, and he took a step back. "Lira, I—"

She angrily closed the distance between them, jabbing a finger against his chest. And he had the *audacity* to look intimidated.

"You've been here before," Lira accused. "You've met Skelly."

Aidryn raised his palms, panic flashing in his eyes. "Let me explain."

Her enraged voice rose. "Why did you keep that from me?"

"There has been—" He nearly backed into a shelf of trinkets. "So much has happened! And not enough time."

"She's *my* grandmother! What right did you have to come here without me?"

"Because it has been seven years since you bothered to," he retorted. "You weren't interested, and I needed to learn as much as I could from Skelly. It's not like I was going to get the information from *you*."

Regret suddenly flooded her, and her lip trembled.

Aidryn sighed. "I didn't mean to let it slip like that. I was going to sit down with you here... cook you a meal, ask you all about your visits growing up—and then I was going to warm you up to the idea."

"I trusted you," she said, her voice trembling. "You asked me to trust that you're still the Aidryn I knew—yet you left *this* out? How much else have you kept from me?"

"Irem required secrecy," he answered steadily. "Would you have refused anything he asked of you?"

"No," she sulked, dragging a stool from the table to sit before the hearth.

"Lira, all of us kept secrets from you—Irem, Eremon, and I. It's unforgivable. But please, try to see it from my point of view: You're at the center of something so vast. We all thought we were doing right by letting the truth trickle out; we couldn't imagine hitting you with everything all at once."

"So you were protecting my feelings because I'm, what? Stupid? Too fragile? A breakable little girl?"

"The opposite," he said, sitting beside her. "You're unbending, like an ancient tree that has withstood thousands of storms. Rigid. Some might say difficult."

She hunched over her knees, still refusing to look at him. "What else was it you said before? Stubborn. Add that to your list."

His tone softened. "Lira, you're so like *her*. Will you at least let me tell you why I agreed to come here?"

"We're under house arrest; I've got nothing better to do." It felt satisfying to hurl a petulant insult or two.

Aidryn huffed softly. "Four years ago, Lord Irem told me your grandmother wanted someone to teach in your stead, until you accepted your birthright."

Had Skelly truly held on for so long, believing Lira would eventually come to her? Only when everything she held dear had crumbled, had she deigned to step foot in this territory again. And now, it was likely too late for Skelly. Lira's eyes burned.

"Irem felt that you were thriving at the Dome," Aidryn

continued. "You were still so bitter about your mother's marriage. You were caring for Talfryn and mastering your work in the archive. At the time, he felt that it was wiser to send me."

Aidryn and Irem were two of the only people who had been close to Lira through her father's death and her mother's leaving. Lira *had* been wholly consumed with her life in Iathium. Clinging to her work was the only way she had survived all the upheaval. It made sense that Irem's assessment might have been a fair one, but it didn't erase her anger.

She took a shaky breath as Aidryn continued.

"He gave you time to grieve your father, to start making your trips into the mountains again—but you never did. By the time he finally came to me, Skelly had bottled those stories up inside of her for years, thinking you'd come back. It was imperative that she have someone to pass them to."

"Why couldn't she just share them with the clan?"

"She was afraid the magic might manifest wildly. Skelly had a very rigid idea of how she wanted everything to go, and no one could convince her otherwise. Irem and I tried.

"Telling me her stories was a safer means of discharging her power until she could give you your birthright. Otherwise, it would accumulate over time."

Lira tried to exhale, resting her forehead in her hands.

"If I'm being completely honest—" Aidryn seemed to hesitate, then continued— "I also came here to learn more about you. I remembered your childhood stories. I also remember when you hardened yourself to this place and stopped speaking of Skelly. I suppose I wanted to learn more about..." He shrugged. "All of it.

"At any rate, I wouldn't have cared if she were *Irem's* grandmother, if I thought I could learn important histories from her. If you weren't going to come out here yourself, the next best person was me."

Lira stood abruptly. "Well," she began, "at the very least, you're good at putting your lies in context."

She didn't wait for him to reply as she stalked into the small bedchamber just off the kitchen and slumped onto the bed. Rolling onto her back, she stared up at the knotted wood ceiling, smooth with age. She thought about what Aidryn had said about her being difficult; she supposed she might have been more open-minded to Skelly. Perhaps she should have continued her visits. But she had been a child, and she had listened to her father. For a moment, her anger shifted to him for deceiving her as he had—as everyone had.

There was a soft knock on the doorframe; she didn't bother looking over at Aidryn before she said, "I left it open. What's the point of locking it with *you* around?"

Aidryn didn't say anything when he entered the room. Instead, he approached a thick, round, tree-trunk stool that sat beside the bed and shoved it with all his might. Lira sat up, gawking at him. "What are you doing?"

"I have to show you something." He knelt, peeling up the hand-woven rug that had been pinned beneath the stool moments before.

"What, the majestic floorboards?"

"There's another reason I was meant to come here," Aidryn said, removing the rug completely and draping it over the stool. "Something we didn't discover for some time."

The aged wood floor beneath the rug looked sturdy and solid. Aidryn knelt and waved his palm over the floor's surface. The cracks and knots in the gnarled wood emitted a bright, crimson light; Lira perked up, leaning closer to watch a line of that same light etch itself into a perfect square.

"By Nami..." Lira whispered, edging closer before she lowered herself to the floor to crouch beside Aidryn as an iron handle materialized on the trapdoor.

"Your grandmother had been trying to open this door for seventy years—"

"But she needed the Key Keeper to open it," Lira breathed, blinking away tears as she stared at Aidryn in wonder. "She needed you here, not me." Her chin trembled, and she swiped at a stray tear on her cheek.

"No..." He gripped the handle, opening the door with a mighty heave to expose a yawning, dark pit below. A rope ladder was tied securely near the opening. "She needed us both. Needs you now more than ever."

Swinging his legs over the edge, he gripped the ladder and began descending into the darkness. Lira gulped.

"Why didn't Skelly write to me?" she asked after him. "If holding all that power was making her sick, why didn't she just ask me to help her?"

"Eremon almost persuaded her to write to you, but she didn't think a letter would reach you without being intercepted. And she didn't think you'd take the news well."

"She was right; I wouldn't have," Lira said, ears burning at the memory of how she'd reacted to the news of magic from Irem and Eremon. "I haven't taken any of this well."

"Who could expect you to? We handled ourselves foolishly."

Lira was surprised at how unruffled he sounded, even after she had raged at him. "I'm still angry with you," she said.

"I know."

She wanted to push the issue further, but there were more pressing questions to ask. For now, it was good enough that he knew she hadn't yet forgiven him for this. "What happens to Skelly's body if she doesn't discharge the power?" she called down.

"She begins to show her true age—at the very least."

For a brief moment, Lira wondered how old Skelly really was.

"Before I came to her," Aidryn continued, "she could barely walk, her legs were so arthritic. After sharing stories with me for a fortnight, she was hiking to the cove again."

He paused for a moment, halfway down the ladder. "Are you coming?"

"Um—yes," she called down. But she shook her head and stepped backward, wiping her sweaty palms on her tunic. Her quivering voice betrayed her fear when she asked, "How long has it been since you last saw Skelly?"

"Two years," he said. "My family started asking too many questions about where I was spending my time. I couldn't let them figure it out."

Aidryn had worked his way much farther down the ladder now—so far, she could no longer make out his expression in the darkness. "I should have come back before now."

Lira fought to steady her breathing. "Do you think she's dying?" She found the top ladder rung, white-knuckling the ropes as she began to climb down. "Like Eremon did."

A long beat of silence—too long. "I don't know."

She swallowed the lump in her throat, concentrating instead on maintaining her hold. If she allowed her fears about Skelly to overwhelm her now, she might miss a rung or lose her already-tenuous grip. "Can't you just tell me about whatever is down there?"

"No; I want you to see it with your own eyes."

Lira squeezed her eyes shut and inhaled sharply when the ladder swayed. "Is it worth me dying on the way?" The last few words came out as a half-laugh, half-sob.

"Just hold on; we're almost there."

"I can't believe I'm following you into a dark pit on nothing but—" she tensed as the ladder swung again—"sticks and ropes."

He chuckled nervously. "A few weeks ago, you'd have just as

soon cut the ropes than climb down after me with no explanation."

"Don't assume that's off the table," she said. Aidryn's movements jostled her again as he climbed farther down.

"I understand why you're angry with me," he called up from the gloom below. "I expected it."

Before Lira could reply, he landed with a loud, "Oof!"

She yelped and went rigid, alert to any noise as she listened for him.

"Aidryn?" she hissed. No answer. Her heart began to pound as she forced herself to keep moving. "Aidryn!"

A strong odor she couldn't place wafted up to greet her just before the passageway below was illuminated. A blaze of fire swept its way around an oil-filled trench that ringed the perimeter of the stone chamber beneath her. Aidryn emerged then, holding a lit torch and smirking proudly. "What do you think?"

Lira stepped onto the stone floor of the chamber and surveyed her surroundings. Her jaw went slack as she took it all in—the massive stone room that split off into seven separate corridors, the dais in the center of the room, and the four stone thrones atop it. Stalactites loomed above; over the crackling of the fire, Lira could hear the beat of water droplets hitting the cavern floor.

"I know this place," Lira breathed, moving deeper into the chamber.

Skelly had spoken of it before: Umhan Cavern. It was a meeting place for clan leaders to gather, far from Iathium's reach.

Lira wandered toward the dais, climbing the steps and reaching for the emblem on Clan Mór's throne: the twin to her pendant. One by one, she took in the carvings on the other thrones: for Clan Tarlach, a rearing horse with a large key between its teeth; for Clan Énna, a massive fish in court livery; and for Clan Beran, a hulking bear with a mace in its paw.

Lira's father had ridiculed Skelly for insisting Umhan existed. Arlen goaded his mother about it often, implying to Lira, and anyone else who would listen, that Skelly wasn't in her right mind. There it was again: another lie she'd willingly believed, from someone she loved.

She sat on the steps of the dais in stunned silence.

"Lira?" Aidryn asked tentatively, moving nearer.

"I believed this place was a myth," she whispered, turning to him. "Skelly tried to tell us—but I believed Da instead." She tried not to dwell on the memories that flashed through her mind: images of her father's face as he reassured her Iathium was truth. Faint flashes of Skelly's devastated expression just before she turned away.

"Why wouldn't you believe your own father?" Aidryn murmured, sitting beside her. "That's what children do."

"I threw myself into school after he died." She nearly choked on the word. "I wanted to make something of myself and make him proud, so I held onto everything he taught me. I never considered he might be wrong."

Her chest clenched and her stomach knotted; she couldn't draw a full breath. Suddenly, the cavern felt like it was closing in on her, and she wrapped her arms around her knees, burying her face as ragged sobs overtook her. She had been so proud—too proud. So sure she was right. How many apprentices had she taught wrongly because she wholeheartedly believed her father's lies?

Aidryn placed a comforting palm on her back. "We all find our own ways to grieve."

"But I was on the wrong side of everything. How can I ever come back from that? I know almost nothing about my power. We fled Iathium before I even had a chance to learn as much as I could about the truth. So much time wasted—"

"Lira, stop." There was a gentle warmth in his voice that gave her pause. He reached for her hand and laced their fingers together, blue eyes brilliant in the firelight. "I'm here with you."

Lira swiped at her tears. "Does it make sense for me to say I'm glad you're here, but I wish you would leave me be?"

"No." He put an arm around her and coaxed her closer, until her head rested on his shoulder. "But it doesn't have to."

They remained on the steps until the fire that encircled them burned low and their bodies were aching and stiff.

CHAPTER 28

That night, Lira bundled into Skelly's bed, wrapping the handmade blankets around her body like a cocoon. Her ears perked at every hint of noise outside the hut, though she knew they were far enough from Acton's Cove that they might not hear the clash of armies meeting below.

She lay wide awake, watching the moon trace its slow path across the sky. Aidryn kept the fire stoked through the night; from her nest in the tiny chamber, Lira could hear the occasional scrape of iron against the stone hearth. The tendril of warmth that wended its way into the bedroom made the chilly air bearable.

During the night, she rose a half dozen times to peek into the kitchen and ask what time it was. Each time, Aidryn shook his head and sent her back to bed.

She woke from dozing at dawn's first light, wrapping a blanket around herself and padding into the kitchen.

Aidryn cast her a weary glance. "You didn't rest at all, did you?"

She shook her head but didn't speak as she rummaged

around Skelly's worktable for the familiar old kettle. It was nowhere to be found, and she sighed. Sharing early morning tea with Skelly was one of her fondest memories from this place. But she supposed the kettle might be gone after so long, just like so many of the other things she'd held dear—things she hadn't realized she missed until now.

The sound of a wooden spoon tapping against iron caught her attention, and turned to find Aidryn staring pointedly at the kettle he'd hung over the fire. Water already boiled in it— fresh, clear water they'd brought up from the underground spring the night before.

Lira smiled. "Glad you found that."

"Which tea leaves would you like?" Aidryn nodded toward a lineup of small ceramic containers.

"Black."

"Excellent." He added a scoop to a tiny copper infuser and dropped it into the kettle. "How do we handle your uncle?"

"He likes to be flattered," she ventured, "but I don't think we can trust him."

Aidryn nodded. "What council would have approved the construction of this keep?"

The unsettled feeling in her stomach bloomed into full-blown, gnawing anxiety. She tried taking a few deep breaths, but mainly succeeded in making her belly hurt. "I don't know. I never dreamed I'd see this clan herded into a muddy, stinking fort like cattle."

Aidryn poured her a mug of tea; she forced herself to take a sip. "I'd wager your uncle's council of twelve has shrunken over the past few years," he said.

"Twelve is tradition."

He shrugged. "We'll see."

∽

Two hours later, Ellwyn led Lira and Aidryn back to the great hall where they'd met Gerallt the day before. To Lira's relief, no hounds guarded the door.

They took seats on a bench at one of the long tables. The lingering scent of sausage and boiled potatoes still hung in the air from breakfast, and Lira's stomach growled. She and Aidryn were counting on Skelly's tea to sustain them until after the meeting was over. Hungry or not, Lira couldn't trust herself to hold anything down.

"I don't want to do this," she confided, leaning back against the edge of the table. "It makes me sick just thinking about it. Being forced to face the council is humiliating; these people have known me since childhood."

Aidryn nodded. "It's not right."

"I'm afraid," she whispered, daring to meet his eyes. "I can't help it."

He shrugged. "Then do it afraid. Pretend. How long will this last—a few minutes? Maybe an hour, at most? Listen, Lira; be afraid, but pretend you're not. No one has to know. Then, if you have to, run outside and vomit when it's over."

She grimaced.

"Trust me," he pressed. "Don't let them see you flinch."

When Gerallt finally arrived, Aidryn was stretched out on the bench while Lira paced anxiously before the dying fire.

"Ah! You finally deigned to show your face," he boomed.

Aidryn sat up slowly, giving the large man a sideways glare as Lira replied tersely, "We've been waiting here for an hour."

"The council has tired of waiting; they're ready to adjourn," her uncle plowed on, grasping the crook of her elbow and steering her toward the hallway. "Come quickly. If we hurry, you'll still have a moment to address them."

Gerallt pushed Lira ahead of him, placing his body between her and Aidryn as he turned a sharp corner and steered her into a chamber, engaging the heavy lock behind them. He took a seat in the center of a small dais on the far end of the room, flanked by two additional chairs.

"Jón! Timms!" he roared. "Our visitor has arrived."

Lira's mouth went dry as Gerallt's two oldest friends emerged from behind a curtain on the opposite side of the chamber and took seats on either side of their master.

Her eyes flicked from one to the other, then back to her uncle. "Where are the Twelve?"

She wondered how long it would take Aidryn to let himself in. It was difficult to suppress the smirk that threatened to curl her lips.

"For the good of the clan, I have chosen a smaller council—at least, for the time being," Gerallt said, grasping a goblet full of wine and taking a long swig. "It's a precautionary measure until the threat from Iathium has passed."

"I was under the impression the *larger* council was for the protection of the clan."

"What makes you think your opinion matters here?" Gerallt asked, leaning forward in mock interest as he propped an elbow on his knee. Jón snorted.

"Little traitor," Timms growled, motioning for Gerallt's goblet and taking a gulp of wine himself.

Lira clenched her fists.

"Enough, Timms." Gerallt waved him off. "Take another drink. Drink the whole bloody flagon, if you wish. Whatever it takes to keep your fat mouth shut."

Timms glared at Lira over the rim of the goblet, but said no more as he drank deeply.

"Now, Silira," Gerallt said, slouching down in his chair—a small, ornate throne carved of cherry wood, from the look of it. "To business. Tell the council why you're here."

"I am here to beg temporary asylum," she answered unflinchingly. "I come as a refugee and a citizen of no territory."

"Not heir to Iathium?" Gerallt asked.

She swallowed hard. "No, uncle. It is as I said."

"Is it?" Her uncle stared pointedly at her hand. "Why else would you flaunt that thing on my lands?"

Lira moved Eremon's ring from view. "My reasons for wearing it, uncle, aren't your concern."

"You should've thought twice before venturing into enemy territory brandishing that symbol," Jón said in a honey-coated tone. "That's very dangerous. Someone could get hurt."

"Yet the first scrape you find yourself in, you come crawling here to hide like a scared rabbit," Timms added.

"No—"

"You never answered the master," Jón growled. "Why are you really here?"

Lira steeled herself. "I gave you an answer—"

"—that was unsatisfactory." Gerallt looked mildly amused as he looked between Lira and Jón. "You must have specific reasons for coming. Your stepfather, the mighty Arthmael, rules Clan Beran. Surely, Fortress Halgeir would have welcomed you."

"I have little familiarity with Clan Beran, and no allies to rely on," she said. "Artur has no love for me."

Timms mumbled something unintelligible into the cup.

Lira ignored him. "And it is a well-known fact that few outside Beran are allowed in or out. If you aren't part of the settlement, you aren't welcome."

Gerallt pursed his lips. "If you were truly as smart as they say, you would have established relations with them."

"Established relations?" Lira asked incredulously. "I'm not a diplomat. My place was in the archive. I never anticipated this."

Gerallt drummed his fingertips on his armrest. "We've heard some interesting accounts from Iathium about your affair with their king."

She flinched. "Accounts that say…?"

"That you murdered him with dark magic and took that

ring for yourself," the councilman answered. "Why else were you arrested?"

"Eremon's own magic killed him. His mother needed someone to blame."

"She has a hefty price on your head."

She raised her chin. "That doesn't surprise me."

Gerallt scoffed. "I could double the size of this keep with the gold I'd get from turning you over."

Lira held his stare. "Then why haven't you?"

"I have my own interests to consider. As yet, Macha isn't a part of them."

Clicking and scraping sounded from behind her. The men sat up straight, on high alert as the door swung open and Aidryn strode in.

"Bugger of a lock you've got there, Gerallt," he said with a smirk.

Lira grinned smugly in spite of herself.

"If it isn't the hound, back from chasing his tail," Jón slurred.

"Only scratching at the door, sir, like a good dog." Aidryn glanced at Lira and winked. "I understood this audience was meant for the two of us."

"You misunderstood," Gerallt said.

"Then so did I," Lira countered, inviting Aidryn to her side. "He has every right to be here."

Gerallt narrowed his eyes at Aidryn. "Young Key Keeper, we were just finishing."

"But—" Lira cut in.

"You may remain here until this evening while we decide what to do with you." He curled the end of his mustache around one finger, turning to Timms in silent demand for the now-empty goblet.

"What does that mean?"

"I have an important audience to attend to," he said, brushing her off.

"But what about Skelly?"

Gerallt rose. "If you wanted to know about *her*, you should've asked before."

He jerked his head toward Jón and Timms, and the three of them disappeared behind a thick tapestry on the opposite wall. Stunned into silence, Lira didn't try to call after him.

CHAPTER 29

"Meeting with the council was a mistake," Lira said once they'd shut themselves back inside the cottage. "I wanted you there, but I wish you hadn't come in when you did."

Aidryn stoked the sputtering fire. "Why?"

"Gerallt had just admitted to having his own *interests* in the matter with Iathium." She shrugged a shoulder. "I suppose if he didn't, he would have already handed me over to Macha."

"Did he give you any clue what those interests are?"

"No. But Gerallt has no loyalty to me. I think we should leave before we find out."

Lira picked up the leather saddlebag and began re-packing their belongings. "You've said before that you can detect magic, Aidryn. Can you use that power to find where they're holding Skelly?"

Aidryn kicked some stray ash from the hearth back into the fireplace. "I felt something when we were in the keep," he said. "I wonder if Gerallt has her in one of the towers."

"Do you think that's what I saw in my vision?"

An insistent knock on the front door startled them both.

Warily, Aidryn placed his hand on the knob—keeping the lock engaged, Lira realized.

"Who is it?" he called.

"Ellwyn."

Aidryn let go of the door, and it creaked open before Ellwyn slipped inside and shut it hastily. Her eyes were wide and glassy as she took in Lira holding the saddlebag, clothing bunched in her fist.

Her cousin held up a cautionary hand. "Papa's in council again. I don't have much time—but he's going to offer you asylum. I overheard it just now."

Lira's knees buckled as she sighed with relief. She braced herself on the worktable, a hand over her heart. "I'd assumed the worst."

Aidryn's wary gaze followed Ellwyn as she moved closer to her cousin, prattling on. "It's not good, Lira. He means to trap you both."

"Go on." Aidryn reached for the leather bag, which Lira relinquished grudgingly.

Ellwyn shifted from one foot to the other. "Sit down."

Lira fumbled for a stool. Aidryn took a seat by the hearth as Ellwyn began pacing.

"You know how Papa is," she began. "He craves influence beyond the Ridge, and you're the heir of all things. He enjoys claiming important people and things for himself."

Lira's stomach turned over, but she pressed her lips together. She didn't want to know where this was leading.

"Aidryn," Ellwyn said, "is it true you're the Key Keeper?"

"Yes," he answered, furrowing his brow. "How do you know that?"

"Papa found out you used to come here—he's been meeting with Tarlach descendants from the city. They trust him because he claims to have an alliance with you."

Aidryn and Lira exchanged a glance; parading Aidryn's

presence before Gerallt didn't sound like something Skelly would do.

"What do you think he's trying to do?" he asked.

Ellwyn shrugged a shoulder. "I think he wants to reassemble the clan and ally with them."

"Why would he do that?" Aidryn asked warily.

"He's going to march on Iathium in Lira's name."

Lira sucked in a sharp breath. This is what Aidryn had warned her would happen.

Aidryn leaned closer to Ellwyn, lowering his voice. "Where did you get this information?"

"Council meetings, snippets of conversation. I glean what I can," Ellwyn whispered. "Papa keeps me on rotation with the archers, though, so it isn't much."

"It's enough," Lira said.

"There's more." Ellwyn took a deep breath. "I heard him talking of a double marriage."

"Whose marriage?" Aidryn asked.

"It's humiliating," she sighed. "He was debating with the council about whether binding himself to Lira would be advantageous."

Lira blanched. "What? Absolutely not!"

The rest of the words burst out of Ellwyn in a rush. "He was also boasting about making a strategic match of me."

Lira felt the weight of the words Ellwyn didn't say. As Gerallt's only daughter, she would be wed to the most beneficial ally. So unless Gerallt had suitors in mind from the other clans—

Aidryn paced by the window, crossing his arms tightly. "So he would marry Lira in a bid for Iathium. And then he would unite his clan with mine through you, Ellwyn?"

Lira flinched at Aidryn's candor. He shot her an apologetic glance.

Ellwyn nodded, leaning against the table. "If I'm not

mistaken, that's his plan. And—begging your pardon, Aidryn—I don't like the idea, and I won't go along with it."

"Well, that makes two of us." He winked at Ellwyn, and she smiled with relief.

Lira felt queasy; she couldn't bear to keep talking about weddings and binding ceremonies. "How can you two joke at a time like this? Are we not going to talk about how me marrying my uncle is a disgusting idea?"

"No," Ellwyn shuddered.

"Of course not, because it's *disgusting*," Aidryn quipped, grimacing.

"Really Aidryn!" Her voice was shrill with panic. "It's not a joke!"

"We're not going to let it happen, Lira," he said gently. "You're in no danger of being married off to him; we'll be gone before he can propose."

Ellwyn looked between them uncomfortably, as if unsure what to say. Lira chewed her bottom lip angrily.

"Ellwyn," Aidryn ventured, glancing sidelong at Lira, "what can you tell us about Skelly?"

She shook her head. "Not much. Papa's had her locked in the north tower for months."

"What's wrong with her?" Lira asked.

Her cousin shuddered. "She doesn't move or speak—almost like she's been possessed."

Aidryn groaned. "This is a disaster."

"We have to get to her," Lira said, turning to Ellwyn. "Can you get us an object from her room? It could be anything, even a bit of straw."

"I'll try, but I can't promise you anything."

"At least promise you'll try." Lira grasped her cousin's hands. "How quickly do you think you can do it?"

Ellwyn's eyes cut to the timepiece on the mantel. "Give me three hours. If I don't return—"

"You will," Lira insisted, pulling Ellwyn into a tight embrace. "Thank you; we have to stop this."

Ellwyn's arms tightened around Lira.

"Be cautious," Aidryn warned.

Ellwyn nodded curtly. "I will."

She pivoted and headed for the door. When it latched behind her, Aidryn whirled on Lira.

"We're going to *turas* into the tower—"

"—as soon as Ellwyn returns. Can you get us something from the cavern? We can take Skelly there after."

He nodded. "I'll be back."

Aidryn headed toward Skelly's room to unseal the passage. He disappeared down the ladder, and Lira collapsed onto her stool again. She ran her fingertips over Eremon's ring.

The weight of everything she had to protect bore down upon her, an invisible force that wrapped itself around her and squeezed like a hungry serpent. Skelly, the clan, Iathium, Rodhlan...

Too much; it's too much. I can't do this.

She crumpled then, folding over herself and resting her forehead in her hands. Taking long, steadying breaths, she willed her mind to go blank. But instead of the soothing silence she sought, flashes of memory danced before her.

The memories were difficult to interpret at first—they led her through a series of binding rituals. In some of the flashes, she glimpsed Skelly performing the rites for couples she didn't recognize. In others, some unnamed priest or priestess performed the ritual. But they performed the same action, over and over, as if the memories themselves were trying to tell her something.

A couple clasps forearms. The priestess wraps strips of emerald cloth, silver, and bronze chain around their joined arms. She begins at the woman's forearm where her betrothed's fingertips rest, and wraps methodically until she reaches the woman's fingertips on her partner's side. The priestess clasps a hand over the couple's wrists.

A flash of light punctuated each shift from vision to vision. Lira was lost to the memories until she felt a warm pair of hands on her shoulders; the gentle touch drew her back, bringing her full awareness to the man before her.

She blinked as her focus sharpened.

"What did you see?" Aidryn asked, expression somber.

"Binding rites," she answered. "Over and over. I feel like there's something I should understand... but I don't. Was there ancient power in the rites? Some sort of magic that manifested —or something the priestesses unlocked?"

"There aren't many written records about it that survived," Aidryn said, "but from what I gather, the rites opened a magical bond between husband and wife that allowed their magic to flow freely, one to another."

Lira blanched, her heart sinking. "That's it, then. That's what he wants. He must think there's some chance he can access my power."

"It's a complicated technique, but I doubt he realizes that. I understand there were precious few priestesses who could truly perform the rites to the fullest extent. Mostly, they were simply symbolic of the old ways.

"Both parties had to be completely open to the exchange. Otherwise, the ritual would be unsuccessful. It's the ultimate test of trust between two people."

Another realization washed over Lira, and she thought she might be sick. "Do you think Eremon—"

"No." Aidryn shook his head vehemently. "He wouldn't have wanted you to harbor the dark magic."

Shame roiled inside her at his answer. "I shouldn't have thought that of him."

"Yes, you should," he said. "You must, even if you're wrong.

Anything is possible when tremendous power is involved. Especially where a ruler's love is concerned.

"You have to ask these questions, even if they lead you to a possibility you don't want to think about. It doesn't make you a bad person to consider all angles or to question who you're willing to put your trust in.

"All the same," he said, rubbing his neck, "Eremon was tampering with things he didn't truly understand. I thought he was being foolish, and I told him so."

He extended his palm, opening his fingers to reveal a chipped piece of stone from the cavern below. "Here." He dropped the stone into her hand.

She turned it over and over. "You openly disagreed with him?"

"At every opportunity." Aidryn sat beside her again. "We didn't see eye to eye on many things."

Lira ignored the curiosity that rose within her; she wasn't sure she could talk about Eremon without bursting into tears.

"I wasn't made for this," she whispered. "I'm a prisoner to all of it—this inheritance, the magic, the memories. There's nothing I can do to make it go away."

"You can't make it go away," Aidryn said, searching her face until she met his gaze. "You must rise to it."

"I should never have let myself love him," she cried. "I want to run from all of this, but I'm shackled to it forever; it will never end."

"Don't despair," Aidryn soothed. "We're all enslaved to our fate. Now, how will you choose to run headlong into yours?"

She sighed. "Find allies, I suppose; though I don't know where to start."

"Start with your friends. You have me, Faolan, Aeron, and Ellwyn." Aidryn reached out, winding one of Lira's curls around his finger.

"What about Talfryn?"

"As soon as we reunite with him, yes; Talfryn, too."

Lira stilled as Aidryn tucked the curl behind her ear. "And Fannin?" she whispered hoarsely.

"Fannin, too." He laughed softly. "I can't believe he tolerates your insolence."

Her face heated as her voice dropped. "I sneak him carrots when you're not looking."

Aidryn drew closer. "Well, that explains it."

He leaned forward, planting a light kiss on her forehead. She swallowed hard at his proximity, keenly aware of the ring she still bore.

As he pulled away, she squeezed her eyes shut and blurted, "You're insufferable."

Aidryn chuckled. "Insufferable, at your service."

He wandered over to one of Skelly's shelves, picked up a small music box, and began winding it.

Lira watched intently as he set the box back on the shelf. "Ellwyn didn't mince words about the idea of marriage, did she?" She laughed uneasily.

"I saw her on occasion, when I used to come here," he said. "She is much more reserved now than she was then—but she'd still make a terrible diplomat."

Lira smiled. "I always wished I could be as direct as she is, with no fear of the consequences."

"Skelly wanted to play matchmaker between Ellwyn and myself, in the event that—well, that doesn't matter." He waved off the thought. "My true interest lay elsewhere, and I always told her that."

"You loved another, then," Lira said. Her voice sounded unfamiliar in her ears.

Aidryn stepped to the window, looking out toward the keep. "Yes."

"And?"

"And..." He shrugged, casting a half-glance back. "It wasn't returned."

"Oh," Lira breathed, a knot twisting in her gut.

She traced the worn wood on the surface of the worktable with a fingertip. Her eyes fell to the tea kettle, and she went to work filling it.

Without a word, Aidryn stoked a fire in the hearth, took the kettle from Lira, and hung it to boil. The cottage warmed with the fire, its crackling filling the silence as they waited for Ellwyn to return.

CHAPTER 30

Ellwyn returned to the cottage two hours later, a small fragment of frayed rope in her hand.

"It's the best I could do," she said, dropping it into Lira's palm. "Good luck."

Without a backward glance, she slipped back out of the cottage. Aidryn locked the door behind her decisively, then turned to Lira.

"Are you ready?" he asked.

Lira bit her lip. "How are we going to get Fannin?"

"I'll call him when we've gotten Skelly out of the territory," he said. "One step at a time."

"All right." Lira heaved a sigh. "Take my hand." She extended her open palm.

Aidryn caught her hand, interlacing their fingers. With a shuddering breath, Lira held the rope against her pendant.

The *turas* happened so quickly, she barely registered it. With a flash of midnight-black, they found themselves standing in the corridor of the north tower, outside a locked cell door. Its iron bars, handle, and lock emitted a low hum that made Lira's teeth grind; it was so repulsive, she backed into the opposite wall, wide-eyed.

"It's dark magic," she whispered.

Aidryn's eyes cut to her for a moment before he approached the door himself. Hesitantly, he allowed his fingers to hover just over the handle. His lips parted in surprise and he hissed a curse before looking back to Lira.

"Aila sealed this," he said. "I'd know her magic anywhere."

Lira swallowed hard. "Then she's one of the Tarlach descendants Gerallt spoke of."

"They're trying to get at Skelly's magic, then," he answered, allowing himself to touch the handle. It sent a jolt through his body; he clenched his teeth until it passed. "We need to make quick work of this and get you both out. She'll know we're here."

He reached for the handle again, but Lira caught one of his wrists before he could begin.

"Wait."

"What?" He searched her eyes imploringly.

"Take this," Lira said, prying Eremon's band from her finger. "It will protect you from the spell Aila put on the door."

Aidryn hesitated. "Are you sure?"

"You're the one unlocking the door."

He accepted the ring from Lira. He closed his fist, and it vanished. "Fine, but you're putting it back on when we get inside."

Lira offered a tight-lipped smile. "Thank you."

He turned back to the door, his fingertips brushing the handle. A bright crimson glow erupted from his hands, entering the keyhole. From the door's inner workings, Lira could hear clicking and releasing as his magic disengaged the lock. Aidryn opened the door slowly.

The stench that emanated from the chamber made Lira gag. With a sinking feeling, she wondered if Skelly had simply died and been left to rot. The room was the picture of squalor, worse than what the people in the keep had been subjected to.

An unfamiliar power hummed from the far corner of the room, and Lira felt pulled toward it. She motioned for Aidryn to follow. They moved toward the magic until they reached a tapestry that separated them from the source. Tentatively, Lira pushed it aside.

Before them, on a crude wooden stool, sat a nearly unrecognizable Skelly—unkempt, gaunt, and staring straight at them with glowing, unseeing eyes of emerald.

As Lira locked eyes with her grandmother, all sound and sensation seemed to suck itself from the room around her. There was a void now, quiet and dark, and the only things she could see were the glowing eyes—the same eyes from her vision. They held her in place, fixing her boots to the floorboards.

"She has come for me, mistress," she heard her own disembodied voice say—the voice from her vision. Yet she felt no movement, no vibration from the sound. She was fully in its thrall, her senses along with her body.

An emerald vine slithered across the floor toward her like a snake, twisting its way up her body and entering her mouth. She wanted to gag, to scream; still, it invaded her as if exploring. Probing. It burned her insides as it searched for what it wanted—then withdrew quickly, as if in disgust.

Lira was thrown violently to the floor, where she gagged and coughed before her grandmother. She hauled herself up to her hands and knees, her entire body trembling uncontrollably. When she dared to raise her face, the crone did not acknowledge her.

"Skelly," she moaned, crawling forward shakily.

From behind her, Aidryn called, "Lira, stop!"

She whirled toward his voice. This time, horror filled her as she heard herself reply, "Ah, you, too. Mistress will be pleased indeed."

Lira blinked, trying to clear the fog that filled her eyes. Suddenly, she was staring out at Aidryn from the place where Skelly had been sitting—rigid and filled with utter hatred. She felt herself blink, then looked down at her own wretched, pathetic body lying on the floor just feet away, frozen and absent.

So small, so weak and breakable. Her lip curled in contempt.

And the man—just as his keeper described. Handsome and wily, to be sure, but distracted. *Good humor and courage overshadowed by the one thing he stands to lose.*

"Give me what you protect," Lira heard herself say. A crooked, gnarled finger pointed toward Aidryn.

He clenched his fists. "No."

Cruel laughter erupted from Lira's mouth, and she sent the vines careening toward Aidryn, slamming his body against the wall and confining him there. His physical strength was no match for this magic, though he made a valiant attempt to escape. The vines pinned him fast, then curled eagerly around his wrists, slithering up his arms.

Aidryn struggled, but a blast of magic slammed the back of his head against the stone wall. He cried out as a green light pulsed from the vines and keys began to fall from the sleeves of his jerkin, scattering across the floor.

"There, child," the voice rasped from between Lira's lips. The body on the stool leaned forward for a better look. A shock of pain tore through Lira's back at the motion; clearly, this was the first time Skelly's body had moved in a long while. Her eyes sought something particular.

"What are these rusted trinkets?" the voice barked. Lira's throat burned. "Trash! Where is it?"

This time, the gnarled hand flicked a finger toward Aidryn.

Lira watched helplessly as Aidryn's head slammed into the wall again.

"Where is my pendant?" the voice shrieked.

"I don't—" *Slam.* "Know what you're—" *Slam.* "Talking about!"

"More lies!" the voice croaked.

Lira felt her very essence beginning to meld with this pitiful shell of a body. This time, when she raised her hands, she raised them of her own accord, hatred coursing through her veins as she willed her magic into a crescendo. She would kill him if he'd lost it.

"Tell me."

She'd make him suffer.

The vines wrapped around his throat, strangling him. His eyes filled with fear. *Good.* Tighter, tighter—

"The girl!" he gasped. "The girl has it! I will bring it to you."

There. Delicious panic. The vines that entrapped Aidryn loosened then, dropping to the floor. His fingers closed over something small before he edged warily toward Lira's body, careful not to turn his back on the crone.

From the tangle of thoughts running through Skelly's mind, Lira managed to grasp her own. They echoed something, over and over... but what it meant, she couldn't—

The ring. The ring, the ring, the ring—

Skelly's voice cut through Lira's thoughts. "Hurry, boy!"

"Yes," Aidryn nodded, his hands moving toward Lira. One hand fumbled with the chain around her neck, and Skelly watched hungrily, practically salivating in anticipation. But with the other, he slid Eremon's ring back onto Lira's finger.

Lira felt her essence being ripped from the enraged old body as Skelly began to understand what was happening. A moment later, she was lying on the floor again, merged with her own body. Her eyelids fluttered open to find Aidryn's face hovering above hers.

"Aidryn," she whispered, her throat burning. Every breath was agony.

"Never take it off again, promise me." His eyes were pleading, full of a frantic fire she had never seen before.

"Promise."

"We have to go. Can you stand?"

"Skelly."

Aidryn's gaze flicked to the crone, then back to Lira. "This magic—it's too powerful. I don't know if we should take her."

"We have no choice," Lira protested. "We need Ljós."

"I think your mother could help us get to him."

"I can't go crawling to my mother."

"Then don't crawl," Aidryn said, searching her face. He grasped her hands. "Don't grovel. Walk in there like the heir you are.

"It's time to stop doubting yourself, Silira," he whispered. "What just happened here would have killed any ordinary woman."

Knees trembling, Lira nodded. She chanced a glance back at Skelly, whose body now slumped lifelessly in the corner. "Is she dead?"

"I don't think so," he said, approaching the elderly woman warily, Lira at his heels. He reached for the Skelly's bony wrist, feeling for a pulse. "She's alive."

"Can you carry her?"

Aidryn leaned forward, tipping Skelly's dead weight into his arms. He grunted as he hoisted her over his shoulder. Once he'd lifted her, he reached for Lira.

Lira's hands shook as she withdrew the cavern stone from her pouch and grasped Aidryn's hand once again. She brought the stone to her pendant and joined the two objects, steeling herself for *turas*. The chamber around them began to fade—

But not before Skelly stirred, and her gnarled fingers latched onto the base of Lira's skull.

CHAPTER 31

As the *turas* swallowed them up, Lira screamed; it felt like diving into a pit of fire, the flames licking at her skin as they were dragged through one horrific memory after another.

Clanspeople burned alive. Iathium's armies laying waste to the outlying lands. A nomadic people begging for mercy as their horses were slaughtered, their wagons burned.

The wailing of men, women, and children filled her head, and her own voice rose to match it. She feverishly wondered whether Aidryn was screaming as well—whether he could see what she saw. Whether she was really burning alongside the visions.

This *turas* felt like it dragged on forever; it didn't manifest in mere moments, like the one that had brought them into the tower. Lira seemed to tumble over herself for hours, through ash and flame. When the fire began to cool and the wailing in Lira's head finally quieted, her throat was aching and raw.

Is this death? she thought. Her thoughts felt disconnected from her mind, as if they were floating somewhere in the ether.

In the distance, she could hear the trickle of the stream in the cavern. Though she felt like she'd been ripped out of her own body, her senses began to return. She could make out fragments of a conversation happening nearby.

"—don't understand; there was no other way."

I know that voice—Skelly!

"What if you had killed her?" Aidryn asked. He sounded as though he could barely control his tone.

"I was a greater danger to her before; transferring the power was a necessary risk."

"During *turas*?"

"I was not myself, Aidryn; surely you understand that."

A long sigh. "At least it's over now."

Lira could feel someone cradling her, and she opened her eyes. A muscle in Aidryn's jaw twitched as he lowered her to the cavern floor.

Lira's hair was soaked with sweat and plastered to her forehead. Her body shook violently, and her teeth chattered as she struggled to draw a steady breath.

Aidryn began to draw away, but Lira wound her hands into his tunic, clutching him close. "Don't go," she whimpered.

"Shh," he soothed, brushing away the sweaty curls that stuck to her face. "We're safe. Just be still. I sent Skelly for water."

Lira had so many questions, but her throat was too parched, and her lips were cracked and tight. Her heart was still pounding in her ears, loud enough that she suspected Aidryn could hear it.

His gaze was intense, blue eyes full of concern as he hauled her closer to him. "Whatever was holding her in the tower, the spell broke when we crossed into Umhan," he murmured, tracing Lira's forehead with his fingertips.

"I didn't think I would survive it," Lira whispered, heaving a deep breath. A tear trickled down her cheek.

"I'm sorry," he whispered.

"Why didn't Eremon's ring protect me?"

"Because the power you received was your own," he answered. "Your birthright."

Lira's lips parted in question once again, but a figure stepped into her line of vision—an outline so familiar, silhouetted against the flames that ringed the room, that she almost cried aloud again. Tears blurred her vision as Skelly stepped forward, cradling a ladle of cold water from the stream.

As her grandmother's face came into focus, Lira noted that she was almost unchanged from their last meeting all those years ago. Gone was the gnarled old crone they'd encountered in the tower and the vacant green glow that had filled her eyes.

All that remained was the woman Lira had known all her life, who had shared her stories and nurtured her granddaughter. Who had tried so hard to break down the walls she'd built around her heart since she was a child.

Lira's hand trembled as she reached for Skelly's. The elderly woman knelt, squeezed her hand, then pressed the ladle to her lips, coaxing her to drink. Once Lira's throat cooled, Aidryn helped her sit up, and Skelly joined them.

"Silira," she whispered, a smile playing on her lips. "Well done."

"Skelly—" Lira began before a sob burst from her.

Her grandmother's soft palm caressed her cheek. "Don't try to talk."

Lira pressed a palm to Skelly's hand where it rested on her face.

"I wish I'd been able to bless you with your birthright in the sacred ceremony," Skelly said. "But there was no time to waste.

"As soon as I came to my senses and realized you'd come for me, I didn't hesitate," she continued. "Receiving magic can be agonizing. I'm afraid I'd forgotten how painful it is, after all these years."

Skelly stroked her granddaughter's hair, peering intently at

Aidryn. "I never thought I'd see you again, young Tarlach. After you disappeared, I feared the worst."

"I believed I was protecting you by staying away," he said, "but I failed."

"Even the best of efforts fail from time to time. Look at my sons. Arlen thought he could protect Lira from her fate; and Gerallt..." Skelly sighed. "He's a monster.

"When something is meant to happen, there's no preventing it. Delay it, we may. But it will come, nonetheless."

Skelly turned to Lira and rested a hand on her shoulder. "Take your Eremon, Silira. It didn't matter what you did, what you risked in trying to save him; he was gone from the first moment his magic rebelled against his bones. His forefathers sealed his fate."

The reminder churned a visceral pain in Lira's gut, but she bit her lips and did not respond.

"And Aidryn—your stepmother would have come to my son no matter what. Magic calls to magic, but dark magic seeks what it may devour. And she comes to devour now."

"What can we do to stop her?" he asked.

"Nothing yet," Skelly answered. "Your job is not to prevent what is happening today, Aidryn."

Something akin to shame passed across Aidryn's features.

"You can't mean for us to go through with these marriages," Lira said, her voice gravelly.

Skelly furrowed her brow. "What are you talking about, child?"

"Ellwyn warned us," said Lira. "She said Gerallt wanted to marry me and march on Iathium—and bind Mór to Tarlach through her and Aidryn."

"She means well," Skelly said, shaking her head, "but she doesn't know what she's talking about."

"She said Gerallt was offering us asylum in exchange for alliances."

"What good would allying with either of you do for him— two fugitives who would never use their magic for evil?" the elderly woman said, waving her off. "He's giving asylum to Aila and Caitir Tarlach in exchange for marriage."

Lira felt like she'd been punched in the gut.

"He's *what*?" Aidryn growled.

"They fled Iathium," Skelly answered. "Gerallt is expecting them tonight."

"And my father..." Aidryn faltered, his face crumping. "I suppose he'd dead, then."

Skelly inclined her head. "You chose whom to save, boy— swore to it, as I understand."

Lira flinched at the implication.

Aidryn rose, pacing toward the crackling fire. "Is there nothing we can do? Can we save Caitir?"

Skelly shook her head solemnly. "Not without a battle, I'm afraid. The rite is set to begin within the hour; everything is already in place. And even if you succeed, your sister will come right back here at the first opportunity."

Silence fell. It felt like the air had been sucked out of the cavern.

"She's only a child," Aidryn murmured, his voice strangely steady, every word measured. "She's just a silly child. She would never agree to this."

"But she has," Skelly supplied. "She believed herself in line for Eremon's hand. This is a power grab, for both women. Your sister must decide to escape on her own."

A maddened laugh burst from between Aidryn's lips as he paced, shattering his calm facade.

"Why are you surprised that Caitir seeks power? You shouldn't be."

"She'll be used as a prize mare for breeding," he growled, "and Aila will rule by proxy."

Skelly leaned forward, an arm propped on her knee. "A prize mare with a crown is still a monarch."

"I know Caitir nearly as well as Aidryn," Lira said. "She's not herself. I think Aila coerced her somehow; maybe there's a way to help her."

"No; your grandmother is right," Aidryn sighed, shaking his head. "You remember the danger Caitir put you in—she went along with Aila's plan to capture you and take your power. No, this isn't the Caitir we knew; but because of that, we can't take the risk."

Skelly nodded sagely. "First, we must protect the magic. Always, the magic is most important."

Aidryn turned his back to them then—stayed that way for so long that Lira found the strength to rise, her legs trembling, and go to him. She swayed with the sudden motion, but centered herself, padding toward where he stood.

Lira wanted to reach for him, but hesitated; finally, she rested her palm on his shoulder. He leaned into her touch.

"I'm sorry, my friend," she whispered.

He sought her gaze then, releasing a long, shuddering sigh. Lira patted his shoulder, then reached for his hand, clasping it in hers. But it wasn't enough; she drew nearer and embraced him instead, throwing her arms around his neck. Aidryn stilled, but returned her embrace, holding her tightly against him. She buried her face in the crook of his shoulder and took in his scent: fresh air and meadows and sunlight.

For a moment, the world around them quieted. There was a safety, a familiarity to this. Comfort in spite of the pain. All this time, he had been her truest friend.

She had been furious with him for keeping so much from her, but she could understand his secrets and lies; they had been meant to protect her. Not her power, her birthright, or her status—just her. In spite of everything, she trusted him with her life.

Skelly's voice cut through the silence. "I wish to share my thoughts. But you're both stubborn; perhaps I'm wasting my time."

"Whatever might help..." Lira turned to her grandmother. "We'll listen."

The elderly woman crooked an eyebrow but patted the stone step beside her. "Sit with me."

They obliged her.

"Skelly, I have so much to say to you—so much to apologize for," Lira said, "but I'm not sure where to begin."

"Soon." Skelly reached for Lira's hand and gave it a squeeze. "For now, I have some things to tell you. It isn't easy to explain, so listen well."

From the look on Aidryn's face, Lira could tell his trepidation was rising to match her own. His throat bobbed as they sat across from Skelly.

The elderly woman laced her fingers together and gazed at them intently. "Aila has made my son many promises—mostly promises she can't keep. But there is one she intends to make good on, and we must ensure she doesn't."

"Tell us," Lira breathed.

"Aila has sworn an oath to Gerallt to drain the three of us of our magic. He believes she'll be giving the whole of this clan's power to him, along with the Key Keeper's remaining gifts."

"The few she hasn't taken already," Aidryn added bitterly.

"Just the three of us?" Lira asked. "How could that be all of Clan Mór's magic? Wouldn't Aila have to take it from everyone else here, too?"

Aidryn stilled, dragging his gaze toward the Lira's grandmother. His eyes flashed with the realization. "Not if someone already did."

CHAPTER 32

It was Skelly's turn to look ashamed.

"Were you hoping to warm us to the idea?" Aidryn asked coolly.

She shook her head. "I was a fool to think I could bear the entire clan's power alone. I held onto it for the one person I trusted: my Lira."

"And now you've poured all this magic into her?"

Lira swayed where she sat; Aidryn looped an arm around her and let her lean into him.

"Not all of it," Skelly said, shaking her head vehemently. "Not enough to do harm."

Images flashed in Lira's mind before she could stop them—and suddenly, she wasn't only reliving Eremon's death, but the deaths of others gone before him. Others who had taken more than their share of magic, and paid the price for it.

Black lightning consumes a woman from the inside out.

A man is reduced to ash as he attempts to steal magic from another.

A mother kills her baby as she tries to siphon its magic, and is then devoured by the power herself.

Lira began to tremble all over again. Aidryn tightened his grip on her.

"How did you survive for so long, with so much power?" he asked.

"Because I named an anointed," Skelly answered. "A person the magic can go to."

"Will I die like Eremon?" Lira whimpered.

"No. You won't," Aidryn said sharply, leveling a glare at Skelly. "We'll make sure of it."

"We have to give this magic to the clan, right away," Lira insisted. "We can't wait."

Skelly's eyes widened. "That's not possible."

"Why." Aidryn narrowed his eyes. "Gerallt knows that you and Lira are the only ones with the power, doesn't he?"

Skelly's head dipped slightly. "Yes."

"And you left these people vulnerable?"

Her grandmother raised her chin. "I have protected this clan."

Aidryn grew deathly still; Lira waited for him to take a breath, but he didn't for a long moment. Skelly didn't speak. The fire crackled around them, its sound amplified in the tense silence.

When Aidryn did speak again, his voice was carefully measured.

"Please tell me if I'm wrong, Skelly," he began, "but if you never gifted this magic to your people, they are empty vessels. Are they not?"

Still, Skelly said nothing. Aidryn continued. "As it stands, you and Lira are the only people here who carry the ancient power. Gerallt knows this, and you say he has offered asylum to Aila and Caitir in exchange for marriage.

"I know how Aila thinks, Skelly. For her to put any effort into a scheme, there must be more than one benefit to her. Actually, there must be several.

"The first benefit is the chance to take this power from you and Lira. If everything goes in Aila's favor, she could gather all of Clan Mór's power for herself. But she's smart enough to know that her chances of getting to both of you are very small.

"So she has plotted out other scenarios—all of which work to her benefit. She knows that she stands a chance at capturing at least one of you. Marrying Gerallt would put both her and Caitir in a firm position to take over this territory.

"Make no mistake, Gerallt will be dead in short order. Aila will then have a captive, powerless people at her disposal. And as the only person among them with magic, she can bend them to her will.

"But do you really think Aila wants near-dead serfs for herself?" Aidryn asked pointedly. "Or is there something more?"

Cold horror crept into the pit of Lira's stomach as she began to understand. Still, Skelly said nothing. When Aidryn spoke again, Lira detected a tremor in his voice.

"Aila is charismatic. And your people thrive on a matriarchal balance—they revere female priestesses and women anointed through birthright. She's powerful, and now, so is my sister.

"Before Aila kills Gerallt, she'll use him to win your people's hearts. Together, they can tell the story of how their beloved Witness Tree hoarded all their magic, but now they're here to deliver something far more powerful."

No... Lira thought—wanted to scream.

"Your empty vessels up there?" Aidryn pointed skyward. "They're primed to receive the dark magic Aila will pour into them once she's won them over. It won't take much—some generosity, a few stories that turn them against their anointed —and they'll accept whatever she offers without question. Then, she'll truly have an army to march against Iathium."

"I am—" Skelly faltered. "I am beloved among my people. They've never given me reason to doubt their loyalty."

"Until they were corralled inside this keep and forced to live like animals," he said. "Perhaps they're fond of you now, but it won't take much convincing from Gerallt and Aila that the squalor here—and their lack of power—is *your* doing.

"People who live in that sort of desperation will believe anything they think will save them. Make no mistake: Aila and Gerallt mean to present a unifying message of hope and deliverance to these people."

"What can we do?" Lira asked quietly.

Aidryn shook his head. "Nothing," he said, "unless you want to risk Aila taking your power. We have to leave the territory and take the magic with us, while we have a chance."

"No." Lira pushed herself into a sitting position. Her head swam and throbbed with the movement, and a wave of nausea washed over her. "We can't leave these people to—"

"It's too late." He shook his head. "They're going to be searching for Skelly, and the feast has already begun. If we stay and you're captured, Aila gets your power.

"These people are doomed either way. But if we can get the two of you clear of this place, we at least stand a chance at protecting your power. And, perhaps, dispersing it back to the clan when the time is right."

Lira turned to Skelly. "Help me understand why you would take all this power for yourself—and for me. *Please.*"

"I have always protected the magic first." Skelly sighed. "Each clan is bound by its own set of magical rules regarding the inheritance of power.

"In Clan Beran, each family swears to remain bound to the fortress in exchange for their own share of magic. As tradition dictates, Clan Énna's powers flow freely to every descendant. The children of Clan Tarlach inherit their power at random.

"The anointed in each clan is also chosen in different ways.

Clan Beran's is chosen based on a show of strength when he or she enters adulthood. Clan Énna anoints one based on a particular resonance with the rivers and seas. And Clan Tarlach's anointed is born into the role, with a deeply-rooted power that can never truly be stolen."

The elderly woman looked pointedly at Aidryn, who refused to meet her eyes. Lira thought of the memory he'd shared with her—and though Aila stole his magic as a child, he still bore some gifts of the Key Keeper.

"But here," Skelly continued, "The Witness Tree is always a matriarch, and she chooses the next anointed at birth."

"How do we inherit our power?" Lira asked.

"In the old days, the master received a measure of power from the matriarch that he would then disperse into the clan."

"But you didn't give that power to Gerallt," Lira concluded. "That's why he has been trying to break you."

Skelly nodded. "My grandmother withheld power from her masters. And her grandmother before her. For generations now, the Witness Tree has been the sole guardian. No one alive in this valley has any memory of witnessing or possessing our magic."

"Except you and me."

Her grandmother nodded.

"We can't linger," Aidryn pressed. "Lira, we have to get you to Beran. The healer can help protect you, and you'll be safe there for a time."

Lira protested, "Is there no way we can—"

"No," he said. "We need to *turas* to Fortress Halgeir."

"Do you have the red pebble?" Skelly asked, looking pointedly at Lira's pouch.

Lira wanted to scream; how could this woman have been such a fool?

"Yes," Lira bit out. She looked from Aidryn to Skelly and back. "If we're going, I suppose we should go now."

"Your chainmail," Aidryn said, his eyes flicking upward, as if he could see their meager belongings in Skelly's home aboveground.

"Leave it," Skelly insisted.

"She deserves protection."

"We have to go, Aidryn," Lira said reluctantly. "We're wasting time."

She shuddered at the idea of another *turas*; she still felt weak and ill from Skelly's burst of magic.

Turning the red stone over and over in one hand, she reached for her pendant. Aidryn looped an arm through hers, and Skelly followed suit.

"Pray this works," Lira said, squeezing her eyes shut. "And pray my stepfather lets us into the fortress when we get there."

She touched the pebble to her pendant, and for a moment, they were tumbling through darkness.

But instead of landing safely inside the walls of Beran's stone fortress, they found themselves lying on the outskirts of the valley, surrounded by Lira's childhood mountains, freshly-sharpened arrows trained on them from every angle.

CHAPTER 33

Artagán pointed his arrow at Lira's heart. His archers surrounded them, waiting for their leader's orders.

"Don't move, on pain of death," he said.

"Artagán, *please*—"

"Quiet," he snapped. "The mistresses are coming."

Skelly sat on her knees, hands folded in her lap, her wily gaze flicking from one young man to the next. With catlike stillness, she carefully calculated her next words.

"Artagán," she said, "you saw what your master did to me. You see me as I am now. How can you serve him without question?"

"I see the same old crone who hoarded our rightful magic," he spat. "The witch who favored a traitor over her clan. We're going to make you pay for what you've done."

Aidryn and Lira exchanged a panicked glance as Skelly sagged. "I was trying to protect you, child," she argued feebly. "I've cared for you since you were a babe. Surely you know I would never bring you harm."

"And yet..." Artagán closed his eyes, taking a deep breath.

As he exhaled, his eyes flashed with a dark power Lira instantly recognized.

Veins of black lightning gathered at her cousin's shoulders, traveling down his arms and into his fingertips. They didn't stop there, though; they flowed down the bow, circling his arrow to the very tip. Then, the veins withdrew into his body once again.

"No..." The dread pooling in her body threatened to weigh her down, to pin her to the earth. She wanted to let it, to give up here and now.

Artagán sneered as he readjusted his bowstring, never taking his aim from her.

"So it's done," Aidryn said.

"Oi, keep your mouth shut," one of the archers, Deghan, said, pressing the tip of his arrow to the hollow of Aidryn's throat.

Lira caught a whiff of a familiar scent then. Not a scent she'd experienced in her lifetime, but one she'd encountered in her visions. Horror etched itself across her features as she realized the source. Her eyes came to rest again on Artagán's arrow; indeed, its tip was slick with a putrid green substance.

At the same time, her cousin laughed as if he'd been waiting for her to notice. "Yes, Lira," he said, laughter rising in his voice, "it's *inoxia*. I suggest you don't move."

"Eremon's magic protects me," Lira whispered, her voice wavering. "Even your poison is worthless against his power."

She hoped it was true.

"Maybe I can't kill you—but I can make you bleed," Artagán whispered. "I can make you wish you were dead."

"And what about your friend? I pierce his throat with this beauty, and he's a dead man," Deghan sneered, applying more pressure to the arrow at Aidryn's throat.

"They're under orders to keep us alive, Lira," Aidryn said, his voice even and smooth. "Otherwise, we'd—"

Deghan pressed the arrowhead just a bit harder, and Aidryn grew deathly still, his nostrils flaring, eyes wide.

"You're expendable, horseman," the archer said.

A female voice cut through the clearing. "He is not."

Lira shuddered as Aila Tarlach stepped into view. She had never seen Aila wear anything except the rich crimson and cream of Iathium; now, the deep green of her gown accentuated her fair skin and her dark, flowing hair.

"Good work, men," she said, with an almost-smile. "I see the spell was effective. Well done, Caitir."

Caitir and Gerallt trailed one step behind Aila, arm-in-arm. Tears filled Lira's eyes as she beheld her former friend, who was now almost unrecognizable. Caitir and her mother wore twin cuffs of emerald-green leather around their wrists; Caitir's expression bore nothing but horrifying contempt.

Her skin was paler than ever before, and had taken on an almost iridescent sheen that stood in stark contrast with her golden hair. And her eyes, once ocean blue, had nearly lost their color completely. Her irises were now the color of the palest surf, almost indistinguishable from the whites.

Caitir's lip curled as she locked eyes with Lira.

"Well, well," she said, her voice like frozen glass, "isn't this ironic. The Witness Tree, at the mercy of her clan."

"And my clan, at yours," Lira seethed. "When they learn what you really are—"

"What we are?" A tinkling laugh bubbled from Caitir's throat then and she released her new husband to glide toward Lira and the others.

The archers made way, and she knelt before Lira, cupping her face with a cool palm.

"Goddesses, Lira," she whispered, her face mere inches away. "Benevolent goddesses come to rescue them from a tyrannical and selfish matriarch."

Caitir released Lira's face, then slapped her cheek with a resounding *crack*. Gerallt roared with laughter.

Lira's head whipped to the side with the impact, and her eyes watered.

"Listen to yourself, Caitir," she cried. "Stop this! Come with us. It's not too late."

Caitir faltered for a moment and paused, her brows knitting almost imperceptibly. She recovered quickly, her gaze growing steely again. "Bow before me," she said, "and perhaps I'll spare you when this is all over."

"I will," Lira answered, "once the archers lower their arrows."

Gerallt barked an order, and the archers reluctantly lowered their bows.

Lira took a shuddering breath, stealthily pressing her fingertips into the soft earth. "Are you sure you know what you're doing, Caitir?"

"No questions," Caitir said. "Bow, or they fire."

Aila held up a palm in warning. "Time, my dear."

She whirled on Aila. "I have done what you asked of me today, Mother," she snapped. "You will indulge me in this."

Though Aila exchanged a brief, doubtful look with Gerallt, she turned back to her daughter. "Very well."

Lira flexed her fingertips in the soil. Slowly, she lowered her forehead to the ground before Caitir.

"Look what you have taken from me, Silira: a place at court, Eremon—even my own brother abandoned me to follow after you like a lost puppy. My brother, who bears the power of the Key Keepers, refused to grant entry to his own flesh and blood.

"But without a thought, he gave everything up for you. Because of you, my father is dead. Because of you, Eremon is dead. Because of you, we have been banished from our home in Iathium."

Lira could feel the land's memory—its power—stirring

beneath her fingertips, and she began to tremble. It felt fuller, more complete—as if the entirety of the forest might bend to a single thought from her.

Please, let this work.

Caitir took a step closer to Lira and crouched, lowering her voice. "But all is not lost. We bring hope to this pitiful people. Gerallt gifts us an army of empty vessels, primed to wield our lightning. And together, we will gather the clans and march on Iathium to claim our rightful thrones.

"I will take my loss and multiply it into ten thousand gains. I will rise from the ashes to build an empire unlike any Rodhlan has ever seen. And you, Silira Mór, will give your power to me. Then you will lie in ruin as I am reborn, and I will make you suffer for as long as your lungs draw breath."

Lira huffed a bitter laugh, looking up at Caitir. "Are you ready to bear the histories of this land on your shoulders? Are you prepared to be tormented by visions of the past during your sleeping and your waking? To taste the blood and tears of our ancestors? To die a thousand deaths alongside them?"

Caitir's lip curled, and she stood again, taking a step back as if to answer. Lira threw caution to the wind.

"You may rise, indeed. You may transform. But not—" she dug her fingers harder into the earth— "without" —*harder*— "a war."

She could hear the panic beginning to rise in Caitir's voice. "Drop your face or I'll have Aidryn killed."

The earth began to rumble beneath Lira's fingertips, and she let a smile stretch across her lips. "I live to serve," she began, "*Rodhlan.*"

There was a rumbling *boom* that silenced all sound in the forest around them. The earth quaked beneath them, throwing the archers, master, and mistresses off their feet.

Lira beckoned Aidryn and Skelly, reaching toward where they knelt.

"Hold onto me," she commanded as the ground shook again. Aidryn grasped her, and she clasped a hand around his forearm. The trees around them popped and creaked menacingly from roots to tops.

The wind ceased blowing through the leaves around them then; the very trees seemed to grow heavy, their limbs groaning under some newfound weight. Then, the first leaf dropped to the ground like a steel dagger, its knifepoint sticking fast in a large root with a resounding, metallic echo.

Lira flicked her fingers then, and the dagger-leaves began to fly from their branches, straight toward their captors.

The archers screamed as the blades flew, some finding their marks as they sunk into their targets, others glancing off skin and leaving bleeding gashes behind. Lira couldn't watch. Instead, she squeezed her eyes shut, stretching her free hand toward her grandmother as the dagger-leaves began to twist themselves into a wide cyclone around them.

Leaf blades sheared the tree trunks as they picked up speed. Skelly tried to hold onto Lira's fingers with a shaking hand, pressing herself low to the ground. The elderly woman was braced on her hands and knees, feeble and unbalanced against the forces that Lira had set into motion.

Lira could feel herself losing grip on her grandmother. But when she tightened her grasp, Skelly slipped and rolled to the ground.

"Skelly," Lira cried, stretching her arm farther.

Skelly pushed herself onto her hands and knees. Roots grew up from the ground to stabilize her as she crawled back toward Lira.

The cyclone's intensity grew, crackling with flashes of emerald and crimson power and pressurizing the world around them. Lira's head throbbed as she struggled to regain control. Her magic ripped a scream from deep within her, and she tightened her grip on Aidryn's arm.

Then, she realized the power wasn't all hers. That the magic mingling with hers was coming from Aila, who stood outside the cyclone, arms raised, murmuring an incantation. She had managed to protect herself, her daughter, and her husband—but only just.

Lira gritted her teeth as the magic—*all* of it—suddenly bent to Aila's will. Aila began drawing the cyclone to herself, arching her back and baring her torso as if to absorb it all.

The daggers transformed back into leaves. The hurricane-force winds knocked Skelly onto her stomach and began to pull Aidryn from Lira's grip. And though Eremon's ring illuminated the clearing, it seemed to only stabilize Lira.

Aidryn's feet rose from the ground first, followed by his legs, then his torso. He tightened his grip on her forearm. Lira reached for his other arm with her free hand, grasping him as hard as she could.

His body lurched as Aila drew a surge of power toward her.

"No," Lira screamed as her magic faltered. "No!"

As her fingers began to slip from Aidryn's arms, some untapped spark of power deep within her raged to life. Roots sprang from the earth and enclosed her feet, holding her fast as she fought to keep Aidryn in her grip. Vines of silver and green surged from the soil, winding around her legs and torso, then up her arms to encircle their forearms, their wrists, their hands.

Don't leave me, she wanted to scream. *Stay!*

The vines tightened then, and for a moment, time slowed and the winds began to calm. Emerald power surged up the vines, then back down again—a familiar warmth that grounded Lira amid the chaos.

There was a shuddering flash of light between them, and Lira felt herself opening, as if she were turning inside out. The warmth she'd felt in the vines that bound them surged toward her middle, bursting inside of her like a shower of stardust. Then, just as quickly as the warmth had entered her, it blasted itself toward Aidryn, illuminating him from the inside out before her eyes.

For a moment, she thought she might watch him die. But his skin stopped pulsing with that power. The vines fell away. Despite the swirling leaves—despite the storm—he released her arms.

He advanced on her, then grasped her face in his hands. She did not falter.

"Witness—a final truth," he whispered.

Aidryn stands before Eremon in the archival chamber, eye-to-eye with the young ruler. They're sizing one another up, circling each other as they launch headlong into a discussion they've both been avoiding.

"With all due respect, I believe you're endangering her," Aidryn says. "I told her—as I'm telling you—that it is against her best interests to be so close to you, but she wouldn't listen."

Eremon lifts an eyebrow in cool amusement. "Perhaps you should stop treating her like a child."

Aidryn bristles, clenching his fists at his sides. "Perhaps you should have stuck to the lessons you agreed to."

"The fact that you've lied to yourself and to her has done you no favors, but neither has it helped me," Eremon answers, tightening a scroll on Lira's desk. "She still hasn't accepted my hand."

Aidryn stills. "What?"

"You were right about her." Eremon sighs. "She's reluctant to seize power—to rush headlong into marriage. She does not fear the passing of time like so many of the women clamoring for my attention."

"Because she is history. She is time itself," Aidryn says, a knowing smile playing across his lips. "Lira is the past, present, and future. She is a living vessel of memory. She will be the bearer of those memories to generations both old and young. And I would be remiss to applaud her relationship with a man whose mere association with her will expose and endanger her beyond repair."

"Then promise me something." Eremon and Aidryn stare one another down, steely-eyed. "Swear to me that you'll protect her."

"I have always protected her," Aidryn says, "and I always will—whether or not she weds you."

Eremon looks ashamed, but only for a moment. "I don't know what the future holds for me. But I want a chance for a life with her, however brief it might be."

"And what about her life?" Aidryn presses, moving nose-to-nose with Eremon. "What does her life become if you die? Have you thought of that?"

"She inherits my throne. My city. My riches." He makes a sweeping gesture around them, as if he doesn't understand Aidryn's protests. "What more could I give her?"

"Peace," Aidryn sighs. "You could give her peace and let her live the quiet life she desires."

Eremon's gray eyes shine, his voice laced with desperation and hope as he replies, "But she is made for so much more."

"That's not good enough." Aidryn shakes his head slowly. "What matters is what she wants for her own life. Does she truly want your throne?"

Eremon straightens, weighing his words before he speaks. "No one has ever loved me for who I am. Except for her."

Aidryn's eyes shutter in resignation. "If she's resolved to be with you, then she needs a protector. Let her protect this archive, but let me guard the vessel until my dying breath."

"Name you as her successor?"

"Not her successor, but her equal. A dual anointing—her sworn protector."

"You mean you'll defend her."

"Yes."

"Swear to it. Swear on your life."

"I swear it."

Defender. Defender.

Defend her. Defend her.

When Lira opened her eyes, the cyclone raged around them once again, pulling them hopelessly toward Aila. She struggled to tighten her failing grasp on Aidryn as he locked eyes with her.

Lira dug her fingers into his arms. "Hold on," she cried, despite her flagging strength.

"I swore on my life," he shouted over the cacophony, "I swore to protect you. And so I will."

Then, he let go.

CHAPTER 34

The last thing Lira saw was Aidryn's determined expression just before he tumbled headlong into the wall of leaves, then farther away from her grasp.

There was no time to react before Skelly clamped a hand around Lira's pendant, yanked the chain from around her neck, and plunged them into *turas*.

The journey was violent; Lira fought it every mile of the way. Fought against Skelly's vice-like grip around her wrist. Fought to get back to Aidryn.

She was consumed by the sounds of his agony, the feeling of searing heat in her chest. The emptiness that built in intensity, compressed her lungs, and threatened to undo her completely as the distance between them grew.

He would be dead before she could get back. It would be too late.

Turas released them in the tall grasses of the western meadowlands, not far from the ocean. They tumbled one over the other until they finally lost momentum, coming to rest in a heap.

Tears streamed down Lira's cheeks. She curled in on

herself, wailing with an anguished cry that echoed far across the meadow. The pain was crushing and deep. She might rather die than go on feeling this way forever.

He has to know. He has to know I tried. I tried but he let go. He let go. He let go. He—

The magic had taken its toll on Lira; she could barely move without trembling. She tried to catch her breath; tried to regain some semblance of control so she could figure out what to do next.

But then she spotted Skelly, still as a statue, watching her fall apart with an acceptance that was so serene, it was almost vile.

"You stopped me from saving him," Lira sobbed. "After everything I've lost, you took him from me too. How could you?"

"All is not lost, child," Skelly said. "He is alive."

"He is lost to me forever," Lira seethed. "They'll murder him because they know it will break me. They're soulless monsters, all of them."

"Yes," Skelly nodded. "Soulless, they are. But they are also wily. They will keep him alive to lure you back. Your job now is to avoid the traps they set for you. As long as you're alive, so shall he be."

"And how can that be, *grandmother*?" Lira emphasized the final word with an edge that made Skelly flinch.

"Can you see the future, too, Skelly? Can I? Because all I can do is feel whatever horrific torture they're subjecting him to. I can't help him, and it *hurts*." She braced a fist beneath her ribs. "Here. Like I could die, too, if I just lie down and invite it."

"When you are bound by a power as sacred as the magic that protects the two of you, you should expect to feel its effort. It's keeping him alive."

"If what you say is true, they will torture him with no end in sight."

Some mysterious, inner knowing illuminated Skelly's face, and she almost smiled. There was a strange joy in her eyes.

"What part of this brings you happiness?" Lira cried.

"Those women aren't the only ones who can master an unusual spell," Skelly said. Now, one corner of her mouth twitched up. "Eremon thought of everything."

With a gnarled hand, she reached for her granddaughter. Tenderly, she turned Lira's hand over to study Eremon's ring. Its stone had burst to life, the cerulean magic inside it burning like blue flame.

"You think the ring is protecting Aidryn? That's absurd."

"Yes."

"How?"

"Ah." Skelly rocked back on her heels, unlatching Lira's necklace and extending it to her again. "It seems the Rí crafted a new spell, one that would allow the ring's protection to extend to another. To bind you to the one person who would crawl through flame to defend you. One that would not only ensure your protection, but theirs as well, as long as you're both alive."

"Aidryn swore to Eremon that he would protect me," Lira whispered, remembering the memory of Eremon he had shared with her.

"I would expect nothing less." Her grandmother nodded. "The true Defender of Histories."

"But how would that extend to the ring? What did Eremon create?"

"A binding spell drawn from the ancient rituals, yet mingled with the power of the ring," Skelly answered.

"The ancient binding rituals like the ones from my vision?" Lira ventured.

"And from your vines in the clearing."

Lira remembered the vines that had encircled their clasped hands and arms. The power that had burst into her, then into Aidryn—and the memory of Eremon he'd shared with her.

Defender. Defender.

Defend her. Defend her.

Lira huffed a disbelieving laugh, shaking her head over and over. Perhaps she was going mad. "It can't be."

"Two people, one magical bond," Skelly affirmed, nodding sagely. "As long as you stay alive, he lives. And perhaps, in the meantime, you can learn to harbor his magic for him—that is, until he returns."

Lira recalled Aidryn's words from mere hours before: *The rites opened a magical bond between husband and wife that allowed their magic to flow freely, one to another.*

"You're telling me that the magic we exchanged in the forest was a Binding. A *marriage*," she pressed.

Skelly inclined her head. Lira felt like the earth beneath her had just given way.

"You're telling me," she asked slowly, "that Aidryn Tarlach is my husband."

"It appears that you are the one telling me."

Her heart sank. "Does he realize?"

"That is possible. I suppose it depends on how much of your power he received during the Binding."

"So he doesn't."

"Aidryn's oath was of the highest order—an oath of devotion. Of love," Skelly hedged. "This magic was crafted to awaken to that love, and to love reciprocated."

Fresh tears slid down Lira's cheeks as she shook her head. "Aidryn doesn't love me."

"Doesn't he?"

"And even if he did" She choked on her tears. "I could never —how could I? I was meant to... to..."

"Meant to what?" Skelly leaned forward, swiping a tear off her granddaughter's cheek. "I witnessed many things while I was captive. I saw what happened to you all in the city. Witnessed Eremon's love for you, and his death.

"I also witnessed your reluctance to accept his hand. The way you wrestled with yourself once he'd asked. The sacrifices you were willing to make to bring a better future to Rodhlan."

"Stop it, Skelly," Lira sobbed. "I can't bear it."

"You cared for him, yes. But there was always another. Always the one you were looking for, the one whose absence you felt keenly once he'd left the archive. And deep down, Eremon knew it.

"You couldn't even bear to wear that ring until he begged you to—and by then, it was too late for him. Still, he'd already planned a way to protect you, even in death. He loved you enough to entrust you fully to *your* defender."

"Yet another choice that was stripped from me," Lira cried. "And from Aidryn."

Skelly tapped the fine, sandy dirt beneath her fingers. "Sometimes, having too many choices can bring harm to even the most well-meaning people. There are times when narrowing the horizon has its advantages. Think of it as Eremon's final decree."

At that statement, something inside of Lira snapped.

"We are not puppets, Skelly!" she shouted. "We're not pawns. Everyone around us has used us both for our entire lives, as a means to an end. And now even Eremon has managed to dictate one of the most important decisions of my life from the grave."

Lira's gaze darted around them, desperate for purchase. The tall grasses surrounding them swayed in the salty breeze, waves crashing in the distance. Another sob broke from her lips when she beheld the Dome, tiny on the horizon.

"My entire life, all I have done is be a good citizen of Iathium. A devoted rule-follower." She looked back to Skelly, jaw set, gaze hardening. "But no more.

"I am not a diplomatic bargaining chip, a weapon, or a tool to be used in some scheme to seize power over these lands. I am the Witness Tree of Rodhlan, and I bow to no one."

For the first time, Skelly looked frightened—desperate. She began grasping for something, anything, to delay what was coming next. But Lira held up a hand.

"I am not yours to command, Skelly. From now on, I live by my own rules. And I'm going back for him."

Defiance glinted in her eyes as she grasped her pendant in one hand, preparing for *turas*. She withdrew the brass key from her pouch—anything that might lead her back to Aidryn.

"Lira, don't! Your magic—"

Lira lifted her chin. "Goodbye, Skelly."

She pressed key and pendant together. The void of *turas* swallowed her whole, but the magic suspended her as if it didn't know where to go. Darkness splintered around her like thousands of cracks in a looking glass, and then she felt herself falling wildly, rapidly, picking up speed with each passing second.

She should have known better. Should have known she couldn't—

The impact of arrival rendered her unconscious.

CHAPTER 35

Lira awoke on an unfamiliar cot. She blinked to clear her eyes, and realized with a start that she'd been sleeping inside a large tent. It was late in the evening, and the canvas interior was illuminated only by a few low-burning candles that guttered in the warm breeze.

She sat up, trembling; a damp cloth fell from her forehead into her lap. On the rickety bedside table sat an array of herbs and tinctures. She was still wearing her pendant and ring, and her leather pouch of heirlooms had been carefully placed beneath the table.

Tentatively, she stood; the room swayed around her as she padded slowly to the tent's opening to look outside. Her limbs cramped, and her lungs burned as if she'd just run all the way across the meadowlands. There was a sharp ache in her chest, and her stomach clenched over and over. She wasn't sure if she was half-starved, gravely ill, or both.

A tent village had been erected in sparse grasslands—on Rodhlan's far eastern border, Lira guessed, from what little she had been able to see. The lay of the land fell somewhere between desert and savannah, the sandy terrain rolling down toward a distant beach in dunes grown over with sea oats and tall grass. The tent where she'd woken up lay on a far edge of the settlement.

The tents that crowded the village were numerous and pitched closely together, but the settlers were quiet and kept to themselves. The few who spotted Lira at the tent door only briefly glanced her way, then went about their business.

Lira looked southward to find the Ridge, then surmised that she was halfway between Fortress Halgeir and the mountains. On foot, she was at least four days' journey either direction—likely many more, in the state she was in.

She was beginning to grow faint, so she made her way back to the cot. Just as she was sitting, an olive-skinned, elderly woman with a long, silver braid entered the tent. When she locked eyes with Lira, she smiled warmly and placed her hand over her heart.

"Witness Tree," she whispered reverently.

Lira's face fell; she was hoping she hadn't been recognized. Now, there was no question; she wouldn't be able to linger. "What settlement is this?"

"This is *Va'hesk*," the woman answered. "the remnant of Clan Tarlach."

Lira wanted to feel relieved, but she wasn't sure she could trust this woman—especially if she knew who Lira was.

"Who else knows who I am?" Lira asked warily.

"My husband, Mytr," she answered, "but to the settlement, you are our niece visiting from Iathium. You grew ill on the journey here, and we are tending you—no visitors. No one here would know you by your face, but that pendant you carry should remain hidden."

Lira felt herself relax a bit, relieved they'd thought enough of her safety to construct a story. "What is your name?"

"Nevala." She nodded toward the pillow. "You should lie back down."

"But I've lost my companion," Lira blurted. "I need help getting back to him."

Nevala's expression was one of genuine pity and concern. "We will do what we can to help you, Silira. But first, you must recover. Lie back."

Lira nodded resignedly, her head spinning as she lowered herself. "Thank you for saving my life."

"We are honored." Nevala propped several pillows and cushions behind Lira so she could recline.

Lira obliged her, settling under the coarse blanket. Her mind raced, but she felt too weak to argue. "Tell me how I got here," she slurred. "All I remember was—the meadowlands..."

Nevala dipped the damp cloth into a bowl of lavender water, then wrung it out and placed it on Lira's forehead again.

"Mytr found you just outside the settlement. Imagine how surprised he was; we rarely get travelers here, and this week there have been two." She smiled warmly. "Your friend Irem departed here just yesterday; tell me that is coincidence."

Her heart began to race and her eyes widened. "Irem Énna was here?"

"Indeed," Nevala answered. "He warned us to stay out of Iathium for a time."

Lira felt the subtle tug at the back of her mind that affirmed Nevala's words. She allowed herself to fully relax.

Just then, Mytr—a slight, middle-aged man at least twenty years Nevala's junior—stepped inside the tent. His face lit up when he saw Lira.

"She is awake!" he cried, shuffling toward the two women. "Praises to Rhona."

"Rhona blessed your arrival, Silira." Nevala handed Lira a cup of steaming tea.

Lira's eyebrows rose as she took a sip. "I thought Rhona was killed; how could she bless anything?"

"Was she not a mortal goddess?" Mytr asked merrily, dragging a small stool to her bedside. "What do you think happens to a mortal goddess when she dies?"

"I don't know," Lira moaned, handing the teacup back to Nevala. "Should I know?"

Mytr opened his mouth as if to answer, but Nevala shushed him with a gentle hand to his shoulder. "Another time," she whispered.

Lira felt her eyelids growing heavy, and realized the tea she'd been sipping must have contained a sedative. But she couldn't go to sleep without telling them as much as she could.

"Beware of the mountain folk," she warned, the words dripping lazily from her lips, "and anyone who claims to be a descendant of your clan. There are dark sorceresses—" she yawned— "from the city..."

The couple exchanged a terse glance.

"But Aidryn Tarlach—he's the one you can trust."

Nevala raised an eyebrow. "Your companion?"

Lira nodded sleepily.

The older woman leaned forward, propping her chin on a fist. "What happened to him?"

A wave of anguish washed over Lira. "He sacrificed himself so I could escape the Ridge with Skelly."

Skelly. Her gut twisted, and for a moment, she thought she might be sick.

Nevala studied her. "So the mad empress in the city isn't our greatest threat, then."

Lira shook her head, her eyelids drooping. "Macha is the least of your worries."

"And what of Skelly? Is this Wilga you speak of?"

"I left her behind," Lira answered, tears filling her eyes. "I shouldn't have."

Nevala rested a comforting hand on her hair. "Hush, now; you are wounded."

"I will go after Irem," Mytr said, "and we will search for her."

"She may be near Clan Énna's caravan—on the western coast." She could barely hold her eyes open now; Nevala helped her lie flat.

Mytr nodded. "That is where Irem was going. I will send a sparrow ahead, then take our swiftest horse. We will make quick work of it."

"I need Aidryn," Lira mumbled. "Need to save him."

"Rest first and heal," Nevala soothed. "Then, do all the saving you want."

Lira tried to nod her agreement, but she was asleep before she could speak again.

FOR NEARLY TWO WEEKS, Nevala doted on Lira. Lira learned that, although Eremon's ring had protected her from the worst of Aila's magic, she had still been gravely injured—a magical injury, as Mytr had called it. Receiving her birthright was the first blow; then, the attack in the mountains. When her last *turas* failed, the damage had been devastating.

She tried to feel remorseful for abandoning Skelly, but found it nearly impossible. While she cared for her grandmother's well-being, she had no interest in being near her for now. If Irem and Mytr had located Skelly, they would be settled with the caravan by now.

"If some disaster had befallen her, we would know by now," Nevala told her—more than once. "Mytr will be home with news any day."

Lira spent hours every day lying on her cot, trying to focus on her magic. Though she could access some of the memories she'd inherited, they were more fragmented than before. She couldn't manage to follow an entire memory from start to finish unless she received it through touch; Nevala had generously shared some of her own memories for Lira to practice.

On the eighth evening, Lira discovered Nevala had once met her mother at Fortress Halgeir. When Iva's face flashed across her consciousness, she drew back from Nevala in shock.

"You never told me you'd met Mam," Lira breathed. "When?"

"I was apprenticed to a healer at Fortress Halgeir, for a time," Nevala answered. "Your mother was quite formidable, but kind."

"Artur's influence, no doubt," Lira said. "Mam was so soft before; being with Clan Beran has changed her."

Nevala regarded her, raising an eyebrow. "Sometimes, change is necessary—as you well know. Iva Beran is your best hope for an alliance."

"I can't think about gathering allies right now," Lira answered.

"Perhaps not yet; but soon, you must."

Lira's heart pounded so erratically, she could scarcely draw a full breath. "We'll see." She had already tried to re-forge a connection with Skelly, and that had failed miserably. There was no hurry for a similar disaster to unfold with her mother.

For now, all she wanted was to get back to Aidryn. From there, she could decide what the next right step was.

As she recovered, Lira found that she was easily overcome with panic. She slept poorly, and when she woke in the mornings, her adrenaline surged. When it became difficult to breathe through the feeling, she tearfully sought out Nevala for help.

"You should go to your mother when you leave this place," Nevala said as she prepared a calming tincture for Lira. "Beran can help you save your husband."

Lira gaped at her, but Nevala only smiled.

"I am also newly married, despite my years," Nevala said. "I would know the imprint of a binding spell anywhere."

"It's not really what you think," Lira stammered. "It wasn't our choice."

"For a spell like that to take hold, it *must* be your choice." She patted Lira's hand and gave her the remedy in a small cup. "You will sort it out for yourselves soon enough."

Lira did not want to think too deeply about the older woman's words—not yet. She pressed the cup to her lips and tipped it back, swallowing the sweet tincture. Almost immediately, her racing heartbeat began to slow. Soon, she could draw a full breath.

After a long moment, she mused, "Mytr must be a truly wonderful man."

"He is," Nevala answered. "The settlement did not wish us bound—he is so much younger than I. I was fifty-five when we fell in love, and he was thirty-seven. It took us nearly ten years to meet a priestess who would perform the rites."

Lira gaped. "Ten years?"

"Magic was scarce—is scarce, still," she said. "It is a sacred and rare thing to be magically bound to the one you love. And I believe you'll find that it always brings you back together, no matter the distance."

With a sigh, Lira reached for Nevala's hand. "I hope you're right."

ON THE MORNING of the ninth day, Mytr returned. He entered the tent with a warm smile, and Nevala rushed to embrace him. Lira sat up, swinging her legs over the side of the cot.

Before Mytr could speak, she blurted, "Is Skelly alive?"

He laughed. "The woman is older than Rodhlan. Of course,

she is alive. Irem took her to the Énna caravan on the coast. She has some healing of her own to do."

Lira sagged with relief. "Thank you, Mytr."

He smiled. "Irem gave her quite a scolding. She was rather brash with *him* to begin, but he was enraged when she admitted how much power she has been holding—and how much she gave to you."

She frowned. "Then I expect he'll be equally angry that I left her."

"You have nothing to fear," Mytr said. "He does not blame you for it."

Her eyes welled up at that. "Irem tried so hard to make this easy on me. He, Eremon, and Aidryn—they all tried."

"Yes," Nevala said, returning to Lira's side. "We all do our best—even your Skelly. She believed she was right. It will be important for you to remember that when the time comes to reunite with her."

"I'm glad she's safe with Irem for now," Lira answered softly.

That evening—and every night after—Mytr regaled them with folklore from Clan Tarlach, and Lira carefully recorded each story with quill and parchment, allowing them to meld with her fragmented power. The action felt both foreign and familiar, weighted and untethered. A plan began to take root, but she held it close as she prepared to travel again.

A fortnight passed before Lira regained most of her strength. Her power began to feel like a surging, overflowing well inside of her—readily available, and almost too easy to use. She grew restless, and she found that she often had to suppress the urge to discharge the magic, just to feel like herself again.

Reluctantly, Nevala and Mytr helped her pack for the long journey ahead. Lira nodded politely when they urged her to ride for Fortress Halgeir and accepted their offer of a brown pony named Tudur to help speed the trip.

Early on the last morning, Nevala brought Lira fresh clothes, a bundle of food, herbal medicines for her travels, and a bladder full of water. Mytr saddled Tudur, singing softly to the pony as he worked.

"Are you certain you should travel alone?" Nevala asked. "Mytr can ride to the gorge with you."

"I'll be all right," Lira said. "Va'hesk needs you both for what is to come."

Mytr nodded. "Our men and women are strong, but our horses have never seen combat. We must begin training them for battle."

Lira gave him a tight-lipped smile. "I will send for you when we have need, if I can't come to you myself. I'll miss you both."

The women embraced, lingering that way for a long moment before Lira tucked the bundle into the saddlebag. Tudur snorted softly, swishing his tail.

"Silira," Nevala began, "your power cannot be trusted completely. You need the Beran healers to right it. Make haste for the gorge, and don't look back."

Lira sucked in a breath as Nevala kissed her cheek.

"Do not forget us," she breathed. "You hold the heart of Clan Tarlach, and we are at your service."

CHAPTER 36

Lira rode as far as the northeastern border of Clan Tarlach's territory before she dismounted near a cluster of willow trees. A light breeze ruffled the leaves as she pulled her hood down and took a deep breath.

The inconspicuous dress Nevala had given her was the color of burlap, and nearly as rough. She could draw up the hood to shield her face from the dust storms that blew up from time to time on this terrain. The only pieces of her old clothing that remained were her belt and the leather pouches that hung from it.

She unbuckled the saddle bag and set it at the base of the largest tree, then turned to Tudur, running her fingers through his coarse mane.

"Go home to Mytr," she whispered.

Tudur tossed his head, agitated, but did not budge. Lira slapped his hindquarters, hoping to jolt him into motion, but he just looked at her incredulously. Then, she noticed the faint hum of magic that emanated from him.

"Clever," she mused. "He enchanted you."

How else would Mytr and Nevala ensure that she'd keep

her word and make for the gorge? She smiled ruefully, scratching behind his ears.

"Now, what do we do with you?" she whispered. "I suppose you'll follow me unless we find some way to break this spell."

Softly, she stroked Tudur's face and forelock. Again, she recalled Aidryn's words: *The rites opened a magical bond between husband and wife that allowed their magic to flow freely, one to another.*

Closing her eyes, she searched for a hint of Aidryn's presence. She stretched a tendril of her power toward the Ridge, where she'd left him. When it met the slightest spark—her first sign that he was truly still alive—she drew a shuddering breath.

Something deep inside of her yawned open; she reached for his power, took hold of it, and focused her intent on sending the pony back to its master.

"*Tana lo,*" she whispered. "Tell Mytr and Nevala I'm sorry."

The humming ceased, and Tudur came to himself, stomping his hooves nervously. Again, Lira slapped his hindquarters, and he broke into a gallop toward Va'hesk.

"Goodbye, my friend," she whispered.

Lira settled herself at the base of the largest willow, leaning against its thick trunk. She withdrew a quill, ink, and piece of parchment from the saddle bag—precious supplies Nevala had purchased for her back at Va'hesk.

Carefully, she dipped her quill into the ink pot and began to write.

Dear Aidryn,

I am further from you now than I have ever been, yet infinitely closer than perhaps you realize. I want you to know that I am safe. I want you to know that

For a moment, she sat, weighing her next words.

I am sorry for what you're enduring on my behalf. I don't know how I will make it up to you, but I swear that I will.

I wish you were with me to see what I have seen. I can't say more; prying eyes are everywhere.

She added ink to the quill, then pressed it to the parchment once again.

For now, please hold on. I am coming for you.

Wind whipped the willow's branches, its leaves brushing together in a soothing serenade. Lira raised her hood and stood, crumpling the letter in her fist. Her magic transformed the parchment into hundreds of tiny dandelion seeds, and she opened her palm.

The soft seeds caught the southward breeze that blew toward Rodhlan Ridge. Lira watched them trail away toward the mountains, then followed on foot without sparing another glance behind her.

~

THE END

Notes & Acknowledgements

THE EARLY SPARK OF INSPIRATION for this series came from an unexpected place, as many stories do. While life often inspires art, however, the details that inspired my story do not resemble true-to-life events or people, outside of the basic family structure I'm about to describe.

My grandmother's uncle was chosen by his grandmother when he was a child to be the family historian—the Witness Tree. Throughout his childhood, Uncle Robert's grandmother taught him the oral histories of her family, entrusting him with cherished heirlooms along the way that she had been safeguarding until it was time to pass them on. He took the role incredibly seriously, spending his adult life painstakingly researching and recording our family histories until he passed away.

Through his research, he came across some interesting and controversial information that some might consider to be conspiracy theory material. Whether the test of time proves these stories to be true remains to be seen (he was only the messenger of these details—not the author). However, the idea of primary source documents contradicting the conventional historical wisdom got my wheels turning.

In addition to being an avid writer and reader, I'm also a historian myself. I started thinking about specific historical narratives I learned when I was a child, and how some of those narratives stood in contrast to the wider breadth of information I gathered later as a history major. I also considered how loyalty to one's country and heritage can often skew historical narratives in favor of the homeland—or in the case of war, in favor of the victor. My wild imagination and passion for history (and conspiracy theories) collided with my love of fantasy, and that's eventually how the story of Lira began.

While the title Witness Tree is a nod to my great-uncle's title as family historian, it is also a widely used descriptor for a tree that has stood for hundreds of years, bearing witness to history. (For example, you'll often hear this term being used to describe trees that withstood a great battle and are still standing today.) I'm forever grateful to my extended family (particularly to Nanny and Myrna, who shared Uncle Robert's research with us) for being a catalyst to this journey.

Taking the steps toward writing and publishing a novel is an incredible undertaking that requires time, patience, persistence, and resilience for all involved—not just the writer. So, if you've been a part of my writing journey in any way, I'm grateful for you.

To my husband, Grant: I'm grateful that I married another creative entrepreneur who understands the deep drive to create. Thank you for helping me to embrace my identity as an author, and for telling more people about my book face-to-face than (probably) I have. You're an encourager and a connector who has always been willing to nudge me out of my comfort zone—an essential component of the life we're building. I love you.

To my children: Thank you for cheering me on and being patient while Mommy has built two businesses in tandem. Many days, I feel like I'm failing in every possible way, but you always make me feel infinitely loved no matter what. I love you to the stars and beyond. Your sweet faces, hugs, and kisses keep me going.

To Mom and Dad: Thank you for helping me with the kids for long hours and seemingly endless days. You have poured yourselves into us and we love you both very much. I'm so grateful for you both.

To Brent: Thanks for that copy of Pressfield's *The War of Art*. After much unnecessary struggle, I finally started reading it— and I think it may have to be required annual reading, at the very least, from now on. It has become a valuable part of my writing journey.

To my editors, Allie Martin and Jolene Perry: Thank you for your straightforward critique and honest feedback throughout multiple rounds of editing. You knew just where to push and to stretch me—and you helped me make my story the best it could be. I'm looking forward to continuing our work together.

Allie, thank you for the guidance and advice you've provided me that goes far beyond editing. Your wisdom and industry expertise have helped me to remain calm and grounded throughout the revision and publishing processes. I'm so grateful we connected.

To my OG readers, Christa, Heatherlyn, Mary Beth, Mika, Tim, and Victoria: Some of you have been on this train since day one, when the story was vastly different than it is now. All of you have been infinitely encouraging over the past four years as I've developed this story. I'm endlessly grateful for the time and enthusiasm you've poured into these characters and this world.

To my family, friends, colleagues, and readers: Thank you for being a part of this adventure. Onward to the next!

- Haley

THE SAGA CONTINUES IN
KEEPER OF KEYS...

Keeper of Keys

HALEY WALDEN

THE WITNESS TREE CHRONICLES

II

KEEPER OF KEYS
THE WITNESS TREE CHRONICLES, BOOK 2

Their combined powers could turn the tides of fate - if they both survive.

Romantic and captivating, brace yourself for this epic fantasy with perilous quests, heartwarming found family, a friends-to-lovers slow burn, and a jaw-dropping twist that will keep you on the edge of your seat.

Lira's newfound magic is broken. Separated from allies and forced to flee the safety of her kingdom's walls, she's alone and tormented by her unchecked power.

When an isolated clan offers Lira shelter, she spends her days mastering her magic, learning how to fight, and finally embracing her true feelings for Aidryn, who is fighting for his life across the continent.

Dark magic has conquered the throne, and the future grows bleaker by the day. With the help of her new friends, Lira must find the courage to save the man she loves, find a powerful new magic, and prepare for inevitable war with the Crown.

Will she reunite with Aidryn in time to heal his wounds, gather allies, and unlock this fabled magic - or will it fall into the wrong hands and lead them all to destruction?

Keeper of Keys is the enthralling, dual-POV second installment of the epic fantasy series, *The Witness Tree Chronicles*.

Find *Keeper of Keys* (*The Witness Tree Chronicles, Book 2*) at your favorite online book retailer.

Learn more:
authorhaleywalden.com

FREE NOVELLA!
BALLAD OF STALLIONS

HALEY WALDEN
BALLAD OF STALLIONS
A WITNESS TREE CHRONICLES NOVELLA

BALLAD OF STALLIONS
A WITNESS TREE CHRONICLES NOVELLA

Historian and horseman Aidryn Tarlach has spent his entire nineteen years waging one silent battle after another. The city archive is the only refuge he's ever known, but even that has begun to unravel. Suddenly, he finds himself struggling to hold onto everything he's fought for.

Aidryn is stretched thin among the interests and people he's spent years trying to protect. His family is bent on controlling the throne. His closest friend, Silira Mór, is oblivious to his feelings for her—and is set to inherit a coveted magic she doesn't believe in. Even worse, the city's young ruler, Rí Eremon, has set his sights on Lira.

Set two years before the events of *Defender of Histories*, *Ballad of Stallions* follows Aidryn to the heartbreaking decisions he must make to protect Lira and secure Iathium's future.

Author's Note:

Although it's a prequel, Ballad of Stallions *is best read between* Defender of Histories *and* Keeper of Keys.

BALLAD OF STALLIONS
CHAPTER 1

Aidryn Tarlach never tired of watching the sunset cast its golden glow across Rodhlan Ridge. The rolling, green mountain range on the continent's southern border was overhung with wispy mist tonight, the sky above brilliant with bright pinks, purples, and oranges. Set against the brilliant green, the sky's hues set the mist into sharp relief.

It looked like the smoke from his grandfather's pipe, Aidryn thought with a sigh. He could almost smell the tobacco—almost wished he enjoyed smoking, just to relive the memory of it.

Fannin, the large, gray stallion Aidryn sat astride, gave a low snort and tossed his white mane, stomping his hooves impatiently.

"Ah, you're ready to run again," Aidryn said softly, brushing his fingers through Fannin's mane with his free hand. "Always in a rush."

The stallion's withers twitched, as if he were considering dumping Aidryn right here in the middle of the meadowlands and taking off without him. True, they had been in one place for too long, but Aidryn couldn't resist taking in the view of those mountains whenever he got the opportunity.

On occasion, he made the journey into the settlement there —but tonight, there wasn't enough time. The horse seemed to sense Aidryn's reluctance to turn back toward the city and snorted again—louder this time.

"Fine," Aidryn sighed, and nudged Fannin into a trot, steering them northward, toward the city-state of Iathium. "Do your worst."

The stallion broke into a gallop, picking up speed across the vast meadowland until the wind was whipping hard in Aidryn's face. They moved so swiftly he could barely draw a breath, but he savored every moment. Riding with Fannin was the only time he ever felt truly free—as though his yearning for endless, reckless abandon might somehow be satisfied, even for a moment.

For a typical horse, Iathium was a full day's ride from where they'd watched the sunset. But for Fannin, it would take an hour—perhaps two—to arrive back at the city gates. Fannin had been a gift from Aidryn's grandfather, from a long line of fabled, magical horses whose existence had been relegated to long-forgotten myth. As had the magic that Rodhlan's people once possessed.

Clan Tarlach called them the *Seanlaoch*—war horses bred for exceptional speed, agility, and intelligence. Iathium's earliest rulers had brought the Seanlaoch's ancestors from across the sea. Clanspeople had then taken to cross breeding the magical horses with the wild ones that roamed the continent's eastern coastline.

Granda Pàl had told Aidryn stories of these horses' ability to defend their clans' settlements and fight invading armies. It was said the horses could move as a unit, communicating with one another as a riderless cavalry.

He'd taught Aidryn a song once, long ago—a ballad about one of the Seanlaoch that died defending his rider during the Felling of the Clans. The rider went on to reunite with his love and raise a family in the east of Rodhlan, but he forever ached for the bond he'd shared with his horse.

> 'Tis setting sun, and light of day
> Gives way to all things dusk and dim
> The sentries 'round us draw their blades
> And fight we now for life and limb

In all his nineteen years, Aidryn had never seen true bloodshed—but he had been forced onto a different sort of battleground for much of his life. For the present, he was determined not to dwell on it, though—he still had a few moments of freedom left before it was time to go home.

It wasn't long before Iathium came into view again, its high stone walls already illuminated by torches to welcome the coming night. The great glass Dome rose high above the walls in the city's center, the torchlight within casting a fiery glow along its smooth surface.

The sprawling city-state was the ruling seat of the continent of Rodhlan, though it was surrounded by outlying clan territories. For centuries, the clans had mostly been left to govern themselves, functioning as separate societies with their own social structures and hierarchies. Aidryn hoped that one day, he might help to reunite his own clan, which had disbanded and scattered in Iathium's infancy.

As Fannin stepped from the soft grass onto the cobblestone path that led to the city gates, Aidryn wished he could quietly flee to some peaceful settlement far from this place. But for now, there were too many reasons why he could not run.

Aidryn's mood grew darker as he rode across the city. The closer he drew to his home, the more he dreaded going inside

—and the slower he urged Fannin to walk. He was tangled in his own thoughts when he heard a familiar voice.

"Tarlach!"

He turned in the saddle to see his friend, Faolan Énna, jogging to catch up. Faolan, one of the Rí's sentries, was flanked by his twin sister, Fiadh, and their cousin, Aeron. All three shared the same rich, black curls, though the twins' eyes were nearly as dark as their hair, set against skin the color of the sand on Rodhlan's western shores. Aeron's eyes were hazel, his complexion a deeper tan.

Aidryn swung a leg over Fannin's side and dismounted, meeting his friends as they arrived at the massive stallion's side. Aeron and Faolan were sentries at the Dome—guards of the ancient palace. As younger members of the ranks, they were often relegated to outdoor duty. Tonight, they were both still clad in the standard black leggings and tunics they wore beneath their armor.

"You can't hear a blasted thing, can you?" Faolan asked by way of greeting. "Did you think I'd run all the way across the city to catch up?"

"It looks like you did," Aidryn quipped with a grin, "as fast as those little legs would carry you."

Fiadh giggled, and her twin shot her a dirty look. Faolan's small build was a running joke among his family and closest friends, and he allowed it—though only just. Despite his height, he was incredibly strong. The sentries called him Little Wolf, though Aidryn likened him more to a lit fuse, always burning steadily home.

Faolan hurled a vulgar insult, earning a sharp look from Aeron. "D'you think Aidryn swears like that in front of his sister?"

"You should know, the way you follow her around like a pup," Faolan shot back. Aeron smirked, completely unfazed.

"Apparently, he doesn't," Aidryn answered, leading Fannin

forward, "or he would've known Caitir swears more than Faolan."

"Could she match up to me?" Fiadh piped up, trotting to Aidryn's side. She walked along at a quick clip, her chin raised as she awaited his response. She was even smaller than Faolan—by several inches, at least—but she was just as fiery.

"That depends," Aidryn answered, glancing sidelong at her before turning his attention back to the road ahead. "How many vulgar insults can you string together before stopping to breathe?"

"Quite a few, I'd wager," she answered. He could've sworn she rose on her toes as she walked—a curious choice, given the worn cobblestones underfoot.

"Now that's a sparring match I'd like to see," Aeron said, shucking off his tunic to reveal three jagged, deep scars that ran from his left shoulder to his chest. He'd been attacked by a wild dog when he was a boy, and he was endlessly proud of the marks.

Aidryn rolled his eyes. "Of course, you would." Aeron grinned wistfully.

"Wipe that stupid expression off your face," Faolan snapped. Fiadh snorted.

"Can I help it that Caitir is uncommonly beautiful?" Aeron clapped a hand to Aidryn's shoulder, leaning in conspiratorially. "Just say the word—tell me whatever I need to do to win her attention, and I will do it."

"Aeron, she's flighty and vain," Aidryn said flatly. His answer wasn't a surprise to his friend; they had been dancing around the topic for months. "She isn't a good match, I promise you."

"What qualities make a woman a good match, then?" Fiadh asked, turning fully toward him as they moved. "In your opinion." She regarded him expectantly while he formulated his answer.

Aidryn had never noticed the delicate iron hoops that hung from her pierced ears. In fact, he'd never realized her ears were pierced. He suppressed a shudder. Needles were not his forte.

He shifted his thoughts back to Fiadh's question and considered his close friend, Lira, who worked alongside him in the Archive. She was the epitome of everything he wanted in a match, so he described her.

"Independence, for one thing," Aidryn began, reaching over to pat Fannin's withers. "Determination. A strong work ethic. A sound mind and the ability to use logic. Fearlessness, too—someone who isn't afraid of a healthy debate once in a while."

"Physical strength?" Fiadh prodded.

He nodded. "To a degree. There's value in it, certainly."

"Not so valuable to a woman *scholar*," Aeron said. "Am I right, Tarlach?"

Aidryn's stomach clenched, his cheeks heating to a blaze. He hadn't spoken a word about his feelings for Lira to Aeron or Faolan—and this was precisely why he had not. It was difficult enough containing his own emotions without his friends teasing and prodding him about her.

Fiadh looked between Aidryn and Aeron and let out a high-pitched laugh. "Well, she would have to be able to lift books, wouldn't she?"

"Oh, she has no trouble with that," Aeron answered. "And she'll rightly box your ears for getting the histories wrong, that's certain."

Aidryn set his jaw, unsure whether to reply.

"Wait—who are we talking about?" Fiadh asked, her brow knitting.

"Silira Mór, from the Archive," Aeron said. "Caitir's friend."

"Oh," Fiadh answered softly.

She fell into step beside her brother, who said, "She seems cold—like her only real friends are books."

"She has friends," Aidryn said, though not convincingly. He had to admit she did prefer books to prolonged company in most cases.

"Who, you and Caitir?" Aeron said. "You should bring them both around more often."

Aidryn snorted softly, not bothering to reply. He wanted Lira to know his friends, but she spent most of her time outside the Archive with Caitir or her younger brother, Talfryn. Aidryn hadn't gotten the nerve to ask her to join them. At this point, it was probably better this way. Besides, it would be just like Faolan or Aeron to blurt out some embarrassing story—or worse, tell her how he felt.

As for Caitir, he knew Aeron's fixation with her. And as much as he admired his friend, he didn't want to see him entangled with Caitir—or their family, for that matter.

His stomach turned as they approached the Tarlach family's tower home on the northeastern side of the city. The estate was built with weather-worn gray stone—the main level served as a dining hall, kitchens, receiving hall, and his father's chambers. On the other end of the structure rose a tall, wide tower with three floors, which held guest chambers and the rest of the family's rooms.

A high rock wall surrounded the property, enclosing the home's vast courtyard. Faolan, Fiadh, and Aeron followed Aidryn through the gates and toward the stables in the back, where he led Fannin inside and began removing his tack.

Fiadh stepped inside the stall with Aidryn, eyeing Fannin's hooves. She stroked the stallion's nose and whispered to him as Aidryn worked, then bent down, inspecting one of his horseshoes.

"It's time to shoe him," she said as she gingerly lifted one of his hooves.

"Yes," Aidryn grunted, hefting the saddle from Fannin's back. "I'll put an order in with your father tomorrow."

"No need," Fiadh replied, rising. "I'll do it now. You'll have them sooner."

"Thank you," he said, running a comb over the horse's back. The twins' father had a smithy just a few blocks from Aidryn's estate.

"Well," she said, backing toward the stall gate, "I'll be off, then."

Aeron, who had been standing outside the stall talking quietly with Faolan, peeked inside at them. "You're not going with us?"

"I'm taking Aidryn's order to Father," she replied, breezing past the young men and walking briskly toward the street.

"Tonight?" Faolan called.

She waved him off as she stepped through the gates, then disappeared around the corner. "I'll see you at home!"

"That was strange," Aeron said under his breath.

Faolan shrugged and slumped against the wall as Aidryn stepped out of the stall and locked it.

"Well, if she's not staying—let's go to the pub. I could use a pint of ale after today," Faolan said.

Aeron nodded, but Aidryn shook his head. "You go on—I'm not drinking tonight."

"Come on," Aeron urged. "There's no rule binding you to the Archive before dawn every day."

"It's my rule for myself," Aidryn answered. "I can't think if I'm hung over from a night with you two idiots." He grinned.

"It's got nothing to do with ale, and you know it," Faolan snapped. "If you're trying to stay close to that girl, just say so. Better yet, do something about it."

"I can't—not really," Aidryn said. "She's my subordinate." It was a pathetic excuse, and it wasn't true. Though he stood to inherit a title, she was considered his equal in the Archive until then.

"Then move on. You could have anyone, but you're stuck on

her," Faolan continued, "and you know you'll never be enough."

The words hit Aidryn in the gut. It was true that he'd had no shortage of young women to show interest in him over the past few years. He'd tried halfheartedly to pursue one or two of them, but he never had it in him to take things very far. No matter what, his thoughts remained fixated on Lira, and he couldn't bring himself to court anyone for long.

Faolan's irritation seemed abrupt, but it had likely been simmering for a while. Before he could ask questions, Aeron said, "Easy—he could say the same thing about me and Caitir."

"He *has*," Faolan said.

Not in so many words, Aidryn thought. "It's getting late," he said dismissively. "If you're going, you'd best be off. I have to get some sleep."

"Maybe next time," Aeron said, raising a hand as he began moving toward the gate.

Faolan began walking too, but he doubled back. "Just—" He crossed his arms over his chest, peering hard at Aidryn. "Think about it, all right?"

"Right," Aidryn said softly. "I'll see you later, then."

His friend huffed, turning to join Aeron. The two disappeared around the side of the rock wall, and Aidryn locked the gate behind them, then turned toward the house.

That night, he lay in bed considering Faolan's words—that perhaps, he'd never be enough for Lira. The thought clung to him, even in sleep, and he awoke deeply unsettled the next morning.

His sense of foreboding grew as he readied himself for the day. Aidryn hadn't only brushed his friends off because of work; there was an important meeting to attend in the Archive, and he was dreading it down to his bones.

～

Want to know what happens next?

Get your free copy at:

authorhaleywalden.com/ballad-of-stallions-free

ABOUT THE AUTHOR

Haley Walden writes fast-paced, character-driven epic fantasy with magical adventures, spellbinding love stories, and unforgettable friendships. As a multi-passionate geek she has many obsessions, including music, martial arts, history, pop culture, and musical theatre. She lives in Alabama with her husband and children.

www.authorhaleywalden.com

THANK YOU!

Loved what you read? Please leave a review on Goodreads or the retailer of your choice. Reviews help readers like you discover new stories, characters, and worlds they'll love.

(Aidryn says he'll race you, and I hear he's pretty tough competition!)